Praise for M. Allen Cunningham

"A fully formed, timeless American writer."
—Square Books, Oxford MS

"Cunningham's prose is perfect—he writes dialogue and sentences that beg to be read aloud."
—Gayle Shanks, Changing Hands Bookstore, Tempe AZ

"A writer both original and well aware of the writers who have come before him. Bold and ambitious."
—Peter Turchi, author of *Maps of the Imagination*

"Cunningham's facility with the language of image and sound casts a spell not unlike Isabel Allende."
—*The Clayton Pioneer*

"Cunningham is a remarkable writer. His prose is delicate, touching, and lyrical."
—Powells Books, Portland OR

"One of the most gifted fiction writers working today."
—Amy Mason Doan, author of *The Summer List*

T0309041

Q&A

M. Allen Cunningham

Regal House Publishing

Published by
Regal House Publishing, LLC
Raleigh, NC 27612
All rights reserved

ISBN -13 (paperback): 9781646030576
ISBN -13 (epub): 9781646030583
Library of Congress Control Number: 2020930423

All efforts were made to determine the copyright holders and obtain their permissions in any circumstance where copyrighted material was used. The publisher apologizes if any errors were made during this process, or if any omissions occurred. If noted, please contact the publisher and all efforts will be made to incorporate permissions in future editions.

Interior and cover design by Lafayette & Greene
lafayetteandgreene.com
Cover images © by Nathan Shields

Regal House Publishing, LLC
https://regalhousepublishing.com

Printed in the United States of America

Q&A is inspired by events of sixty years ago and today. It's a true story, but many details have been changed and each character is an act of the imagination.

The camera was a man-eating monster.

—Jack Benny

Q:

Mr. Winfeld, what is fame?

A:

I think the definition, sir, is "well-knownness,"
or something of that nature.

Q:

Is fame not the sum total of the misunderstandings
that accrue around a person?

A:

Yes, exactly, sir. I would agree with that
definition one hundred percent. In my own
experience, sir, that definition would
prove *very true*.

Q:

You've been misunderstood?

A:

I've been… Can I say it this way: I've been misrepresented.
You ask me about fame, sir. What is fame but a sort of
falseness, a performance? I've been doing a kind of *performance*,
you might say, a misrepresentation the likes of
a paid actor, as I believe I said before.

Q:

Performing, as you say you were—
may I ask, Mr. Winfeld, what was it
about you, then, that failed
to be put across?

A:

Oh, well, sir, far too many things. Far too
many things to name here, right now. I mean
we would need a very long time to go into
the matter, wouldn't we? I might just make one
comment about that: for instance point out
that a person—on that little screen, a
person is necessarily a rather flat image.

Q:

Flat, as opposed to three-dimensional?

A:

Yes, sir, and 3-D glasses would not
help with the kind of flatness I mean.
I'm not referring to the technology
of it, in other words.

Q:

You mean to say, then, that
the screen itself flattens—

A:

I mean to say, for the purposes—
and these would not be *my* purposes,
personally, but for purposes of the TV
screen, flatness is desirable.
It plays best.

Q:

And, Mr. Winfeld, in your judgment of the
events with which these proceedings have
been concerned, why did things happen
in the way that they happened? In other
words, for what reason, in your judgment,
do we expect or demand not only
a winner, but a winner who will
"take all," as they say?

A:

Well, sir, you could look at it the other way. You
could say, at least in my opinion you could, that
as much as a winner what we need and
require is that somebody lose and lose badly.

Q:

And in your judgment, Mr. Winfeld, must
television become the lottery system it
appears to have become now?

A:

I wouldn't say, sir, what television should or
shouldn't be. I only have my own experience.
My experience, however, is that Americans
love the big win—but just as much, we

can't help ourselves from wanting
to watch a big loss. Or can't turn
our eyes away, I should say.

Q:

Mr. Winfeld, do we risk, more and more,
seeing the *price* of everything and the *value*
of nothing?

A:

I believe, if I'm remembering correctly here,
that those words were somebody's
definition of cynicism, sir.
Do we risk cynicism?
Sure. I'd say yes.
No question.

Q:

Is the TV screen to blame?
Is the screen destined to make cynics of us all?

A:

Well, certainly television is training us to
lump together things that aren't
related, naturally speaking—or to mistake
one thing for another.

Q:

What kinds of things?

A:

Knowledge and money, for one.
But answers are something we
like very much, aren't they? That's
what was happening on the screen
all the time, wasn't it?—I mean winning
big thanks to having the answers. I mean, you're
asking me for answers right now.
I'm no different. I love knowing
an answer to something,
I'll admit it.*

*Congressional Record, House Subcommittee on Legislative Oversight, October 6, 1959.

1.
A VERY YOUNG MEDIUM

September/October 1956

SIDNEY

Mint and Greenmarch Productions, Inc.
667 Madison Ave.
New York, NY

Sept. 27, 1956

To whom it may concern,

I watched the broadcast of your new quiz program last week and I write to request a chance to try out for the show. I am an ex-GI and a student at CCNY. I happen to have thousands of odd and obscure facts and many facets of general information at my fingertips. People have always told me I must have a photographic memory. My uncle likes to call me a "walking encyclopedia." So, I believe I would do well on your program. I could try out anytime.

Sincerely,
Sidney Winfeld
Queens, NY

"How would you like to make $25,000?"

The TV man leans back in Sidney's sofa, his silky blue suitjacket parted to reveal pinstripe and glistening shirtbuttons. He's not an ostentatious fellow this Mr. Greenmarch isn't, but TV means money, and good taste is important as Sidney can appreciate.

On the coffee table Greenmarch's fine leather attaché case lies open, the test question cards loosely stacked beside it. Already Sidney knew the answers to all but a few, and those he didn't know he's now got stored away, can all but read the cards already in his mind.

Q:

For nine points, who was Samuel Morse's early partner in the development of the telegraph, and what were the words of their first telegraphic transmission?

A:

The partner was Alfred Vail, and contrary to popular belief their first telegram was not "What hath God wrought," which came later, their first telegram was the words "A patient waiter is no loser."

That one Sidney knew, had stuck in his memory ever since he first heard it years ago, maybe 'cause Sidney himself is patient like that, not so lucky as some maybe but willing to patiently wait kind of on the sly and not miss an opportunity once it knocks. Leaning back, Greenmarch gave him a pleased little smile. Then without even clearing his throat the TV man said it, said, "How would you like to make $25,000?"

He isn't joking and Sidney knows it, but what a question, and how do you answer except to laugh in the face of luck itself because after all Mr. Greenmarch knows these aren't the usual—how to put it—*terms of discourse* for Sidney or for that matter anybody in Sidney's postal code.

So Sidney laughs. He laughs and watches the weird brightening of the TV man's eyes, and laughing Sidney answers: "Who wouldn't!"

Next thing, they're in the back bedroom and the TV man is shuffling through the shirts in Sidney's closet, shirts which none of them are in snappy shape. His back to Sidney he's like a man in an assembly plant, hands moving in the hangers, head jerking left right left. He murmurs, grunts dissatisfaction. The closet's odor seeps out as the shirts and jackets sway: musty, sweat-locked. A second-hand shop, this whole place.

"Here," says Mr. Greenmarch, and out comes the maroon jacket, Sidney's late father-in-law's double-breasted. How many ring-studded handshakes did that suit bring old Josef Winks? How many stockholder meetings did Josef show up in those flared lapels, sucking down smoke after smoke at the head of the table? Sidney tried it on exactly once, night of the man's funeral, then into the closet. Bernice wouldn't hear of selling it.

"No, no. Much too large," Sidney says. "Isn't even mine."

"Doesn't matter. It's a costume. Let me see you in it."

The shoulders float beyond Sidney's frame and give the effect, he knows, of shrinking his head.

Mr. Greenmarch eyes him like a tailor. "No, it's good. It's good." Sticks his nose in the closet again. "And this." He passes Sidney a pale blue shirt, shirt which the frayed collar means it's only for weekends now.

"But, Mister Greenmarch—"

"It's Ray, please. And I'd like to call you Sid. Can I call you Sid?"

"Sure. Fine." Though even to Bernice he's Sidney. "But, Ray, you know, I could get another suit." For a chance like this they can afford it.

"Don't do that," says the TV man. "It's a costume, like I said. Trust me. This is my job, OK? I create people. We don't want *you*, we want the *television* you, understand? College student, GI, scraping by in Queens until, gee whiz, here comes the opportunity of a lifetime—to show the whole country right through their televisions just what you're made of! Now, is this your watch?"

Greenmarch swipes it from the dresser top and gives it a look, and Sidney thinks but how he *is* a college student and a GI and how he *does* call this Forest Hills stoop his home...

Greenmarch holds the watch to one ear. "Good golly but it's loud!"

"Well, ain't Army issue."

"No, it's perfect." And taking Sidney's wrist in hand the TV man pushes the watch on. "Couldn't be better. The mike'll hear every tick, enhance the tension, you see."

And now Sidney feels it: the TV man coming here, the questions and answers, the clarity of Greenmarch's directions—here, right here in the back bedroom of some lousy little duplex, a fella's getting remade.

"Now, Sid, we'd like you to go on air in tomorrow night's program. Can you manage that? Good. Can you report to my office at one-thirty? We'll go over the show, you'll have it all down pat. You'll take nine points, then a second nine for eighteen and stop the game there while you're in the lead. We'll walk through it tomorrow. But listen, I want you to get your hair cut. Ask them for a whitewall, understand? Tell them you need to look like a marine. Oh, you'll do fine, Sid. You'll win right through. Just play ball with us, kid, and you'll have that prize money."

He's gathered up his things, Greenmarch has, and he's making his way out and all the way behind him Sidney's ears are aglow and he's putting in, "Sure, sure, you can count on me, Ray, will do" and such like, and just as they reach the door in comes Bernice.

"Good evening," says Greenmarch, smooth as his suit sleeves. "I believe you're Mrs. Winfeld."

"Honey," says Sidney, "honey, this is Mister Raymond Greenmarch from NBC. The man I told you about."

"Your husband has some good news," says the TV man with a smile, sliding out. But he stops on the stoop. "Oh, Sid, one last question. You're not claustrophobic, are you?"

"Me? Nope."

"Good. We put you in a booth, you know. Feels a little like a telephone booth. And it's *hot* in there."

"Fine, Ray, fine!"

"Very nice to meet you," blurts Bernice, though Greenmarch is down the steps already. "Gee, Sidney, now he's a pretty sharp dresser! What's all this about—a booth, did he say?"

"I'm on tomorrow," says Sidney.

"What? Tomorrow?"

"They're giving me a chance, Bernice. Our chance."

"The quiz show?"

"This is it, honey. This is our start."

"All you have to do is answer the questions?"

"The real start for me and you."

"What's that jacket, Sidney?"

"Gimme a kiss, honey, come here. Then I'm going to the barbers."

Nine o'clock on Wednesday October seventeenth and Sidney is live in the box in Studio 6-B —'isolation booth,' it's called, but it's a box—Klieg lights turned up to blind and roast, the glass before him all glare, and the piped-in voice of Fred Mint coming through the headset tinny and histrionic, like some phone operator jumped-up on Benzedrine, that or too much Geritol —America's Number One Tonic!—and out in the black, past Fred Mint's podium, the rows of the studio audience pitch upward to the control booth also black, and up there is Greenmarch, invisible, unheard, but working the levers—

"Now, Sid," says Mint's voice in his ears, "you have nine points. I am going to turn your headset and microphone off, and I'll be back to you in just a minute"—then *click* the voice becomes a series of muffled tones as the hunched shoulders in Mint's serge jacket turn while he addresses Sidney's opponent, and the fan is off and Sidney, alone, is panting in the box—*isolation booth*—with sweat cascading from his white-walled temples, down the back of his neck, down his sides underneath the dark red flanks of Josef Winks's oversized suitjacket, and though he's live and traveling right this minute to living rooms in (as Greenmarch says) every market across the country, the face *out there* is sweat-filmed and bloodless in black-and-white, the hair is all wrong, and it isn't Sidney Winfeld at all, and meanwhile here in the flesh behind every one of those screens, right here in Studio 6-B behind the blinding glare in his glass box, Sidney's on his own, unhearing and unheard, breathing heavily and pouring out sweat, alone in his own light, and in the void darkness where the audience should be there's only the weak mirroring of the booth's glass, an image of a man in earphones and a bulky red suit, a see-through man standing in a bright blank space, waiting, just waiting to say, "Nine please, Mister Mint, I'll try for nine," the way he's practiced.

"Now, friends," says Fred Mint, his gray face smiling as the camera moves trustingly closer, "have you been slowing down, feeling tired and run down, especially after a cold, flu, or a sore throat or virus? Well, your trouble may be due to what the doctors call iron deficiency anemia, a very fancy term for what we call *tired blood.* Check with your doctor, and to feel stronger fast, take GERITOL. In just twenty-four hours, Geritol iron is in your bloodstream carrying strength and energy to every part of your body. Just two tablespoons of liquid Geritol or two of the Geritol tablets contain twice the iron in a pound of calves' liver. So remember, if tired blood is your problem, take either the good-tasting liquid Geritol or the handy Geritol tablet, and take them every day, and believe me you'll feel stronger—and mighty fast too: within seven days or you'll get your money back."

CONTROL

The studio audience applauds and a little fanfare of woodwinds and kettledrums is heard.

   —Give me Camera One—

As Fred Mint spirits away his bottle of Geritol, cut to the full set in its silvery monochrome: Sid Winfeld in his soundproof booth at right, Maurice Pelubet in his booth at left, Fred Mint and podium at the center.

   "Before we go on" says the host,

   —Camera Two—

"I would like to say that all of the questions used on our program have been authenticated for their accuracy"

   —Ready Camera Three, real close now, Camera Three—

"and the order of their difficulty by the editorial board of the Encyclopedia Britannica. All right now, Sid Winfeld, how are you holding up?"

   —Where's Sid, fellas? I said Three—

"Just fine, thank you, Mister Mint."

"Sid, you have nine points."

   —There he is, about time, gents, stay on him now, don't let'm go—

Ding! goes a little bell as Mint plucks up the next blue card.

"The category is the History of Communications. How many points do you want to try, from one to eleven?"

"Nine please, Mister Mint. I'll try for nine."

"For nine points: Who was Samuel Morse's early partner in the development of the telegraph, and what were the words of their first telegraphic transmission?"

—Hold him now, hold him—

COMMENTATORS

"Some people have said our contestants are too good to be true. Well, the typical American has many facets, and those who doubt it show little faith in the American way."

Q:
Are all things isolated under glass?

A:

Q:
Forever now, will all things be mediated?

A:

Q:
Can you see me? Am I there on your screen?
Am I there at all? Where are we now, and
was it the questions or the answers that led us here?

A:

Q:
Am I there? Hello?

AND NOW A WORD FROM OUR SPONSORS

If you often can't sleep your nerves on edge try this new sleeping tablet one hundred percent safe sleep helping to calm down jittery nerves …

"After I did the pilot, we went out to dinner and the sponsor said, 'We may have to change your name because nobody will believe a man named Sonny who's giving away all that money.' And I think I said something like, 'Well, for the money you're prepared to pay me you can call me anything you want.' Anyway, the first night of *$64,000 Challenge* the announcer said, 'And here is your host Bill Fox,' and I stood there for a moment until somebody said, 'That's you!'"

"The individual—the one with a surname, the one with a unique personal history and perhaps a few secrets to keep—fades happily into virtual space."

"It was the most impactful show we've ever had."

"The sponsors probably quadrupled their sales in one year. You're talking about $100 million."

"It was a con game, that's all—a scam from start to finish."

"I'm telling you, on the nights the show was on, you could shoot a cannon down the street, 'cause *nobody* was on the street."

"As a matter of fact, there is no audience, not in reality."

"I remember one night walking down—walking down on a summer's night in the streets of New York and the windows were open. And out of every window, I heard the same sound and the sound was the show, *our* show!"

"There are only some millions of groups in millions of living rooms."

"The deception we best understand and most willingly give our attention to is that which a person works upon himself."

Safe sleep, one hundred percent, or your money back.

"Every two minutes of every hour of every day, an image from a camera in Jenni's apartment was loaded onto the web."

"We're all secretly practicing for when we, too, will join the ranks of the celebrated."

"The camera begins to attract its own subject matter."

"Tell me the large technologies humans have stopped, diverted, or put a break on."

"It's no longer a passive recorder but actively attracts the people it records."

"I've often been tormented by the vision of a future in which we have invented, uh, we have really *perfected* mass communication to the degree that it will be possible to bind together in one great instantaneous network all the human beings of the earth, and that by a system of translation machines such as we have up at the United Nations, they'll all be able to understand anything that's being said…"

"In her FAQ, Jenni said, 'The cam has been there long enough that now I ignore it. So whatever you're seeing isn't staged or faked.'"

"… And they're all tuned in at one moment to listen to a central message—and here are billions of people all listening—and the nightmare is very simple: *What are they going to hear? Who's going to say something worth…?*"

"While I don't claim to be the most interesting person in the world, I do think there's something compelling about real life that staging it wouldn't bring to the medium."

"Well, I'm all for the multiplication of mass impressions. Now don't misunderstand me. I just think that at the same time we ought to be trying to work out better and better things to say, as well as better and better ways of saying them."

"She laughed in a sweet, natural way that was a testament to television existence."

Three medical ingredients all working together like a doctor's prescription to help bring safe, natural-like sleep.

"Reality, to be profitable, must have its limits."

"The world was becoming a television studio and those who wished to rule it would have to become actors."

"Friends, we don't have much time. Remember Geritol and Geritol Junior..."

"The age of humanism may be burning off."

Contains no narcotics and is non-habit-forming. Now don't you deserve a sound sleep?

"Goodnight everybody—see you next week!"

KENYON

As he comes along the sidewalk toward the family house on Bleecker, Kenyon Saint Claire spots his own reflection in the front window, a passing figure sparkling on the glass. Valise in hand, he's thirty years old and on his way. Even now he could turn through the gate up the steps inside, receive his mother's kiss and stand before his father's shelves while Dad stands at the mirror in the other room knotting his tie. They could ride the train together. But no, Kenyon will keep walking, thoughts to himself. He wants to get to Hamilton Hall in time for a cigarette before class.

He remembers the very early days with Dad in the front room by that window, so often standing there as a boy, head cocked to read the titles on the countless spines along the shelves—the books Dad had read but also those he'd written. Kenny would take them down and admire the title pages. Before he could read he'd understood how Dad's name looked when made of letters. One cover bore a monogram in gold leaf: MSC. Maynard Saint Claire.

Or younger still: sitting on Dad's lap at the window, watching people pass by on the street, and Dad's wise tobacco breath: *See them, Kenny? More going by than you could ever count. It's like a play, isn't it, how they all go by? Oh, it's like a great drama.* It was a silvery screen, the window, its projection grandly three-dimensional. And that drama beyond the glass—the bustle of bodies and cars—was in some way protecting, consoling. Kenyon would discover that all the great dramas shared these properties: however they might chill or frighten you, in the end they were a form of protection and solace— their effect and intent was just this. Dad did—as Kenyon eventually would—see himself in the scenes out there. But the window was never just a mirror. Something in his father's deportment, his fascination as they peered through the glass, taught the boy this crucial thing: *never just a mirror.*

Probably the old fellow watched him go by just now.

Kenyon rounds the corner to the whoosh of traffic on Broadway, the awakening city before him like a stage whose curtain is rising. God, he loves the energy of these crisp golden mornings, the fall air so enlivening, the jaunty march amidst his fellow citizens, and the sense of purpose this town confers on its people.

Through Dad's unspoken guidance Kenny and his brother were led to understand that they were living and growing up inside a culture. It was just one of a great many cultures but it possessed dignity, intelligence, and a legacy of philosophical, moral, and artistic achievement that it gave to the world for keeps: Shakespeare, Jefferson, Emerson, Whitman, Dickinson. Always Dad had given them books. *Robinson Crusoe. Treasure Island. Sherlock Holmes.* The tales of Kipling. Mark Twain. The Homeric epics. Tacitus, Plotinus, Plutarch, Epictetus, and Aurelius. Darwin's works, Newton's works, Voltaire, Dostoevsky, Thomas Hardy, William and Henry James. He never pressed the boys to read them all, they were simply gifts. He wanted his sons to know the gift that the world of literature and ideas could be, to never fear the gift or be intimidated by it.

Andersen's *The Little Fir Tree* was the first small volume Kenny read front to back, a nasty old tale as he recollects it now. What were the words? *And how glad the little fir tree was when at last they came to cut it down!* Where the child reading finds a story about fulfilled wishes, the adult sees a tale of misguided hope and betrayal. Mom, at his arm, must have read it that way, though she never let on.

Reading was luxurious in those first years, an engrossment warm and maternal. Perhaps it still is. How well he remembers, during his Army service, his comfort in keeping Palgrave's *Treasury* on his person all the time. The little octavo, green with triangles of red leather at each corner, fit snugly under the flap of his field jacket pocket. That book was a constant gift, and more, a talisman: Kenyon never was shipped overseas.

Now it's his privilege to foster this lifelong enrichment for his students. This fall marks the start of his second year on faculty. Columbia, imagine! Dad's colleagues are now Kenyon's as well: Trilling, Barzun, Miner—or if not yet actual colleagues, then soon to be. Already, surely, he's no less than their peer. A matter of a few years and he'll have his Ph.D.

For now, Kenyon earns eighty-six dollars a week. In his own Village apartment four blocks from the family home he eats, nearly every other night, grilled cheese and a fried egg—"Croque Madame," he calls it, to dignify the act. On the off nights he dines with his folks on Bleecker or eats out. Chop Suey. It is a decent life. Though one could wish the neighbors didn't bang their cans or let their cats spray the stoop. And he's happy. He's happy. He is.

At Broadway he boards the crowded uptown train. Inside the car's bottled light, hugging his valise and gripping a strap, his body is jostled like all the others. Here below, as the train hurries after its yellow beam, a person becomes anonymous, a body in motion, little else—identity in limbo amid the masses.

Dad had won the Pulitzer at forty-six. Kenny was fourteen and became conscious of friends and relations slapping his back. *His* back, Kenny's. Suddenly they were slapping his back and smiling as if something had changed for him too, not just for Dad. And the telephone was jangling. And Dad's name was in the papers. And one weekend a gaggle of reporters trailed the family clear from the city to the farm in Connecticut. All this woke Kenny up—somehow put an end to his boyhood. And newly awake, he understood that he needed to pay attention now, real attention to the years and to the world and to his place in it all. He began thinking he might have a place, began asking way down somewhere inside himself, *what place?*

The dank motor-oil smell seeps in through the train windows, the rhythmic clacking of wheels numbs the ears. Isolated lights blink past and disappear. There are tunnels off these tunnels—for the workers or in case of emergency. The darkness between stations is a kind of public sleep. But the city is awake. The city is everywhere above, in motion all the time. Kenyon rises to its streets again at Broadway and 116th and strolls the half-block to campus and to Hamilton Hall—and as he passes through the doors, lighting a smoke as he goes, he can actually feel the anonymity sliding off his shoulders.

"Morning, Kenyon," says a colleague, shoes clapping past. "You're early today."

"Am I?"

"Beat your father anyway."

"Oh?"

The first thing Kenny did in this house was fall down the stairs.

In Dad's office Kenyon sluffs his overcoat. Installed at Dad's desk he spends twenty minutes reviewing his notes. Finally he gets up to have another smoke, standing in his jacket at the window. Students are trotting here to there around the neat rectangle of the south lawn, bright and resolute on the paved ribbons of the paths. The morning light seems to frame them with special care here, in the school's safe enclosures.

Probably the old fellow watched him walk past the house this morning. Why didn't Kenyon stop? The old house is—always has been—narrow and deep. It pulls you in. Four stories, the fourth they always rented out, on the third a study for Dad, and on the second Kenny and George's room, which the folks keep just as it was, twin beds neatly tucked in the quilts his grandmother stitched.

The first thing Kenny did in this house was fall down the stairs. The voice is Dad's. Five or six Kenny must have been when he fell. He doesn't remember the moment itself. But even now Dad will recite the words—at holiday gatherings, midtown luncheons, picnics on the farm—the anecdote retold as long as Kenny can remember. What's a family but a swirl of inside jokes, of stories shaped and reshaped? This story, though, is curiously firm, so familiar its words could be a refrain from one of Maynard Saint Claire's poems:

The first thing Kenny did in this house was fall down the stairs.

And then George, not yet four, famously rejoined: *No, Daddy, but first he had to go* up *the stairs.*

At hand to hear the boy's remark was Lionel Trilling, the Saint Claires' Sunday lunch guest. On the spot Trilling ordained George a high critical intelligence destined for a life of close reading. Friends and relations, upon hearing Dad tell this, always roar and smile. "Way to take the fall for your brother, Kenny!"

And Kenyon smiles as they slap his back.

"Well now, isn't that Mister Saint Claire?" Maynard Saint Claire bustles in, briefcase under one arm, a steaming paper cup in each hand.

"Morning, Dad."

"Earlier every day, aren't you? Here's some coffee."

Kenyon checks his watch. The coffee hot in his hand.

"You can't keep out-punctualizing me, Kenny. They'll retire me on the spot."

"You're the punctual one, Dad. I'm just early."

"Yes, I saw you go past the house this morning. You ought to have knocked, early bird." Dad hangs overcoat and hat, digs out pipe from breast pocket, pats his side pockets, bends to his desk drawers. "Oh, but I remember that feeling, that eagerness. It's a wonderful secret: the fun of it all—the energy teaching can give a fellow." He shuts the drawers. "Damn! I may have to ask you for a cigarette, son."

Relievedly puffing, Dad sits, but Kenny remains on his feet.

"Seminars this morning, Kenny?"

"Yes. Shakespeare, then Henry James."

"The *Portrait*?"

"*Ambassadors.*"

"Ah. And how will they take it?"

Kenyon shrugs. "They're a sharp group."

"Will you also do *The Princess Casamassima*?"

"I'd like to."

"Lionel's introduction is very good, you know."

"Yes, I think so too."

"Poor James. Can you teach them to love him as he deserves?"

"I think I can. I'd like to."

"Oh, but that's always the question. Will our young ones, when they've left us, love them as they deserve?"

"You know what I was thinking, Dad? Do you remember when I was in Europe?"

"Mm."

"And you and Mom couldn't reach me?"

"Ah, yes. Your prodigal year."

"What did you two make of that?"

"Well, I told your mother, 'He will not go to Nineveh. He isn't the first.'"

"Did she worry?"

"Mother? Oh, she's a rock."

"It couldn't have been easy on either of you."

"Well, anyhow, we put George on your trail."

Kenyon and Dad chuckle, Dad perched on the radiator in woolen jacket and trousers, reading glasses tucked in breast pocket, cigarette in hand. Deep smoky laugh, crow's feet and smile lines. He's led a happy life. In all Kenny's memories Dad is a laugher and a mild soul. His poetry, measured and meditative, has the same lightness of spirit. How does he put it in that memoir he's been toiling on? *Good art weighs nothing; it knows its way among the mysteries of wit and humor. Its reference to truth is its smile.*

"But you know what I was thinking, Dad? Students of mine, some of them, they seem to struggle with Shakespeare so, as if they're missing some essential preparation. I wonder if what's lacking is just some world experience, like what I got in Europe."

Maynard flicks his ash into the glass tray on the sill. He shakes his head. "Everyone, Kenny, is prepared to read Shakespeare by the time they're eighteen. As teachers we must remember that, son. At eighteen, you've been born, you've had a father, a mother, you've been loved, you've had fears, you've hated, you've been jealous." He shrugs, turns up his hands as if to say *think clearly, you'll see it is so.*

Oh Dad, demystifier of the beautiful and the grand. For thirty-six years in these Columbia classrooms Maynard Saint Claire has labored to instill the guiding values of appreciation: that the fault is not in Shakespeare but in ourselves, and not a question of being equipped but merely of being alive and awake; that good art weighs nothing; that the word was spoken, and because it was printed may go on speaking and, if only we use our hearts and listen, we will hear it speaking to *us*.

Remember this. Remember.

Kenyon stubs out his cigarette. Coffee in one hand, he takes up his valise in the other. "I'd better walk over." He likes to claim the quiet of the classroom before anyone arrives. Always so many thoughts to put in order, layers to excavate. He wants to be devout about this work. "Sorry I didn't stop and knock, Dad. Nervous energy, I guess. Let's ride together tomorrow."

Behind his coffee, Dad just nods and smiles.

World experience. What did Kenyon mean by that? In his youngest days, he'd harbored an immediate suspicion of the laughter of strangers. Most children do. With Kenny the proportions were tragic. Anyone who laughed was laughing at him and he'd burst into tears. *You mustn't get so upset,* Dad would say. *Other people's happiness isn't at your expense.* Maynard Saint Claire would have his boys know that the world is a place of welcome with goodness and laughter to spare. But something inside the boy believed, stubbornly, reflexively, that everything in the world had something to do with him. It was in Europe that Kenyon finally managed to shake these old notions, and when he saw that they'd left him at last, he saw that other things had fallen away with them. In a world where everything concerns you directly, you are prone to injury, yes, but watched over too. He realized in Europe that for all his life he'd felt himself held, assuringly *held* in the palm of a hand. Life, though sometimes it laughed, would never let him drop. He'd even had a destiny. He'd moved steadily toward it under that benevolent protection. But in Europe—in Paris—he learned how, eventually, if one is to live, one becomes lonely and unprotected—that this is everyone's lot. Somewhere, finally, the great hand gives way and one finds oneself in free fall.

Kenyon was never supposed to be in Paris at all. He'd fled there from Cambridge, six months into an ill-fitting fellowship. He'd learned in Cambridge that he wasn't one for the English scholar's robes or hushed cloisters, all the farm-like intellectual industriousness of those gothic halls and chapels. He'd begun to feel surrounded by the lifelong choir boys of academe. What he wanted to do was *live* somehow, live and write. He had a novel coming on, his first novel, and he couldn't get the whiff of the continent out of his curious nostrils. So he fled, first to Sidie's room in Montparnasse, a girl he'd met on a gallery tour in London.

She lived in a low-ceilinged rear atelier on the Avenue des Gobelins. There was a toilet in the open beside her bed. When one person required its use, the other would wait in the hall, a surprisingly sexy little routine. Kenyon slept the first night on her floor and thereafter they shared her narrow mattress and musty duvet. She made a lithe and lively first lover, and she took clear pleasure in leading him out of his inexperience, teaching him the ways of the body. He would wake with her sweat-scented hair all spilled across his face, straw-yellow hair that clashed pleasingly with her dark and fulsome eyebrows.

She was studying English literature and art, so he was spared speaking French all day. He could read it well enough, but out loud he tended to chew the words. He couldn't manage to forget that it was a foreign language. He and Sidie never lacked things to talk about. She loved Paris and gladly led him all around. In the Montparnasse cemetery just blocks from her flat stood the plain little grave of Baudelaire, and some mornings they would sit there on the stone ledge beside it with their baguettes, breadcrumbs accumulating for the excitable little birds. He walked with Sidie to the Sorbonne, he wandered amid the giants in the dusty crypt of the Panthéon, he went up and down in the rue Mouffetard, the air thick with the smell of roasted chicken. He loitered under the slanting houses in the Place de Contrescarpe and in the shady bandstands of the Luxembourg Gardens, poked at the mildewed volumes of the Left Bank booksellers. He was like Lambert Strether in *The Ambassadors*, a surprised child. Nowhere else had he ever felt the developed interior world of civilization expressed so naturally in the daily setting and rounds.

> The air had a taste as of something mixed with art, something that presented nature as a white-capped master-chef.

He did not carry James's book with him, but he had the words by heart. And somewhere there, also in his mind, was the voice of Bill Westhouse, his old professor at Saint John's, lecturing on James's late novel: "Now, gentlemen, it is well you recognize that these Paris marvels are a cliché.

The loveliness of the Tuileries—and they are lovely. The grandeur of Notre Dame—and it is grand. By themselves, even collectively, they are a magnificent surface—and surface only. It is what one does with them. It is, as in all things, how one *sees* that matters."

More than once, Kenyon went with Sidie to the Old Navy or the Café Dome, where they would wait over smoky coffees for Sartre to waddle in. Even in the present, their own time, this place went on happening. The lights were lit. The books were open. If this was Paris, what was Europe at large?

Kenyon had started his novel. He'd been in Sidie's room two and a half weeks, and they could go on forever, god knows. In bed, she would give him her fingers to suck—his tongue pressing the bulb of each salty knuckle one by one to the roof of his mouth. She would turn and give him the smooth cleaved peach of her rump, shivering when he kissed the back of her neck, the downy darkness at her hairline there. In her building was a single-occupant elevator, a little slow-moving booth of glass that the open stairway encircled, and they made a small ritual of Kenyon's climbing the stairs around her as she glided upward, Sidie rotating on her heels inside the glass to watch him, their eyes on each other all the way to the fourth floor. He was hardly aware of his own efforts, didn't notice his reflection laboring up the steps. And then, in her bed behind her door, they were always ready.

It was this way between them—or he believed so—until the day she started pressing him for money. He didn't understand at first—he thought them little quips, these comments about all she'd given him.

—Haven't I provided for you?

—I'll give you something for the rent, yes.

—And for my bed? My body?

Finally he saw that she'd mistaken him for a son of rich Americans. He did give her a little money, as much as he could spare, but now their time together was tainted. Or rather, he'd come to understand what she'd expected all along. He'd known she had other lovers. She'd never pretended this wasn't so. He'd thought of her as a teacher—her body teaching and teaching generously—he'd believed himself her pupil in some pure form of tutelage. Now he understood how blind that was, how blind they'd been to each other.

And his novel was growing, so he found a room of his own in the rue de Seine. His concierge, a faded little lady in a flowered frock, sympathized with his aims, or maybe pitied him for them. She said she had a daughter in America, a writer like him. The girl had gone to California to write, she'd told her mother, because in Paris, in Europe, so much had already been done. Which was, Kenyon reflected, exactly what had brought him here.

In his room was a bed, a table, a tiny stove, and a sink. The plaster of the walls was flaking away. He would brush it into little piles every other day. The windowsill had rotted in the weather. There were rats, and slimy droppings from other vermin, and a minor pestilence of fleas. But he told himself he would write in the cafés, the gardens, the library. The days were cold. Out walking, his hands and feet would often grow numb. Settling in on a park bench with notebook and pen was soon out of the question. And soon the cafés, too, cost more than he could spend. That left the library. But even enshrouded in the library's delicious quietude, he found he couldn't divest his thoughts of the lures of the city outside. Also preying on his attentions were the unknown lures of the continent. What must Vienna be like? Or Czechoslovakia. Or Istanbul. He'd stopped seeing Sidie altogether. He roamed the arrondissements, a nominal writer in shabby clothes, a hungry, writerly sponge soaking up all that he saw. The novel was started, and it persisted in his mind, troublesome, indeterminate. What would it take to write it? When would he really feel a sense of purchase on life to make that possible?

He'd developed some painful sores behind his zipper.

He hadn't written to his family. They knew only that he'd left Cambridge and gone to Europe—that much he'd told them.

Alone in this chilled and beautiful city, ministering to his sores and wishing he could write, he now began to feel he was waiting out the weather. Haunting his thoughts were all those characters in literature who live in little hovels and die of the cold. He tried to put them out of mind. At the table in his small room, cloaked in a coarse woolen blanket, he ate spaghetti and read books and thought about his novel. In what he'd written so far he saw that somehow, shockingly, he'd fixed on the idea of patricide. There were allusions to Oedipus in the father's house, to Isaac seizing the stone, the knife, the axe, and turning, right there at the altar, upon Abraham—and upon the old man's damned angel too.

He still resisted wiring his parents. Whatever venereal sickness he might have, however quickly he might starve once his money ran out, he didn't want to be located. Why? He hardly knew, but it was like a conviction within him. What was he up to in Europe? Of how many young Americans has this question been asked? Was he hiding?—hoping, even as he wrote, that somehow his own ideas would not find him?

One day in Paris, in his sometime diary, he wrote:

> *Now and then you'll hear people say, "So and so seems to be doing very well for himself. Did you hear? He's moved to Rome or Paris, someplace, and he's writing a book."*
>
> *No one ever knows how anyone is doing, of course.*
> *We are all uncreditable and delusional voyeurs.*
> *We never know.*

In the end his novel remained unfinished. George had come to Paris and brought him home. And in all that time abroad, had Kenyon *lived*?

SIDNEY

Sidney Winfeld is inside the door that's inside the door of 667 Madison Ave. Midday in Manhattan and look here: tonic water and cherry in hand, he's perched on the couch in the master office of Mint and Greenmarch, Inc. Three weeks running he's been on the air, three consecutive Tuesdays he's glided past the concierge up the elevator and past the secretary into this room at the heart of it all, to stand on Mr. Greenmarch's—Ray's—Persian carpet shaking the man's hand, take position on the silvery-green corduroy of the couch, receive a glass clinking with ice, and talk details, nuance, the finer points.

From a drawer in the gleaming frigate of his desk Greenmarch brings out the blue question cards. Turning them in his hands, he settles himself in the low-slung leather chair adjacent to the couch. Behind him the large window is a frame, the windows in the opposite building his backdrop, rectangular glass portals stacked in columns and rows. Beside the window, in a frame of its own, hangs a headshot of Lucille Ball. Across her brow runs the black valance of a wig, black pigtails covering her ears. She's doing her crazy lady disguise, her smile huge and toothless in front.

"That's new," says Sidney. "Do you know Lucy?"

Greenmarch glances over his shoulder. "No. I mean yes, who doesn't, but no. Now, Sid, you've got your continuity cards by now, haven't you?"

"Mm-hm, Mister Lacky had 'em ready for me after last week's program."

"Fine. Although in future you won't get them so early. Better we have till Tuesday, to allow for putting in reference to very current things. That means, of course, you'll only have a day to memorize before broadcast."

"Sure thing, Ray. My memory's not so shabby anyway." *In future,* are the man's words. Meaning, Sidney realizes with a shiver of joy, that they're keeping him.

"All right then, I'll speak to Mister Lacky."

"Oh, and Ray, I'd like to correct a little thing on the cards, which is where Mister Mint comments how Sid Winfeld hits the books every night. It isn't the books so much, you see, as it is my photographic memory."

"These are production decisions, Sid. The chitchat on the cards is strictly for Mister Mint, Mister Lacky, and myself to decide."

"I thought I'd bring it up is all."

"Well, there's no need. Now, Sid, we've only got a little time and we need to talk mannerisms. For instance, with a three or four part question, don't ever take the parts all in a row, OK? That's flat. It gives us nothing to watch, see. What we need from you is to always leave one part out, something to struggle with. In other words, say you take the first part, second, *leave out the third*, take the fourth. Then when you come back to the second—"

"The third," says Sidney.

"What?"

"You said leave out the third, so you mean when I come back to the third."

"Sure, fine, when you come back to it—"

"Not the second."

"Look, Sid, it doesn't matter third or fourth—"

"Second or third."

"Excuse me?"

"Second or third is what we were saying, not third or fourth."

"Sid, look, I appreciate your exactitude, but let's make sure you're getting my point, which is to say that it's all in the indecision. Got that? I need you to be *indecisive* and I'm going to tell you how. Do this for me now, Sid, OK? Close your eyes."

"What? Here?"

"Yes, put down your glass."

Sidney sets his tonic water and cherry on the lacquered wooden coaster on the end table, sits back in the couch, tugs at his lapels, shuts his eyes.

"Now, Sid, I'm gonna ask you Part Three, and before you answer I want you to squeeze your eyes tight, count to six, and mumble all the answers over again one at a time on your fingers. Ready? Here's Part Three. Name the mythological beast of the ancient Greeks that was part lion, part goat, and part serpent."

"Oh, that's the Chimera."

"No, Sid—"

"But, Ray, I'm quite sure that it is."

"Sid, please. Please. Squeeze the eyes, count to six, mumble."

"Even if I know the answer, you're saying?"

"People don't want you to know everything, Sid. This is the point."

"I know what I know, Ray."

"Of course. But we're making television here. Will you close your eyes again please? OK. Listen, in this case you'd still say Chimera, which is correct. You still get the points, the cash, all that. I only want you to slow it down, think it out in a way we can watch."

"You mean pretend to think it out, like acting."

"Bingo."

"Well, I guess I know something about that."

"We all do, Sid, we all do."

"So, Lucy—she an inspiration or what?"

Greenmarch sighs. He drops the blue cards in his lap. Two-handed, he removes his glasses, like they're very heavy or delicate. He palms his forehead, drags his hand over his eyes, nose, mouth, chin. "You wanna know what Lucy is? I'll tell you what Lucy is. Lucy is Number One."

Greenmarch speaks with nauseated quietness, under some kind of duress, glasses dangling in one hand.

"Five years she's been Number One," he says. "Her viewership shot from ten to fifty million in her first three years on air. When Little Ricky was born? The number watching was twice the number as watched Eisenhower's inauguration."

For Greenmarch these facts are gut-rotting, rote.

"Lucy has made television the biggest thing in the world. And you know what that means? It means whoever is Number One on television, there's nobody bigger. Anywhere. Nobody."

Greenmarch replaces his glasses, and now there's a razor-like glint in the lenses. He seems refortified and coiled to spring. "And that picture, you know what I like about it?" he says, though it hangs behind him, out of his sight, as he turns his attention back to the cards. "She's had her fucking teeth knocked out, is what I like."

COMMENTATORS

"We call it trivia but it's not trivial at all. I say that it's better to know something about everything than everything about something."

KENYON

Kenyon feels restless, undeniably ill at ease, whenever he finds himself in a house whose walls are not conspicuously lined with books. This apartment is such a place. He's come for dinner at the invitation of his old friend Clover, a mutual acquaintance. She secured him a brief writing job back in the spring, a pamphlet for the U.S. Information Agency to be entitled *What is American Culture?* It proved easy enough to write, he recalls, and paid reasonably well considering. He'd had the pleasure of citing Carlyle (*The great law of culture is: Let each become all that he was capable of being*) and making reference to Stevenson's *The Amateur Emigrant*, where the Scotsman said: *Culture is not measured by the greatness of the field which is covered by our knowledge, but by the nicety with which we can perceive relations in the field, whether great or small.* Tonight would be, as Clover had put it, a gathering of television and movie people, and might prove interesting if not helpful to him. "They're always looking for writers, these folks."

Arriving, Kenyon learned that Clover herself would not be present. "In absentia," said his hostess, "she's offered us your company, Mister Saint Claire." The hostess wears a smart collared shirt and beaded necklace and her gestures are quick and graceful. He understands this vaguely familiar woman to be an actress of some kind. An air of practice in everything she does. "You're a marvelous writer, Clover tells us."

She'd led him in among the guests, the roomy apartment packed and chattering, and soon he was turning here and there holding a wine glass and shaking hands. He knew nobody, though it seemed they all knew one another, and he'd arrived several minutes too late: everyone in mid-conversation. He began drifting about, the interloper, wishing there were bookshelves on which to train his focus. It's an urbane and moneyed crowd, the women in wraps and bangles, with Audrey Hepburn hair, the men's shoes impeccable. In his professor suit Kenyon feels dowdy and defensive. There seem to be, even amid the evening repartee, deals in the making.

He stands at the large living room window that looks out on the twilit park and wonders, not for the first time, about the varying altitudes in New York: their differing qualities of light, sound, vibration. Underground. Street level. Office. Penthouse. Pigeon roost. The city itself strikes him sometimes as an act of patricide on a vast collective scale. Its main idea is dominance. And now a change in the focus of his gaze reveals him to himself in the glass, his transparent figure stretched massively over the park. But he is only one framed human, he knows, in a grid of identical frames.

This is how we store our people here, thinks Kenyon.

Last night he dreamt he was walking all around the city, weak with anxiety, taking many wrong turns. Threatful figures awaited him in alleyways. Lost, dazed, he'd found himself inside a greasy bottling plant or pump room, crud-caked pipes and valves in all directions, endless flights of metal stairs. Then: standing on a sidewalk before the great wooden doors of a church, talking to a bystander. *It's the strangest thing,* he'd said, *to be in a place so familiar and to feel totally lost.* He'd awakened himself speaking these words, after which he lay for a time in the dark, amazed by the fluency of his articulation, the clarity of his own voice that had carried him over out of dream.

Kenyon is remembering this when he becomes aware of someone beside him at the window, a small dark figure in the glass. A voice says, "Helluva view, ain't it?"

. . .

Sam Lacky is a small man, something boyish about him, energetic, except with a suave composure. His suit very nicely cut, his cufflinks large, he carries his cigarettes in a silver case. His hands are manicured, smooth-looking, hairless. Kenyon notices the hands first thing. They draw the attention. Clearly Lacky is comfortable in this setting, the people here are his people. But he seems, somehow, apart from it too. He is in television, he says, his company develops the trivia shows.

"I don't own a set myself," says Kenyon. But he's heard a little about these programs. The players answer questions for cash prizes, much like some of the old radio shows. Kip Fadiman, Dad's old friend, had hosted such a show when Kenny was a boy. *Information Please,* they called it. The idea was to stump a panel of experts, whereupon you'd hear the ring of a cash register, which meant that whoever had submitted that question had just won twenty-five dollars or some amount. Unforgettable in a way, the clank and chime of the drawer serving up its money.

Lacky is apparently a great information gatherer: already he knows several things about Kenyon. You live in the Village, he says. You've written a novel. You and your father both teach at Columbia. For a moment or so Kenyon feels like the evening's honored guest. Has Clover put this in motion? Has everyone been briefed? One hears that this is the way of things, that those who rise rise first by association, but how strange to go into a setting brightly aware, to stand here, how many stories up, and feel yourself being lifted. Dad's name, Uncle's name, these naturally play a part, but Kenyon knows that would only give his father joy—Dad has always wanted passionately all the best for Kenny and George, and he worried, Kenny could see, more than he'd ever admit. When it became clear that Kenny would join the Columbia faculty, Dad wrote him: *The rewards, I don't need to tell you, are scandalously slight. I have enjoyed it, even though I am quitting soon; but the enjoyment was the greater part of my pay.* Honest, earnest father—if his name proves a help to his sons, then that, as he sees it, is the higher value of his winning The Prize. What else could The Prize be to a man like Dad but a general glow upon the family, a light in which they all might warm themselves?

When will Kenyon's novel be published, Lacky asks. A difficult question, but Kenyon answers, "Well, I'm still working on it." They talk for maybe half an hour. Because Lacky is holding no drink, nothing in his hands but a cigarette, he has nothing to divert his eyes. There's a deliberate steadiness in his look. "Do you ever find it hard," he says, "to share your dad's office?"

And just then their hostess rings the dinner bell, and Lacky and Kenyon turn to fall in with the stream of guests. Leaning, Lacky murmurs, "What do you make over at Columbia, Kenyon? Mind if I ask?"

Kenyon does mind, of course, but he also feels a strange and defensive pride in furnishing, immediately, the figure: $4,400 a year. Because Lacky ought to know that the figure is not why one becomes a teacher. If Lacky hears his answer—and he must—he gives no sign.

One evening early the following week Kenyon answers the phone and there is Sam Lacky's voice on the other end.

"Penelope gave me your number. I hope you don't mind."

Who Penelope is Kenyon doesn't know—another friend of Clover's maybe? Clover herself has gone to Los Angeles for some months on business. "No, no," Kenny says. "How are you, Sam?"

"Well, I'm calling, Kenny, because I believe you'd be a fine fit for one of our shows. What would you say to coming on up to our office to try out?"

"A trivia program, you mean?"

"That's right. See, we're looking for new contestants and you're the first I thought of. I'm convinced you'd have a great success."

"Well, Sam, I have my teaching."

"Shows are in the evenings."

"I've never even seen the programs, to tell the truth."

"You know, they're entertainment. A man of your education, you'd do fine. And you'd send a very positive message."

"I'll give it some thought," says Kenny.

"Let me buy you lunch," says Lacky. "What do you say? Are you free tomorrow?"

. . .

Here comes Kenyon Saint Claire, thinks Kenyon Saint Claire, approaching his own shrunken figure twinned in the dark lenses of Sam Lacky's sunglasses. The men shake hands, there on the sidewalk in front of the luncheonette at Madison and Sixty-Third. "Damn, am I glad to see you, pal," says Lacky. This familiar manner is so perfect a non sequitur that Kenyon can only smile—his walleyed image in the lenses unmoving amid the swim of the avenue.

Inside they order sandwiches and coffee. Lacky pays the ticket. They sit.

"Lemme get right to the point, Kenny. One of the trivia shows I co-produce needs a new contender. Short story is, there's a guy from Queens goin' on five weeks now as the big winner and it's time to freshen the bed, so to speak. People like a winner, sure, but not all winners are a bag of laughs, and this particular person is starting to . . . well, worry the sponsors. Now, here I am at this dinner party last week, and here's this sharp young man from a good family, well-educated, such a believer in education he's doing the Lord's work like his father before him bestowing knowledge on the next generation, even though—and you'll excuse me, Kenny—even though a man can't raise a family in New York on the salary they're paying him. So I meet this young man and I think, you know what a man like that is? A man like that is a *winner*. He's a *winner*. He's doing all the right things, got all the right values, why shouldn't he be rewarded for it? See, I work in television, Kenny, as you know—but what you may not know is what kinda stuff people are seeing on their TV sets at night. Well, let me tell you, OK? What's today, Tuesday? Take a typical Tuesday night on ABC, what do you get? Seven-thirty to eight-thirty, *Cheyenne.* Guns. Eight-thirty to nine, *Life and Legend of Wyatt Earp.* Guns. Nine to nine-thirty, *Broken Arrow.* Guns. Two hours of guns and that's just Tuesday nights. Now, we're talking tens of millions of viewers, Kenny, *tens of millions,* and that's what we're giving them? Cowboys and Indians? When you start thinking in those numbers, especially if you're somebody of your very educated nature, it's pretty demoralizing, wouldn't you say?"

"Well," says Kenyon, "at the least it's a wasted opportunity."

"A wasted opportunity, that's right. A real travesty too. I work in the business and even I would say so. But then I meet a young man like yourself, Kenny, and I think, here's the real thing, here's the kind of person we ought to see on our television screens. I'm thinking, I could work with this guy. Now, hear me out. Our company, Mint and Greenmarch, we produce a very different kind of programming. Is it entertainment? Sure. It's even thrilling in its way—but these thrills, you could call them intellectual in nature. Not a gun in sight. It's all about what's happening in the heads of the contestants, it's all about knowledge. They're called trivia shows, but you know better than I do, you being the teacher and all, that education is no trivial thing. I don't know if you've ever watched *The $64,000 Question*, Kenny, but they've got this slogan on there, goes, 'Where knowledge is king, and the reward king-sized.' Well, that's very nice and all, but in point of fact the show's just onesy-twosy, little questions come and gone—real *trivia*, you know, and the rest of the time it's Hal March standing around shooting the breeze or telling the ladies about Revlon. Everybody's got their sponsor, sure, and that's all well and good, but our shows are doing something different, doing more for the public, I say. And it's entertaining, like I say. Don't get me wrong. But even Shakespeare's entertainment, you know. No, what Mint and Greenmarch is doing, really, is to push this medium forward—TV being a very young medium, see— and we are confident that a higher level of programming is possible. Take one example, we produce this little children's program, *Winky Dink and You*, it's called, and it's the nature of this show that kids don't just sit and stare at the television, but that they actually *participate*. All the kids have a little Winky Dink Kit at home, see, which comes with these four magic crayons and this magic window, as it's called, which is a sheet of acetate they stick right to their television screen. And during the program all the kids are right up at the screen and Fred Mint is helping them draw different pictures and things. Now isn't that, for example, a beautiful use of this medium, helping kids become artists? Doesn't that beat the regular TV diet of shootouts and silliness? Well, with our trivia programs, too, the idea is education. What I mean is, we're showing knowledge to be a desirable thing. Our current champ, this guy from Queens, he's won himself $60,000."

"$60,000?" says Kenyon.

"And counting," says Lacky. "Unlike the other show, we don't stop at sixty-four. Now, like I say, Kenny, I look at a man like you and think, now *there's* somebody who deserves that kind of money. See, I've given this a lot of thought, Kenny, and I'm telling you, you're the guy to beat Sid Winfeld."

"That's the champ you mentioned?"

"Sid Winfeld, mm-hm. It's time he goes, he's making the sponsor nervous. Bring a man like Kenyon Saint Claire on the program, though, and it's good for everyone concerned. A man of real education, man from a good family who ain't a snob—the sponsors, the viewers, everyone loves it. And you get to earn some of the dough they ain't paying you up at the college. You take sugar?"

"Sure." Between them their small table is a mess of deli papers and napkins. Kenyon watches a solid white cascade stream into his paper coffee cup. "Thanks, that's plenty. I do appreciate your invitation, Sam. But who's to say I even manage to beat this Winfeld?"

"You'll manage, no question. I wouldn't make the proposal if you couldn't. Like I say, at the end of the day it's entertainment, it's television. We don't just throw you in there, is what I'm sayin'. And no one leaves empty-handed. Worst case scenario, you only do one show, a thousand bucks."

"A thousand?"

"Guaranteed. But you'll do even better, Kenny. No question. Us producers, our job is to know what you know."

"Wait," says Kenny. "Let me understand. You decide who wins?"

"Look, you're a teacher. We understand that. We're not looking for actors here, if that's your concern. You go on to the show as yourself. You're the educator, the man of good family, that's you."

"Yes, but you—"

"We help you be *you*, even on television. 'Cause television, it's a different dimension, see. It's got its own rules and requirements, every program does, and if you break these, well, there goes your show. It's a controlled medium or there's no excitement, and remember, we wanna show the *excitement* of education. What we do for the program, Kenny, is create people. But the person we're creating here, well, that'll be *you*. *You* know what you know, and *we* know what you know. It's simple, see?"

"I think so. I don't know. When would this be?"

Kenyon walks to Columbus Circle, following Fifty-Ninth along the edge of the park, turning over Lacky's words in his mind. Already, somehow, there's a new clarity in his outlook, a kind of liberating honesty inside him, and it lends buoyancy to his walk along the rumbling street. For the first time in several years, he sees himself plain. *What would you do,* Lacky asked him, *if you won a thousand, a couple thousand dollars?* Without hesitation Kenyon said he would write a book. Four words: "I'd write a book." That's it. He loves teaching, he believes in teaching—just like Dad—but *winning,* that is something else. Winning means money, and money means having choices.

And isn't Lacky right? Wouldn't Kenyon be teaching *while* winning?

He's breathing clear now. He can see himself and own his own feelings. Sometimes, of late, he's sensed down at some buried level of his being the presence of omens, weird little harbingers, something not right somewhere in his bones, the tremors of a preliminary doom. And now, today, thanks to his selection by the most unlikely of saviors—television!—there is a change. His body moves forward to the subway station, but inside he's turning about to get a better look at himself, to pose the question to Kenyon Saint Claire, there in the anonymous stream of the New York street: Has it all been a premonition of *success?*

He's come to the subway stairs. With sprightly little hops he descends, not even holding the rail, floating down into the roar of the trains and thinking, *$60,000! $60,000!*

2.
APPLAUSE

November 1956

Winky Dink and you
Winky Dink and me
Always have a lot of fun together

Winky Dink and you
Winky Dink and me
We are pals in fair and stormy weather

All the kids who heard
Winky's magic word
Make a wish and then they all shall wink-o

What a big surprise
Right before their eyes
Wishes do come true from saying wink-o

Presto change-o, that's a thing of the past
Wink-o wink-o works twice as fast

Winky Dink and you
Winky Dink and me
Always have a lot of fun together

Winky Dink and you
Winky Dink and me
We are pals in fair or stormy weather.

—Theme song, *Winky Dink and You*

AND NOW A WORD FROM OUR SPONSORS

"You know, ladies," says the *$64,000 Question*'s Hal March, looking straight at you as the camera cuts to a closeup, "no matter how often you use a greasy cream or scrub your face with soap—if you'll forgive my saying this—you still leave some dirt behind. So I'd suggest getting your skin thoroughly clean with…"

Music sounds and a chorus sings: *Clean and Clear!*

The vertical hold gives way: the picture scrolls upward—
and upward—
and upward…
For a moment the sound is scrambled…

"There must be a moral in this someplace," says a program host, as the audience laughs. "I don't know what it is. How many points would you like?"

"Now Helen's unpacking her Winky Dink Kit right now, getting out her Magic Crayons and now she's going to get out her Magic Window. Now you do just as she's doing, boys and girls…"

"Revlon puts beauty within your reach," says Hal March, "with Snow Peach!"

"People with low blood iron often feel the cold more, and now that we're entering the winter season, here's a suggestion…"

"Watch Helen now, watch as she rubs her Magic Window and you do that too, that's the way to get some of our magic into the Magic Windows. You see how she rubs it? Fine…"

"Lose ugly fat fast with RDX stomach reducing plan!"

"And now this is Bob Shepherd wishing you good health from Pharmaceuticals Incorporated…"

"Now Helen's gonna put her Magic Window right up on the screen of the television set. That's right. Now you do it, just the way she does it, boys and girls, it's very important…"

"Bill, as if I don't know, who is Revlon's next guest?"

"Everyone knows who the sponsor is, but no one is sure who the boss is. The sponsor meets the payroll but that doesn't make him the boss."

"We'd sit in the sponsor's meetings and they would say, 'Well, that one— that one's gotta go on to win,' or, 'I don't like that one, let's get rid of him.'"

The lights are on—
    and the lights are on—
    and the lights are on …

"You cannot ask random questions of people and have a show. You simply have failure, failure, failure, and that does not make for entertainment."

"Would you like to win some money now, Meryl?" says Hal March.

"Sponsor, agency, network, producer, director, and even audience—all do certain kinds of bossing at different times and in different ways."

And in the booth the light is on, and the studio is dark.
    "Can you see and hear me, Meryl?" says Hal March.
    "Yes, I can."

But this magic window is always a mirror.

"Ready for your $16,000 question?"

Always a mirror.

Who's at the switch?

What happened to the signal?

CONTROL

Full-front is Fred Mint's strong angle—trim figure, features sharp, chin like a rock. When he turns you see his slight hunch and the face in profile goes doughy.

—Pull in, Camera One, nice'n slow—

He faces the camera now, looking you in the eye, close as a kiss, dapper tie done up snug.

—There, hold it, that's beautiful, and—

"Good evening. I'm Fred Mint. For six weeks on this program a twenty-nine-year-old college student, Sid Winfeld, has beaten all his opponents and run his winnings up to $69,500. Hundreds of people from around the country have offered to challenge him. Tonight some will get their chance to do so, and during the next thirty minutes we'll find out whether they can win against the unstoppable Winfeld. So now"

—Ready Camera Two—

"presented by Geritol, America's Number One Tonic, let's meet our first two players. From New York City, Mister Kenyon Saint Claire, and returning with $69,500 from Queens, New York, Mister Sidney Winfeld."

—Camera Two—

KENYON

Dark in the wings, hurriedly finishing a smoke, Kenyon watches the silver face illumined on a monitor overhead, the voice transposed to a distance of several yards, Mint himself facing away in the bath of light beyond the booths. *Tonight some of these people will get their chance,* Mint is saying, though Kenny alone stands by in this dark, the floodlit contest to come already decided. Or so he's understood. In which case, why so horribly nervous now?

Somewhere opposite, in the dark behind the other booth, stands Winfeld, watching him perhaps, Kenny's own face lit gold with every pull on the cigarette. Does he know, poor Winfeld, what's coming? Surely he does. Surely they've made it worth his while, the arrangement settled. He and Kenny are to shake hands afterward, in the light before the cameras as the audience applauds.

And they're applauding now, and here goes, and Kenyon drops his smoke into the Dixie cup an assistant offers. Moves ahead into the light and there before him materialized like an image in a mirror is Sid Winfeld, small and stout in oversized jacket, tortoise-shell glasses gone milky in the brightness. Eyes averted, the players pivot to pass shoulder to shoulder between the booths. Four steps forward in the lens glare and static of clapping hands to find their footmarks beside Mint at the podium, to crowd in and stick for the three-shot as instructed. The camera's red light is a hungry eye fixed upon them.

"Welcome back, Sid Winfeld, and a cordial welcome to you, Mister Saint Claire. Now, Sid, you're faced with that same awful decision that begins every game. You have $69,500. You can take it and quit right now and a check will be waiting, or you can continue playing. Of course, if you go on playing and Mister Saint Claire beats you, his winnings will be deducted from the money you have. So, to help you make up your mind, here are some things you should know about Kenyon Saint Claire."

Now a second camera lights up red, pulling in close on Kenny as the voice of Bob Shepherd, low and weirdly intimate in register, comes over a microphone from somewhere in the darkness above. It's like a voice in one's head: *He teaches music at Columbia University and was a student at Cambridge University in England. He's written two books and is currently working on his third, and his hobby is playing the piano in chamber music groups.*

They said to look in the lens, but Kenyon can't do it. He can feel the frame pressing in around his head and strives to compose his face in its cake of blush and powder, sweat already beading in his hair. Teaches music, did they say? A student at Cambridge for a time perhaps—but *three* books? And as for the piano, how his family would laugh: at most he'll sometimes noodle around after dinner on his parents' old upright, cigarette still in hand. But now Fred Mint is turning to address him.

"Out of curiosity, Mister Saint Claire, are you in any way related to Maynard Saint Claire up at Columbia University, the famous prize-winning writer?"

There's a burning in Kenny's throat. Did he put out his last cigarette or swallow it? He stoops, one hand resting awkwardly on the wing of the podium where his microphone is mounted. He feels he can't possibly be squeezed into the same shot with these two men, over whom he towers by a head.

"Um, yes I am," he answers. "Maynard Saint Claire is my father."

"He is your *father!*"

"Yes."

"Well, Saint Claire is a very well-known name. Are you related to any of the other well-known Saint Claires?"

He needs to swallow but his throat won't function—anyway they're reeling the words right out of him.

"Uh, well, Emily Saint Claire, the author and editor, is my mother, and Curtis Saint Claire, the historian, was my uncle."

"Curtis Saint Claire. Also a prize-winning writer, wasn't he?"

"That's right."

"Well, you have every reason in the world to be proud of your name and family, Mister Saint Claire. Now, Sid Winfeld, you've heard some things about Kenyon Saint Claire. You have $69,500. Do you want to take it and quit, or risk it by playing against him? What'll it be?"

"I'll take a chance, Mister Mint."

"That's the spirit, Sid. OK then, gentlemen, take your places in the booths. Don't forget to put on your earphones, and good luck to both of you."

Music sounds. The hot lights are on. Turn now, through the narrow door, into the glass box. There's the upright microphone, slender as a charmed snake. The shut door muffles the studio orchestra and seals in the heat. A private terrarium, televised. The camera's red eye in the dark, the viewers beyond the lens. How many? Duck to don the headphones and all is doubly muffled. Inward and inward inside the glass, deaf to the world that watches.

CONTROL

As the players enter the booths, twin spokesmodels appear as though conjured by the music. Affixing each contestant's name to his scorebox, they glide back on their heels, withdrawing, every movement synchronized. The music ends.

"Neither player in the booths can hear anything," says Fred Mint, "until I turn their booths on—which I am going to do right now."

KENYON

A *click* in Kenny's ears, then Mint's voice coming through like a telephone: "Can you hear me, Sid Winfeld?"

"Yes, I can," answers the other voice.

"Mister Saint Claire?"

"Yes, loud and clear."

"All right, Sid, I'm going to turn your booth off. I'll be back to you in just a moment."

Click.

"Mister Saint Claire, I think you know how to play this game. You try to get twenty-one points as fast as you can by answering questions with a point value from one to eleven. The high-point questions are difficult, the lower-point questions a bit easier. The first category is World War Two. How much do you think you know about World War Two? You can tell us by saying how many points you want from one to eleven."

You'll take seven, Lacky had told him. *You'll tie the first round.*

"World War Two," says Kenny, as if contemplating. "I'll try seven points."

In their dry run, to his own surprise, he'd answered a number of Lacky's questions correctly. *You know what you know, and we know what you know. It's simple.* Lacky's office doors shut and Lacky's on his feet before the desk, dabbing his brow with a handkerchief. *It's gonna be hot in there, that I can promise you, so after the big questions you'll press your face like this.*

Already Kenny can feel the sweat around his eyes. The questions he missed he went and looked up on his own. *We help you be you, even on television.* And here comes Lake Ladoga.

"For seven points," says Mint's voice. "Lake Ladoga played a large part in a particular phase of World War Two. Name the countries whose troops opposed each other at Lake Ladoga."

Isn't that more of a geography question? he'd said to Lacky. *It's Finland and Russia that border Ladoga, of course.*

Lacky just gave him a look. *Geography or war, what sounds more exciting, Kenny?*

"Let's see," says Kenny. The words in his own earphones are like an inner voice and every deep-drawn breath booms in the mike and he knows the mike feeds his voice to the camera and the camera feeds the television sets—how many?—all speciated around the country. "Let's see, I remember the German-Russian line ran from Lake Ladoga to the Black Sea, but Ladoga, I guess it's in Finland, so would the answer be Finland and Russia?"

"It would be," declares Mint, "and you have seven points!"

And here comes the audience applause, and Kenyon breathes and smiles, his smiling face so tight with makeup it's like a mask he can't quite crack.

Then *click*, the applause is gone, Mint turns his back, and Kenny is alone and left to wait in his light behind the glass.

COMMENTATORS

"You want the viewer to react emotionally to a contestant. Whether he reacts favorably or negatively is not that important. The important thing is that he react. He should watch hoping a contestant will win, or he should watch hoping a contestant will lose…. People tune in to see someone unpleasant defeated."

LIVING ROOM

Wouldn't be all that bad to see this new fella win.

The picture switches to Sid Winfeld. Bloodless gray behind glass, greased hair askew under his headset, he takes the ten-point question, sweating visibly around his mouth.

Get the guy a hankie.

"Sid Winfeld, you're right—and you now have ten points!"

Applause, and Sid in his booth pumps both fists downward as if landing a jump. His lighted scorebox winks—the numeral 10 appears.

Just might be unbeatable, this guy.

Fred Mint flips his lever and turns again to Kenny. "Kenyon Saint Claire, you have seven points." *Ding!* goes a bell as he snaps up another card. "The second category is The French Revolution. How many points do you want from one to eleven?"

"I should take eleven but I don't dare. Let me try for ten anyway."

"Ten points. Here is your question. The French Revolution brought to prominence men of varied backgrounds. Name the following: first, a lawyer nicknamed The Incorruptible, whose idealistic views ironically encouraged the Reign of Terror. Second, a lawyer who as Minister of Justice under the convention advocated The Revolutionary Tribunal."

This one's a doozy.

"Third, a physician scientist who published a revolutionary journal called *The Friend of the People*. And fourth, the man who was considered the greatest orator of the constituent assembly. He was of noble birth and his aim was a constitutional monarchy."

"Oh my goodness! Well, my father would know that."

He's smart but not uppity, this fella.

KENYON

Through the earphones Kenny hears the ambient ripple of laughter from the audience. Amazing, but they're pulling for him already, the laughter a delicious warmth in his head. He smiles at the sound and coughs a laugh of his own into one hand.

Should I really say that about my dad? he'd asked Lacky.

Just try it, OK? They're gonna root for you, you'll see.

"It's a four-part question," says Mint's voice. "First, the name of the lawyer nicknamed The Incorruptible."

"Yes, of course. He said, 'The King must die that the nation may live.' That's Robespierre."

"Right. Second, a lawyer who as Minister of Justice…"

There's that statue in Paris, have you seen it?

Lacky's mouth twitched, a deadpan look. *Can't say that I have, Kenny, no.*

"Well, the thing I remember about him," says Kenyon into the mike, "is the wonderful quotation on his statue. 'After bread, education is the primary need of the people,' it says. That would be Danton."

"That is right," says Mint. "And indeed you're proving his statement was true."

Again comes an encouraging chuckle from the audience, positively electric amid the fuzz of the headset, and Kenyon can't help smiling in the hot light as he blots his brow and eyes.

"Third," says Mint, "a physician scientist who published a revolutionary journal called *The Friend of the People.*"

"Yes," says Kenyon, on a roll now, and every bit a teacher whose father is a teacher too. "Yes, that paper was very important. It got the people behind the revolution. That has to be Marat."

Poor Marat, they found him in the bath, sunk down in his own blood.

Huh. Killed himself?

No, stabbed to death. There's that painting by David.

Let's not touch on all that. It's enough to say, what was it, about the people?

His pamphlets got the people behind the revolution.

Yeah. That's plenty.

"That's correct," says Mint. "Fourth, and finally, for your ten points, the man who was considered the greatest orator of the constituent assembly."

"Well, this one I'll have to guess. I suppose the greatest orator there was…"

Count to four. One. Two. Three. Four. Like that. Then blurt it out like you're positive.

"The Count de Mirabot."

"You're right for ten points—which brings your score to seventeen!"

And here comes the applause in a great surge of relief. Kenny can hardly understand it, but how clearly they're on his side, how lucky they seem to feel, as if he carried them through. He's blotting his face, their roar in his ears, and even in the claustrophobic swelter, the sweat down his back, there comes a cool rush, a chill.

Click.

SIDNEY

"Sid Winfeld, you have ten points," says Mint, that hopped-up voice in Sidney's ears. Then the little *ding!* of the bell and: "The category is Medicine. How many points do you want?"

November twenty-eighth tonight and that makes six weeks running he's stood in this box, sweating in the old maroon coat and the earphones clamping his skull while he bites his lips, twiddles his fingers on his chin, squeezes his eyes, grimaces, shakes his head, counts to four, always to four. Well, small price to pay, all that.

"I'll try seven," he says.

Small price to pay for a run like this, the prize money, the recognizing, all those looks when he walks the campus to classes, the chance to show he knows a thing or two, Sidney Winfeld and his copious memory. Small price, albeit he won't deny there's been hiccups—the prize money for instance.

"For seven points, Sir Alexander Fleming and Doctor Selman Waxman are each associated with a famous and potent antibiotic. Name these two antibiotics."

The prize money—talk about a hiccup—and that long involved speech from Greenmarch last week as to how the sponsor only pays them a flat sum and he's got his budget to consider or there's no show and so on and so forth, which the gist was telling Sidney in so many words, *we never said you'd keep ALL the money*, and serving up the paper he called "the settlement" or something to that effect for Sidney to sign where it stated

On winnings from sixty to eighty thousand I will take fifty, eighty to a hundred thousand I will take sixty and such like.

He's counting now. *One. Two …*

It's entertainment, said Greenmarch. *A show. There's the prize money, then there's your net take. And anyway, you're already well beyond the twenty-five we first discussed, which gives you no ground to be fussy.*

And if I'd rather not sign? said Sidney.

To which Greenmarch only grinned, a look like *poor sap,* and said, *Let's remember whose show this is.*

Three… Four…

It was all on account of the advance, no question. It had been, what, only three days before that Sidney came asking for the eight and a half grand. Four weeks he'd been on the program, it's only reasonable he'd want a *retainer,* so to speak, his winnings piling up with every game but until then not a buck in his pocket. Well, Greenmarch couldn't shake him till he had a check. Deposited that night and Sidney and Bernice, how they'd fucked after that, like honeymooners.

Five… keep them waiting, show them real suspense. Six…

"Sir Alexander Fleming," says Sidney into the mike, "is a discoverer of *Penicillin notatum,* or *Penicillin.*"

Notatum's just icing. To show them up there in the control room that Sidney Winfeld's the real thing, not some little project of theirs.

"Right," says Fred Mint. "And Waxman?"

They think Sidney doesn't see what's happening here?—the wheels they've got in motion now, Mister Professor over there all dressed and done up for the big debut.

"Selman Waxman is the discoverer of Streptomycin, for which—"

"You're right!" says Mint, cueing the applause to drown Sidney out, but Sidney ain't through speaking and bears down on the microphone almost shouting—

"For which—"

"You don't hafta say anything more, and you now have seventeen points!"

"For which he received the Nobel Prize!" The producers anyway will hear him, applause or no—they think he didn't know Selman Waxman already? And Sidney smiles so they'll see it, sweat-drenched and boxed up in their tank as he is. But he knows now to do it, the minute the cameras go off, backstage at the first opportunity he'll get Lacky or Greenmarch off to the side and demand another advance—tactful, professional, but not to be brushed off or denied—$10,000, he'll say. I've earned it, he'll say. You owe me.

Q:

How much did you receive in total
as your winnings?

A:

$49,500, sir.

Q:

This was more than the
arrangement called for?

A:

Yes, sir. Mister Greenmarch told me
he was giving me a bonus, as he put it,
because of my great histrionics.[*]

---

[*] Congressional Record, House Subcommittee on Legislative Oversight, October 6, 1959

CONTROL

—Camera Two Camera Three split screen, let's see 'em sweating now, fellas, show me their pores—

"Gentlemen, I caution you not to divulge your scores. Your booths are both on the air and you can hear each other. We're at the end of the second round and neither of you has reached twenty-one points. You both get a chance to stop the game right here and now, and if one of you stops, whoever has the high score at this point will win. You'll win at five hundred dollars a point for the difference in your scores, but I caution you, don't stop the game unless you think you have the high score. I'm going to turn your booths off, give you time to think about it, and I'll tell you when your time is up."

The studio orchestra plays, a brooding ascendant vignette.

The frame is split with the players in closeup side by side, sodden with sweat, gray faces wracked.

—Stay on Winfeld Camera Three don't let'm out of frame Jesus-H the guy's jittery isn't he—

COMMENTATORS

"The living rooms were hushed, bluish from the little cube that looked very cold—its pictures were malignant and toneless—but was warm to the touch like any working machine. We all clustered around the cube, silent, intent, solitary—unlike ourselves."

KENYON

Mom and Dad do not, of course, own a television set. To know they aren't watching is in one sense a relief. In another way, though, it adds to Kenyon's surprising loneliness.

Loneliness? With five, ten million watching?

In fact he can't know how many, and it wouldn't help to know. How does one hug a million people, let alone ten times that number? To be watched in this way is to lose all agency.

Q:

When the world and its machines
are so busy creating you, how
are you supposed to create yourself?

A:

Create yourself? Sounds like
a whole lotta trouble.
Let's go for a ride. Now relax…

A terrible feeling, to realize this medium itself might broadcast a person you barely resemble. There's a black hollow in the pit of Kenny's stomach. It came upon him unawares but is finally unmistakable—the feeling exactly of nauseating homesickness. The Klieg lights are no help, god knows. The glare on the glass. The applause, he must admit, is pleasurable. It puts a body in a glowing state: you can almost believe they love you—but even that is just a layer, a kind of lotion. The smallness of the booth, and being shrunken down that way—to a picture on a screen—some part of you knows, even while some good feelings wash over you, that you can't be any more alone. Even George, who does own a small television, is not watching. And what is Kenny doing out here, so far beyond the edges of the values the Saint Claires embody? All the lights are on and powered to full brilliance. The books on his shelf, though, on his father's shelves, are closed. He's doing his best to keep his mind on the money. He's told his parents, "I could win a couple hundred dollars." They took this as pleasant news, amusing enough, worthy of their good wishes. *At least eight thousand,* though, is what Lacky had said when they signed the contract. *Possibly much more.* But how do you tell your parents such a thing?

CONTROL

"I'll stop," says Sid Winfeld, squat, gray, and bespectacled in his booth.

—*Camera Two Camera Three hold the split*—

"Sid Winfeld, I have news for you. This time you don't win—now don't get excited, you don't lose either. At seventeen points you are tied with Mister Saint Claire and we have to play another game. As I'm sure you both know, this second game will be at one thousand dollars a point, which means that in the next few minutes one of you could win as much as $21,000."

—*Hold the split*—

"Conversely—I don't mean to scare you here—you could *lose* $21,000. There's a lot of money at stake right now, gentlemen."

—*Ready Camera One*—

"So what do you say we just sorta slow down, and we'll start the new game in just a moment. All right?"

—*Camera One*—

Close on Fred Mint's face as he takes a deep breath.

"I'm telling *them* to slow down. I'll have to slow down myself. Whew! You know, this *slow down* is a word that's very much in vogue now, 'cause a lot of you have been slowing down without even thinking about it. That's because you don't have much vitality left. It's a problem that faces many this time of year, feeling tired and run down, especially after a cold, flu, or sore throat or virus."

—*Ready title*—

"Well, your trouble may be due to what the doctors call *iron deficiency anemia*—boy, there's a mouthful to slow you down. We call it by the simple term of *tired blood.*"

—*Title up. Good, oh that's lovely fellas*—

"I have a wonderful suggestion as always. Take Geritol. In just twenty-four hours Geritol iron is in your bloodstream carrying strength and energy to every part of your body."

KENYON

The questions Kenyon missed he went and looked up on his own—like the Churchill question coming at the end of this round, the nine-pointer in which he's to say, *I'll go all the way, Fred, I'll try for nine.*

First, of course, comes Fashions. *I don't know anything about fashions. Can I take three points?* Answer: *Nylon.* That one hadn't stumped him. Then will come the first nine-pointer, category Founding Fathers, about the Massachusetts man who said, "taxation without representation is tyranny." He'd known it was one of two people but couldn't remember whom, Daniel Delaney or James Otis. It was Otis, though he'd said Delaney.

Say it just like that, Lacky told him. *Say, hmm, it's either Daniel Delaney or James Otis.*

So, Otis for nine points, which will carry him to twelve. Then the Churchill question and *I'll go all the way, Fred.*

Ding! goes the bell.

"The category is Churchill. How many points do you want?"

"Do you mean Winston Churchill?"

"Let me look and see myself. I assume it's Winston Churchill. Yes, it is."

"I'll go all the way, Fred. I'll try for nine."

"Nine points, you say?"

"Yes."

"Well, Kenyon Saint Claire, if you answer correctly you will have twenty-one, but you'll still have to wait while we give Sid Winfeld his chance to answer. Because we are at a crucial moment here, let me ask you again, you wanted nine points, is that right?"

"That's right."

"Then here is your question, for nine points. Winston Churchill wrote a series of six brilliant books chronicling the events leading up to and including World War Two. I want you to name any three of them. Because you are trying for twenty-one, you're allowed a little extra time to think about it. I'll let you know when your time is up."

The studio orchestra plays. In the earphones the three-tone melody is a wheezy blare, mounting forebodingly through its octaves.

Kenyon moves his lips, furrows his brow, rubs his chin. He's sweating everywhere, with another round still to go. *You'll tie at twenty-one in the second,* said Lacky. *The third, you'll get the same score and win.*

"Kenyon, your time is up. For your nine points, which would give you twenty-one, name any three of the six brilliant books I mentioned a moment ago."

"One of them, I think the first one, is *The Gathering Storm.*"

"That is one."

"Another is *The Grand Alliance.*"

"That's two. You need one more to give you twenty-one points."

Turn your head a little aside. Murmur. "I've seen the ad for those books a thousand times. I can't have any more time, huh? Oh, I have it. *Triumph and Tragedy.*"

"That's right, and you have twenty-one!"

Applause like a refreshing splash, the pressure so beautifully let off, the audience so thankful.

"Now, Mister Saint Claire, you have the twenty-one points needed to win, but of course Sid Winfeld still has one chance to answer and we'll see what happens. I'm going to allow you to listen in because you've got twenty-one, but please do not say anything, OK?"

Click.

"Sid Winfeld, you have eleven points. The category is Churchill. How many points do you want to try for?"

SIDNEY

Sidney can already hear him breathing over there. Mr. Professor listening in, which means he's at twenty-one. They think Sidney doesn't know!

"I'll try ten," he tells Fred Mint.

And now the big reveal, which he's supposed to look surprised, Mint saying, "I can tell you now that your opponent has already scored twenty-one. If you answer this question correctly we'll have another tie. If you miss you'll be back down to one point with a difference of twenty points in your scores, meaning that at one thousand dollars a point you'll lose $20,000. Remember now, there's a lot at stake and take your time. Here's your question for ten points. Prior to his election to Parliament in 1900, Winston Churchill was with the British Army in three foreign countries. Name them. Do you want some extra time to think about it, Sid?"

He knows the television picture is split to a two-shot now: himself and Mr. Saint Somebody side by side in closeup.

"No, thank you, Mister Mint, I have the answers."

They think he didn't know Selman fucking Waxman already? No hems and haws now, he'll run right through these Churchills and Mr. Professor can go right on and listen.

"South Africa in the Boer War," says Sidney.

"That's one."

"India."

"That's two. One more left for twenty-one."

"Sudan."

"That's right, and we have another tie at twenty-one!"

But in the ensuing applause Sidney doesn't even grin.

LIVING ROOM

And now the third game, for fifteen-hundred a point.

Constrained in the oval of the TV screen, drained of color but glistening silver with sweat in that field of gray, each player remains in his booth, earphones on, listening, or not listening, as the master of ceremonies flips the switch to mute him or let him speak.

Ever so slightly the picture wobbles, each figure striated and wavy at the edges, the shadowy areas very black. Oh, but how white and cleansing is the light. How rapturous the transmission. What wattage must they use to bring the faces forward from the dark?

The first question is for Mr. Saint Claire, tall, dapper, and dignified in his booth. Is there anything he does not know? Sid Winfeld must hope there is, for he stands to lose more than $30,000.

Ding! goes the bell.

"The category is Queens. For $1,500 a point, Mister Saint Claire, how many do you want?"

"Do you mean mythical queens or real queens?"

"Well, goodness, I'll have to look. I think these were real queens. Yes, they were."

"Eleven. I'll go for eleven points."

"All the way, the most difficult question. Here it is. The wife of King Ahab was a cruel and willful woman. She favored the idolatrous worship of Baal and persecuted the prophets of Jehovah. What was her name and what country did she rule?"

Always when Fred Mint reads a question an extra zone of silence surrounds his voice, a tight breathless silence you can almost see on the screen. The man in the booth and the whole world listening.

"You say the wife of Ahab?"

"Yes."

"I was afraid of that."

He looks uncertain, Kenyon Saint Claire. His brow is all furrowed and the sweat around his eyes suggests tears. He seems so vulnerable. He just might miss this one. He moves his head around in thought and you can hear the little clang of his earphone cord against the microphone. The closeup is cruel, all but cannibalistic.

"Mister Saint Claire, I'll have to ask for your answer."

"I suppose I'll have to guess."

His wide mouth looks stretched, the strain of worry. Give the poor guy a smoke.

"The only person I can think of…could it be Jezebel?"

"It could be, you are correct! And one more part—what country did she rule? I'll have to ask you to answer more quickly now."

"That must be Palestine."

"You are right, and you have eleven points!"

They let you hear the audience applause, but it's not like *The $64,000 Question*—on this program you never see all the people clapping, their amazed faces.

"Sid Winfeld, for fifteen hundred dollars a point, the category is Queens. How many points do you want?"

"I'll try ten."

Winfeld, so tense-looking, so out of sorts, his hair sticking up or his voice all wrong, nevertheless always seems sure of himself.

"For ten points. Placed on the throne unwillingly, this girl ruled England for nine days before she was imprisoned and killed by the government of the queen who succeeded her. What was her name, and who was the queen who followed her to the throne?"

What must the one or two-point questions be like? Nobody ever asks for those.

"Her name was Lady Jane Gray."

"Right."

"And she was killed…"

"All we need is, Who was the queen who followed her?"

"She was succeeded by Mary Tudor."

"Queen Mary. You are right. That gets you ten points!"

Applause, and Sid Winfeld, not quite smiling, nods with closed eyes.

SIDNEY

Click: the applause is gone and Mint turns to the other booth.

Queen Mary, they'd told Sidney to say. As if he didn't already know she was a goddamn Tudor.

He'll take eleven points on the next, finish off at twenty-one, which one question left means Professor over there is getting twenty-one right this minute to set up the third tie. Because of course Saint Kenny isn't going anywhere, no, it's all laid out so nice, and Greenmarch sure loves these tie games, a fetish like.

Off-camera, boiling away, mopping his neck and mouth and brow, Sidney awaits his eleven-pointer. How good to get another one right, no matter what's coming next week. Hasn't he had a helluva run anyway, and he'll make sure to get his money, and there'll be future appearances of one kind and another—TV ain't done with Sidney Winfeld and his encyclopedia brain. *A champ like you*, Greenmarch told him, *you won't just disappear. We'll need you occasionally at least, if not regularly.*

Eighty grand in winnings all told, the most money ever won on TV. Even if Sidney's net take is a different number entire, well, to win all that on the air where anybody can see, that's a helluva run. And naturally it far exceeds $64,000.

"Sid Winfeld, you have ten points. The category is Opera. How many points do you want to try for?"

"Eleven."

"You want to go for twenty-one. Then I can tell you now that your opponent—it's the same thing that happened before—your opponent has twenty-one points."

Sure enough, he's listening in again from that booth next door. Might as well say, *Hi there, Kenny, you think I don't know opera? Get a loada this.*

"Now, Sid, I caution you to take your time and answer carefully. If you should miss you'll be back down to zero, and your opponent at twenty-one points with $1,500 a point will win somewhere in the neighborhood of $32,000, which will be deducted from your $69,500. So be very careful."

Should've been a banker, that Fred Mint. Spends half of every show crunching numbers, hanging dollar signs on every little comment. If they'd just stick to the questions Sidney could really show them.

"Here is the question, Sid—and you can have extra time if you need it. I want you first to listen to this aria."

In his earphones now: the music, a woman's up-pitched voice, but Sidney's not hearing it. What he's hearing already, beyond the fizz and crackle of the tape, is his answer. Now the music stops and Mint's voice cuts in.

"Sid, for eleven points I want you first to tell me the name of the aria. Second, the name of the opera. Third, who wrote it. And fourth, the name of the character in the opera who sings it. Would you like extra time to think about this? I'll tell you when your time is up."

Cue the studio orchestra, which the music always goes *doom doom doom*, up and up, like something copped from a Hitchcock movie. Sidney does his concentration act. Then Mint's voice is back.

"For your eleven-point question, which could either make or break you on this, Sid Winfeld, first give me the name of the aria."

"I'd like to try the opera's name first."

A nice twist, which those producers, Sidney's got to admit, they know their show business.

"Right, give me the opera's name."

"The name of the opera is *Rigoletto.*"

"Right. Now the composer's name."

"Guiseppe Verdi." Sidney says it correctly even though Greenmarch told him to pronounce it like *Guy-seep-ee.* They want it like everything Sidney knows comes from a book and he mispronounces because he's not properly educated. Oh, and that humiliating spiel last week where they made him say on air about missing the answer on gothic architecture the week before, *Well Mister Mint, I went home and I checked my encyclopedia and found out that gothic architecture originated at the Abbey of Saint Denis—*"Saint Dennis"—*outside of Paris in 1144. Up until then I was sure it was Germany.*

"Verdi is right," says Mint. "And the name of the character who sings the aria?"

"Am I permitted to hear the song again, please?"

"Yes, I think we can play it again. May we hear the aria again?"

Nevermind that during his service Sidney was stationed in the Porte de la Chapelle, practically in view of Saint Denis for six weeks. Again the music fills his earphones, the woman's voice. Not so different from Bernice—she's done some singing of her own, classical like this and not at all bad. They don't know cultivated, him and Bernice? Who says they don't?

"All right, Sid, you have to tell me two more things—the character's name and the aria's name."

"'Cara nome' is the name of the aria."

"You're right. You need one more, the character's name, for twenty-one points."

"Sung by a girl. Gilda."

"Right again, and you have twenty-one!"

Applause, applause.

"Sid Winfeld, will you come out? Mister Saint Claire, come on out here. Gentlemen, this is terrific; we've played three games and we've got another tie. What an exciting show of knowledge you've given us."

Out at the podium for another three-shot, Sidney can see in the professor's face he didn't expect this. Well, they don't tell you everything around here. They're shaking hands like good old sports and Mint's saying, "Can you both come back next week? Sid Winfeld?"

"Yes, sure, Mister Mint."

"Mister Saint Claire, can you come back?"

"Yes."

"Next week you'll play again, this time for $2,000 a point, which puts as much as $42,000 at stake between you. Goodnight, Sid Winfeld. Goodnight, Kenyon Saint Claire. And congratulations."

And it's back to the darkness in the wings for Sidney and Professor while Shepherd does the last commercial, and as they're walking amid the applause Professor turns and murmurs a little something—hard to hear, but to the effect of *you sure put up a mighty fight*, only Sidney just says, "Yes, excuse me, I need to find Mister Greenmarch."

AND NOW A WORD FROM OUR SPONSORS

If you had your Winky Dink Kit and played along with us, well, there's no reason for any of us to miss all the fun.

It's so easy to get your Winky Dink Kit, and you know something, the fun starts as soon as you get your Kit.

Of course, you can watch the program without a Kit, but you can't really be a part of the program without it.

And you can't have the same fun that the boys and girls who have their Winky Dink Kits do have.

Now, I know you're used to watching television shows, you just sit back and watch all the other shows, but not this show.

This show you really get a chance to be a part of, because it's different. You get a chance at home to play right along with us.

But to be a part of the show, you *must* have your Winky Dink Kit. You send fifty cents, boys and girls—got that?—with your name and address, and send it to Winky Dink, Box Five, New York nineteen, New York.

Now I do hope you'll all get your Winky Dink Kits right away and have fun with those boys and girls that do have their Kits, because you really can't have the same fun if you have no Kit.

KENYON

The outside world is something of a shock—the cold night air, the whoosh of cars, all the anonymous faces around Rockefeller Center even at this hour. To come out of the NBC building onto the sidewalk on West Fiftieth is to come out of a daze. Something has just happened, though it seems impossible to say what. Though saying what seems important.

Kenyon starts moving right away, down the cold sidewalk toward Fifth, still sodden in his suit beneath the overcoat, winding his scarf, hunching his shoulders, hurrying to keep his heat. He lights a smoke as he goes. He'll walk to Forty-Second at least, maybe farther, before taking the subway. He needs the low-level shock of the city, its nightwalkers, its stacked windows careening up into dark, all the looming proximity of those secretive lives.

Lacky had seen his surprise and smiled, clapping Kenyon's shoulder. "What a showing, Kenny! A helluva showing!"

They were standing in the brightly lit hall off the studio, stagehands and assistants swirling, not the time or place for discussion, but Kenny simply said, "I'm a little confused, Sam."

"Confused? What's confused? That was a helluva contest! Now come back next week and show us more of that old IQ, huh?"

My IQ? Kenyon thought to say. *We both know that's not what this is about.* But he held his tongue. Lacky beaming pure beneficence, projecting how all's gone according to plan, how successfully they've extracted the desired performance.

Kenyon is walking very fast, a minor ache in each long stride, outpacing something, pursuing something, not sure. He'd made peace with the answers, it was the way of television, he could accept that—they were *his* answers in the end, after all, he'd done his reading, god knows, he's a teacher, that settled it. And they'd expected a performance—the mumbling, the counting, the kerchief—he'd known this and obliged. But that there was still so much he *hadn't* known, so much they had not told him.... He had *been performed by them*, that was it. They'd left him so surprised. And by such a simple trick: by keeping him in the dark.

They have him, he sees now. They have him and they will surprise him again, surely, in order to feed his reaction to the cameras. This will be, as long as it lasts, unsteady ground—Kenny at their mercy, with viewers watching everywhere. Through his mind in a single rush comes the voice of the Dane—*you would play upon me you would seem to know my stops you would pluck out the heart of my mystery you would sound me from the lowest note to the top of my compass ...*

He's reached the corner at Forty-Second Street now and, crossing, he comes to stand on the broad concrete apron before the library. There in the streetlight are the twin lions atop their pedestals, great temple guardians aglow in the white repose of stone. Between them the upward sweep of the steps that carry you to the three doors beneath the engravings on the high entablature: "To HISTORY LITERATURE AND THE FINE ARTS—FOR THE ADVANCEMENT OF USEFUL KNOWLEDGE—TO SERVE THE INTERESTS OF SCIENCE AND POPULAR EDUCATION." The building is very still amid the motion of the city. Inside, the books are at rest, awaiting the discovery of those who will come by morning.

It may be that night is the province of television. Morning, though, is still something else.

Kenyon, on his second smoke and wound up, all damp around the collar, continues on toward the Empire State Building. He'll catch a train at Herald Square, but he needs the eight or nine blocks still ahead of him. He's decided he'll ring up his parents once home. They're at the farm this week. They didn't see the program and he wants to talk to them while that's still the case. It seems important somehow. It's late, and maybe they're in bed already, but he will.

"Kenny!" says Dad's voice. "Oh, Emily, it's Kenny."

"I'm not waking you, I hope."

"No chance of that, son. We've been answering the phone every few minutes. Everyone saw you, it seems."

"So you know the outcome."

"Not that it surprised us, Kenyon. We had no doubt you'd do well."

"A tie, yes. Three actually."

"Son, you're a cause célèbre! It's remarkable. Had you any idea how many would watch?"

"The outcome, you know, there's no outcome yet."

"And is the money what they're telling us it is, fifteen hundred dollars per question or some unthinkable sum?"

"Who told you?"

"Oh, just everybody! They've all been calling. Earl Jordan, Betty Vincent, the Fletchers, the Singleys, Fadiman—who else, Emily? Doctor Addison. Addison was totting up the numbers while he watched."

"Well, it's fifteen hundred a *point*, actually."

"Oh, and every question at a point?"

"Uh, no, some are worth eleven."

"Dear god!"

A gasp, a pause, Maynard Saint Claire's mouth drifting from the receiver to report faintly to Kenyon's mother.

"It's…it's strange, Dad. It's a high-pressure kind of situation."

"Whose money is it? Where does it all come from?"

"Advertisers, you know…"

"That's an awful lot of eggs to sell."

"Pharmaceuticals mostly."

"Those numbers, you can hardly add them up!"

"Next week we start at $2,000 a point. To break the tie."

"Wondrous strange! $2,000 next week, Emily. Your mother says—we both say—we hope you win it all, of course. Who've you been playing against?"

"Don't know much about him. He's a college student. He's had quite a run. Seems to know everything."

"Well, you've made an impression, there's no doubt."

"It's a game. You know. High-pressure or not, it's a game. I'll need to remember that."

"Wisely so, son. But we have no doubt you'll do well."

"Even if I win, it's funny…even if I win, well, no one stays champion forever."

Another pause. Dad's familiar slowness when he listens. The taking in, the reflecting, the thoughtful, almost hesitant reply. "Mm, yes. Winners, losers, that's the jargon of sport. What really counts, as you know, is the impression one makes. You'll always do fine with that, Kenny."

And if the impression one makes is not one's own?

"Thanks, Dad."

"From what I know of it all, I should think you'll be good for television."

But oh, Dad, the dark wings, the isolation booth, the blinding light's dissimulation. If I am good for television, can television be good for me?

"I don't mean to keep you up. I just got in and thought I'd call. How's the farm?"

"Well, last of your mother's squash is in…trees are all turned…we're using the furnace at night. The Gantley place is sold, did we tell you? Bought by a builder who's come in and taken out all the trees along the drive. Can you picture it? They wanted to put in grass and they did, all in a single morning. They bring the grass out in rolls. Have you seen this? They just roll out the lawns and done!"

Q:

How awful is it?

A:

$2,000 a point—the climb
of the money on and on, the lights
ablaze, the orchestra blaring...
And there are no one- or two-point
questions on those cards.
They never tell you this.

Q:

No, no, I mean, how awful is it
to live in a world where
everyone believes in you?

A:

3.
FIFTEEN MILLION
December 1956

SIDNEY

"Feel this one, Sidney. Here. Feel it. Oh, aren't they just gorgeous?"

"They're very fine, Bernice."

"Do you feel that? Oh, did you ever know something so soft? Mother had one of this type, I seem to remember."

And here is where, before, Sidney would've said, *Then let's ask your mother why don't we* and *Maybe she's still got it you never know* and *Why do we need a new one?*, which their circumstances and all—though he never did like charity, he'd have felt the responsibility to say such things. Instead, now he follows as she runs her hand along every fur on the rack, and when she says, "Oh, how will we ever choose?" he doesn't even hesitate: "You choose, Bernice. It's all yours, your choice, whichever one you want, don't think of the price."

She turns, smiling, and brings her body close. "Sidney, you spoil me, honey."

"That's good, honey, that's exactly what I want."

He smells her now, breathes her in deep. She's doused herself in that scent—*Je Suis Fois* or whatever it's called, the little cut-glass mister she brought home the other night, the one which she let him watch while she spritzed herself in the nude and rubbed it in. An aphrodisiac, no question, because he was harder inside her than ever—she said so—and then the sheets and both their bodies smelled so sweet with the scent all night.

So what if he is, after all—spoiling her. She bought the silver fox coat only two weeks ago, but right now she's positively glowing, all giddiness, like a girl, and Sidney can hardly believe what that does to him inside. He hasn't seen her like this since before her father died, which all their problems seemed to start soon after. Josef Winks that old pushover always slipping his precious daughter money even knowing how Sidney objected, even after Sidney sat the old man down and made clear he wouldn't have it, because generosity and gifts was one thing but so was consideration for a husband's feelings on the matter—and when it came to Josef dolling out straight cash it was more than a fellow could be expected to stomach. But even a speech like that couldn't change a thing, which the next time Sidney caught her stuffing a roll of bills into the kitchen jar he all but flushed them down the toilet, Bernice shouting, *How dare you!* acting sick at his ingratitude, telling him, "You're practically *terrified* of money, Sidney, that's

the problem with you!" Coldest voice he'd ever heard from her. And for
the first time it made him wonder would the way they were raised come
between them in the end?

Then the old man passed and Sidney put his foot down with her mother:
jewels and silverware and furs he could abide up to a point, but no more
straight handouts—not from the mother especially. Which, her mother
did back down, and finally Sidney and Bernice had those fights behind
them.

Except then Bernice started up about kids—another subject that
terrified him, she said...

Well, here they are at Saks surrounded with furs and Bernice is bringing
her body very close and there's a whole new look in her face—nothing like
those months of grieving after her father's passing, and her flat stare all
the times she pressed herself on Sidney like he would do her a service. No,
her eyes are so different now he can hardly believe, and she whispers close,
"I want the white one, Sidney, the ermine. The swing coat. Can I have it,
baby?" and down there her hand is moving where their bodies touch, the
fingers playing so nice on his stiffness, and she says, "And something soft
for you after that."

Q:
Mister Winfeld, do you remember that
preceding your loss you had a meeting
with Mister Greenmarch?

A:
Yes, sir.

Q:
What happened at that meeting?

A:
Is this the day I lost, sir?
Is that what you're referring to?

Q:
When you were *told* that you
would lose. Let us fix the date
when you were told you would lose.

A:

This would be on the fourth
of December, nineteen fifty-six.
This was the day before the
program, the usual Tuesday meeting. *

Sidney knew this was coming and now here it is. No tonic water and cherry today, Mr. Greenmarch too preoccupied for little preliminaries. Sidney on the green corduroy sofa and Greenmarch on his feet, and between them, on the coffee table, a teetering pile of files and records, and though Sidney knows he shouldn't, he goes ahead and asks. "What's all this, Ray?"

"Documentation," says Greenmarch flatly. "Memoranda. Trendex reports. All pertaining to the span of your life on the program."

"So I'm over. That's it for me."

"Are you surprised? It can be a shock, we realize. After a winning streak like yours."

Sidney won't be ruffled. He waves a hand. "Don't look so serious, Ray. These files, this isn't…it ain't a police report." Important to show he's professional. He saw it coming after all—and he got his ten grand advance last week, it was in the bank by the following morning.

Greenmarch stays grim. Already everything about him—that stern face, his tie done up and jacket on, the square of his shoulders as he crosses the office to the wheeled blackboard—it all says *non-negotiable*.

"Here's the thing, Sid." Chalk in hand, Greenmarch bends and starts a diagonal line going upward across the board. "Trendex shows you've been very good for the program. September and October's reports reflect an upward movement. But now…" From the center of the board Greenmarch's line levels off—a canceled heartbeat. Flat horizon. "Now November's ratings clearly show a plateau."

"I'm over."

"It's the cyclical nature of entertainment, Sid. A program like ours, people don't want one winner forever."

"I get it, Ray."

"It's good to see that you understand. The viewers, they need rises and falls."

---

* Congressional Record, House Subcommittee on Legislative Oversight, October 6, 1959

"My turn to fall, sure. I get it." He got the ten grand anyhow. And more to come. And there's the arrangements still to be made: future appearances, a retention agreement, and such like.

Greenmarch, retrieving the blue question cards from a drawer in his desk, comes to sit in the leather chair by the sofa. "So let's hash out how it's gonna happen, shall we?"

Still no mention of the tonic water.

"Oh, and, Sid, that incident with your wife last week—I've been meaning to apologize. You understand, of course, why we couldn't have her in the studio. And I realize, I do, that she was very upset, rightly so—it wasn't very gracefully handled on our part."

Bernice was livid, hurried offset for wearing the silver fox coat, just minutes before the broadcast. Greenmarch himself met her in the hall, she said, where the three production assistants held her *under guard* as she put it. *And that smarmy little producer, he tells me it's my coat, my coat is just too beautiful he says, for the purpose of the program he says, people know I'm Sidney Winfeld's wife he says, and how will we explain such a coat on the wife of our poor ex-GI?* Greenmarch offered her the greenroom, but she was in too big a tizzy and told him no, she'd prefer to go. Sidney found her out front after the broadcast, standing on the cold sidewalk, still furious. For more than two hours she'd waited there in the wind, smoking, and right away she poured all the poison into his ear—the humiliation, the indignation, the third-class horror of the situation: *Who are these people, Sidney? They think they can run anybody's life?* In his pocket was the check, still wet from Greenmarch's fountain pen, and when he told her she quieted down, the rage in her face giving over to confusion, and said, somewhat breathlessly, *I'm still not sure I like them any better.*

But they got the ermine the very next day.

"No apology necessary, Ray," says Sidney now. "No hard feelings. And listen, before we run through the questions, I'd hoped to discuss the matter of my future appearances."

This is how you do business, Sidney knows. Relevant matters discussed at the relevant time. *You put my wife out in the cold?—an unfortunate incident but I'm not the kind to hold it against you. Now let's talk turkey.*

Q:
You think I don't know this is
how you do business?
Come to mention it, you think
I didn't know Fleming won
the fucking Nobel?

A:
We badly underestimated you, Sidney.
Let us make it up to you.

KENYON

"Got something for you," says Sam Lacky with a smile. From behind his desk he hoists a bulging canvas sack and thunks it down between rolodex and Dictaphone.

"What's this, Sam?"

Lacky shrugs, ironic but watchful. The sack is labeled U.S. MAIL.

"What…letters? All of these? You mean these are for *me*?"

"I figure, who needs Trendex? We got the U.S. Postal Service."

The sack is deep with them. Kenyon can plunge his hands under. Hundreds at least.

Lacky watches, grinning, as Kenyon brings out a fistful. Jonesboro, Arkansas; Freeport, Illinois; Sterling, Colorado; Lakeland, Florida; Clarksville, Tennessee; Redding, California. They're already opened, every single one.

"Wait, you read them?"

"Well, not me. The secretaries. Company policy."

"But they've been read?"

Lacky shrugs. "Looked at anyhow—anything bearing on the public image of the program, you understand. Myself, I only read a few. You'll like these two especially."

He hands some papers across, each neatly flattened and paperclipped, rubber-stamped in green with the date of receipt.

The top one is typewritten, several short lines on stationery.

Abbey of Santa Lucia
Paterson, New Jersey
November 28, 1956

Dear Mr. Saint Claire,

I and my sisters here had the joy of watching your fine performance on television tonight. There was a consensus afterward that we would write to you. Clearly you are a blessed young man, and it is plain to see what good effect you will have on the nation when you secure your win, as we have no doubt you will. We wish you to know that you are a source of pride and faith to all of us here, for though we have never met you we know you in God. We are raising your name in prayer.

With blessings,
Mother Agatha Locatelli

In Lacky's amused look Kenyon sees a gauge of his own reaction as he read. Weakly he says, "Nuns watch television. Wouldn't have guessed."

The second letter is handwritten, a small precise script in blue ink.

Dear Kenyon,

You came out tied last night, which I realize is not the same as a straight victory, but congratulations all the same! I think you must be one of the nicest fellows any girl could meet—and please do not be too embarrassed if I should add one of the handsomest. My parents and I were delighted to learn of your writing, your teaching, and your interest in music, and we wished uniformly that Fred Mint had said something, anything at all, about your Romantic eligibility. You are not already spoken for, are you? I sincerely hope not. I am nineteen years old and a student of one of the best schools here in Wassau.... I write this with my parents' blessing and include my photo...

The letter continues for two pages. Flipping, Kenyon finds the girl's small photo affixed to the final page with rubber cement.

"Kind of on the young side, that one," says Lacky. "But there's plenty more in there, they tell me. By the way, is your number listed? Well, you'll wanna reconsider that. And we'll need to find you someone—to handle these letters. Should expect 'em by the truckload once you're the champ." He's come around the desk to tip a smoke from his pack for Kenyon. "I'm afraid you're a celebrity, Kenny."

Mailbag aside, they run through the questions, the point values. Categories: Boxing, the Civil War, Movies and Movie Stars, Explorers, Newspapers, Kings. He and Winfeld are to tie the first round, but Kenny's to stop in the second at eighteen points and win. It's the same thing they told him last week.

"You'll need to miss a few," says Lacky. "You aced them all last time, remember. We'll make sure it's ones you won't know."

He misses several in this dry run—Boxing, the Civil War, Newspapers. Lacky wants to tell him but Kenyon says no, he'll look them up. He jots them on a notepad for that purpose.

Commanding Gen. Union Army early 1862
Boxing promoter first million $ game
Owners of Chicago Trib, NY Daily 1914

How well they'll come to know his weak spots.

Q:
Kenyon, incidentally, I've had a lot of
questions about you since last week,
about whether or not you're married or single.

A:
I'm single.

Q:
You are, eh? Are you
in the market, so to speak?

A:
Well, Fred, I don't know if I'd put it
so commercially. I'm in the market, yes…

SIDNEY

He's gonna renege, Greenmarch is. Sidney feels it. They're gonna put him right out. *I can't promise you, Sid,* Ray kept saying. *I can't promise you, but there's lots of options.* The *Steve Allen Show* was mentioned, a panel show was mentioned, a job in the office with weekly pay and other benefits was mentioned (*Let's talk again once you've finished your studies, Sid*). But no, they just wanna placate him, after the winnings settlement and the pesky advances, after the incident with Bernice, after the questions he's humiliatingly supposed to miss—of all the questions, the name of a movie he saw three times and a subject he studied in American History class just two days ago. They're done with Sidney Winfeld in his bad haircut and oversized suit. Now they got Mr. Ivy League, who needs the City College kid? Well, it wasn't even *his* haircut, wasn't even *his* suit—didn't he do everything they asked?

Sidney picks up the phone and dials.

"Mister Greenmarch's office please, this is Sidney Winfeld.... Hello, Ray? Listen, about the program, I've given it a lotta thought and this college vendetta business, it just doesn't sit right. It's being put across, oh you know, as a college fight—City College against Columbia—and what I'd really like to do, Ray, because I don't feel good about this as things stand now, what I'd really like to do is play it honest. I know, I know this comes a bit late, but listen, listen, Ray, I'm happy to refund you a portion of the prize money so I can play it honest, a thousand dollars, how's that sound? I refund Mint and Greenmarch a thousand bucks and Mint and Greenmarch give me a shot to play it honest against Saint Claire, what do you say? Huh? But you understand, Ray, I'm sure you understand my discomfort with this business of City College versus Columbia and which I'm City College means I lose even if it's unnatural. You understand that, Ray, don't you?"

Silence.

The silence of their not hearing—so much louder than the silence if Sidney had never said anything at all.

Sidney decides.

In the phone book he finds the number.

"Yes, I'm calling with a story, breaking news, really. You see I'm directly involved in events…yes, I'll hold.… Yes, hello, I'm calling with a story for the paper—directly involved that's correct—it concerns the National Broadcasting Company—NBC that's correct. Yes, thank you… Hello, Mister Gelman, my name is Sidney Winfeld. I have a story for you— certain facts—about NBC. Yes, NBC television that's correct. You see I am currently a contestant on their Wednesday night quiz program—Sid Winfeld, yes, that's me. Sidney. Well, that's very kind, thank you. In fact I won't be on the show much longer.… Hello? Mister Gelman? Can you hear me better now? Yes, sir, that's what I said, you heard me correctly, sir. *I've been instructed to lose to Kenyon Saint Claire on tomorrow's program.* I wanted to see that *The Post* got the story before the broadcast. Yes I'd be happy to. OK. Sidney Winfeld. Forest Hills. Tomorrow night at ten-thirty. That's correct. We're to play two rounds and I am to miss two questions. My score—would you like me to tell you what my score will be? *Fixed.* Yes exactly, *it's fixed is the reason I'm calling, yes.* Yes. Yes."

• • •

In the evening, after dinner, he rings up Janofsky. Good old Janofsky, which his betting days being over don't mean he can't have a little fun with Nadine, and it's only right Sidney's own unpleasant situation bring some fun to somebody.

"Dick, hi, how the hell are you? Well, I've had some unpleasant news, they're throwing me off the program, that's right, no it's the truth unfortunately…you've got it, that's exactly what they expect…well, they're telling me future appearances and so on, one thing and another, no promises but they mentioned *The Steve Allen Show…* I know!… No, I wouldn't say *happy* about it, but what the hell can you do?…It's hard to know, something like forty or fifty thousand, depending on Saint Claire's score in the second round… No, not so happy, but listen, Dick, how'd you like to surprise Nadine with a show of erudition tomorrow night? Well, I'll miss one in the first and one in the second—I figure those answers oughta be put to use for *someone's* benefit—could be it'll get you a lay, who knows? OK, so the category in the first is Movies and Movie Stars but that's an answer anybody'll know—it's the movie *It's a Wonderful Life…* I know, I know, but see, they want that the know-it-all should miss the easiest question by far, more dramatic they think—but the Round Two question is category Newspapers. Yes, Newspapers, and this is the harder one but just remember when I throw it, you tell Nadine *What's the Matter with Kansas.* That's right, well, *William Allen White* is the first part. Uh-huh, she'll love it, she'll love it, maybe you'll even get a lay, ha ha. *What's the Matter with Kansas,* uh-huh, because where I'm concerned who knows when I'll get laid again after tomorrow's indignity… Well, sure, I suppose there's always the chance of that *Steve Allen Show…*"

Q:

Mister Janofsky, when you were
watching the program that evening
were the questions and answers
exactly as Mister Winfeld had told you?

A:

Yes. In particular I knew there would
be the great opportunity to answer
one of the questions he was going to miss.

Q:

Did you have that little fun with your wife?

A:

Well, yes! [*]

December the fifth, the day of the broadcast, and Sidney's in his undershorts in Dr. Brody's office. That ulcer-like pain in his gut—started a month ago—which the timing of it all makes sense, says the doctor.

"These things are stress-related, Sidney. Quiz kid like you, sweating it out on national television every week, all that money at stake. I were you, I'd have symptoms even worse."

To which Sidney says how he'll be off the show after tonight.

"That so?" says Doc. "They say when you go, do they?"

"Lemme just tell you, Doc, if you asked me which movie was nominated for five Oscars in nineteen forty-seven but didn't win, I'll tell you *It's a Wonderful Life.* But it ain't you that's gonna ask me, too bad."

"I guess I pretty well figured those shows were rigged. No offense, Sidney."

---

[*] Congressional Record, House Subcommittee on Legislative Oversight, October 6, 1959

"And if you asked me, say for instance, the name of William Allen White's editorial, I'd tell you *What's the Matter with Kansas*. These things are not unknown to me, Doc."

"Get yourself some Milk of Magnesia, Sidney, OK? That ulcer, something tells me it'll be gone in a week. You can get dressed now."

Brody steps to his desk, slaps down his clipboard, fishes the smokes from his shirt pocket under the white coat. "Hard to believe," he says, lighting up, "the kind of things they've got on television. Just any kind of thing, any hour of day. It's a changing world, Sidney. My kids, for instance. When they were young they'd read three, four books a week, easy. That was the kind of house we lived in. Nowadays, they watch all the evening programs with their own kids, even supper doesn't stop them—they eat in the living room watching one of those westerns. Of all my grandchildren I don't have anybody'll talk with me about Robert Louis Stevenson or Mark Twain. It's a different kind of world."

"Milk of Magnesia, you say."

"That's right. But wait, if you know the answers, Sidney, why not just say them? Well, better for that ulcer probably to be done with it all."

Q:

They asked you
to do a lot of things?

A:

That is correct, sir.

Q:

Did they ever make you
drink any Geritol?

A:

Frankly speaking, I couldn't see spending
two dollars and ninety-eight cents
for twenty-five cents worth of cheap medicine.

Q:

You say you never did try the product?

A:

No, sir, I would rather take some reputable product.[*]

---

[*] Congressional Record, House Committee on Legislative Oversight, Oct. 6, 1959

CONTROL

The studio orchestra plays, the lights turned up hot. The contestants in their boxes sweat and sweat. In studio blackness floats the red eye of the camera. The audience applauds. The little bell sounds and Mint reads out the questions. *The category is The Civil War, the category is Boxing, I'm sorry you lose nine points, we put you back down to zero, better luck on the next round. You are correct and you now have sixteen points. Gentlemen, I caution you not to speak I'm going to give you time to think it over.*

Click and the booths are off, the lighted boxes deadened to sense, the glass a glinting wall and the earphones a form of deafness.

Mint is almost whispering: *If either player stops the game now Sid Winfeld will win $101,500, but he doesn't know it because they don't know each other's scores—let's see what happens.*

And no one stops, and Mint says, *No? Neither one of you?* And as the audience sends up a ripple of titillation and surprise the master of ceremonies needs a breather and says so and the camera pulls closer for a word from the sponsors.

Oh, questions, questions—I guess I've asked thousands of questions here on television. But there's one simple question that everybody asks everybody else, and I think you know what that is: What's the weather gonna be like? Well, here in New York it looks like we're really in for a tough winter—and I think you know what that means too, it means plenty of sickness. So will you remember, if you feel tired and run-down, especially after a cold, flu, sore throat, or virus, you may suffer from iron deficiency anemia, a very fancy term for what we call tired blood...

Commercial accomplished, the lights brighten again and the game resumes.

—Camera One, nice'n close—

Mister Saint Claire, you have no points at present.

Ding! goes the bell.

The category is Movies and Movie Stars. How many points do you want from one to eleven?

—Camera Two, show me his sweat—

You are correct, and you now have ten points! Sid Winfeld, how many points do you want to try for?

—Stay on him, Camera Three—

No, I'm sorry, the answer is "It's a Wonderful Life," you lose five points, putting you back down to eleven, better luck on the next round. Mister Saint Claire, you have ten points.

Ding! goes the bell.

The category is Explorers. For eleven points and a shot at twenty-one, here is your question. Pizarro was an early Spanish explorer who discovered and conquered an advanced civilization. Tell us the civilization he discovered, the country this civilization was in, and the leader of the civilization at the time of the conquest. Would you like time to think it over?

—Camera Two, that's gorgeous I feel his nerves, even closer if you can—

Your time is up. That's your answer, Atahualpa? Then you score twenty-one points! Sid Winfeld the category is Explorers. You're gonna try to go for twenty-one?

—Camera One, let's see Mint with Winfeld's booth, give me some contrast, oh, that's beautiful and awful, the guy trapped in there—

I can tell you now that your opponent has already scored twenty-one points. If you answer correctly, we'll have to play another game at twenty-five hundred dollars a point. I'm not even gonna bother to figure up the sum cause it's quite gigantic. I'll tell you when your time is up. Gentlemen, it happened again, you both have twenty-one points. First of all I wanna say congratulations to both of you, I don't care who wins or loses you guys really know your onions. We're gonna take a moment out here now for you to settle down. My good friend Bob Shepherd has some important and helpful news for anyone suffering from common rheumatic and arthritic-like pains.... Thank you, Bob. Before we go on I would like to say that all of the questions used on this program have been authenticated for their accuracy and the order of their difficulty by the Editorial Board of the Encyclopedia Britannica.

Ding! goes the bell.

Kenyon Saint Claire, the first category is Newspapers. You're correct and you have eight points!

—Camera Three, we're gonna stay with you on Winfeld—

Sid Winfeld, with your $69,500 still at stake, now at $2,500 a point, the category is Newspapers. I beg your pardon? You have no idea?

—Close as you can, Camera Three, the guy's just dyin', show us the corpse now don't let us off the hook—

You don't wanna take a guess at it? Then I'll have to give it to you, Sid. The title of the editorial was "What's the Matter with Kansas." I'm sorry you stay at Zero. Mister Saint Claire, you have eight points.

—Camera Two—

Ding! goes the bell.

*The category is Kings. Catherine Howard is correct, and what happened to her?
He did divorce her, and you've got eighteen points! Sid Winfeld, the category is Kings.
You're right, you now have ten points!*

—Camera Two, Camera Three, split screen, line the poor suckers up for me, fellas—

*Gentlemen, may I caution you now not to divulge your scores because you can hear
each other. I'm going to give you some time and I'll tell you when your time is up. Click.
If either player stops the game right now, Mister Saint Claire will win back $20,000
from Sid Winfeld. They don't know each other's scores, let's see what happens…*

COMMENTATORS

"The emcee is not precisely dishonest…. He's not a fake but he is a bit
artificial—in a nice way, of course…. Announcements are safe. Real talk
is dangerous."

SIDNEY

"Gentlemen," says Mint's voice in the earphones, "if one of you wants to
stop the game you must tell me so right now."

He's hardly finished saying it when here comes the other voice: "I'll
stop."

And just like that it's over and Sidney can only shut his eyes. He stands
in the hot booth with the headset still on, eyes squeezed closed, shaking
his head, as Mint's voice declares, *You win $20,000!* He keeps his eyes shut
even as the spokesmodels open the booths. He knew this was coming,
sure, only how do you prepare for the moment itself? He opens his eyes,
peels away the earphones, lays them down next to the snakelike wiring
exposed on the backside of the scorebox, and steps numbly from the
booth. Somehow, at the podium, he manages to shake Saint Claire's hand,
to listen to Mint's obsequious little speech—*we may have a lotta contestants
in the future but I doubt that anybody will ever display…*and to say his own little
part when Mint gives him the cue: *You're going home with $49,500, Sid, what're
you gonna do with your dough?* "Well, Mister Mint, this all came so suddenly.
The first thing I want to do is outfit my family… I would also like to make
a small contribution to the City College fund…then I'm gonna guard the
rest of my money, put it in the bank. And I would also like to thank you
and the members of your staff for all the kindness and courtesy you've
extended to me."

"Thank you, Sid, for being a wonderful contestant. Sid Winfeld, ladies and gentlemen!"

Applause, applause, and Sidney is wheeling and heading toward the wings, toward the hard edge of the blazing stage light which is only shadows.

Q:

Mister Winfeld, you felt you had rightly
earned all that prize money and had
no obligation to give it back?

A:

May I say, I was not—in my opinion—
I was not a quiz contestant. I was an actor.

Q:

Mister Winfeld, does the kinescope
of the television quiz program which you have
just seen accurately reproduce the questions and
the answers given to you—and by you—
at that time?

A:

Yes, sir, it does.

Q:

Does the kinescope also accurately reproduce
the mannerisms and acting gestures used by you?

A:

Yes, sir.

Q:

Does it reproduce the perspiration coming off
your brow when you attempted to answer
what were theoretically most extremely
difficult questions?

A:

It does, sir.

Q:

Mister Winfeld, did that film reflect the condition
within the booth that made you apparently so warm?

A:

Yes, sir. They have an air conditioning system in there,
but when I asked them to turn it on they gave the excuse
that it would make too much noise. Naturally, keeping it off
caused me to perspire profusely.

Q:

They do have air conditioning in the booths that they can
turn on or off as they desire?

A:

Yes, sir. But at all times they refused to turn it on, claiming
it made too much noise and interfered with
the production of the program.

Q:

Being in such a closed space without any air at all,
you would naturally perspire quite extensively?

A:

Yes, sir.

Q:

Were the booths locked?

A:

No, sir. But you were not to leave the booth
until the door was opened for you from outside.

Q:

The door could be opened from the inside, though?
You could leave the booth at any time if you chose?

A:

Not exactly, sir. Doing so would greatly disrupt
the program, you understand. *

---

* Congressional Record, House Committee on Legislative Oversight, October 6, 1959

KENYON

Come back next week, will you, Mister Saint Claire, and tell us if you'd like to keep playing, said Fred Mint on the air. But they knew—everyone this side of the cameras knew—that Kenny would be back on Tuesday for the meeting in Lacky's office. As for tonight, by 11:30 he's out of the building, still made up, walking alone down West Fiftieth. Good to be outside and in the dark—a profound relief, really, after the blinding lights, the blazing booth, the cameras' red eyes, the answers at the ready but always swallowed down (*count to four*), the outrageous clarity and precision of it all.

Let us give thanks for shadows, goes a line in his head—is it a remembered line of poetry?—*let us thank the edges unseen, the heights and deeps of the never revealed.*

Has it really happened? he thinks. Did I really win $20,000 tonight?

And they tell him he's safe to keep playing. So it's to continue. There's more to come.

But suddenly, somehow, his mind turns to his time in Europe—he is seeing Sidie's low-ceilinged flat, and his crumbling room in the rue de Seine. Despite his efforts to write, he was an aimless, feeble thing in Europe. Plagued with anonymity. But how he'd felt his freedom then. He hardly even knew it at the time, but my god, how he'd felt it.

Tonight in the bright hall outside the studio, amid the bustle, the popping of flashbulbs, he shook Mr. Greenmarch's hand, and Mr. Greenmarch, smiling, said, "Fifteen million tonight. How's that feel, Kenny?"

"Beg your pardon?"

"Fifteen million. *Viewers.* Number of people watched you conquer Winfeld!"

Kenyon boards a train at Rockefeller Center, sits with the windows at his back. But there in the black window opposite he sees himself in the illumined car; his coarse and curly pompadour, the mask-like definition of the face in its makeup. Always now, every window a mirror. That booth most of all. And the cameras, always throwing you back at yourself.

Fifteen million—among them, he knows, were Maynard and Emily Saint Claire. Their neighbor Dr. Addison invited them over for the broadcast, knowing they had no TV set of their own. And surely what they saw on the screen will dismay them—a man so unlike their son, a mere performance. *We help you be you.* Oh, Kenyon can hardly borrow such an explanation for use with his father—*I know, I know, it's awfully false, Dad, but you see they're helping me be my best television self.* No, never. And so, what to say? He told his parents he'd call and he will, but best to *listen*, as always.

At Thirty-Fourth Street he changes trains—out the automated doors, up the grimy concrete steps, down again into stagnant brimstone air, onto another car.

He's had to change his number, a personal visit to the telephone company. And still, somehow, his line kept ringing. So he unplugged the phone+ and plugs it in only to call out. How strange, those first few days, the constant siren of that ring and no one there to get it but Kenny. This, and then the sacks and sacks of letters. He's only one person, but now they'll make him their own, in fifteen million ways.

Up the subway stairs into the night again, down along darkened storefronts, the overstuffed trashcans lining the curbs. And there ahead, outside his door, a small clump of people loitering in the streetlight— college kids, by the look of them. Kenyon stops, safe at his distance of half a block, and hears one of them—a girl—implore: "Knock again, Claudia."

"This isn't his place," says another.

"I'm telling you it is. Go on, Claudia, knock."

And so Claudia steps out and raps at his door.

Kenyon crosses the street, rounds the corner, and walks the two extra blocks to Bleecker.

The old house is—always was—narrow and deep. The close darkness of the hall is immediately a comfort. The stairs down which he tumbled. And up there his boyhood room, unchanged. Through the parlor doorway he passes into blackness. The curtains are shut. Fumbling, he finds the lamp and the light illumines—as if before anything else in the room— the shelves and shelves of books. He does not move through the other rooms, each one still dark. He does not take off his coat. He merely sits in lamplight, sinking into Dad's armchair by the window, amid the books. The telephone, on its table beside the sofa, is silent. His parents, some years ago, nearly sold this house—put it on the market and allowed every interested party to traipse through. Someone even made an offer, which only had the effect of bringing Maynard and Emily to realize they didn't want to sell at all. They apologized, took down the listing, settled back into having the old place on their hands. In all their time here the house has never proved much of an investment—they bought it just before the crash. Now it stands, whenever they aren't staying in it, like a perfect time capsule, their always-home, ensphering the old furniture and belongings, unchanged from Kenny and George's boyhood years. For Kenyon, alone though he is, to be in this parlor is to expect Mom or Dad's voice to call out any moment. From where he sits he can hear Dad's smoky murmur, the mysterious tobacco breath and the low words in Kenyon's ear as they look together out the window. *See them, Kenny, going by out there? It's like a play, isn't it, how they all go by.…* The window a portal, the drama beyond it all three-dimensional, never just a mirror. Across the closed curtain now, in the valley of one of its heavy green folds, a little spider has started a web.

Kenyon stands and steps to the shelves and looks at the numerous spines labeled MSC. He lights a cigarette, the breathed smoke dispelling along the books. *Praise little boys,* he remembers, *who think their father perfect.* A line from one of Maynard Saint Claire's contemporary Psalms. He turns to the wall clock in the corner above the upright, unlatches the glass door, sets the pendulum going. No need to move the hands to the proper hour—the ticking is enough.

Finally he shrugs out of his coat, sits at the sofa, takes up the phone and dials.

"Wonderful, Kenny," his father's voice is saying, "oh, wonderful! But the *intensity*, I had no idea—I can't imagine what you were feeling, my own heart was pounding the whole time we watched. Doctor Addison said, 'Maynard, are you in need of medical attention?' He was only half-joking."

"Goodness, Dad. Maybe you shouldn't watch."

"That's what your mother says—but oh, weren't you wonderful!"

Kenyon's been braced for their insights, their inevitable reaction to his performance, and now—rather than relieved, he's purely confused. How could they see the man in that glass box and believe they saw their son? Do they know him so scarcely? Even to his own parents, is he to be a celebrity?

"Will you go on playing, Kenny?"

"I expect so, yes. And how did Mom take it?"

"Well, we clasped hands through it all, Mother and I. But you know, she's so very solid—a *Gibraltar*, she says in my ear now. Oh, and she—she says you must be very tired."

"She's right as usual. But guess where I'm calling from. I'm sitting in the parlor on Bleecker. I thought I'd sleep here tonight, would you mind?"

He'll stretch out just here on the sofa. No going upstairs to the perfect, regressive room, the neatly tucked twin beds of yesteryear. When his parents inquire, he explains the conditions at his door.

"Oh," says Dad, chuckling, "the liabilities of fame. Probably even those have their advantage. Your mother—your mother says maybe you'll meet somebody."

"Fame," says Kenyon. "I don't know. Celebrity, more like. But listen, Dad, how did you handle it?"

"I?"

"Yes. I mean—being famous."

He listens as Maynard Saint Claire draws a long breath. "Ah well, what is it Montaigne says? *They do not see my heart but only my demeanor. I exist only in myself.*"

· · ·

The phone in its cradle and their loving goodnights in his ear, Kenyon stands again at the shelves, his father's Montaigne open in his hands. And here in solid type is the passage—"Of Fame."

> Everyone can make a good show outside, full within of trembling and terror. They do not see my heart, they only see my demeanor.
> To be known is, in some sort, to have one's life and its duration in others' keeping. For my part, I hold that I exist only in myself.
> To expect my name to acquire fame, in the first place—I have no name which is sufficiently mine.

TV NOW

A man in a wrestling suit, running at top speed, deliberately careens into a massive block of ice.

In slow motion, the sequence is replayed.

In slow motion, the sequence is replayed.

In slow motion, the sequence is replayed.

4.
OTHER CONSIDERATIONS
January 1957

KENYON

A crowd, a crowd, and sunlight on the street—hard white Sunday sun like they haven't seen for weeks—winter sun, it renders the stone of the NBC building a watery tan. Photographers move in the crowd. "Kenny! Kenny!" The police in their blues and brass buttons hold back the perimeter. His parents are somewhere there among the spectators.

On the red-carpeted sidewalk Kenyon stands alone, a zone of empty space between himself and everyone else. This kind of staging, this choreography for the cameras, it's the nature of publicity. *Just smile*, Mr. Greenmarch told him. *Smile, wave a bit to the girls and grandmas. That's all. Won't be hard.* So Kenyon smiles.

Greenmarch himself stands back along the perimeter now, his face sternly managerial in sunglasses.

Kenyon, cast in the role of spectacle, goes on smiling despite the chill. It's 28 degrees in the sun, and though all the onlookers are sensibly bundled up, he wears a thin suit jacket, asked by Greenmarch and the others to remove his overcoat—for the cameras.

And now the police bustle to divert the crowd. A barricade is carried away and through the opening, engine gurgling, sunlight flaring on glass, comes a glistening red convertible. The crowd applauds and so does Kenyon as the car is piloted along the curb just in front of him. Deep black tires suck beautifully at the pavement. From the white interior behind the wheel, the driver, Mr. Masterson, unfolds himself, waggling the key in one hand. "Kenny," he booms, turning about with Kenyon beside him, to better address the public. "In celebration of your great display of knowledge, it is the pleasure of the Mercedes-Benz Company to give you this 1957 190 SL convertible, complete with 104-horsepower engine, fog lamps, leather interior, and a three-piece white leather luggage set." From the periphery comes a blonde spokesmodel in headscarf, sunglasses, and traveling coat, bearing in each hand a white suitcase and under each arm a large white vanity kit. These she places in photogenic arrangement on the red carpet beside the car, genuflecting, then turns to open the driver's door for Kenyon.

And the keys are in Kenyon's hand, and the crowd is roaring as he slides into that foamy interior behind the wheel, the seat cool beneath his legs.

"Kenny, for the sake of our New York traffic enforcement," announces Masterson, "I shall hope your driving isn't as fast as your brain!"

The Mercedes people, for the gift of the car, requested one dollar and, as they put it, "other considerations."

What does this refer to? Kenyon had asked Greenmarch, looking at the contract of sale. *Other considerations.*

Greenmarch shrugged. *Oh, public relations, etcetera. Pure boilerplate.*

The engine rolls over and purrs again and the crowd rejoices anew. And now the photographers surge to encircle the car, Greenmarch conducting at their rear.

At the wheel with nowhere to go, the engine idling under him, Kenyon keeps on smiling.

Greenmarch was right. It isn't hard at all.

Only last week did Kenyon buy a television set. Monday morning, coming past a department store window, there was his own face multiplied in bloodless black-and-white. He stopped before the display, a pyramid of identical screens. He had to look twice to be sure that was himself he saw. Shrunken, striated and wavering, gray as death, the kaleidoscopic image was nothing like a mirror. On the screens he furrowed his brow and gnawed his lips, head clamped in ridiculous black earphones. Then the picture cut to the man in the other booth, Clarence Holloway, the black social worker with whom he'd played a tie game the week before. Then Fred Mint's face appeared, his mute mouth addressing the viewer—but Kenyon, looking on from the sidewalk, was not the viewer, no, the viewer was not the man who stood there now beyond the glass, deaf to Mint's words amid the uptown traffic.

Who was the viewer?

By some unnerving division that caused a sudden sweat to bloom in his palms as he peered through the glass, Kenyon felt himself standing inside those little screens, in that underwater gray, shrunken in the small booth at Mint's back, waiting there while Mint spoke to the cameras. The doubleness was almost physical.

When the picture cut to another advertisement, Kenyon went inside. Before the bells on the door had stopped jangling a salesman greeted him.

"I'd like to buy a television set," said Kenyon.

"Certainly, may I show you the models we carry? Wait a minute, now, aren't you Kenyon Saint Claire?"

"I am, yes."

"Well, goodness, what a pleasure to have you visit the store."

"Thank you."

"The sets are right this way, Mister Saint Claire. And if you wouldn't mind, I know that our floor manager Mister Spellman would be delighted to meet you. May I call him down?"

"I'm afraid I'm in a hurry. Perhaps another time?"

"Of course, of course. Our newest models are just here. Each has the latest VHF dial and aerial attachment…"

"This is something of an impulse. I hadn't planned to buy a set today. Can I pay for this one here and have it delivered?"

"The twenty-one-inch Zenith? Certainly, sir. Are you sure you'd prefer the tabletop model? We do have the RCA console models…"

"This will be fine, thank you."

To feel so divided—it had frightened him—to be scattered to some space beyond his own recognition or reach. He told himself that by keeping a set he would keep himself close.

The set arrived the following day. The deliveryman unboxed it, placed it in the corner on the low bookshelf whose top Kenyon had cleared, and plugged it into the wall.

"Your first television set, sir?"

"Yes."

"Simple enough to use," said the deliveryman, whose jacket was emblazoned with the name of the department store. He clicked a knob on the metal panel above the greenish screen. The television made a bird-like squeak, then an electric hum as the picture emerged, very dim at first, but gradually coming clear: a speckled field like blowing snow. "Volume here," said the deliveryman. He turned the knob until static hissed, silenced it again. "VHF dial here." He rotated the dial, but there seemed to be only snow.

"No picture?" said Kenyon.

The deliveryman shrugged. "You'll get something with the aerial. Need to toy with it usually. You have twelve channels, regular programming on three of them: CBS here, NBC here, and ABC here." Each station, as he clicked through them, displayed a bulls-eye pattern. "Mostly test patterns right now. But tonight you'll get Steve Allen, Ed Sullivan, no problem."

In fact it would be Kenyon himself on that screen, playing live against Clarence Holloway.

He signed the man's clipboard and closed the door after him.

He crossed the room to the set and stood with one hand on the dial. The set was warm to the touch and gave off a faint odor of heat, of burning wires. He turned the dial through each snowy station, all twelve. Then he stepped back to stare at the screen as if watching the snow fall outside a window.

Still the photographers circle the car, strands of white exhaust crawling around their ankles.

"Mister and Mrs. Saint Claire," calls Greenmarch from the sidewalk, "would you come forward for a picture with your son?"

Kenyon hears his father, out of sight, calling back from the crowd. "Is it necessary?"

"Well, sir, it's not *required*," says Greenmarch with a laugh—and the onlookers laugh too. "But you must be very proud."

Bodies shift about and Maynard and Emily emerge in their overcoats and hats, looking somewhat adrift, in need of instruction.

Greenmarch, loud and charming, says, "Are they always so shy, Kenny?" He's stepped across to take Emily's arm.

"I'm afraid so," says Kenyon.

"Now, won't you both stand just here beside the driver's door? There. Oh, that's very nice, isn't it."

Emily's gloved hand rests on Kenyon's arm where he's propped it along the door. Maynard holds his hat in one hand. Kenyon smiles as the cameras clack and stutter.

The onlookers, for some unbeknownst reason, begin to applaud.

· · ·

Afterward, upstairs in the studio, there is a brunch social with the program team and some members of the press, a crowd of thirty or so. At Greenmarch's invitation Kenyon's parents have come up too. Fred Mint is there, and Sam Lacky, and Clarence Holloway, against whom Kenyon will play a third game this week, most likely their final faceoff given what Lacky told Kenyon a few days ago: *He's likeable, but he ain't a champ.* How much does Holloway know about it? Kenyon wonders as he shakes the man's hand and introduces his parents. He *is* likeable, Holloway. He has a glass eye and something of a lisp, and a homespun way of knowing his facts. *Likeable.* Kenyon hardly understood the word the first few times he heard Lacky use it, but now, five weeks on the program and counting, he's beginning to see what they mean. He himself, apparently, is likeable.

The brunch is a handsome spread of sweet rolls, sliced melon, strawberries, scrolled salami rounds, deviled eggs, olives, and assorted pâtés. All the studio's utility lights are on and the crowd mingles around the serving table in the space where the audience usually sits, the risers having been cleared away. In this light the set looks absurdly lifeless, one-dimensional. The bulky cameras, pushed against the wall, stand asleep. A small group has gathered around Fred Mint's podium, plates in hand, glasses propped beside the host's levers. Kenyon leads his parents on a little tour.

"The dreaded booth!" says Maynard.

"Try it out, Dad."

Holding his father's glass as Maynard steps in, Kenyon shuts the door. With Mom he circles to the front. The booth is semi-dark, more like a closet than the specimen box it becomes during the broadcasts. Through the window Maynard waves at them boyishly. They laugh and wave back. Maynard dons the earphones, looking out as he stoops and talks into the mike. Kenyon points to his own ear, shaking his head. "We can't hear you, Dad. Soundproof!"

"Do we have our next contestant there?" Greenmarch appears at Kenyon's shoulder, buttered roll and napkin in one hand. "A hell of a show that would be, father versus son."

Emily chuckles. "Maynard used to have a radio program, you know."

"Did he?"

"It was some time ago. How long now, Kenny, ten years?"

"Fifteen," says Kenyon. "*Reader's Hour*, it was called. CBS radio."

"Is that so? Not a trivia program, I'd guess," says Greenmarch.

With a mildly theatrical show of relief, Maynard steps out of the booth now. "My god, you feel you're going to be gassed in there. How do you stand it, Kenny?"

Greenmarch says, "It's not so good if you're claustrophobic."

"I didn't think I was," says Maynard. "Now I wonder."

"And Kenny will tell you, it's even hotter with the stage lights on."

"Dad, we were just talking about your radio days."

"Oh?"

"I never knew you'd had a show, Mister Saint Claire," says Greenmarch.

"Well, hardly mine. It was a conversation. That was the point."

"A teaching program, was it?"

"You could say so, I suppose. More precisely it was an on-air book club, a venue for appreciation."

"Books," says Greenmarch. "I see."

"When I say books, of course, I mean…ideas."

"Mm," says Greenmarch. "Philosophy and that sort of thing?"

"Philosophy, yes, and literature. Ethics, politics, history, science, religion."

"How long did it air?"

Maynard's brows go up. He points a finger at Greenmarch as if to acknowledge he's hit the bullseye in asking. "Nowadays it wouldn't, would it?"

Greenmarch chuckles, running a hand down his tie. "Well, I don't know that it wouldn't. Just look at what we're doing here after all. What was your eleven-point question last week, Kenny, the one about the nineteen-twenties?"

"Oh," says Kenyon, "you mean the one I missed? Uh, four different presidents occupied the White House in the nineteen-twenties. Who were their vice presidents."

"That's it. And you got three of them, didn't you?"

"Mm-hm, couldn't remember Hoover's man, sadly."

"Well, it was a damned challenging question, is my point. And you got three of them. But this is a pass/fail kind of program and three out of four, I'm afraid, does not pass. Now wouldn't you folks call that a respectable exam? You see, it isn't all easy questions around here, not by any means."

"Not easy," says Maynard, "no. And that's to be admired. But an *answer*, Mister Greenmarch, well, it's not the same as an *idea*, is it?"

Greenmarch tips his head, nodding as he chomps the last of his buttered roll. "Television," he says between bites, "is a special medium, Mister Saint Claire, with special requirements. Entertainment—in this line of work, entertainment's the primary concern. You can't ever afford to forget that your viewers, they're looking to be entertained. But the trick is, I say, not to become another *I Love Lucy*—all empty silliness. I say let's squeeze some knowledge into the entertainment. If we can do that, then we've done something. Then everybody wins, I say. See, you and me—the classroom, the TV set—I'm not sure these things are all that different."

"Squeezed knowledge," says Maynard, somewhat absently.

"Well, not that it's a grapefruit or something—"

"And to what end is this knowledge?" says Maynard, with a placid smile. Cool as ever, he will not be roused. As Kenyon knows, though, it's his father's lifework they're discussing—the books he's studied, the books he's taught, the books he's written, and the place of such work in the world. Whether Greenmarch can see this is not so certain.

Kenyon says, "All this reminds me now, Dad, of something I've been meaning to propose to Mister Greenmarch and Mister Lacky. Say the program were to include segments on some of the topics that come up in the questions…"

Without even turning his head, eyes still fixed on Maynard, Greenmarch asks, "How much did you win last week, Kenny?"

"$87,000." To his bones Kenyon knows the sum.

"There," says Greenmarch. "There's the answer to your question, Mister Saint Claire. We're giving your son—excuse me—your son has *earned* $87,000 on our program so far. And counting."

"A great deal of money," says Maynard.

"Yes, and a fair end result, wouldn't you say? Television isn't radio, true enough. But I wonder…" Drawing a breath, turning to Kenyon with a smile, Greenmarch claps his shoulder warmly. "I wonder if your father's giving television enough credit, Kenny."

"Oh, I don't begrudge you your profession, Mister Greenmarch—"

"Call me Ray. Please."

"I've got nothing against your program, Ray. I'm probably speaking out of turn. You see, Emily and I, we don't own a television ourselves."

"Oh my! But you've watched this fella, haven't you?"

"Of course," Emily chimes in. "At our neighbor's home. We're terribly proud."

"I only got a set myself last week," says Kenyon.

"So you folks saw last week's program. Now tell me, who was that VP of Hoover's?"

"Curtis," says Maynard, just as Emily blurts it out too.

"There you have it. If you'll forgive me, I'd guess that you both learned a little something."

"In fact," says Maynard, "I happen to remember that answer in particular because Curtis is also my brother's name."

Greenmarch is deadpan. He turns to Kenyon. "But you mean you went and bought a set yourself, Kenny? We would've sent you one! Listen, why don't you return yours. I'll get you a set delivered this week."

"But, Ray, I—"

"On second thought, why not keep both of them? One for the bedroom, one for the sitting room."

"It's really not necessary, Ray…"

"Nonsense. It's our pleasure. Consider it done!"

Then, for a moment, they all fall silent, standing under the white utility lights, drinks in hand.

"Well," says Greenmarch. "Cars, TVs, $87,000… Can I get anybody anything else?"

Amid their chuckles Greenmarch claps Kenyon's shoulder again, then slips away through the crowd.

. . .

Kenyon half-expects the matter to be forgotten, but the set from Greenmarch arrives the very next day. It comes in a much larger box than his Zenith. According to the deliveryman, who wheels it on a hand truck, it's a 21-inch RCA, a beauty with a walnut console and woven speaker. "I hate to be a bother," Kenyon tells him. "But can I give you another address for this?" He gives the address of the Bleecker house. His parents are spending half of every week in the city now, while his father teaches the spring term.

"How do you like it?" he asks Mom on the phone the following night.

"It's sort of lovely, isn't it? It sort of glistens, even when it's turned off. We've put it in the living room."

"Oh? How'd you find the space for it amid Dad's shelves?"

"Well, we moved some things around. Anyway, thank you, Kenny. It's a lovely gift. And how nice to just—turn it on and there you are."

They've watched the night's broadcast, of course—at last, after three weeks of tie games, he's vanquished Holloway.

"And aren't there a lot—we'd had no idea how many programs there are. All the time, so much to see. Does it ever pause?"

COMMENTATORS

"In frenetic quest for the unexpected, we end by finding only the unexpectedness we have planned for ourselves. We meet ourselves coming back."

"It was the picture that mattered, the face in black and white, animated but also flat, distanced, sealed-off, timeless.... I tried to tell myself it was only television—whatever that was—however it worked—and not some journey out of life or death, not some mysterious separation."

"Everything on TV is somewhat of a lie, but it's still entertainment."

SIDNEY

At the lamplit breakfast table in the dark kitchen, in slacks and undershirt, hair slicked from the shower, Sidney bends forward looking over the photos in the NY Post: Kenyon Saint Somebody in his nice trim suit gooning and clapping his hands as they lay a $3,400 convertible at his feet. And the background—who are all those people in the background so pleased to clap and smile along? What's in it for them? Even the New York police have been called out on Kenyon's account to hold back the crowd.

For Sidney of course it was never so much as mentioned, such a thing. Not even a consolation prize. Not even a bribe to keep him from spilling the beans. No, for Sidney they never offered a new coffeepot even. Anyway, they counted on he wouldn't spill the beans, which doing so would only be to spill in his own lap. In other words it was, *You want the world knowing you didn't in actual fact know all those answers? That you gamed them for six weeks running? Give that some thought, why don't you, Sid,* was their attitude on that front.

But here they go heaping prizes on Mister Professor—prizes he doesn't even have to answer questions for, doesn't even have to *earn*, while Sidney's up early to get to the transit office before daylight—a whole day's work ahead of him and then night classes after—and here's the NY Post of all papers reporting on the professor's goony smile. They sit on Sidney's story for a month, then print this instead. Greenmarch is behind that, Sidney's positive. Dave Gelman, the reporter—hadn't Gelman said over the phone he'd be calling Greemarch himself?

Sidney folds the paper, pushes away his cream of wheat. That old stomach pain still hasn't gone. Guzzle Milk of Magnesia by the bottle, no use. And the pain is flaring now, and there's an angry sweat breaking out under his arms. The day ain't even started yet, the day's real work still ahead of him. He takes the folded paper and flings it, throws it hard at the kitchen door but in midair it just flutters open and the pages scatter softly across the floor, the smiling picture of Kenyon Saint Claire coming to rest at Sidney's feet.

Greenmarch not only reneging on their agreements, not only refusing to take Sidney's calls, but defaming him probably to Gelman on the phone. Why else would Gelman take a scoop like that and spike it?

And this stomach complaint, which the reason is Sidney being under so much *pressure*. What does Saint Smiles know, him with his convertible, about pressure like this? All the money gone, gone—what'd *Saint Suck-Me* ever know about a thing like that? Those thugs and their so-called racing syndicate, the shady dropoff up in Yonkers, which Sidney should have trusted his misgivings on that subject, except that his cousin Arthur was there through the whole deal, Arthur who'd recommended the bookie in the first place and kept saying, *Alberto knows these guys, I'm tellin' ya*, though only God knows how well Arthur knew Alberto. And then the guy in the tight jacket crossing the street from the train station to the little gravel lot behind the deli—and before the guy even reached the sidewalk on their side, Sidney could see the shape under his jacket, the shape which they were meant to think, *Hey that ain't no belt buckle*. Right then, who knows what Arthur saw, but Sidney—who'd still had some questions, who'd hoped to discuss further the exact terms and nature of this transaction—could see these guys weren't the types to leave a meeting empty-handed. So there went the money like they'd planned, awful quick, no more than a minute. The guy took it, checked it, then hooked a thumb and finger between his lips to whistle. From someplace behind them a black car circled around, he jumped in, and goodbye prize money. Arthur thought they'd simply done business, had no idea, and Sidney didn't say a thing, didn't even let on, something just drained right out of him and what was the point? Even late as last week, Arthur was nagging him to call them up, check in on their "investment," and Sidney couldn't say it clear enough, couldn't say, *That money is gone*, without Arthur insisting, *No, no, you don't understand these fellas, Sidney. They gotta be like that, but it don't mean they ain't good for it.* Sidney having told Bernice precisely *nada* of the whole arrangement, Sidney not sleeping so well lately, Sidney being emptied out and hollow since that handover behind the deli, Sidney's gut just about killing him some mornings—what'd he do but start to see Arthur's reasoning. What'd he do but pick up the phone and dial their number. What choice did he have but to hope it wasn't like he thought. After three rings a woman answered, a secretarial voice, and he was wonderstruck. But he realized he didn't have an actual person's name. He mumbled some. Then he said simply, *I'm calling to inquire about an investment I've made.* The woman asked him to hold. There was a click, then silence. A few minutes later he understood they'd been disconnected. He dialed again, and this time, stern-like, the secretarial voice said, *You called a few minutes ago, didn't you?* Again she made him hold. And now, after several minutes, a man's voice came on the line: *Who is it?*

An investor, he answered. *Sidney Winfeld.*

Listen, Winfeld, we don't know you, OK? You better think that's a good thing, OK? Don't make us know you, and don't call here again.

So the money's gone. The thugs don't know Sidney Winfeld, thank God. But Mint and Greenmarch is another story. They think Sidney's gonna sit tight with their little secret? What's he got to hide?—it's not like he lied every time they asked him a question, he knew plenty of those answers before Fred Mint ever pulled a lever. Furthermore he was an actor under contract, this ain't a matter of saving face or saving a reputation, it's a matter simply of what they owe. What's he got to show for all he's done for the program? What right do they have to renege on their guarantees?

From the transit depot on his lunch hour Sidney once again calls up Mint and Greenmarch.

"Hello, Denise? Yes, yes, it's Sidney again. Now you know why I'm calling, I know you know it, Denise, and please don't tell me Ray can't take my call at the moment. If he's there he needs to get on this line and talk to me—because to be perfectly honest, Denise, I've lost my patience—now I know you're only doing your job, only doing like Mister Greenmarch asks of you and I understand that so don't take this personal, Denise, but you can't keep protecting the man, understand me. It's time he gets on this phone and talks—because really it's only fair to Ray at this point, it's only fair he be made aware of the steps I'm planning to take beginning this week, beginning *now*—now don't misunderstand me, no, it's not a threat or anything of that nature, but what I'm referring to is real substantial steps I will take beginning *now*—as *recourse*, you understand, public and legal *recourse* for Mint and Greenmarch's failure—yes, yes, no, I wouldn't think you're lying to me Denise, fine yes please be sure that he receives the message and please let him know that I expect him to call me in the next twenty-four hours—no, that's all thank you, Denise, I know you're only doing your job, honey, I understand that—OK then, bye."

Sidney is halfway through his turkey sandwich when Ray's return call comes through.

"Listen, Sid," says Ray. "I've been very busy and I apologize you haven't heard from me…" Blown out of proportion, says Ray. I'm sure we understand each other better than all this, he says. Confident, he says, we can reach an agreement. Why don't you come in, he says, so we can talk.

KENYON

Kenyon has a blind date. She comes on the recommendation of Mint and Greenmarch, Inc. It's in his contract, surprisingly enough—under the purview of that same signal phrase, *Other Considerations*. While he's never wholly understood its meaning, he's never suspected till now that the phrase could pertain to his sex life.

He'll take her to see *Rear Window*, the latest Hitchcock film. She is, Lacky says, from an old New York family of distinction, the daughter of a gentleman with important holdings in east side shipping. They want Kenyon to drive her in the 190. He's to bring her to Washington Square before the show to meet the program photographer for some publicity shots. It's all a sham. Kenyon garages the car clear over in New Jersey, can't cover the cost of storing it in the city—after all, he's only had one small advance payment from Mint and Greenmarch thus far. So he taxies out early in the evening, already dressed for the date, to retrieve the convertible from its concrete crypt. Then it's through the Lincoln Tunnel to her family's place on Park Ave.

She's waiting in the lobby, alone—he's relieved he doesn't have to meet her parents. She's lovely. Her gloved hand clasps his and without hesitation she pulls him close to kiss his cheek, irradiating him with strong perfume. It's 52 degrees, so they ride with the top down. She covers her hair with a mantel of golden silk, tips him a cigarette, lights his and hers both from the car lighter. "Oh, boyee," she drawls, apropos of something he seems to have missed. Her laugh is a smoky chortle. While they cruise through the city, she holds her head back as if luxuriating, the glove stripped from the hand that holds her cigarette. They don't say more than a few words, taking the wind and city noise as an excuse.

At Washington Square, with the great white arch and a spangle of city lights as backdrop, they spend an hour leaning against the car in their evening clothes, arm in arm. Pacing around the car, arm in arm. Sitting in the car, smiling at the night. Laughing and smiling all the time. Finally they can go—just in time to get to the cinema and hand the keys to the valet.

Up on the screen, Jimmy Stewart is in a fix, hobbled in a massive cast, confined to a wheelchair, and bound to learn the hard way how awful it is to be noticed. *Why doesn't he read a book?* Kenyon thinks, as he watches Stewart fixate more and more obsessively on the view out his back window. "Oh, dear," says Stewart's scrappy masseuse, "we've become a race of peeping toms. What people oughta do is get outside their own house and look in for a change."

Give the man a book, for god's sake!

Maureen is the blind date's name, and she's a free spirit. At dinner following the movie, she tells Kenyon her parents are abroad for the winter. A property in Ticino, Switzerland. She hardly comes home while they're gone. How can she? The city is endlessly exciting.

As for Kenyon, he's taken to sleeping in his parents' house several nights a week, whenever they're away at the farm. In the empty rooms he sometimes sits awake for hours, alone in the quiet, all the contained years palpably manifest around him. The worn furniture. The dusty spots under the lamps. Beyond the walls the city thrums, but in the house nothing moves. He knows that in the kitchen, behind the cupboard doors, all his mother's servingware sits neatly stacked, inanimate, dumbly waiting—and though he cannot say why, this is extremely comforting. He doesn't tell Maureen any of this, but late in the night, after they've had plenty to drink, he brings her to the Bleecker house. There by the dim glow of the parlor lamp, on the sofa between his father's wall of books and the curtained window, she leans against him in her chiffon, paws him with her gloves off, then undoes his belt, pries him half-hard from the elastic waist of his undershorts, and shoves her wide mouth down over him. Like a senseless eye the dead green screen of the television set looks on, dully reflecting their miniaturized bodies.

They make love. It seems to be expected of them.

Afterward they drowse together on the couch, smoking.

"Boyee," says Maureen, with a pleasurable sigh. "You must like being famous."

"This isn't...customary, if that's what you mean."

"Oh, did I mean something? I don't know."

"Anyway, aren't *you* famous?" says Kenyon. "Do *you* like it?"

"Not famous. Only rich. It's different."

"Notable then. How's that?"

"Notable? OK, I suppose notable."

"And do you like it?"

"Oh yes! Be crazy not to."

"Well," says Kenyon, "not that you have much choice."

She chortles. "What's that supposed to mean?"

"It's a kind of duty, being notable, being famous. Isn't it? You have to make the most of it, or it makes you…"

"What does it make me? What?"

"You lose control of it." Kenyon shrugs. "Better to control it than be controlled, correct?"

"Boyee," she yawns. "I have no idea what you're saying."

"Me neither," he says, and grunts. "The Answer Man himself hasn't the foggiest idea."

"I'm still drunk. How about you? Can I sleep here?"

"I suppose. Not sure it's in the contract, though."

"Oh now, that's an awful thing to say."

"Sorry. Shouldn't have. Who is it you know at NBC?"

"The chairman or somebody. I forget his name. Father knows him. They're gonna put me in a movie, that's what somebody told Father. But hey, this wasn't some kind of obligation, you know."

"OK, I'm sorry."

"I like some excitement is all. I'd be good in the movies, I'll have you know. I like to have new experiences. I'm not a tuck-me-in type, you understand."

"How old are you? Have I asked you that yet?"

She laughs. "I'm twenty-four. What's it matter? Well, I'll forgive you this time, Ken Ken, but won't you be nice and get me a drink of water?"

He groans to his feet, pads into the dark kitchen, fills her glass from the faucet.

"It's your parents' place, you said? It's very quaint."

"Well, they're a quaint old couple, Mom and Dad."

"I've never seen so many books."

"You don't have books up in that manor of yours?"

"Oh, Mother does. Some anyway. Have you got another cigarette?"

"Yeah. Here you go. I just remembered how tired I am."

"I couldn't be more awake. Hey, listen, I don't suppose your folks have some liquor tucked away behind all these books?"

"I'm remembering how tired I feel. I have to give a lecture tomorrow. This morning."

"What's the subject?"

"Camera versus Agora. Dear me."

"Oh, Ken Ken."

"Don't call me that, please."

"Poor baby. Just put your head on my shoulder. Would you like to watch some television?"

"No."

"It'll help you sleep. I don't have any idea what we can watch at this time. Let me switch it on."

"No, leave it off."

But she's not listening.

The knob goes *click* and the room fills with voices.

MAILBAG

Dear Kenyon,

I am a classroom teacher at Mabel Bishop Elementary here in Fleming, Wisconsin, and I write on behalf of my fifth-grade class to congratulate you for your success on television. My students and I have a great admiration for the breadth of knowledge you have demonstrated, and they have made and decorated the enclosed card in appreciation ...

Dear Mr. Saint Clare, [sic]

You remind me so very much of my grandson Philip whose grasp of history, geography, and literature has always impressed me. Unfortunately Philip, now in middle-age, is something of a recluse and I wonder would you ever call him up? I can't say how much it would mean...

Dear Mr. Kenny,

How did you ever learn all the things you know? I love to read books and I only hope that some day I can be as bright and smart as you are. My mother says I may get to an Ivy League college someday. Won't you remind me, Kenny, what college do you teach at?...

KENYON

"On one side we have the tradition of the *Camera,*" says Kenyon Saint Claire from his podium in front of the blackboard as the photographer circles the lecture hall, shutter clacking. "Before the age of television or Kodak, the word Camera meant a room, a chamber, an enclosure, a sanctum. Writers and philosophers of the Camera include Plato, Seneca, Marcus Aurelius, and perhaps more than any other, Montaigne."

Kenyon turns and scratches *CAMERA* across the blackboard, and beneath it the names. His red-rimmed eyes are burning, a headache severing his skull.

Clack clack goes the shutter.

"On the other side of the literary philosophical tradition is the *Agora*—the marketplace, the public sphere, the realm of the common man and collective experience. In the Agora we find Socrates, Lucretius, Rabelais, and Erasmus, to name a few."

Under *AGORA* he adds these names.

"It's worth noting that in ancient Greek the word *agora* is directly related to the adjective *gregarious*. A Hebrew permutation of the term came to signify a coin of small denomination—currency, the coin of the realm, etcetera. But let us dwell a minute on polarities.... The Camera is solitary, the doors drawn shut, and its writer composes by candlelight, by firelight, or in the wintry daylight seeping through a nearby window. He keeps a blanket drawn up beneath the desk to cover his knees. The loneliness of the Camera is the necessary prerequisite for his thought. The state of mind induced by the Camera's quietude is his ideal. That state of mind, that brand of thought, is primarily *introspective.*"

In large letters Kenyon chalks: *INTROSPECTIVE.*

He managed a meager hour of sleep before it was time to shake himself out of the night's delirium, pull on his trousers, and chauffeur Maureen home. *Ring me up,* she said, before getting out of the car. Then, seeing his face, said, *Well, anyway, it was very nice to meet you.* He arrived on campus rumpled in last night's clothing—and no time for a cigarette.

"Also common among a great many philosophers of the Camera is an element of stoicism. These are *stoical* thinkers."

STOICAL.

"The philosopher of the Camera communicates ex officio, by virtue of silence—in other words, he uses *writing.* He is a *writer* foremost. His medium is the page, and *writing is an end in itself.*"

WRITTEN.

"Let us note that all of this could not be more different than what comes to mind when we hear the word 'camera' today."

He makes a crude drawing of a Kodak, then chalks an *X* over it.

"As for the Agora, its environs are practically without limit. The philosopher of the Agora walks abroad. He lives and breathes the open air, the air of the people. His sensibilities are *public.* His mode is conversational, dialectical, *Socratic.* For the philosopher of the Agora, the medium of choice is *speech,* and writing, if he writes, is merely a means to an end."

AGORA

PUBLIC.

SOCRATIC.

SPOKEN.

"To whom does the philosopher of the Agora speak? He speaks to the common man, and that man is a listener—a man who learns by listening. Unfortunately, the Agora is often noisy, and frequently the philosopher's voice is drowned in the chatter and exhortations of the marketeers around him. This is the cost of gregariousness, of dealing in the coin of the realm."

Dog tired as he was, this morning Kenyon noticed with a kind of disorientation a crystal quality in all the daylit scenes around him. Sights as mundane as a corner grocery, a blinking red crosswalk signal, or the stream of jacketed bodies hunching forward down a subway stairwell—

they all looked suddenly aglimmer, rendered up in immaculate celluloid, shot through with a new purity like the light of some great invisible projector. He wonders if the studio lights have done something to his eyes? Or is it an afterglow of that film—*Rear Window*—which seemed to him, as he sat in the great darkened movie house, an explosion of color. Are all these chromatic spectacles bound to work some irreversible change on people's retinas?

"As for the philosopher of the Camera, to whom does he speak? He speaks to the ideal man, and that man is a *reader*—he learns by introspection. Unfortunately, there's a cost to dealing in ideals, as many of us know only too well. Communication by silence, by the written word, is an act of persistent idealism. Are the readers out there? After all, there are quiz shows to watch!"

Kenyon couldn't resist, and now there comes a rumble of recognition in the lecture hall—laughter, laughter in every crowded row. He's packing them in. He'd worried that the photographer would cause some distraction, and it's true the man circles the room constantly, that shutter clacking without pause—but in this moment Kenyon wonders, *What does it matter?* Who would believe it, but they're lining up outside the door every time he lectures, many of them merely auditing, not even registered. And isn't that beautiful? Oh, so what if they come merely to gawk at a celebrity? They're still bound to glean something, aren't they? And is the photographer's presence any concern, really? The studio did not insist on this, merely suggested, and Kenyon thought it preferable to the stilted publicity photos at NBC. Better he be seen in his natural environment for once, dealing in ideas. Well, they're all here together, and they all know why the photographer is circling, and Kenyon couldn't resist. They love him, after all, and he smiles large as they laugh.

In suit and tie at the front of the lecture hall, Kenyon Saint Claire is photographed at the podium, smiling large. With one hand he turns the pages of a heavy book. Behind him on the well-chalked blackboard are the names of several philosophers.

Later, in the wings of Studio 6B before the broadcast, taking instructions from the photographer, Kenyon Saint Claire poses beside a wheeled blackboard where someone has drawn a massive sum in digits as large as Kenyon's head.

$104,500

A happy Kenyon Saint Claire beams at the sum. *Click.*

A wide-eyed Kenyon Saint Claire ogles the sum. *Click.*

A playful Kenyon Saint Claire stretches out his arms to take measure of the sum. *Click.*

A delirious Kenyon Saint Claire is hoisted in Fred Mint's arms before the sum. Both men pitch their heads back and laugh, open-mouthed. *Click.*

CONTROL

—Camera One, nice'n snug now—

Fred Mint and Kenyon Saint Claire stand close at the podium for the two-shot, Mint leaning in as if Kenyon's hard of hearing. In the camera, all images are flattened and all is false proximity.

"I just wondered," Mint says, "last week you told us that you had written a book, and it is still not published, called *Country of the Father.* Isn't that right? It's not published?"

"No," says Kenyon Saint Claire, "not published."

"Well then, you'll be interested in the telegram I've received, and I'd like to read it for you, here on the air—sent to me today, and it says, 'You can advise Kenyon Saint Claire that we would like to take a look at his unpublished book *Country of the Father.*' It's signed William Dover, story editor, Universal International Pictures, International City, California. Now, isn't that nice?"

Applause, applause.

—Camera Two, show us the happy man—

Kenyon, bashful, beams in the hot lights. From Mint's hand he takes the telegram and kisses it, waves it in a small triumphant flourish, then tucks it safely in his jacket pocket.

"And we hope it will be successful," says Mint. "Now, Kenyon Saint Claire, we have a new contestant here: Mister Dearborn. You come to us from Long Island, Mister Dearborn, is that correct? And you practice law there?..."

Presently they are in the booths, Kenyon and Dearborn, the white-hot lights burning down on each of them through the glass, and Fred Mint, the impresario, is in full form.

Ding! goes the bell.

"Kenny, the category is Furnishings. How many points do you want?"

"Hm, I don't know anything about Furnishings," says Kenyon, his voice somewhat metalized through the microphone, the bass tones deepened, every breath extra sibilant. "Can I take three points?"

"Yes, you can. Is that what you wanna take? Three points? For three points, What is the name of the cloth draped over the back of a seat to resist staining the fabric with hair oils?"

"Well, that much I know. An antimacassar."

—There's our winner, gents, isn't he gorgeous—

"Antimacassar is correct, and you have three points."

Applause, applause. The scorebox flashes to **3** as Mint clicks off Kenyon's ON THE AIR sign and turns to the other contestant.

KENYON

As Mint and Dearborn do their drill, Kenyon's mind is fairly wheeling, that telegram a source of heat in his pocket. *Advise him that we'd like to take a look at his unpublished book.* Goodness! But wait, this William Dover is in the *movies*? It is a movie studio and not a publisher that wishes to read the book? Isn't that queer! Oh, but what writer wouldn't want a movie made of his book? Yes, who would not want that? I want that, Kenyon tells himself. Of course I do.

Amid this burble of thought he all but forgets that the book is not yet written. Rather, not yet finished. He does have a stack of manuscript pages in the top drawer of his desk at home, but he hasn't looked at them in more than a year...

The producers have deemed a tie game unnecessary. Kenyon's victory over Dearborn is quick.

LIVING ROOM

That was quick.

The men come out of their booths, shake hands in cordial manner—*a fine contest, sir, you have my admiration, etcetera*—and off goes Dearborn toward the wings. But before he's out of sight here comes the new contestant: tall svelte blonde in high collar and pearls. Mr. Dearborn, kind of a short guy, rises up on the ball of one foot for a quick nip to her cheek, one hand at the small of her back. Smiling, she steps to Fred Mint's podium.

"Well now," says Mint, "we've just said goodbye to Mister Dearborn and now we have, do we not, Missus Dearborn? Missus Victoria Dearborn?"

"That's right. Hello."

"That fella there, he happens to be your husband."

"Yes, he does."

She's all smiles, a glowing beauty. Those cameras love her, the screen loves her, the TV set is all but vibrating.

"This will be the first time we've had a husband and wife on the program, now isn't that nice. So, Missus Dearborn, naturally you also hail from Long Island. And like your husband you also practice law there, is that correct?"

"Yes, although a different line. I represent Warner Brothers Motion Pictures Company."

"Oh, have you been involved with any interesting pictures lately?"

"Yes, in fact I'm presently working on the new Tab Hunter film, *The Spirit of Saint Louis.*"

"Oh, a fine picture it is too. I saw it on the opening night. Well now, Kenyon Saint Claire, you have won $122,000 to date. Tonight you have the opportunity to take your winnings and never play another game, or you can play against Missus Dearborn here and stand to win or lose as much as $10,500. Before you make up your mind, here are a few more things you should know about Victoria Dearborn."

They go close on Mrs. Dearborn—what a face!—and here's Bob Shepherd's voice: *She graduated summa cum laude from Sarah Lawrence College. She is an expert speed-reader and a prize-winning ballroom dancer. She is the chairwoman of her local chapter of Soroptimist International.*

"Well, Kenyon, what do you say? Will you play Missus Dearborn or—"

"I'll play," says Kenyon. Affable old smile.

"That's the spirit. OK then, I'll ask both of you to step into your booths and put on your earphones."

CONTROL

—*Camera Two, lay of the land please, very nice, it's just glittering, gents, would you look at that*—

Cue music. And here comes a spokesmodel to affix the name MRS. DEARBORN to the new contestant's scorebox. As the music winds down, the spokesmodel glides backward as if rewound on a fishing line. Disappears behind the booths.

And now they are started.

—Camera Two—

"Missus Dearborn, I'll begin with you."

Ding! goes the bell.

—She's beautiful, Camera Two, my god they're all just gorgeous tonight—

"The category is The Civil War. How much do you think you know about the Civil War? Answer by telling me how many points you'd like from one to eleven."

"I'll try for nine points."

"You'll try for nine. For nine points: Because he did not sanction secession, this man was the only senator who refused to leave the United States Senate when his state seceded from the union in June of 1861. Name him and the state he represented."

"Andrew Johnson of Tennessee."

—Camera One—

"You're right, and you now have nine points!"

Applause, applause.

Mrs. Dearborn's scorebox flutters to **9**. Mint silences her earphones.

—Ready Camera Three—

"Kenyon, you have three points. The category is Holidays. How many points would you like?"

—Camera Three, make us feel that sweat—

"Holidays," says Kenyon, swabbing his brow. "I could use a holiday right now."

Laughter from the audience. Under the oppressive lights, a little smile flits across Kenny's mouth. "I'll try seven points, Fred."

"For seven points, here is your question… You're right and you now have ten points! Missus Dearborn, you have nine points."

Ding! goes the bell.

"The category is Elections. How many do you want? All right, for nine more points, here is your question. That's correct, and you now have eighteen points! Kenyon, the category is Elections. How many points will you try for? For eight points, here it is: In the election of 1912, the vice presidential candidate of the Republican Party died shortly before Election Day. Who was this candidate, and who was named to replace him?"

—Don't even think of letting'm go, Camera Three—

Close on Kenyon as he breathes deep, fidgets, shifts his weight to one leg. "Well, 1912. That was the year that Taft and Wilson beat Teddy Roosevelt…" He gnaws his bottom lip. He squeezes his eyes closed, opens them. In the microphone his long exhale is like a sea roar. "The name of the man," he says tentatively, "who was the actual vice-presidential candidate who ran for the office was Nicholas Murray Butler. Now that's the man who replaced the original candidate who died."

"That's right," says Mint. "I presume you know Butler because of the association with Columbia."

"Yes, he was the president of Columbia for many years."

"Uh-huh. Now the original candidate was…"

But Kenyon Saint Claire doesn't know. He's squeezing his eyes again, casting his head back, his face all pale and glistening.

"I'll have to ask for your answer, Kenyon."

"Sherman," says Kenyon suddenly. "James S. Sherman."

"Sherman is correct, and you have eighteen points!"

The audience pours forth a wave of relieved applause.

KENYON

The holiday line, Kenny had thought of that. Seems to be a hit too!

Lacky had wanted him to miss Nicholas Murray Butler. *Who except a historian would know a thing like that?* said Lacky.

A Columbia man, Kenny had answered. *Any Columbia man would know.*

CONTROL

—Ready, Camera One, we'll stay with you—

Swiveling again to the opposite booth, Fred Mint begins to speak, but— Cue bell.

"Whoop! Missus Dearborn, Kenyon, we've just heard a sound which means that our time is up. Won't you both come out here, please. My, you both have played mightily tonight and you've come to a tie at eighteen points each. All I can say is that this has been one of the most thrilling contests we've ever had. How do you feel, Kenny?"

"Hot."

"How do you feel, Missus Dearborn?"

"Just fine, a little warm."

—*Camera Two, close on our starlet now*—

"Well, you both answered very difficult questions and you deserve a little break. Are your children at home fast asleep, Missus Dearborn, or may they be watching?"

"Oh, they're asleep at this hour."

"They're just youngsters, aren't they? And, Kenny, any members of your family watching the program?"

—*Camera One*—

Kenyon laughs. "About thirty."

"Well, they all have much, much reason to be proud of both of you for your tremendous display of knowledge. You'll come back next week, and I know everyone will be waiting to see the outcome of the match. At $1,000 a point, I congratulate you both."

Cue orchestra as the audience applauds. Kenyon and Mrs. Dearborn make their way offstage and the camera pulls in close on Fred Mint for the Geritol placement.

—*Ready sponsor title*—

Mint's in a terrible rush and keeps speaking as the orchestra plays out, but manages to finish just in time to wave to the audience at home.

—*Sponsor title go*—

Cut to a globe encircled by a whizzing plane whose jetstream spells the word GERITOL. A GERITOL bottle appears and the plane continues its orbit: one, two, three swipes across the bottle: FEEL. STRONGER. FAST.

Cue announcer, and Bob Shepherd's voice comes on: *To Tell the Truth! You'll really enjoy the exciting new panel show, To Tell the Truth! with Bud Collyer. Brought to you by Geritol and Zarumin every Tuesday night over another network. And now, this is Bob Shepherd wishing you good health from Pharmaceuticals, Incorporated, who brings you Geritol, Zarumin, and other fine quality drug products!*

A final flourish of the tympani drums and…show's over.

—*Now that's television, gents*—

5.
THE NEW REAL
February 1957

"That was the fun of it—the confusion and mixture of televised fantasy and voyeuristically apprehended reality. A dose of fantasy. And the insinuation that we might be watching something real. Which has turned out, fifty years later, to be television's perennial, still winning formula."

—Susan Sontag

Q:
Mr. Winfeld, have any pressures
ever been brought to bear on you
to keep this whole matter quiet?

A:
Actually in a way, yes. In other words,
all sorts of blandishments and promises
were made to me, as I have stated before; that I
would get certain jobs if I shut my mouth; I would make
certain appearances on shows and become part of
the Mint and Greenmarch staff and so forth, if I would just, very
bluntly, shut my mouth and not say anything

about this to anybody.*

---

*Congressional Record, House Committee on Legislative Oversight, October 6,
1959

Roll Tape

Greenmarch
Come in, Sid, come in.

Winfeld
Hello, Ray. I guess you know— we've discussed this I realize— what brings me here today.

Greenmarch
Have a seat, please. Can I get you a drink?

Winfeld
I guess I have time to sit, thanks. Sure, OK, but nothing alcoholic, I've got to go back to work after.

Greenmarch
Thanks for coming in like this, Sid.

Winfeld
As we discussed on the phone, Ray, you've received my messages.

Greenmarch
I realize you've had a hell of a time reaching me, Sid, and—

Winfeld
Finally I didn't know what else to do but to insist on seeing you in person—

Greenmarch
The program, there's just not enough hours in the day some days, it's been a very busy time for us here—

Winfeld
Because since I went off the air as you know things have been a little, how do I say, irksome or—let's just say I've been through the wringer a bit, Ray.

Greenmarch
But listen, in spite of all this I wanted to reassure you that we're here for you, Sid.

Winfeld
—and meanwhile all the time I'm remembering your guarantees.

Greenmarch
I realize you've been waiting regarding those post-appearance opportunities—

Winfeld
The shows and appearances you'd stipulated, yes. See, my wife is— well, very naturally, she's started asking me for some kind of enlightenment on our situation, how we're going to manage and so on.

Greenmarch
And I want to assure you I've been working on your behalf behind the scenes, so to speak.

Winfeld

You see, her parents are quite wealthy but I won't have any of it. Can you think what that must be like, Ray, to have your mother-in-law always standing there with a handout? What other stance can a guy take, what else can a guy tell his wife in a situation of that nature?

Greenmarch

I'm sorry to tell you this, Sid, but although I did submit you as a candidate for the new panel show I'd mentioned, you were not one of those selected to advance to the next phase. Now, these decisions, they're extremely calculated—there are formulas, algorithms, demographics. Analyses of all kinds are taken into account—things the candidate can have no control over whatsoever. But listen, I'm still looking into a number of other possibilities for you, Sid, including further guest appearances and quite possibly a position of some kind in the office on the pre-production side.

Winfeld

Well, I would not be opposed to a position of a behind-the-scenes type, I mean I'm not going to be choosy at this point, Ray, only I still remember the guarantees that were held out to me quite clearly, so you understand that it's my preference to maintain some on-television work of some kind.

Greenmarch

At the moment we have no offers for you, but this doesn't mean we've forgotten you, Sid. Now, once you're done with your college schooling—how's that going anyhow?

Winfeld

I'm doing fine in all my courses, thank you, and in fact I'll be graduated on the sixth of May—

Greenmarch

Good, good. Well, once you're done, May sixth, if we haven't managed to secure you a spot on any shows—

Winfeld

It's been something of a challenge I admit since being on the show, and now I can't walk across campus without someone calls out to me about Henry the Eighth's wives or the discovery of penicillin or some such business, which what are you gonna do?

Greenmarch

—and I intend to keep working on your behalf on that subject—but if we haven't managed to secure you a spot anywhere, you need to come right up and see me on May sixth, got that, Sid?

Winfeld

Sure, I'll come up in May, but you understand that I'm still looking and hoping for something more immediate. I mean don't five or six new panel shows come on the air every week? Sitting at home and watching, that's how it looks anyway.

Greenmarch

As things stand now, Sid, I'm looking into a few other possible productions, so we may still have panel show opportunities for you in the near future.

Winfeld

Whatever the nature of the appearance, I would not object.

Greenmarch

If we utilize you, Sid, it will look something like this: you will appear once per show, every day on the air. We'll cut to your face, you'll say a few words, you'll be referred to by name when the occasion arises.

Winfeld

I could hold a bottle of Geritol and say all the business about tired blood, I'm not choosy. But would this be like an announcer essentially?

Greenmarch

Not an announcer precisely. A recurring featured guest, more like. Now, Sid, there's another point we need to discuss, and I'm sure you can guess what it is.

Winfeld

Sure, I'm happy to talk over all points, it's why I came in after all.

Greenmarch

It's my understanding that you called up a few newspapers.

Winfeld

As we both know you are referring to Dave Gelman at the *New York Post*—

Greenmarch

I'm trying to understand, Sid, what might have motivated you to do that.

Winfeld

—which I'm fully aware he called you up and you had a conversation the two of you.

Greenmarch

Had we made you angry in some way? I mean, you have your prize money. I would hate to look at this as being some kind of blackmail scheme.

Winfeld

That would be false, Ray. No, but let me tell you my whole situation in gist. You see, it turns out that Bernice—Bernice and me—we're expecting.

Greenmarch

Oh, well now! I had no idea—well now, isn't that wonderful!

Winfeld

I didn't know myself until very recently.

Greenmarch

Congratulations, Sid. Let me pour you another. When is she due?

Winfeld

Thank you. OK, sure, but again nothing alcoholic please. And seeing as you've had kids yourself, Ray, you must know how tense these months leading up can be, especially if you're short on funds.

Greenmarch

Certainly, sure, these times come with their share of pressure—wait, do you mean to say that your money's *gone*?

Winfeld

Ah, yeah, this was the matter of some bookie my cousin knew—unfortunately I piddled away my winnings through my own stupidity.

Greenmarch

Jesus Christ, Sid.

Winfeld

And frankly I am physically afraid of this guy, the guy is a real murderer.

Greenmarch

Jesus Christ. Don't you realize that in backing a syndicate, it's an illegal thing? And those kinds of people—they can be dangerous people, Sid!

Winfeld

Yes, I know it, Ray, but what's done is done I'm afraid.

Greenmarch

OK, OK, listen…ahhh…would it help if you had someone to talk to,

Sid, somebody to just listen to all you're going through, the pressures and so on?

Winfeld

Well, I'm here talking to you, Ray. Unless a shrink's what you mean—

Greenmarch

Well, yes, a *shrink* is one way of referring—have you ever seen an analyst, Sid?

Winfeld

I've already got one, see him twice a week in fact, though god only knows how I'm gonna pay him except, like with everything else, from what's left of my savings.

Greenmarch

No, sir, I want you to go five days a week, not twice. We'd be happy to put you in touch with an excellent analyst. Consider it done, OK?

Winfeld

Well, sure, I would appreciate it, Ray.

Greenmarch

All you need to do is talk with Denise on your way out. We'll foot the cost.

Winfeld

But I'm not asking you to do this, I hope we'll be clear on that, OK—

Greenmarch

It's the least we can do, Sid. We recognize that we are in part responsible for your emotional upsets—we opened the door to these problems for you.

Winfeld

But in other words, it's other things I'm still asking of you, and only because you gave me your guarantee. A fellow just needs assurance from time to time, as you understand, Ray, honest assurance, which otherwise you get this gnawing feeling with all the pressures and whatnot.

Greenmarch

The world, Sid, is a cruel world, and fate plays an even greater part in such things. What can we say? I don't know whether *I* can cope with life or not, but I don't think you're in a condition to do so all by yourself at this stage, and I say we have help, Sid. And meanwhile we're here working on your behalf …

Winfeld

And may I say a few things before we continue? For example, I'll admit I flipped. And I'm saying to myself now, I'm saying, I'm perfectly willing to need help, that's why I'm here. I'm saying, ahhh, Ray gave me a damn good break.

Greenmarch

You're welcome, Sid, of course.

Winfeld

No, but listen, Ray. Just for a minute. See, it all went back much further for me. I felt in the end that here was this guy Saint Claire with his fancy name, Ivy League education, parents of distinction all his life, and I had just the opposite, the hard way up. Here was my own sort of mental delusion that this should all be coming to me.…

Greenmarch

So you're owning up to it then? That you've been acting badly. It's a good first step to be able to say it, Sid. To just say, for instance, yes, there was a blackmail scheme afoot.

Winfeld

[*sighs audibly*]   Ray, these are very different things, as I think you know already. Needing help is one thing, but you're talking a criminal matter, which you can understand I am not going to come out against myself and say—

Greenmarch

Yes, well…now there's one other topic we need to discuss today, which is that there are certain stages to how we proceed here. I'm not going to disclose what the stages are because I don't want to hold out any bait or anything like. But listen, I want you to write down on a piece of paper now to the effect that contrary to what you have said in the past or written in the past, Raymond Greenmarch has at no time disclosed questions, answers, points, anything like it. Here's a pen, Sid.

Winfeld

I'll be glad to, Ray, of course. I'm glad to write whatever you say. Can I just set my glass down right over here for a moment?

[sound of a ballpoint pen on paper]

Greenmarch

Have you thought of how you might reduce a bit more, by the way?

Winfeld

What can I say, I'm already reducing, Ray. I'm down to 179, I mean to start with I've never exactly been heavy—

Greenmarch

No, not heavy *per se*, only the TV camera, you know, can be a fairly unforgiving thing—

Winfeld

But if you put me in a big jacket that was never even mine then that's how I'm gonna look…

Greenmarch

And in terms of wanting to represent the best of yourself to the young people out there, etcetera…

Winfeld

Anyway, I'm reducing in preparation. When I go on I want to look like a gentleman, not that little short squat guy I was before.

Greenmarch

I knew you'd understand.

Winfeld

Now, I wanted to ask you another thing, Ray.

Greenmarch

Sure, I think I have a few minutes. What's on your mind?

Winfeld

There's that match I'd still like to do, just fair and straight, with Mister Saint Claire.

Greenmarch

Well, this idea of a rematch, I think we've discussed this before, Sid. In all honesty I don't see you and Saint Claire doing such a thing—

Winfeld

And it needn't even be a cash contest, better to do it for some kind of charity probably.

Greenmarch

A *charity* match, well, that could be different. That we might consider…

Winfeld

In fact I've already talked to one or two people at City College and they said later this spring, say March, they'd be happy to host something like this.

Greenmarch

Around March, you say? Hm. I'm not sure we'll be a position to ask Mr. Saint Claire to do such a thing come March, Sid, but if, say, Mrs. Dearborn were still on, we could certainly ask her.

Winfeld

Wait a minute now, do you mean Saint Claire's going to lose to Mrs. Dearborn?

Greenmarch

Now, Sid, I really don't understand what you're referring to. As you know very well, contestants play until they're defeated and we have no way of knowing…

Winfeld

No, no, of course.

Greenmarch

Mr. Saint Claire has been the reigning champ for some time already, but no one lasts forever, as you know.

Winfeld

Yes, sure, he could take a fall any day now, that kind of winning streak can't be kept up forever, sure. Well, Mrs. Dearborn would make a good contestant, certainly, but you understand my interest in going up against Saint Claire one last time, I know we've spoken on that subject already you and me.

Greenmarch

Let's all continue to give it some thought, shall we? All right, Sid, now make sure you stop and talk to Denise about that analyst, OK?

Winfeld

OK, we'll be in touch then, won't we, Ray?

Greenmarch

Mm, and if at any time, Sid, you're sitting at home in the evening and something starts to gnaw on you—

Winfeld

Yes, well, like I say, these times are not the easiest what with the expectancy—

Greenmarch

Call me up. Just call me up.

Winfeld

I'll just call you up if it ever comes to that.

Greenmarch

Hang in there, Sid, won't you? And congratulations!

Winfeld

Thanks for seeing me, Ray.

[*End tape*]

KENYON

The letters keep coming—sack full after sack full—so they've hired a girl, Ernestine, to answer on Kenyon's behalf. She's at her desk in the lobby of Sam Lacky's office, a sheaf of open letters beside her typewriter, when Kenyon arrives for his Tuesday meeting.

"Fourteen today," she calls.

"Pardon?"

"Fourteen. Marriage proposals. That's in this little batch alone."

He backtracks to her desk, plucks up the top letter, and reads.

> Dear Kenny,
>
> I write to you of my own volition. No one is urging me on to this action, and though it is unlike me I have the personal conviction that fate or something of that kind has demanded that I put pen to paper to tell you this: I so sincerely wish to be your bride....

He says, "She comes to the point, doesn't she?"

"None of them waste much time."

He smiles at her over the letter, but Ernestine has turned away to fuss at the platen on her Royal. She's a bit older than most of the secretaries—and always very upright, a little prim, but it's not for lack of confidence. Her eyes, he's noticed, are a deep and living blue, and they project a surety unlike the younger girls.

"I'm lucky to have you," he says, and watches as she turns those eyes on him now. "To have you as a...buffer."

"Is that what I am, though? Mister Saint Claire, you don't know how I worry sometimes."

"Over what?"

"Over *whom*, is the question. Over these poor girls. How many hearts do I break every day?"

"Oh, but it isn't you...doing the breaking."

"What makes you say so?"

Her shoulders come forward. She's wearing a speckled maroon sweater and with this gesture he notices the shoulders for the first time: smart, expressive. He can't think of another person whose shoulders, by their shape and slope, seem to speak of such an integrated intelligence of body and mind.

"It's really me, in a way," he says. "Anything you write on my behalf—I'm the responsible one, aren't I?"

"I'm not sure that helps me much, Mister Saint Claire."

"Oh, but don't you think…" He stops. He lays the letter down atop its stack.

"Don't I think what?"

"Don't you think it's all just silly?"

She shakes her head. "I don't want that on my conscience!"

He doesn't understand this and she sees it.

"They're *people*, aren't they?" she says. "It's a responsibility. To see each one of them for the person she is."

He can tell she means it. There's a tension in her face, a slight pallor. She looks at him squarely, an expectant stare. *Show me*, the look demands, *that you're not a cad.*

"You're right, of course," he says. "Like I said, lucky to have you."

"You're very welcome."

In the office Kenyon and Lacky run through the blue cards. They've perfected and distilled this routine to a matter of ten or twelve minutes.

"Sam," says Kenyon, when they're through, "I'd hoped to make a suggestion. May I?"

"Couldn't hurt. What's up?"

"Well, I realize we're in the home stretch here…" They've discussed this. Victoria Dearborn will unseat him. Lacky and Greenmarch are sorting out the details—a long series of tie games is in order, they've said. *We can't let go of you in anything but the most dramatic style*, Lacky has told him. *You're TV's biggest winner ever!* "I realize we're in the home stretch, but I've had an idea for some time now—I've mentioned it to Mister Greenmarch …You remember, early on, how we talked of the program's potential, Sam, for teaching. For knowledge and learning."

"Sure, sure. I'd say we're doing pretty well on that note."

"Hear me out, though, Sam. You see, as a teacher I think of all the things that… For instance, say the program had an informational segment every week—just one segment where we explore a topic more fully, one of the topics from the cards. Say, just a minute or two on Emily Dickinson, or antebellum America, or a scientific question of some kind. It seems to me that would be a very natural outgrowth…"

As Kenyon talks, Lacky's eyes fall closed. Almost imperceptibly his head wags side to side. Kenyon, warming to his own idea, goes on a minute or two more, but Lacky seems to be waiting it out.

"Think of it, Sam," Kenyon concludes. "Wouldn't it be wonderful?"

In the silence, eyes still closed, Lacky draws a deep breath. Very slowly one of his hands moves forward over the desk, palm down, fingers splayed, and settles atop the leather blotter—the gesture of a man patiently putting a complicated case before a child.

"This program, Kenny, the format, the delivery—we've put all the moving parts together very painstakingly. The isolation booths, the lights, the sponsor, even Fred's suits—it's all of a piece. Hundreds upon hundreds of factors and considerations go into a production of this nature and, with all due respect, it's not your line."

"Well, of course, Sam, you're the TV guy here—"

Now Lacky sits up and reaches for his calendar book.

"Incidentally, Kenny, have you got any idea how many people are tuning in every week? You seen the mail for today alone? You're topping the ratings—not just on NBC, all the networks. That brings up something else, speaking of how big this thing is—effective next week we're moving the show to Monday night. We're going right up against Lucy. Ray's determined to bring Lucy down. It's a fight to the death for him. And you know what? We happen to stand a good goddamn chance."

Lacky springs up and comes around to grip Kenyon's shoulders squarely with both hands. "I hope you're enjoying this time in your life, Kenyon Saint Claire, 'cause it's a hell of a ride you're on. Jesus H. Christ, kid, you're the biggest thing next to *I Love Lucy*!"

Out in the lobby, Ernestine is steadily at work. Kenyon stops to watch her from a few paces behind—her narrow back in the maroon sweater. The keys strike and clatter, the tiny bell dings, the carriage return zips along on its lever. What is she saying on his behalf? Whose affection is she gently refusing, and with what reassurances?

Kenyon turns again to Lacky's office. Door in one hand, he leans in. "Hey, Sam, listen. Tomorrow night, could I go without makeup?"

Lacky, in his chair, falls still. "Say again?"

"Could I skip the makeup tomorrow and go on, you know, just with my face?"

Lacky takes this in, flattens his mouth, shrugs. "That's a fight for the dressing room, Kenny. Not my jurisdiction."

"Got it. See you tomorrow."

Kenyon shuts the office door and turns to find Ernestine watching him, swiveled around from her typing table.

"Making progress?" he says.

"Dolores Fletcher," she says. "A widow in Des Moines. She's watched you every week and feels that she knows you. Ms. Fletcher writes, where is it?—oh, here: 'I expect you won't be on the program forever, but would you laugh if I were to say how much I'll miss you when you go?'"

"Goodness. Why would I laugh?"

"Very trusting, isn't she? They all are, actually."

"What are you going to tell her?"

"What can I? I'm saying thank you, like with all the rest."

"Yes, and please tell her I would never laugh."

"Certainly, Mister Saint Claire."

"Thank you, Ernestine. And call me Kenyon, please."

"OK." She smiles, a real and fulsome smile. "I sign you that way anyhow."

It's the first time he's seen this smile, he realizes, and by the way it lights her blue eyes he understands that it's her only smile, fully authentic, never squandered or dealt out in half portions.

"Ernestine," he says, before he can give it any thought, "would you let me take you to dinner?"

Still smiling, she pauses, appraising him. Then she shakes her head.

"No luck?" he says.

"Next round, maybe. How's that?"

"Pardon?"

"You may try again later."

A man accosts him on the sidewalk as he comes out of the building.

"Kenny Saint Claire! Oh my God, it's you!"

"Hullo," Kenyon mumbles, demurring. And though he keeps walking, the man comes alongside, shoulder to shoulder. They seem to have stepped onto the same moving track. The man wears an overcoat and tie, good shoes, carries a briefcase.

"My God, I watch you every week, Kenny! You're a hell of a champ. Hey listen, I'd like to give you a little something, could I? Would you hang on just a second and let me give you something?"

"You're very kind," says Kenyon, "but I have to be going."

"Of course, no, I understand. I'll just walk with you a bit. You see,

I'd just love to give you a little something and I think you'll appreciate it—knowing you're a writer and all—the reason being that I watch you every single week—you understand, don't you?—just a little show of my appreciation—here they are, Kenny. I'd like you to take these—would you allow me to give them to you?"

In the man's outstretched hand are two gleaming ballpoint pens, thick and metallic, of very fine quality.

"You're too kind," says Kenyon. "I couldn't possibly—"

"No, please, it would mean the world to me if you took them, Kenny—you understand, don't you?—and I know you'll make good use of them."

"I'm afraid I can't accept. You're too generous—"

"Listen, Kenny, c'mon, what am I gonna do with them—I sell radiators for pete's sake. My boss gave me them, some kind of bonus, and they're awfully solid made of real gunmetal or something, but really what am I gonna do with them whereas somebody like you—"

They've reached the subway entrance. People pour past them down the stairs as Kenyon stops and turns.

The man draws back a bit, hand still outstretched. He's an older fellow, retirement age or beyond. His eyes are a yellowish green recessed amid the folds of a weathered brow, but they have a bright look, an innocent gleam.

"Just take them, Kenny," he says, almost softly.

"I could buy one from you, how about that?"

"No, sir. They're a gift."

"I—I'm not sure I understand."

The man shrugs. A small smile. "What's to understand? You could write me a check but I wouldn't cash it, just hang it on the wall." His stare is very steady. "A token of thanks," he says. "For your inspiration."

So Kenyon, helpless, puts out his hand.

Time wants a story (rumors of a cover, Lacky tells him).

The Detroit News wants a story.

NBC is looking, says Lacky, into how they can keep him on. The *TODAY Show* wants him to call.

It's as if they've all started to worry that his winning streak cannot last.

Meanwhile, the glass booth has become a kind of sickness. Standing in that sense-deadened box, ears clamped under muting headphones, sweat-slicked shirt clinging beneath the jacket, he will crease his brow, grimace, kiss his kerchief repeatedly, counting, always counting to the maximum quantity of suspense—and always already the answer is installed in his brain. These nauseating contortions, and the prospect of doing it all again (and he must do it again, and again after that, for another few weeks at least) makes him ill.

Yet here he is once more, flayed under studio lights, the teeth of the cameras gnawing hungrily at his suited figure, the camera's sinister red all-seeing eye confirming his reduction in the lens. Once more the audience applauds, gasps, and the tympani boom, and the studio orchestra crescendos upward, and Fred Mint soliloquizes on Geritol, while Kenyon agonizes in his isolation booth before them all—before how many millions?—and professes to know the answers, or pretends to *not* know, and drives the numbers of his scorebox up, down, and up again.

But first the easygoing banter, as rehearsed from the cards...

"And, Kenny," says Fred Mint, "with your $122,000 really at stake now, how do you feel tonight?"

"I feel nervous tonight."

"Oh, you really are nervous? But you've been nervous before."

"I don't know. I feel nervouser."

The audience laughs as planned. He winces out a smile, groping the wing of Mint's podium, hunched inside the camera's frame.

"Nervouser? That may cost you about $100,000 there, that little grammatical error. But I'm sure you said it just kind of in the spirit of cuteness. And, Kenny, you have no decision to make this week, which should be a blessing, because last week you were tied by Missus Dearborn. You both understand that instead of the customary five hundred dollars a point, and since you tied twice last week, you'll be playing for fifteen hundred dollars a point. Which means, Kenny, that you can either win or lose $16,500. That is possible in the next few moments. Or it could be anything up to that amount too. Are you both ready to play? Missus Dearborn, are you? Kenny?"

The question is only a courtesy. Fred Mint has already said it for all to hear—Kenny Saint Claire has no decision in the matter.

Q:
You're gonna try to go to twenty-one?

A:
Yes.

Q:
I can tell you now, Kenny, that your
opponent has already scored
twenty-one points. If you answer
this next question correctly,
you'll also have twenty-one and
we'll have another tie, which means
we'll have to play another game.
If you miss, of course, I don't want to scare you,
but she will become our new champion.
Here is your question and take your time.
You may have some extra time if you need it.
Four great voyages were made by Christopher
Columbus and many different places were among
his discoveries. Tell us on which voyage, the first,
second, third, or fourth, each of the following places
was discovered: the Virgin Islands, Martinique, or Santa Lucia,
Hispaniola or Haiti, and South America.
Do you need a little while to think this over, Kenny?

A:
I sure do.

Q:
I'll tell you when your time is up…

He'd called the number on the telegram, Universal International Pictures.
Who wouldn't have done so? He remembers the surge of confidence with
which he picked up the receiver, the clarity of purpose with which his
finger guided each numeral around the dial, the rotary whirling back.

He was nonplussed to hear the secretary say, "I'm sorry, who?"

"Kenyon Saint Claire. Mister Dover asked me to contact him."

"Did he phone you, Mister Saint Claire?"

"No, it was a telegram. You see, he expressed some interest—"

"Please hold."

And then a rather long wait…

Until there came a gruff voice: "Bill Dover here"—and then Kenyon was fairly chattering: *…in response to your telegram.…A manuscript…your telegram, yes…on national television…Country of the Father, it's called…Yes, that's me…well, it is quite hot in that booth, sure…Kenyon Saint Claire…no, it's still unfinished, but when you expressed interest—*

"Unfinished, you say?" Dover seemed to be gnawing a cigar—or chomping handful after handful of cashews, hard to tell. "Well, that is somewhat irregular. But how's this, Mister Saint Claire, you send the manuscript along I'll give it a glance, OK?"

And Kenyon had hardly thanked him before Dover's receiver clattered down. Embarrassed, confused, Kenyon hung up. He mailed the manuscript to International City the following day, without hope of response.

Q:

… Your time is up, Kenny—for ten
points which will either give you twenty-one
or put you back down to one point,
four great voyages were made by Columbus,
different places were among his discoveries,
tell us on which voyage each was discovered.
Want to take a crack at
the Virgin Islands?

A:

Uh, I'll try Hispaniola.

Q:

All right. Which voyage was it?

A:

That was on the first voyage.

Q:

All right. And another?

A:

South America was on the third voyage.

Q:

Let me see now…that is correct for the second part.
Now Martinique or Santa Lucia and the Virgin Islands?

A:

Martinique is on the fourth voyage.

Q:

That is right, and then—

A:

So the Virgin Islands must be the second.

Q:

You're right and you have twenty-one points!
Kenny Saint Claire, Mrs. Dearborn, we have another tie game!

AND NOW A WORD FROM OUR SPONSORS

"The great networks are sharpening their weapons—competitive performances at the same hour—you simply can't jump all around the dial and take a small bite—there's too much to miss! But DeForest double or triple screen TV lets you see it all—all the time—when you like what you see better on one, you touch your remote button and switch sound only, or flick the super magic infra-red remote for channel changing. It's more fun than you dreamed about—try it tonight! Enjoy it up to one year if you like without paying anything!"

TV NOW

A bare-chested man in bicycle shorts empties a bucket of silver thumbtacks onto a stage. He pumps his arms three times overhead, breathing and bracing himself, then leaps and bellyflops atop the tacks.

The studio audience gasps…

KENYON

Early Thursday morning and Kenyon stands in the lobby of Sam Lacky's office, Lacky not yet in and Kenyon somewhat afloat in the middle of the green neatly vacuumed carpet as Ernestine arrives. She must have caught the very next elevator after his. Her hair is in a kerchief and she's carrying a bunch of yellow chrysanthemums in a funnel of paper.

"Mister Saint Claire," she says, surprised.

"Kenyon."

"Kenyon. Were you hoping to see Mister Lacky? He won't be in till after lunch."

"No," he says. "Round Two."

"Excuse me?"

"I'm here for Round Two. And already I'm remiss. Should be me bringing those to you."

"They're for the lobby." She holds the flowers out. "Would you mind? I need to fill a vase."

"My mother grows these," he says.

"Oh?" she says, but she's already moving down the hall and turns through a door out of sight.

Kenyon waits.

After a few moments she comes back and stands in front of him, a cut glass decanter in her hands, water lapping its sides.

"Did you empty Fred Mint's whiskey to get that?"

She smiles, holding up the decanter. "In they go."

"Before I ask you anything, before you answer, let me assure you that I'm prepared to go several rounds with you if necessary."

"Fair warning," she says. She moves to arrange the flowers on a low end table in the corner.

"Where do you come from, Ernestine?"

"New York." She straightens, stands with hands on hips looking at the flowers. "Why do you ask?"

"I wouldn't have guessed New York. I was thinking Wisconsin, Ohio, maybe Maine."

"That'll cost you four points, Kenny Saint Claire. I watched you last night. Were you feeling unwell?"

"Did I look it?"

"I wouldn't call it hale and hearty, whatever it was."

"Could have been the makeup. I mean, the fact that I skipped it. Maybe that was it."

"Won that little battle, did you?"

He smiles. And then, to his surprise, she crosses the carpet and stands directly before him, no flowers between them this time.

"Well, it's your own face, isn't it."

In the bright tunnel of her blue eyes he sees himself contained, very small, like a man high up at a twentieth-story window. But there's no doubt that the man is him—not his television stand-in, not some other person.

"You said something about Round Two?" she says.

They both still have their coats on.

"Yes, for eleven points, here is my question—"

"Oh stop. No one's watching."

He looks around the room, over her shoulder, over his own. "No sponsor?"

"No sponsor, no audience, no ratings."

"Dinner?" he says. "Please. I'd be flattered."

She draws a breath and seems to hold it, her eyes on the knot of his tie. "Tell me something first."

"Sure, anything."

"Can I trust you?"

"Pardon me?"

"I asked if I—"

"Of course you can trust me. Of course."

"I'll tell you frankly, Kenyon. I've heard a few things."

"Have you really?"

"Yes."

"Well, it's nothing. Whatever you've heard."

"Park Avenue princesses? That sort of thing."

"It's nothing, believe me."

"I'm a different breed, Kenyon. So long as you understand that about me."

"Understood."

"And I have one condition," she says.

"OK."

"No photographers."

"Oh, you've seen my contract."

"Can you meet my condition or not?"

"It might cost me. Are you camera shy?"

"*I'm* not the issue. Stand up to them, Kenyon. Stand up for real life. Disobey."

"We don't have to tell them. They may find out, though."

"Just refuse to cooperate. Have you thought of that? I mean, how are we supposed to get to know each other with some photographer lurking around? How are we supposed to talk?"

"I don't think that's the point. Not for them anyway."

"But what *is* the point?" says Ernestine. She steps behind her desk, slips out of her coat, and drapes it on her chairback. Then, planting her fingers on the desk, she leans forward. "What's the point for *you*, Kenyon?"

He takes this in, silent before her—breathes it in as she holds him with that uncanny blue stare. It seems a very long time since someone asked him a question as real as this.

"You're remarkable," he says.

"Lucky to have me, I know."

"Dinner with my parents," he says. "How about that? The most unphotogenic evening imaginable."

"Thank you," she says. "I accept."

FAMILY TABLE

Dad says the grace as always. Thanks for the gathering of family, for friendships new and old, and for the first sprouts in Mom's garden. On the supper table, pork loins and mashed potatoes steam. In the old Delft tureen simmers Emily Saint Claire's traditional winter stew—leeks, turnips, squash. A February evening in the country, on the fifty-five-acre farm. The eighteenth-century house is sturdy, though the floors creak like mad. Kenyon and Ernestine have driven up from the city and everyone is charmed to meet her. George is down from Newport. Kip Fadiman is visiting too. Always to Kenyon he looks the same, old Kip: clean-shaven and handsome in double-breasted jacket, dark-rimmed glasses, the impeccable swoop of that pomaded hair. It's just the way he looked when Kenyon and George were boys peering down through the banisters in the Bleecker house, back in those days of frequent gatherings: Adler, Fadiman, Krutch, Wilson, and Lewis altogether in the living room talking away. He's never aged a minute, Kip. And how familiar, too, are the rich deeps of his speaking voice, heard so often on the radio.

Kip: Does it shock you, Ernestine, to be with a family that still says grace at dinnertime?

Ernestine: Why, no. *(Smiles)* Should I be shocked?

Kip: I was, I confess it, first time I sat down with these good people.

Dad: Were you really, Kip? I never knew.

Kip: Oh, that was a long time ago. I'd imagined you a Marxist, Maynard.

Dad: I?

Mom: You hadn't read Maynard's poetry then.

Kip: I admit I hadn't. I've long since been corrected, of course—by the poems and the man. We were all communists of a kind, though, back then. Malcolm Cowley still is. But never Maynard.

Ernestine: Well, my family has always said grace.

Kip: Have they? Protestant or Catholic?

Ernestine: Protestant, though not for any particular reason.

Laughter.

Kenyon: Marxists or not, it's always been a religious country.

Kip: Nominally, Kenyon, nominally. Our real religion—it's what all those party members were protesting back then—has always been the dollar. We're putting God on our money, in fact. You've heard, haven't you?

Dad: Yes, I'd heard that. Care for some pepper?

Kip: Thanks, yes. Congress decided last fall. *In God We Trust.* All our coins and bills will carry the words. The dollars trust God, while we trust the dollars.

Dad: Oh, Kip, it hasn't always been so. We used to be made of other stuff.

Kip: True, true. I mean since the industrial revolution—that's where we start to see more interest in the counting of dollars than...the subtleties of Shakespeare.

Ernestine: Oh, but was Shakespeare ever a religion?

Laughter.

George: For some of us he still is.

Dad: Ernestine has a point, Kip. Are you talking about Marxism or money or religion or literature?

Kip: All of the above! And also *attention*—the faculty of attention.

Dad: Go on, now. Elucidate. Gravy?

Kip: Mm, thank you. What I'm saying is—*(to Emily)* oh, incidentally, these potatoes are simply delicious.

Mom: You have Maynard to thank, not me.

George: They're Dad's specialty.

Kip: Well done, Maynard. How do you get them so silky?

Maynard: Secretly, I'm afraid.

Kip: And my compliments on the pork, Emily. Perfectly succulent.... Now what was I saying?

George: The faculty of attention...

Dad: Yes, and you have the attention of the faculty. *(Waves his fork to acknowledge Kenny and George).*

Kip: Good, good. So, *attention*. Most of us, don't you think, want to be part of contemporary history, but what if contemporary history doesn't demand any rigor in how we control and direct our attention? Won't we let our attention decline? Or won't we simply fix it on money, or on those objects that most interest the majority, which by the way is the same thing as decline.

George: Objects such as…

Kip: Spectator sports, pulp fictions, picture magazines, gadgets and machines, movies, television. Non-rigorous things.

Dad: As opposed to…

Kip: Well, as opposed to *Hamlet*, or Socrates, or Aquinas, or Voltaire.

Kenyon: Rigorous things.

Dad: Oh, but are those *rigorous*, Kip?

Kip: Comparatively, yes. It depends on how one brings oneself, which is my point.

George: But those first things you mentioned, sports and magazines and television, don't those also require attention for anyone to enjoy them?

Kip: They *attract* attention, George, that we know. I wouldn't say they *engage* it. That is, they communicate to and stimulate the audience, but we can't say there's any real *connection* made or much benefit provided. The stimulus is immediately forgotten.

Ernestine: As a matter of fact, Mister Fadiman, there are hundreds of people every week who feel such a connection to Kenyon from watching him on television that they write him the most personal letters imaginable.

Kenyon: Ernestine answers them on my behalf.

Ernestine: Girls propose marriage, teachers praise him, young men ask his advice—

Kenyon: She handles them all so graciously.

Ernestine: What do you make of that, Mister Fadiman? Doesn't it mean they're paying attention? Isn't that a connection?

Kip: I suppose it would be. Except that it can't, because it is never *intimate*. I'm sure you do an admirable job, Ernestine, but you're the one writing back. Not Kenyon. So whatever connection these viewers may feel—and I'd never blame them for feeling it—it is incomplete. It is illusory. And even if Kenyon were to answer them directly—

Kenyon: Sometimes I do.

Kip: Oh, well, I commend that, Kenyon, but I'm afraid it can't change the nature of the correspondence—I mean its basis. What the viewers have responded to is not an *actual* connection, but a stimulation.

George: *(Nudges Kenyon)* Mister stimulator.

Kip: Or simulation, we might say.

George: *(Nudges again)* Mister simulacrum.

Emily: But what about you, Kip? You've hosted your own share of programs. You've always made a fine impression on the audience yourself.

Kip: I see your point, Emily, and *impression* is the key term. What the audience sees is always a representation, hardly ever the real thing. And the audience—as a matter of fact there *is* no audience, not in reality.

Emily: How do you mean?

Kip: Well, I mean, it's the nature of the medium, whether radio or television. Take television: for those watching, it's not at all like going to the theater or to a concert, is it? They are not a unified audience in that sense. They are a *viewership,* which is different. They are only some millions of groups in millions of living rooms, and through the courtesy of the television networks these groups each feel themselves to be in contact with the performers. They have not made contact at all, only gathered an impression, usually a false one.

Dad: In fact that's nothing new, Kip. False impressions have been a stock in trade forever. Montaigne said it four hundred years ago: *Dissimulation is one of the most notable qualities of this century.*

George: But back to the faculty of attention. This audience, whatever form it takes—these viewers, they're still paying *attention* of a kind.

Kip: Perhaps, but it's very unlike *actual* attention. It may be honestly felt, but it has none of the virtues of attentive reflection or of grappling with abstract ideas. It's a passive and disempowering attention, really an act of amused consumption. Wouldn't you say so, Kenny? You've spent weeks on television now. Wouldn't you agree?

Kenyon: Certainly a quiz show and Thomas Aquinus—I mean viewing and reading—are very different. And it's true that it's become a real challenge for me—to make sense of my work in education alongside this role on television. Can the two ever be integrated? I don't know....

George: And you're always stuck in that horrid booth!

Dad: And that's no breeze, let me tell you! I've tried the booth myself. Almost fainted! I don't know how you do it, Kenny.

Kip: I remember the first time I hosted *What's My Line*—how it surprised me to learn that we were to rehearse the whole thing beforehand. You must rehearse quite a bit, Kenny, on the quiz program.

Kenyon is taken aback.

Kenyon: Pardon me?

Kip: I mean, the show always runs so smoothly. Mustn't you rehearse each week?

Kenyon: Rehearse? Why, not at all, Kip, no. We don't rehearse.

Ernestine: But, Kenyon, you do have your meeting with Mister Lacky every Monday...

Kenyon: We have production meetings, that's true—

Ernestine: They're very detailed meetings, I always assumed...

Kip: All that clever banter before and after each program—you don't rehearse any of that?

Kenyon: Oh, that. Yes, of course. That part we rehearse.

Kip: Did you think I meant the answers? Forgive me. I wouldn't question that archival brain of yours. *(Smiles.)*

Pause. Clank of dinnerware. Kenyon drinks from his water glass.

Dad: No, no. Kenny's a natural. A naturally marvelous answerer. I believe it's because he's always respected the value of knowledge. Like my father, the country doctor—everything interested him. Nothing was unimportant. Kenny was always that way too. Did I tell you, Kenny, I heard from Hector, my cousin out in Illinois. He wrote to say he watches you every week. When your turn comes he closes his eyes and listens to your voice and says he can just see your grandfather talking.

Kenyon: My goodness.

Dad: But, Kip, I think what you're saying is that television, sports, and these things—they do influence our ways of thinking, our behaviors. In the end they hold up a mirror to us all.

Kip: To our powers of attention or lack of them, yes.

Dad: They're nothing in themselves but a reflection.

Kenyon: Whereas a book, or a seminar...

Dad: Whereas a book, for instance—a book can also be a mirror, of course. But the truly great book, as we all know, is never simply that.

Ernestine: No? What, then?

Dad: The truly great book is—

Kenyon and Dad: *(In unison)*—a window.

Kenyon: *(To Ernestine)* Dad taught us this a long time ago. Me and George. Didn't he, George?

Dad: The truly great book, unlike the mirror, will never isolate you.

Kip: And never render you passive! Profoundly true, yes, profoundly.

George: Let me help you with the plates, Mom.

Kip: I'm afraid I've been talking all this time, and we haven't learned anything at all about Ernestine.

Ernestine: Oh, don't worry about me.

Kenyon: Ernestine is a gem. A brilliantly sensitive soul. I can tell you that about Ernestine.

Kip: Ernestine, you ought to come next month to the Town Hall. I've asked Maynard to join me in speaking there one evening, for a radio broadcast. Bring Kenyon along.

Ernestine: What will your topic be, Mister Saint Claire?

Dad: Don Quixote's profession.

Kenny: That's the subject of Dad's new book.

Ernestine: You'll talk about knighthood then?

Dad: Well, in a sense. As I see it, Don Quixote is neither madman nor knight. What he is, is an actor—although not in the way that we've come to understand the word. He's an actor because he strives with all his heart and soul to *act as if* he's noble, as if he's virtuous, as if he's perfectly heroic. Whatever the actual circumstances may say about him, whatever abuse he faces, he never stops acting the highest role, and so he becomes it.

Ernestine: There's an inspiring thought. We'll have to go, won't we, Kenyon?

Kenny: *(Blushes)* Sure. Wouldn't miss it, Dad.

George: Mother wants to know, who'll have some ice cream?

KENYON

Outside, the moon is large above the old house. In the icy dark the leafless trees look stony as columns. Only a few birds call. Kenyon walks out with Dad along a freshly mowed path through the field, the scattered hay a refulgent blue. Dad loves getting up on the tractor to cut these causeways over the grass, perched high in the seat in his overalls, duffel jacket, and red hunting cap, the engine's stovepipe spurting exhaust in florets of gratifying black. Dad's a farmer at heart, though with no trace-horses or even chickens to speak of. The local foxes charm instead of vex him and he indulges an unkempt verdancy in all corners. He wears his hunting cap now, the flaps down to warm his ears. He and Kenyon are heading to the property line to watch the neighbor's cows. In that farmer's heart of his there's a special place for the sight of bovine breath steaming in the dark. A vestige from his rural boyhood in Illinois, maybe. He puffs an after-supper pipe as they go.

"Good old Kip," he says, "was every bit himself tonight, wasn't he?"

Ice cream eaten, cigarettes smoked, fireside yarns exchanged, Fadiman
has taken his leave for the night. Kenyon and Dad watched his taillights
diminish from the drive. George had retired upstairs and Ernestine was
snug in the parlor listening to Mom at the upright. The music carries
faintly into the field even now.

"It was good to see him," says Kenyon. "It'd been some time."

"Had it? You know, if you should ever need anything, he's very close to
you in the city. Kip would never fail you."

"I know it. I've been so tied up these last few months."

"Well, keep him in mind."

Their feet rustle in the mowed clippings, little piles of hay kicked ahead
with every step. Even in the night freeze, the smell is rich and fruitful.

"You know, Kenny, I don't like seeing you tied up. You can do anything
you want, son. I wonder if you realize that."

Kenyon burrows deeper into the coil of his scarf, the cold seeping
through his jacket. "Dad?"

"I've never asked—this television business—I've never asked you about
it. I've wondered though, Mother and I both, whether it's good for a man
like you—or the kind of man we think you are."

Kenyon's heart sinks. *The kind of man we think you are.* "Well," he says,
"there's so much *opportunity* in it. NBC wants to put me on a salary—
when I'm done with the quiz show—did I tell you? I'd be a consultant
for their public service programming, an educational position. And *Life
Magazine* has asked me for an article." Pointlessly he adds: "There's always
the money to consider."

"A tremendous amount, I know," says Dad. "And I know how tempting
that is. I understand that completely."

Dad stops in his paces. Kenyon slows and turns. The old man's face
glows golden in the flare of a match, the light cupped in his hands over
the pipe. Drawing deep, Dad looks up at the moon as if making a wish. "I
just hope you'll always do the right thing, Kenny. The thing that will make
you the happiest. You *can* do that, you see. Whatever the circumstances."

A quick sting in Kenyon's sinuses now, and something welling in his
chest. "I want to, Dad. It's all been pretty confusing, I admit."

"Well, if there's anything about this business making you unhappy,
maybe it's time to stop."

"I don't know. Do I seem unhappy?"

"You seem…put upon."

Helplessly now the corners of Kenyon's eyes go cold with tears. What is this sudden emotion? Dad sees it.

"You must be under an awful lot of pressure, Kenny."

"Everything happened at once. I never had much time to think."

"Mm. Just don't forget that you can stop—if that's what seems right. You can…" Dad extends an arm sideways, his pipe sweeping the air. "…wipe the slate clean."

"You think the slate's dirty?"

"Oh, it's none of my business. In any case, I'm not sure what 'dirty' would mean."

"I'm doing my best, Dad. Yes, I've been confused, but just stopping— it's not so simple."

"No? What do you mean?"

What do you mean, Kenyon? What do you mean? How to say it? How put into words the futility, the sense of loss despite your accumulated winnings, the sense that the moment of surrender has long since passed?

It's shame. That's what this feeling is. *Shame.* And now Kenyon sees it clearly. All this time he's been lying outright: to the cameras, to the amorphous television audience, to the people who stop him in the street. But never until tonight has he lied outright to his family. While talking with his parents these last few months, he's been all evasion—roundabout answers, changing the subject. Tonight, though, is different. Tonight came his first bold-faced lie, spoken in front of everyone at the table. *We don't rehearse.* And such awkwardness in that moment of lying, and Dad had smoothed it over—but the old man knows. He knows.

With a fullness in his throat now, Kenyon blurts it out: "What chance is there, Dad? I mean, the things Kip was saying at dinner—television, attention, all that—"

"Oh, I don't think he meant to chastise you, Kenny—"

"I know, but—"

"He's spent so much time on television himself—"

"But he's *right*," says Kenyon. "That's the thing, isn't it? We all know he's right. And we never had a chance, did we? Those of us who would live another way, teach another way. I see that now."

Even with the moonlight at the old man's back, Kenyon can see the fall of Dad's shadowed face as he listens. This troubles Kenyon profoundly, down on some deep level where a father's authority is supposed to last forever. Still, in the hopelessness of the moment he says it again. "There never was a chance, Dad, was there? For people like us—to make a difference."

They start forward again, slowly, shoes rustling the grass. Kenyon sleeves the wetness from his face before it can crystallize in the cold. They've almost reached the fence line, shoulders of heifers coming into view, secretly, black against black—and the plumes of their breathing, dark gray until caught in bluing moonlight.

Dad's large hand comes to rest on Kenyon's shoulder.

"Oh, son," he says, and breathes, breathes. "What can I tell you?" His own smoke mirrors the breathing of the gentle beasts out there. "I've never been absolutely sure you wanted to live my life over again."

"No, no, that's not what I'm saying, Dad..." But Kenyon feels so far gone now, so adrift in misunderstanding, that he falls silent.

"You know," says Dad. "I may as well admit, I don't completely regret my coming retirement."

Beyond the fence in the moonlight of the neighboring field the large dark bodies, made anxious by their presence, are turning and turning in circles.

"Ernestine is lovely," says Dad.

"Yes. She is."

KENYON, ET AL.

fix. *v.tr*—1a. To place securely; make stable or firm. b. To secure to another, attach. 2a. To put into a stable or unalterable form. b. To make (a chemical) nonvolatile or stable. c. To kill and preserve (a specimen) intact for microscopic study.

In the dark of the narrow shaft, in the illumined booth of the elevator car rocking on its cables, Kenyon Saint Claire flies upward...

The Detroit News
Feb. 18, 1957
By Russell Harris, Staff
Correspondent
Boyish-looking Kenyon Saint Claire, who happens to be television's biggest money winner as well as a pretty fair blackjack

player, would like to duck from under
TV's horn of plenty before he owns the
network itself and his sponsor's tonic
factory. The a-little-gawky, self-described
"shy" teacher is doubtful about his ability
to helm NBC. As for the tonic, he says in
judicial fairness: "I imagine it does a good
job. Has alcohol in it."

Mr. Bigler awaits him in the reception area on the thirtieth floor, greets
him with outstretched hand as soon as the doors slide open. "Kenyon.
Thanks so much for coming up."

His tie-clip is a tiny silver television set glinting against brown and yellow
houndstooth.

"This is Miss Gray, my secretary. She's prepared the paperwork."

Together they proceed across the thirtieth floor, stopping along the way
at several desks and office doors to allow people to shake Kenyon's hand.

Although Saint Claire's winnings total
$122,000, he does not get a nickel from
the program until he either quits or loses.
It seems unimaginable that he should lose,
but will he quit?

"I can't afford to keep winning," he says.
"It's exhausting my savings, and the tax
implications are surprising. I'm told I've
reached a point where additional winnings
will be worth only about 10 cents on the
dollar."

"He is an engaging, curly-headed, lanky image of the all-American boy—
'so likeable,' gushed the Chicago American's TV critic Janet Kern, 'that he
has come to be a "friend" whose weekly visits the whole family eagerly
anticipates.'"

The windows up here are small, and yet the building at this height seems
bathed in a lambent natural light totally unlike the drab shade in which
one walks at street level. It is celestial in effect, a purifying element, golden
where all else is gray.

d. To prevent discoloration of (a photographic image) by washing or coating with a chemical preservative. 3. To direct steadily: fixed his eyes on the road. 4. To capture or hold: fixed our attention. 5a. To set or place definitely; establish: fixed his residency here. b. To determine with accuracy; ascertain. c. To agree on; arrange. 6. To assign; attribute: fixing the blame.

Seated at one corner of the conference room table's gleaming expanse, Kenyon, Mr. Bigler, and Miss Gray review the contract.

"This clause stipulates the three-year term," explains Miss Gray. "This one stipulates the salary of $50,000 per annum. ... The exact nature of your position as contractor is outlined *here*: Public Programming Consultant, with appearances on the *TODAY Show* at a frequency maximum of daily.... Content delivered will be educational in nature—"

"Wonderful," says Kenyon.

"—subject to the approval of the Production Office—"

"OK—"

"—and never to exceed the designated allotment of programming time."

"I see."

"The Saint Claires represent a tradition of people that is almost dead now, like Thoreau and Emerson. They have their roots in the nineteenth century. They are content and confident in themselves."

7a. To correct or set right; adjust. b. To restore to proper condition or working order; repair. 8. To make ready; prepare. 9. To spay or castrate (an animal).

"'In our senior year,' says one of Saint Claire's college roommates, 'Kenyon used to have a recurring dream about a billfold in which there was a twenty-dollar bill, and when you took the bill away there would always be another one there.'"

"You'll sign again next month, of course," says Miss Gray.

"Sign again?" says Kenyon. "Even though it's a three-year term?"

"Yes, you'll sign next time with Mr. Denning," says Miss Gray.

"Our vice president," says Mr. Bigler.

"For the photographers," says Miss Gray. "The publicity signing. Until then, we need to secure your complete confidentiality, so we've prepared this non-disclosure agreement."

10. Informal. To take revenge upon; get even with. 11. To influence the outcome or actions of by improper or unlawful means: fix a jury. –intr. 1. To direct one's efforts or attention; concentrate: fixed on the goal. 2. To become stable or firm; harden: the plaster is fixing. n. 1a. The act of adjusting, correcting, or repairing.

Agreements duly executed, they rise from the table to shake hands again.

"Welcome aboard, Kenyon," says Mr. Bigler. "NBC is happy to have you. I believe Miss Gray has a little something with your name on it."

"Here you are, Mister Saint Claire."

The pale blue check bears the neatly typed sum: 4,400.00.

"Your first month's pay."

2. A clear determination or understanding. 3. A difficult or embarrassing situation; a predicament.

"And we wish you continuing luck with the quiz program," says Mr. Bigler.

"Thank you. To tell the truth, I'll be relieved to have all that behind me. Whenever the time should come."

"I'd imagine it's a good deal of pressure," says Bigler.

"Yes. And less than ideal in other ways."

"Ah. Tax implications?"

"There are those, to be sure. But this…" Kenyon waves the check, blushes. "A position of this kind, I mean—it's much more my cup of tea."

"Oh," says Bigler. "Of course. You're a teacher, after all."

"I'm a teacher, yes. I hope to make a difference, you see, however small. Spouting answers—I'm not so sure that's served anyone but me."

"Well, good for you, Kenyon. Your intentions are very admirable."

Mr. Bigler pats his arm, and then Miss Gray takes her leave as Bigler walks him back through the office to the elevators.

Down he goes, his first month's pay tucked safely in his shirt pocket.

The figure on the check is equal to Kenyon's annual salary at Columbia.

4. Slang. An amount of something craved, esp. an intravenous injection of a narcotic.

Coming back from the farm, seated passenger-side in the 190 as Kenyon sped them onto the turnpike, Ernestine put her head back against the headrest and said, "They sure love you dearly."

"Hm? Mom and Dad?"

"Your mom and dad, your brother, Mister Fadiman."

"Kip's practically family."

"Can you remember a time," said Ernestine, "when you didn't feel the love of everyone around you?"

"I'd have to think..."

"I mean from all sides. Have you ever known anything else?"

"I'll think about it. The military maybe. What makes you ask?"

She shrugged a little, head back and eyes half-closed. "Different lives. That's all."

"You and me? You mean your life's been different?"

She let out a small sleep-thick laugh that was half a groan. Without looking she reached over and touched her hand to his neck. "*Most people*, Kenyon. Most people's lives are nothing like yours."

"Well," he said, after a few moments. "I'm sure that's true."

"Lucky boy," said Ernestine.

"Lucky boy," he said.

The next day they met for lunch at Columbus Circle and she told him that when she was fourteen her mother had died of a head wound after slipping down a set of hospital stairs following a checkup, and that her father, a high school metal shop teacher, never recovered from the shock and grief. At seventeen Ernestine left the city and lived with an aunt in Pittsburgh while attending secretarial school. In her first year away her father was killed by a taxi on Third Avenue. There was just enough money for a plot and a simple bronze plaque, but nothing for an adequate funeral, and anyway Ernestine had never known his side of the family. Quietly she saw about his burial and went back to Pittsburgh. That same year her aunt, after being widowed a decade, remarried and moved in with her new husband and his four children from a prior marriage. Left to her own devices, Ernestine transferred to a secretarial school in New York, living in a ninth-floor single-bedroom apartment in Queens that she shared with the two girls who'd placed the classified.

"I still think about it sometimes," she said. "Why I ever came back here. This city killed both my parents."

"Why did you?" asked Kenyon.

"I still don't know. No family. No real home. But I was born here. That seemed like reason enough."

"I'm glad you're here," he said, and reached across the table to take her hand. "And listen, you can have my family. They love you already."

"Oh, you're giving them away, are you?"

"No, no. Sharing them," he said.

He watched her take this in, squeezing her hand. She looked very serious and didn't even blush. "That's a lovely thought, Kenyon."

They left it at that.

IN LIVING ROOMS ACROSS AMERICA

Here again is Kenny Saint Claire in earphones and shut up tight in his glass booth under all the lights. Again he holds his breath or hardly breathes as Fred Mint brings on the questions for nine points, ten points, eleven.

Name each of the six Balearic Islands.

Tell us the common names for: 1) caries 2) myopia 3) missing patellar reflex.

Name five members of George Washington's cabinet.

The screen is all whites, silvers, and grays, airtight.

His face fills the frame, crushed close against the glass—glass in several layers: isolation booth glass, camera lens, television screen. Kenny Saint Claire a specimen in a box: scrutinized, admired, idealized, panegyrized, celebretized, and subjected to the projections of every viewer—all 20 million craning forward from the edge of their seats at home—a man watched more closely, maybe, than anyone of any time before him.

To watch him *being watched*, to see how he bears up, that's half the stimulation.

To be asked to *perform* like that, it would be a nightmare and a fantasy all at once.

Can he really know all those answers? This question is also part of the fascination.

You look at him and ask yourself, if it were *me* in that booth…

And really he *is* you already, you and all the other millions who watch—Kenyon Saint Claire, sweating and murmuring behind glass, is taking upon himself everything you've ever wished for, worried over, dreamed of, or dreaded. *Am I smart enough? Calm and collected enough? Good-looking enough? Likeable enough? Can I hold up under pressure? Can I make it look easy when I need to? Do I have anything worth envying? Have I figured out how to sport it? Would I answer the call—or take the fall—for a higher cause? Am I sufficiently ambitious? Do I banter well? Can I manage glamour and sophistication without growing arrogant or giving up plain talk? Would anybody ever call me inspiring? Am I a cause of anyone's pride? Could I fake it if I needed to? Well, don't we fake it every day, every last one of us? But me, am I convincing? What exactly do others think of me? What do I think of me?*

Now Fred Mint announces it: they've got another tie! Kenyon in his booth and Mrs. Dearborn in hers—they smile tensely, disbelievingly, at this news in their earphones. And here come the spokesmodels to let them out while the crowd applauds. Always a relief to escape those hotboxes, you feel this as you watch the players step out through the doors. Even the losers, they're *relieved*, and you're relieved with them. But this one's another tie—how many does that make now? Four, five? So Kenny Saint Claire is still in the game with winnings up to $143,000 tonight—in case you don't believe it they display the sum right there on Mint's podium, right under the word GERITOL.

"Missus Dearborn," says Mint. "You're really giving this fellow a run for his money, and I mean that quite literally. Is there some secret to your success so far? I guess you'd be wise not to tell us if there were."

"No, no secret," says Mrs. Dearborn in her soft-spoken way, pearl earrings glinting under the lights, "only a good deal of luck."

"I'm sure you're far too modest," says Mint. "And, Kenny, you've made it through once more."

"I've scraped by, Fred, yes."

"Would you ever have thought, those months ago when you first came on against Sid Winfeld, that you would find yourself here with $143,000, the most money ever won on television?"

"Never, Fred. Never. I never would have dreamed."

"You've just taken it one game at a time."

"One question at a time, yes. That's all I could do."

"Well, you continue to be a great inspiration to the many millions of viewers watching this program every week. I thank you both, in fact, for another very exciting game. And we'll see you both again next week as you each try to break this nearly unbreakable tie. Goodnight."

The audience applauds as the players go their opposite ways. Then the lights darken to leave only a pool of brightness on Mint at the podium.

"Now, friends, until next week won't you remember that if these winter days are getting you down, it may be due to iron deficiency anemia, or *tired blood*—a very common condition this time of year—and I have just the answer for you..."

. . .

Q:

How do you bear to watch this stuff?

A:

What do you mean?

Q:

Don't you know it's all a setup, fixed from start to finish?

A:

Fake, you mean. Sure, I know it's fake.
Doesn't everybody?

Q:

So you watch it for the theatrics?
A stage play, like?

A:

A *teleplay*, yep. I watch and laugh.
But then I think, wait, what if it isn't?

Q:

Isn't what?

A:

What if it isn't, you know, artificial? Fake.
Or what if it isn't *only* that? You know,
what if it isn't just for laughs?

Q:

I don't follow.

A:

Look, here's one of the producers—
yesterday's *Times*—and they're asking him, like
you're asking me, are these programs fixed?
"No," he tells them, "they're simply controlled.
We know our contestants from exams—their
areas of expertise—and this gives us
a certain control." *Control* is the word.

Q:

I don't see the difference. Fixed.
Controlled. It's doublespeak.

A:

Anyway, presuming they're *all* fake—
The $64,000 Question, Dotto, Tic Tac Dough—
then *fake* is the *new standard.*

Q:

The status quo, like.

A:

Right. Bingo.
Fake is what we want.

Q:

Hold on now.
Is it what *I* want? No.

A:

Well, you gotta ask yourself that.
We all do. Not that it'll change
anything we see on TV.

Q:

Fake is the new true?

A:

Brilliant. You said it.
Fake is the new true.

Q:

The new real.

A:

The new real.
What could be more entertaining?

Q:

God help us.

A:

What else could be this much better than the old real?

COMMENTATORS

"The controversy about the effect of TV on vision is likely to go on for some time to come. Until definitive tests have been made, the exact effects will not be known. In the meantime, certain simple precautions can be taken…"

"Well, of course we want problems but they had better be insoluble ones, because we want to keep on asking questions that can't be answered. There's no sense in asking a question that *can* be answered. That's not an interesting thing to do."

"Like a good American, he fought hard, taking advantage of every rule. Like a good American, he won without crowing. And like a good American, he kept on winning."

MAILBAG

Dear Mr. Saint Claire,

I wish to tell you that as a result of your success answering those many difficult questions on television my twelve-year-old son Marvin has become quite another person. He seems to be plagued with a new kind of seriousness and never goes outside anymore. In the past it was everything we could do to get him to open a book, he much preferred to be playing out of doors all the time. Now he spends every hour he can with reference books and has designs to go on television at his earliest opportunity and win until he is rich. That's all well and good except that we're beginning to fear for his health. Won't you write to him to say that there is more to life than facts and money?

Sincerely,
Roberta Johnson
(Plainfield, VT)

Dear Mr. Kenyon,

I am going to be on the honor roll this month for the first time, and this is all on account of you.
Love,
Dora
(Springfield, OR)

KENYON

There have been rumors and murmurings, for weeks they've been leading up to this, and now here it is, flat on Ernestine's desk: the latest edition of *Time* magazine, its cover trimmed in red and white, and there under the stately Roman lettering of the title is his own face, the face of Kenyon Saint Claire framed against a field of patriotic blue. Wired up in bulky black earphones, inclining toward the slender serpent's head of a microphone, he's fixing his gaze on an answer, determined that the answer not elude him, his lips parted to say his line. Above his left shoulder a legend reads QUIZ CHAMP ST. CLAIRE, and further up in the top corner a yellow banner says: BRAINS V. DOLLARS ON TV.

Kenyon's heart is racing. "My goodness."

Do I look like that?

"First time you've seen it?" says Ernestine.

"Yes."

Is he overreacting, or is he really short of breath? He feels her watchful eyes as he picks the issue up. "I don't remember taking this picture."

Is that my face?

"Would you like a cup of water, Kenyon?"

"When does this come out?"

"Today, I think. Let me get you that water."

Suddenly, somehow, the water glass is in his hand, and he's still holding the magazine. He hasn't even opened it. He's thinking, somewhat irrelevantly, how little he resembles his father, despite what people say.

Does he really look like this? With that face? Whose is it?

"The story's only a few pages," says Ernestine, from somewhere just behind him. "In case you were wondering, you're not the whole issue."

"No? Good. I'm not that important. I'm not *this* important." He's realizing now how stunned he must look.

"Mister Lacky's ready whenever you are. Do you need a minute?"

He lets the magazine slap down on the desk. He breathes out. "Oh, I don't know. No. I think I'm ready."

"A car will take you over afterward."

Following their production meeting, Kenyon is scheduled for a photo shoot with Mrs. Dearborn at the NBC building.

"OK. Will you come along?"

"I hadn't planned on it."

"But will you?" He turns to her. "Am I permitted to ask?"

"I'll see," says Ernestine. She squeezes his arm, a look of mild worry in her eyes. "Go on in."

Lacky is at his desk, craned forward over another copy of *Time* open before him. He doesn't look up. "Come in, Kenny."

"I just saw Ernestine's copy. I don't remember taking that picture."

"It's a file photo. These headphones, they're superimposed, see?"

"Don't tell me what it says, OK, Sam?"

Lacky glances up. "It's all good though, you don't need to worry."

"I don't want to know."

"It's great fucking publicity, that's all any of us need to know. Jesus, are you all right?"

"Surprised, is all." He's still holding the water glass. He keeps one hand underneath it, his fingers so slick with sweat.

"Listen, like I keep telling you, make the best of this, Kenny. Enjoy it!"

"Excuse me, Sam, but what do you know about it? Did they ever put *your* face on the cover of *Time* magazine?"

"Never been so lucky, no. Do you need a smoke, Kenny?"

"No, no. My stomach…I'm sorry to lash out."

"Don't apologize. I'm sure it's a shock. Let's take a few minutes, why don't we, just a few minutes to, you know, catch our breath."

"OK."

Lacky folds the magazine, leans to drop it in a side drawer, and trundles the drawer home. *Click.* He lays his head back, clasps his hands over his stomach. "Buddy, listen, this is the final lap, OK? This is it. One more show and you're done. Done with the isolation booth, photo shoots, these meetings. It's all behind you after that, OK? You've got your gig at NBC. You'll have your winnings. A new kind of life. Hm?"

"Yeah," says Kenyon, sipping from the glass. "Yeah, I see that. And I realize I'm terribly lucky. I do. You just wonder—I wonder, anyway—how much louder it all could get. How to turn the volume down."

"Maybe you need a getaway, Kenny—you know, once your run is over here. Someplace nice, somewhere sunny. Treat yourself."

Kenyon unbuttons his coat, slips it over the chairback.

"You need some more water," says Lacky, "before we start?"

They run through the cards, the point sequencing, the mechanics of his loss to Mrs. Dearborn, and Kenyon feels better and better by the minute. *The final lap*, he tells himself. *The final lap.*

The car awaits him downstairs, sent over by NBC. Lacky will come along to direct the photographers. Ernestine can't leave her desk, but she hands Kenyon a letter, an invitation from the New England Broadcasters Association. Kenyon gives it a glance before tucking it away. It appears they'd like him to speak at their upcoming conference in Boston—*a few remarks from a well-respected television personality and educator.*

It's a ten-minute ride through midtown to West Fiftieth, then up the elevator to the sixth floor. Mr. Greenmarch meets them in the hall, leads them through the studio doors, calling out and clapping. "OK, people, our champ has landed. Let's make this quick." The Klieg lights blaze. In the off-camera dark amid photographers and various production crew stands Mrs. Dearborn.

"You two know each other by now," says Lacky.

"Of course," says Kenyon. "You're the woman who knows everything. You are positively terrifying." Mrs. Dearborn smiles warmly as she takes his hand. He sees anew that she's a beautiful woman, quite glamorous, like a more wholesome Lauren Bacall.

She says, "And you look very familiar. I think I saw you this morning on a magazine cover."

"Oh goodness," says Kenyon. "Don't believe that for a second. It's all pretend."

"Oh?"

"I never even took that picture."

"Well, there's one cat you won't get back in its bag."

In her face now, suddenly, he sees a fellow passenger. Just like him, she must know everything of what's ahead. "And now for more pretend," says Kenyon. "Shall we?"

She laughs a little. "I'm afraid so," and steps with him into the lights.

They've wheeled out the blackboard again. Someone has chalked the sum of Kenyon's winnings in massive digits—**$143,000**—and beneath it a huge question mark.

Cross all your fingers, Kenny, and bite your lip like this. Good.

Now look at that money and show us how bad you want it.

Missus Dearborn, can you give him your best challenger's smile? A look like, You're really in for it, pal! Can you try that, honey? There you go, that's very nice.

The flashbulbs burst.

Missus Dearborn, would you stand back here on this chair and pop your head over the blackboard? Careful getting up there now.

Okie doke, now smile, won't you?

Kenny, keep those fingers crossed now…

Flash, flash, flash.

For a quarter hour they go on, and then Mrs. Dearborn is asked to report to wardrobe and change for a new round.

"The black and white dress, please," says Greenmarch. "And let's change that board now. Let's have it say *TIED AGAIN.*"

Again, they ham for the cameras.

Now, Kenny, you stand behind her just here and press this kerchief at your forehead like you're really sweating. Good, now bite your lip. There.

And, Missus Dearborn, look at the words on the board like you're not afraid in the least. A real challenger's stare. Very good, OK, both of you hold it just like that…

Flash, flash, flash…

Lacky offered to have the car take him home, but Kenyon preferred a walk. Now in the bustle of the streets his own face confronts him at every newsstand. He won't dare try the subway—not today. To see himself multiplied, to be duplicated and propagated and carried in so many briefcases, under so many arms—the image itself is oppressively authoritative. Against all reason the image renders the actual him, the *only* him, a simulacrum. The image is the truth, and all things conspire to take you out of yourself.

In the gray mist he turns up his collar, tugs his scarf snug, and bores forward down the sidewalk, moving fast, eyes kept low. He is jigged up and distracted, but he's got a yearning this morning, a yearning as clear and sharp as any he's ever felt. What he yearns for is the old chaotic freedom of this city, the noise and restlessness, the stony indifference, the constant dangers, the lives in teeming masses all around. Until very recently he was lost in all that. Always the caverns of Manhattan called up a special resourcefulness. You had to carry, somewhere inside yourself, an answer to the city's vast anonymity. You did it by *striving*—striving for something exact or for something vague and elusive, but striving all the same. But now how different: to know, well beforehand, everything that lies ahead.

Maybe he does need a break, a getaway, like Lacky said.

Still walking, he withdraws the broadcasters' invitation from his inside pocket, unfolds it in the wet. The letters blur and bleed little halos of ink as he reads.

Coming to the Forty-Second Street library he's decided. He jogs up the steps and through the huge wooden doors. In one corner of the marbled lobby there's a public telephone. He dials Lacky's office and within seconds Ernestine picks up.

"Let's take a trip," he says. "Please. I have this invitation and I'd like you to come."

"You mean Boston? Are you joking?"

"Yes. No. In a few weeks."

"Are you asking me to elope, Kenyon?"

"I need to go—to get away. I'll pay for your room."

"My room?"

"Yes. Your own room. No expectations. I need to get away. Won't you come?"

Silence.

"Ernestine?"

She makes a noise like a sigh, or maybe a small laugh. "You really think you can escape it all? It's not just in New York, Kenyon."

"I know. But you'll be there. I mean, I want you to be. I want you to be there."

6.
TODAY
Spring 1957

AND NOW A WORD FROM OUR SPONSORS

"To be part of the show," says Fred Mint to the boys and girls at home, "you must have one of our Winky Dink Kits."

"When the clock strikes three in the morning," says Bob Shepherd, "are you often still wide awake, your nerves on edge, unable to fall asleep?"

"Here we have three young girls who—it looks like they've all been shot through the heads by Indians, but actually two of these girls are wearing those trick arrows, you know, that fasten to their heads with the spring hoops in them."

"Of course if you don't have a Winky Dink Kit you can't have as much fun."

"I suggest that you take the Kent carton test and see for yourself just what a difference Kents can make."

"Wake up, America! Time to stump the experts! This is the program in which you, the public, turn the tables on the authorities..."

"Remember, and this is important, Sominex contains no barbiturates, no bromides, no narcotics, and it's *non-habit-forming.*"

"You switch to Kent and smoke one carton—now I don't mean just a pack or two, but a carton—you'll find that Kent's micronite filter gives you *high filtration.*"

"Now Helen's gonna put her Magic Window right up on the screen of the television set. That's right. Now you do it just the way she does, boys and girls, it's very important."

"Remember, we're not selling the program...we're selling the audience for the program."

"This is a very critical moment. I caution the ladies and gentlemen in the audience not to call out answers."

"Finally, ladies and gentlemen, remember that *Information, Please* is unrehearsed, unprepared, happy-go-lucky, fancy-free, and enough adjectives—we're off!"

"We're here to deliver the audience to the next commercial."

"Now, boys and girls, you remember the Magic Word?"

"One girl has a real arrow shoved through her ear—no, shoved through her hairdo. And she is the one we're looking for…"

"Now if you don't have your Winky Dink Kit yet, I'm sure you'll wanna get one. You must if you wanna have all the fun on this program."

"Now you can avoid hunger tantrums, lose weight naturally and fast, with RDX full stomach reducing plan."

"Shakespeare—he was so prophetic, he always knew what was gonna happen. Imagine so many years ago saying 'TV or not TV.' That is our future, and that's a pretty bad one I'd say right now."

"Now I'm gonna step out of here and I'm gonna count to three and when I say three I want you to say the Magic Word with me, all right?"

"High filtration to help you keep your smoking moderate."

"You can fill your stomach, and fat just seems to melt away."

"You know, it takes a mother to know the way to her family's heart, and here's what we mean…"

"When you get your Winky Dink Kit you'll be able to play along with us instead of just watching."

"And now a golden opportunity is yours. Are you shaking or is that me?"

"To get your Winky Dink Kit for yourselves or your friends, you send fifty cents, boys and girls, send fifty cents—got that?—fifty cents with your name and address…"

"And, mothers, after sickness help your child gain strength fast."

"She's just vibrating all over! My goodness, calm down! Calm down! It's all over now, you've got 700 dollars so things get easier from here on in."

"Give him Geritol Junior, the ideal tonic for growing children."

"Of course it's very easy to get your Winky Dink Kit, boys and girls. All you have to do is send us fifty cents with your name and address. It's very simple and that's all there is to it. Fifty cents with your name and address."

"So remember, friends, for a real night's sleep, take Sominex as directed for natural-like sleep with 100 percent safety."

"One…two…three. *Wink-O!*"

KENYON

"A way of misrepresenting this book is to say that its hero is mad, is under delusions as to his identity, *thinks* he is a knight."

At the podium under the high red velvet of the proscenium, Maynard Saint Claire is a thin post in a gray suit. Lights glance off his silver hair, the dark stage an abyss behind him. He consults no notes, extemporizing in his seasoned way. But he projects well, his voice deep and clear.

"No, our hero has merely read the books, the ideal books. And he decides to go forth and act everywhere as if he were a knight. He doesn't *think* he is one, but he thinks he can act the part. And the story is of how he acts the part utterly without success."

A chuckle moves through the audience now, a surprise to Kenyon—to hear this description of failure charming them so. Sunday evening, 10th of March, the night before his final quiz program, Kenyon listens from his place in the second row, Ernestine's left arm entwined in his right. At their backs, the plush red seats of the town hall slope upward, every row filled. Even up in the broad scallop of the balcony there isn't a single empty seat for the first ten or eleven rows. And the microphones are carrying Dad's words out over the radio waves right now, live, for how many more listeners at home?

"We would not believe a story," says Maynard Saint Claire, "which told us that a man walked into this decidedly unphilosophical world and made it philosophical."

Now, unexpectedly, Kenyon is hearing Dad's words of two weeks ago.

The kind of man we think you are.

Their nighttime walk through the frozen field. In that cold, Dad's voice a warmth in itself.

We've wondered if it can be good for you, this television business.

Dad's saying those words again now, within or behind the words he's saying onstage.

Kenyon's hair bristles. He sits up straight.

"Sometimes this would-be knight encounters people who decide just for fun to play along a little while with this person who is playing this astonishing role. So in this book we find many persons hoaxing, they think,

Don Quixote, by pretending to be the kind of people that he expects to find. I personally do not believe that he's hoaxed. I think he sees through all those hoaxes. They sadden him a little bit at the spectacle of folly in the world. No, he wants to keep on being—seeming to be, and talking and acting like—a perfect man, an ideal man."

Loud and pure, Dad's words are ribboning out above Kenny's head, letters actually printed upon the air, perfectly legible, like a banner of words in an ancient manuscript—and Kenyon, attentive reader, knows that the words are meant for him alone.

Our shows, Lacky had said, *are doing something different, doing more for the public. The idea is education. What I mean is we're showing knowledge to be a desirable thing…*

"He was not hoaxed, this would-be knight," says Dad, and now Dad's eyes find Kenyon in his second-row seat, and Kenny is looking into Dad's face as if they are not in the town hall amid a thousand people but alone at the breakfast table with Mom's blue porcelain creamer between them, or talking in the honored privacy of their shared office, the air dense with smoke.

Listen, Kenny, Dad is saying. *Listen now.*

"No, I think he knew what he was doing all the time. I think he was being a professional actor, an excellent one. And that brings me to my final point about him, that he is human in the richest sense of that word."

I saw you, Lacky had said, *and I thought, here's the real thing, here's the kind of person we ought to see on our television screens…*

Dad's glance breaks away and again he's a man at a podium, a lifelong teacher in a simple suit, unaccustomed to the bright lights but talking simply, forthrightly.

When will Kenyon learn, if ever, to speak as simply as that? What will it take to make that possible?

"As all men are actors, all the world's a stage. And when a father says to his son, 'Act like a man,' he's not asking him to be dishonest. He's asking him, as a matter of fact, to be honorable in the highest sense of the word. About all we can ever do in this imperfect world is *act* as if it were perfect. It means we have to talk that way and we have to think that way and we have to move that way. In this respect, Don Quixote remains, I think, the perfect man."

Dad pauses, and there is a ringing silence in the hall. Then: "Thank you." And he steps away from the podium.

Applause, applause, as Maynard Saint Claire crosses the stage. At the stairs just beyond the light the old man goes slow, gripping the railing, watching his feet the whole way. Kenyon joins in the applause, stung to the quick. Yet as he watches Dad's hunched back he's also thinking, admiringly, how the old man lives almost entirely out of his time.

You're still at liberty, Dad, he thinks. *You're still free—to be sincere. But today— for the rest of us, these times make it harder than ever. All but impossible.*

And then to his depths, with an anguish that sweeps over him like a wave—even as he knows he cannot disown it—Kenyon mourns his own thought.

All but impossible.

Intuitive as she is, Ernestine notices. She's squeezing his arm, checking him with a searching look.

Are there tears in his eyes? No, but he's sure there's a pall of panic in his face.

All too often these days, something takes him out of himself.

How to get back?
How to get back inside and stay there?

Q:
Why impossible?

A:
Sorry? Why *what?*

Q:
Sincerity. You said sincerity was
all but impossible.

A:
Well, look around—the mass entertainments,
the spectacle, the gewgaws and gadgets.
Everywhere those things that absorb
our focus most of all—the majority of
them are superficial, temporary.
And one can't—

Q:
—and one can't be sincere by superficial means?

A:

Exactly.

Q:

Who says?

A:

The dictionary says. The literal meaning of superficial
is *the top-most face*. The mask. That which hides,
disguises, misrepresents, or *seems*.

Q:

Not what *is*.

A:

Yes, sincerity is what *is*.
Genuineness, wholeness.
It has completeness, truthfulness,
meaning.

Q:

We don't *mean* enough.
We pretend too much.

A:

We play a role, or roles.
One role after another.

Q:

The masks.

A:

The top-most face, yes.

Q:

Can't *some* roles be sincere?

A:

Sure, the roles we take on authentically.
Not all these roles thrust upon us.

Q:

These masks.

A:

Yes, these masks going up in
front of us every day.

Q:

Where do they come from, the masks?

A:

They're in the air. In everything we
give our attention to. There's no escaping them
anymore. It's a surfeit of *seeming*.

Q:

And sincerity is out the window.

A:

Mm.

Q:

And yet if sincerity is out the window,
how can I trust these assertions of yours?

A:

KENYON

Tonight again the lights, the lights, the layers of glass, the camera lens that
shrinks him in his box, the tympani, the applause, the puffed-up questions
and all the contortions this spectacle demands before, at last, he can just
say the answers. But finally, finally Kenyon has reached the end of his long
public audition…

LIVING ROOM

How many tie games is too many?

Ding! goes the bell as Fred Mint plucks up another card.

"The category is Political Leaders. Missus Dearborn, you have ten
points. How many do you want to try for?"

"I'll take eleven."

"For eleven points, here is your question. The following men were
rallying forces behind varying political movements during the last ten
years. First, a Frenchman born in Saint—I'm not sure of this word, C-E-
R-E—the owner of a small stationery and bookstore who wanted to

reform the tax system. Second, a pro-Greek archbishop who wants his island home freed from British rule. Third, an Egyptian army officer who first headed his country's government after the exile of King Faruk. And fourth, an African who while serving a prison sentence was elected prime minister of what has since become the new nation of Ghana."

She takes the second part first.

Her face—the crease in her brow—you just can't tell what she's thinking. She bites her lip, moves her head side to side. Yet she's cool and collected too. She doesn't sweat in that booth like all the men, not that you can see. The men, god how those little booths must just *smell* of them by the end of every game. But she takes her time. And that crease—is that worry or concentration?

KENYON

Throughout the broadcast, every time Mint turns, the green gabardine of his jacket shimmers at the shoulders and back.

Now with a *click* his voice is in the headphones: "Kenyon Saint Claire, you have ten points."

Of course no one sees the green jacket at home, let alone the shimmer. The screens leech the colors away, the faces and scenes all bloodless variations of shadow and light.

The little bell chimes and the blue card is in Mint's hand.

"The category is Biblical Families. How many points would you like to try for?"

The pressure of the headphones at Kenyon's head, the tension of the bent metal band and the rims of his ears pressed flat and stinging, and the soft weight of the dangling wires tugging his whole skull downward ever so slightly, and his own breathing resounding back at him through the mike. The heat, the heat, the sweat that drenches his undershirt, the incessant stare of the cameras and the red eye anchored in the darkness of the studio—the things we accustom ourselves to!

"Biblical families," says Kenyon's own voice in his ears. "I think I'll try for eleven."

"For eleven points, and since you are trying for twenty-one I can tell you that your opponent has already scored twenty-one. Now you know how this works, Kenny—if you answer this next question correctly we will have another tie and you and Missus Dearborn will have to play another game. If you miss, then you will lose something in the neighborhood of $27,000, and we will have a new champion. Now I don't want to pressure you, so you'll have some extra time if you need it. Here is your question: The oldest man in the Bible is Methuselah, who died at age nine hundred and sixty-nine. According to the Book of Genesis, who was his father? We're going to give you some time to think it over, and I don't have to tell you that the game is weighing on this. Now good luck."

The music plays. Kenyon gives his best grimace, mouthing the words over and over.

Father of Methuselah, Father of Methuselah.

He stares at the exposed tangle of wires on the backside of his scorebox. The ragged edge of the industrial carpeting on the isolation booth floor, the threading all frayed—it doesn't meet the wall all along the base but veers in places to leave a gap of two or three inches, exposing shoe-scuffed plywood, particles of sawdust and dirt.

In the lower left-hand corner of the booth's front glass, clear as day, there's a thumbprint—a workman's thumb, slightly brown with grease.

Father of Methuselah, Father of Methuselah.

All the time his brain is answering *Enoch, Enoch, Enoch.*

Or is it a spokesmodel's thumb?

Has it been there all along?

Would anyone believe the stale and burnt-smelling air inside this glass cell, the Klieg lights—*Krieg* lights, he always wants to say, War Lights— baking the particleboard and carpet, the Formica and aluminum and steel.

Methuselah.

Enoch.

Would anyone believe the blindness behind this glass, all the blackness beyond the scorching Klieg lights?

To stand here and look out is to see nothing at all. A nonexistent vista, nothing like a window.

Look at them, Kenny, how they all go by. Oh, it's like a play, isn't it, how they all go by?

The window was like a screen, but its projection was grandly three-dimensional.

Methuselah. Enoch.

The first thing Kenny did in this house was fall down the stairs.

Click.

"Kenyon Saint Claire, your time is up. For eleven points, which would bring you to twenty-one and another tie game, please tell us the name, according to the Book of Genesis, of the Father of Methuselah."

First thing Kenny did...

With the white square of his doubled-over handkerchief, Kenyon is swabbing his brow, his eyes, his mouth.

...fall down the stairs...

"Well, Fred," he says into the snakelike microphone. "I know my scriptures, but right now at this moment the name is escaping me."

In his earphones he can hear the anxious rustle and murmur of the crowd.

"There's an awful lot riding on this, Kenny. Would you like to venture a guess?"

Enoch. Enoch.

"Because we're having a bit of an indication from our studio audience, I have to caution them not to call out or make noises of any kind. Kenyon, I'm afraid I have to ask for your answer now."

Enoch...fell down the stairs.

With a clarity almost sickening in its intensity, Kenyon senses the forthcoming relief, finally, of failing to answer.

COMMENTATORS

"A degree of deception is of considerable value in producing shows."

"Those concerned with this matter also recommend that viewers sit far enough away from the TV set to give their eyes a chance to focus properly."

MAILBAG

Dear Kenyon,

Since it's all over and done with, I thought now would be as good a time as any to write and say, "Who do you think you're kidding?" It's many occasions now that I have watched you on TV and I just want to tell you I am not fooled, nor can you expect the whole American public to be fooled either. Not for long. Hold tight, sir, your moment of truth has not yet arrived but it is coming.

Sincerely,
Linwood Youngers
(San Marco, TX)

Stockton Junior College
Office of Communications
1998 Pershing Way
Stockton, CA 95206

Dear Mr. Saint Claire,

On behalf of Lincoln Walters, Dean of Stockton Junior College, the Office of Communications writes to congratulate you on your display of erudition on American television, and to extend to you our cordial invitation to speak before our graduates at our commencement ceremonies in May of this year.

On average, four hundred students graduate from Stockton Junior College every spring, with a majority continuing on to our nation's finest four-year institutions of higher learning. Among the current student body you may count your fans and admirers in the hundreds. It gives us no small pleasure to inform you that your television success inspired the formation here of a thriving Quiz Club last year. Twice monthly the Quiz Club sponsors "quiz show" contests in our campus quad, events which draw great crowds of spectators even from the general public in Stockton.

It would be our honor to host you in May. You can be assured of the warmest welcome. In the secondary document attached please find our invitation and proposal laid out and itemized in full, including your prospective itinerary.

With cordial regards,
Miriam Whittaker, Secretary to the Dean
Office of Communications
Stockton Junior College

Dear Kenny,

I write on behalf of my baby sister Elaine Cheryl Vaughan, who is in love with you but too terribly shy to write and tell you so herself. Elaine is a good girl, twenty-three last month, and a Christian in all ways, although very lonely. She is often downhearted and I believe that a letter from you would mean the world to her. It needn't be awfully long either—just a few kind words to lift her spirits. Won't you write to her?

Sincerely,
Jackie Vaughan
(Terrence, OK)

KENYON

In Boston, Kenyon and Ernestine stay on the fourth floor of the Beacon Hotel off Tremont Street. True to his word, Kenyon has booked her a room of her own. Their doors stand at opposite ends of a seemingly endless hall that runs half the length of the city block at least. They couldn't be more chaste.

Both rooms have a view onto the Boston Common, the lawns parched a yellowish green and the many old trees still bare and the ponds all brackish black. Beyond the park, scoured bright in the early spring daylight, the gilded dome of the statehouse glints like ice. Everywhere all the puddles are still frozen, the gutters are petrified runnels, and the wind whips over the sidewalks and the stark concrete paths of the Common with such polar ferocity that everybody hunches down under scarves and upturned collars. Even in the bitter air, men and women in the costumes of eighteenth-century patriots stand at the park's perimeter distributing leaflets and soliciting tourists. Watching them from Kenyon's window, Ernestine says, "Do they ever get anyone, do you think, in this cold?"

"Who?"

"Those poor tour guides down there. Those Paul Reveres and Abigail Adamses or whoever they are."

Across the room at the small tea-service, Kenyon is filling their cups. He brings Ernestine's in its saucer, then moves the muslin drape aside to see for himself. "Look at those tri-cornered hats," he says.

"And those bonnets."

"Let's pray they're all wearing two pairs of long johns."

"Mm, especially the women."

He turns back to the table for his own saucer. "You've got to respect them, being out there."

"You don't think they're just fleecing the tourists?"

"They could find warmer ways to do that. No, those tour guides are my kin—I'd recognize them anywhere. I'd bet they're all amateur historians, teachers."

Ernestine makes a doubtful noise. "I think I'd take a history class before I hired one of them."

Kenyon snickers. "It's that old problem of educator versus entertainer."

"Is it too cold of me?"

"They're the cold ones, remember?" He comes up close and rests his chin on her shoulder, murmuring, "No, I understand completely. I won't make you take a tour, how's that?"

She chuckles.

Kenyon carries his tea to the desk in the corner, sits and picks up the green steno pad. He's had it at hand since they left New York this morning. LIFE has asked for 2,000 words, a personal account of Kenyon's quiz show experience and rocket to fame. But he's been wrestling with how to say something more—something suitable of a Columbia man. For most of the train ride he was jotting notes while beside him, so beautifully calm and calming, Ernestine read Maynard Saint Claire's Quixote book.

Kenyon jots a few notes now:

> *Educator/Entertainer*
> *Classroom/Living Room*
> *Teacher/Television*
> *Living Presence/Screen Projection*
> *Knowledge/Facts & Answers*

Then:

> *I'm glad it's over, but now I see that the hardest work is*
> *to come: I'm going to have to think about what happened.*

He feels Ernestine's hands at his shoulders, her stomach and breast pressing warm against his back. "Still thinking about the article?"

"Mm-hm. That, and trying to decide what to tell them tomorrow."

He's to give the nine a.m. keynote to open the broadcasters' conference.

"Tell them the truth," says Ernestine.

Sitting very still, the steno pad in his lap, Kenyon is silent. Her hands warm and palpable on his shoulders. Her words burning in his ears.

Could he be any more grateful that she's here, that she's with him, standing over him in this way? Won't Ernestine finally bring him out of that constraining screen in all its monochrome and dissimulation? Briefly, in the moments following his last game, as he walked away from Fred Mint's podium and out of the blinding studio lights toward the dark wings and the dying out applause, he had thought, *Now I am out, now it is finished, now I'm myself again.* But it wasn't to be, because it isn't so simple. Still the letters keep coming. Still his fame betrays him every time he walks the streets. Still the red-eyed cameras await him in the *TODAY Show* studios. Every morning he's to be boxed in the grays and blacks of the shrunken frame, the screen's entrapment. But in stepping toward Ernestine, in answering to her solidity and warmth, won't he finally return to himself, a man in full color again?

He's been rereading Marcus Aurelius, a tiny pocket edition of the *Meditations*. *Come back now to your sober senses*, he read last night. *Recall your true self. Awake from slumber, and recognize that they were only dreams that troubled you; and as you looked on them, so look now on what meets your waking eyes.*

Isn't Ernestine just that? The sight he's to see upon his awakening?

Oh, but he wants to be careful—not, for all his winning, to lose her in the end. He believes, believes strongly, in her understanding. But how to admit it, everything there is still to admit, without displacing it all upon her?

"The truth, huh?" he says.

"Yes. I mean don't hold back," she says. "Tell them what you think."

He knows what he thinks, he does, and he could say it tomorrow, say what he thinks about television and all the rest. And yet with what right? What right does he have to say such things, a teacher who's been pretending all this time?

Well, he does have the right—doesn't he?—of *a man awakening*.

"Do you ever feel guilty?" says Ernestine.

"Hm?"

"It's like a conspiracy, isn't it? Hasn't it been a conspiracy all along?"

He shifts in his chair, pulling away to look up at her. What is she saying, exactly?

"I mean, here I am," she says, "answering all those doting letters—and they have no idea, those girls, that the person writing to them—"

"—isn't me?"

"Is in the exact spot they're all wishing for."

Kenyon breathes. Curling over the back of the chair, he kisses her wrist. The scent of floral soap.

"You have a very pure conscience," he says.

"Only because I know my own deceptions."

The next morning, reading his notes from a podium at the front of a Unitarian meeting hall near Downtown Crossing, Kenyon declares, "I believe in TV as a medium of communication. I think it is potentially the greatest of all."

Before him sit rows upon rows of attentive men in suits—radio men, television men.

"For a while," says Kenyon, "I had the feeling that quiz shows might have an effect on American education—they might be the secret weapon the educators needed. But I've concluded that in the long run the effect of the quiz shows can only be bad. The reason for this is that these programs do not have any faith in their audiences. They do not encourage the audience to ask questions, only to listen for answers."

"A quiz show," says Kenyon, "can teach us almost nothing, and it certainly cannot educate. The world of the educated man is not full of answers, as our television screens would have us believe—it is full of mysteries, it is foggy and dark, with lots of unlighted passages leading off to no one knows where. The more educated a person is, the more such passages the person discovers."

"But all this does not mean," says Kenyon, "that television is incapable of educating its viewers. The problem is one of faith. *Your* faith as broadcasters. I believe you can have faith in the audience."

"I've heard," says Kenyon, "from so many people who say, 'please, let's have something that stretches us a bit. Let's have something that wakes us up and even keeps us awake,' because television so often is a kind of soporific—we use it to go to sleep. But 'please,' they say. 'Teach us. We want to know things!'"

In the front row Kenyon finds Ernestine's eyes. Glinting, alive.

His notes are incomplete and he's reached their end, but with Ernestine watching him he feels he can go on, and he does, something opening up inside him. And how good it is, how completely nourishing, to speak publicly without a script, to believe the words he is saying.

A reception follows the keynote—a wood-paneled banquet room with urns of coffee and platters of fruit. The broadcasters press close around him in their identical suits, lapels badged and hair immaculately parted. They want him to elaborate, some of them. Some want to challenge him. Some want to bandy the names of mutual acquaintances at NBC. At the perimeter, reticule in one hand, coffee cup in the other, Ernestine seems suddenly tired, withdrawn. Every few minutes Kenyon glances over, tries to reassure her with a look. But soon through the bobbing heads he sees that she's gone.

He stands his ground, stammers out answers, shakes their hands, receives their thanks and thanks them in turn. Finally the crowd begins to drain from the banquet room, the broadcasters hurrying to the next scheduled panel. He's free to go.

Ernestine is not in the lobby, her coat gone from the coat check. Kenyon bundles up and hunches forward through the narrow, ice-blown streets.

At the Beacon's front desk he learns that she's collected her key and retired to her room.

Upstairs he taps at her door.

After a moment her voice answers: "Yes?"

"It's just Kenyon," he calls through the door. "Everything OK?"

"Fine." Her voice is very flat. "I'd like to rest a little."

"Me too. I'll see you later then."

Down the long, long hallway, weaving amid the maids' trolleys, room key in his hand, footsteps hushed in the deep carpet. The room, freshly made up, anonymizes him as he closes the door. And then he's overcome, unexpectedly, by his own fatigue. Performing, performed upon, you always forget how tired you are. He wants to think some more about the *LIFE* piece, but his system is in revolt. He'll shut his eyes. There's time. They needn't check out till three. Their train leaves at six.

Kenyon hangs his suit and shirt. In undershirt and shorts he turns back the covers, settles in, plunges to sleep.

He's in the booth, the lights ablaze, the studio crew zipping about in the dark. An hour before broadcast, an all-systems check: *These our actors as I foretold you were all spirits and are melted into air into thin air.* Fred Mint's voice in his earphones, the back of Fred Mint's shirt beyond the glass, not yet in his jacket. The host is testing the mike, the tissue ruff still circling his collar from makeup. *One acts a Ruffian another a Soldier this Man a Cheat and that a Merchant one plays a designing Fool and another a foolish Lover, but the Play done and the Actors undressed they are all equal and as they were before.* Beyond the glare Mint's face twists back across one shoulder to wink, his fingers making a sign: *A-OK?* Kenyon nods, thumbs up, earphone audio confirmed. But still Mint taps at the mike, and in the earphones the tapping is oddly wooden *tap tap…*

Kenyon stirs, whips his head across the pillow to check the bedside clock. Has he slept the day away? But it's not yet noon.

Another *tap tap* at the door, then Ernestine's voice in the hall. "Kenyon?"

He finds a monogrammed robe in the closet, folds it closed across his undershirt, cinches the belt.

When he opens the door, Ernestine still looks remote. She doesn't ask if she woke him. She comes in and immediately sits down in the desk chair, facing him across the room.

"Are you feeling all right?" he says. "Can I get you some tea?"

"No. Kenyon, I need to ask, is there something you want to say to me?"

Now comes a cool disturbance, low in his belly. The rush of fear. Has he been too inattentive, too distracted? He wanted her to be here with him, beside him, but for fear of pressing himself on her he's been overly timid, overly slow in his attentions.

She says, "Since we got here I've been thinking, thinking, *Why did Kenyon bring me to Boston?* And this morning during your keynote, in your face, I saw it. I listened to you. You were telling the truth. Maybe for the first time you were telling the truth. But you haven't said a thing to me."

"The truth—"

"Yes. You still haven't said it, Kenyon—to *me*."

She knows. She knows that it was all a fix, all along. It's so very clear to him now. But there's something else to tell her—something that must come first.

"Then I'll say it now, Ernestine. The truth is, I think I love you."

In her face, everything clears. She looks stunned, overcome. She says, "You *think*?"

He's still standing all the way across the room, barefoot in the ridiculous robe. "It isn't a winning answer." He shrugs. "But this isn't television."

Ernestine straightens. She takes a breath. She gets up and walks across the carpet to stand close in front of him. She is looking him over now, something churning in her thoughts. She is shaking her head almost imperceptibly. "I think I love you too. But that's not what I meant at all."

"It's the first thing that came to mind," he says. "It's not what you meant?"

He can't tell her all the rest: the fixing, all the pretending before the cameras—he can't yet say these things aloud, though she already knows—not yet.

"No, it's not what I meant," she says. She moves still closer and now their bodies are pressed together, her breath on his lips. "But it's enough for today. And, no, this isn't television."

She kisses him, her lips very full, her mouth all warmth, and they are embracing now.

"One truth at a time," she whispers, breathing the words into his mouth, over his tongue. He swallows them down.

For all his lying, he has never lied to *her*. He never will.

"I'm still tired," she says. "Can we rest?"

"Here?"

"Yes."

"Ernestine, I don't think we should…"

"I don't either. Just lie down and rest with me."

She draws him to the side of the bed, kicks off her shoes, and reclines across the covers fully clothed. "Come on. Take off that silly robe."

"Ernestine, I never thought…I wasn't expecting this…"

"I know," she says. "But go ahead. Take it off. No one's watching. Just me."

So Kenyon uncinches the robe and hangs it, and then he is before her in nothing but his sagging undershirt and baggy undershorts, knobby elbows and long legs exposed.

For a long moment she stares at him standing there—a steady, compassionate look. Then she waves him closer. He stoops and crawls into her arms.

They fall asleep almost immediately, then wake again just in time to check out and make their way to the train station.

LIFE (ATTEMPT)

Having seen me win $129,000 over the course of twelve weeks on a television quiz program, people often ask me not how I managed to answer all those difficult questions, but how I first came to be on their TV screens. Though I am asked innumerable other things every day, everything from "Can I have your autograph?" to "Will you kiss my baby?" to "Will you marry me?", this is by far the most common question: How did you get on television? What I hear them saying is simply this: "How can I make money on TV like you?" Unfortunately, my answer won't be much help, because in my case it was all thanks to a friend and a toothache.

Last fall, I was on the telephone saying goodbye to a friend who was moving to Europe, where her husband had received a new job. This friend told me that she'd had a turn on a television quiz show the week before (I forget the name). Though she hadn't managed to win anything more than a watch, she recommended that I take a stab at it myself, and she gave me the producers' names and phone numbers and the address of an office on Madison Avenue.

At this time I knew next to nothing about television. I did not have a set of my own. At any rate, I misplaced the scrap of paper on which I'd written the information, and soon the whole thing had slipped from my mind. But several weeks later, on a Friday morning in November, I woke up with a vicious toothache. It happened to be a lovely fall day, so following a visit to my dentist, I spent a half hour or so wandering through midtown. I happened to have with me a book into which I'd tucked the scrap of paper weeks before, and then I found myself on Madison Avenue, standing across the street from the very address I'd scribbled down and forgotten until now. This seemed a serendipitous experience, and something in the crisp sunlight seemed to be suggesting freshness and regeneration, so in a spirit of adventure I crossed the street and walked through the door.

High up in an office on the fifteenth or twentieth floor, I was given some forms to fill out before being seated at a desk for a rather grueling paper exam. The questions seemed to be of the wildest variety and almost comically difficult at times. Having never seen a quiz show I did not yet know how representative of these suspenseful programs those exam questions really were. It was several hours before I'd completed the tests, and I dropped them in a receptionist's tray with the feeling that my day had gone to waste.

Only a few days later, I received a call from that production office. My exams, they told me, showed me to be a good candidate for a quiz show. But instead of the program for which I'd tested, they said, they would like me to appear on another one with a slightly different format, a newer show that was broadcast every Wednesday night at ten-thirty. It was Tuesday morning. Could I be at the studio the following night at eight?

That's how it started. And in the last several months I have had to get used to a great many things that are new and strange. The truth is that I have gotten used to almost none of it. People ask me now about money, about fame, and I hardly know how to answer. I cannot simply say, as I want to say, that it feels unreal—that the *unreality* of it all is my main sensation.

But finally, after the many weeks of bright lights and prize money in that glass booth, I have begun to have the time to think. A few things have grown clearer to me in this short time—the question of television, for example. As everybody says, TV could and should be better than what we have at the moment. On the other hand, I've had the chance to see firsthand how many bright young people there are behind the scenes, hard at work trying to improve it. If you were to ask me now whether I worry that television will become only a great venue for hucksters, I would tell you no.

—*No, no, no*, his mind is saying, and Kenyon stops writing.

He must scratch it all—this lying superficiality, this "celebrity" dross! *Scratch it all!*

It's time he writes something true, goddamn it, something worthy!

He reads back through his words, back to that one promising note: the subject of *unreality*. There it is. He'll start over now…

I am told that there are now over 500 television stations in this country. I am told that 85 percent of American homes are equipped with a television set. Most disturbing of all, I am informed that the average household watches <u>five hours</u> of television every day. Five hours! Since completing my run on the quiz show, I have had some time to think, and what I am thinking about most of all are those hours upon hours, which amount to 150 hours per month per household. This in turn amounts to nearly 2,000 hours per year for almost nine out of ten homes in America. Nearly 2,000 hours.

For eleven weeks I stood locked in a glass box. It was in many ways a very uncomfortable, deceitful, and humiliating experience—and yet all around me, all the time, were people eager to assure me that my situation was enviable, even glamorous.

Thinking again of those 2,000 hours, of the unreality of my own experience, I must ask you: aren't we, each one of us on both sides of a broadcast, stuck in our own little boxes, our own little isolation booths?

An admired senior colleague of mine at Columbia University, Mr. Trilling, has written: "The deception we best understand and most willingly give our attention to is that which a person works upon himself." Have we ever understood that as well as we might today? With those 2,000 hours in mind I ask you this.

[End attempt]

COMMENTATORS

"Kenny is almost a Greek tragic hero, a vast commercial property being used by Geritol. He has strong opinions about the debasement of values by commercialism, but he can't condemn commercialism now."

Q:

Mr. Lacky, is it a fact that on some occasions, some of
these contestants to whom you made this offer, to
supply them the questions and answers ahead of time,
initially refused to go along with it?

A:

They were reluctant to, yes.

Q:

But on no occasion did a contestant actually refuse.

A:

That's correct.

Q:

So you persuaded them?

A:

I can be very persuasive, sir.
It was my job.

Q:

Did you attempt to persuade them using
appeals other than monetary rewards?

A:

I would like that question over again, please.

Q:

I will rephrase. Did you offer them the inducement, or
the altruistic suggestion, that they would advance
the cause of humanity in some way?

[Discussion off the record]

Q:

I will rephrase. Did you tell them they could advance
causes in which they were interested—for the good
of mankind—by appearing on this program?

A:

This was one of the considerations. I had them
take it into consideration.

Q:

You would agree then that you used all kinds of
appeals to the best instincts of people to get them
on this program?

[Discussion off the record]

Q:

I will rephrase. Were there inducements offered
to contestants that would appeal to them—inducements
concerning the furtherance of knowledge, information,
and assistance to the American public?

A:

This was one of the considerations, yes, sir.

Q:

And did you use that type of appeal to them in order
to overcome their scruples against receiving
advance questions and answers from you?

A:

Yes. But I am not a super-salesman.
I didn't club anybody over the head.

Q:

Did you also tell these contestants that, after all,
this was only entertainment and
everybody was doing it?

A:

I may have said that, yes, sir. *

---

* Congressional Record, House Committee on Legislative Oversight, October 2, 1959

KENYON

He's waking up. He's coming back—isn't he?—back into himself. It's gradual, but it's happening, a bit like the water rising in a rain gauge, almost imperceptible. Very soon, he's sure, he will recognize himself again—he will *be* recognizable, and not only to strangers, whose attention means less and less to him every day, but to his family, to George and Mom and Dad. How he's missed that.

He's rounding the corner off Sixth Avenue now, proceeding across the plaza at Rockefeller Center. Down in the rink, skaters crowd the ice, getting in their last figure-eights of the season. Almost mid-April already, April 12th to be exact, and Kenyon has a six p.m. engagement at the NBC offices. He's to sign his contract—*again*, the contract he already signed, but this time in the presence of the press: the "publicity signing," with Mr. Denning, vice president of the network, seated beside him. They're to smile and smile as they pen their signatures—redundantly, meaninglessly— across a dummy contract, photographers pressing in.

Must it be a signing? Kenyon had said to Mr. Bigler and Miss Gray. *That kind of pretending, is it actually necessary? I mean, I would think an announcement would suffice—*

It's a photo opp, said Bigler. *To see you sign is the whole idea.*

I've already signed, though. It won't be true.

It will be slightly true, said Bigler.

And so he'll be fed to the cameras again, always the feeding of those lenses, those flashbulbs and flapping shutters and the hungry red eye of the television cameras—so that his image can go outward, outward always, along the wires to the so-called press, the so-called public.

Kenyon is early: it's only a quarter of six. He pauses in the plaza to watch the swarm of bodies across the ice. The scratch of the skates is muted under the music piped through the loudspeakers, an antic Benny Goodman number. Up ahead, beyond it all, looms the crypt-colored stone of the NBC tower. And directly in front of Kenyon, at waist-level, is a great slab of polished granite engraved with the words of John D. Rockefeller, the man's famous *I believe* litany:

… I believe that every right implies a responsibility; every opportunity, an obligation; every possession, a duty.

I believe that truth and justice are fundamental to an enduring social order.

I believe in the sacredness of a promise, that a man's word should be as good as his bond; that character—not wealth or power or position—is of supreme worth....

Thirty minutes later, on the thirteenth floor of the NBC building, Kenyon Saint Claire sits next to James Denning at a polished conference table, the pen poised in his hand, the dummy contract laid open before him, and both men smile and smile. Across the table, the phalanx of photographers goes to work.

SIDNEY

May the 6th and here he is at 667 Madison Avenue, waiting politely in the carpeted lobby outside Greenmarch's office while Greenmarch wraps up some other business. Ten minutes, fifteen—and not a sound yet from Greenmarch behind those doors, not so much as a *sorry to keep you waiting, Sid, but I'll be just a few more minutes*. Which, Sidney being *expected* and all, having an *appointment* and all, it's not as if he's come *barging* in here—well, it puts a bad taste in a fella's mouth, how could it not?

"Denise, honey, could I have a glass of water?"

"Sure, Mister Winfeld," says the secretary, stepping away from her typewriter to fetch it. And she brings it with a little paper napkin but no comment such as *he'll be with you very soon, I'm sure*, no such thing, nothing at all, so he tells her again, says, "I did make an appointment. I'm in his book for today." To this she returns a small noise, hard to interpret, and sits herself down again.

Sidney gulps half the glassful—lukewarm and tastes of galvanized piping.

Some days he's dying, Sidney's sure of it, dying quick of some condition with hardly any symptoms at all. Started in the gut, that so-called ulcer which hasn't got worse but not better either—and he's no hypochondriac. This is the stuff he's talked over to no end with the shrink. Worries like his, they'd sicken just anybody, even the shrink said so. Would *level* most fellas, in fact. But now look at him getting started—*hey, don't start down that road that road leads no place and you know it*. After all, it's not the worries that bring him back to this office, it's the simple fact of certain guarantees having been made, a man's pledge, Ray Greenmarch himself back in February saying *come see me in May, Sid*—it's not as if Sidney's here unannounced or uninvited or showing up just to gush out his worries. No, he's in the man's book which when you're in the book you deserve the respect—

But now the office door bursts open.

"Sid. There you are. Have you been waiting awfully long?"

And Sidney's on his feet and pumping Greenmarch's hand—a cold and curiously soft hand, the padding of the palm gives way under your clasp, just sinks like a partly deflated balloon and almost no grip at all in Ray's shake. Have they never shook hands before now? It's possible they haven't, it's just possible, which would explain an awful lot.

"It's been a frantic afternoon, Sid—this and that, he and she, them and us. But come in, come in, sit yourself down. I've got a few minutes before they rope me back again."

The door clicks shut behind them.

Greenmarch glides to his desk and sits. "You must be finished with your studies, Sid."

"That's right, Ray. I figured you'd remember. Today in fact. As of today I'm graduated."

"Congratulations! And how's your wife?"

"Fine, fine, and you remember—"

"I remember she's expecting. And when's the tike arrive?"

"Oh, middle of September."

"That's swell, Sid. I'm sure you're both very happy on that note."

"We sure are, Ray."

"Good. Well…"

Sidney sits ready now, upright and listening, all ears. It ain't for him to broach the subject himself, it's May the 6th after all and they both know damn well what brings him in. So he levels his eyes across the desk at Greenmarch—at Ray—and waits.

Greenmarch runs a hand down his tie, leans forward, and plants his forearms across the desktop.

"Well, Sid, as I say, things have been frantic around here, and we may as well get down to business, shall we?"

"Yep."

"Which is to say, Sid, that Mint and Greenmarch has—only very recently—brokered some deals with NBC. These were major growth opportunities for this office, you understand—"

"That's good news. That's great, Ray. Congratulations."

"You see, though, Sid, that the upshot in your particular case, I'm afraid, is an abstention of dealings with regard to quiz show and panel show programming. That's to say, I'm afraid, that those opportunities we'd discussed prior, you and I, I'm afraid it's now out of my hands."

"Out of your hands?"

"Mm. My hands are tied, in other words."

"The deal's off, you're telling me."

"Those particular properties, Sid, the panel and/or quiz programs we'd discussed, they're no longer our property, you see."

"You sold the shows."

"We were given the chance to capitalize on these productions and in the interest of growth we no longer hold creative stake—"

"Tell me in fucking English, Ray. Tell me what you did."

"Look, Sid, it's business, all right? There was a buyer—"

"It's fucking *monkey business*, Ray. Why don't you tell me *that*?"

"Sid, I can appreciate you're disappointed—"

But Sidney's on his feet already and moving, his back to Raymond Greenmarch, his hands already outstretched to fling open the office doors—and though Greenmarch back there at his desk is saying something to the effect of *I'd be more than happy to put you in touch with our liaison at the network*, already Sidney's body is wheeling through the corridor, charging onto the elevator, dropping like a meteorite to the street—already the crush of the sidewalk surrounds him, already he's moving through the people, the people down here on the ground, and already he knows those promise-breakers upstairs are in for it, those TV guys jerking their levers day and night thinking they make the world go round, one way or another they're in for it.

KENYON

May 6th, six p.m., Kenyon Saint Claire stands on the steps of the house on Prince Street. He's been here a few minutes already, watching through the tender leaves of the plane trees the coming and going of people along the sidewalks. He told the agent, Halverson, six o'clock, and Ernestine quarter after. He checks his watch: 6:03. But here comes Halverson now, the heels of his Florsheims clapping.

"Am I late? She isn't here yet, is she?" Halverson mounts the steps in two strides—two at a time, breathing heavily. His coat hangs open, the bulk of his belly pushed out as he digs in his trouser pocket for the keys. "Good god, wouldn't that have been awful." A ring of beaded sweat has just started to dampen his collar, where the gray shadow of whiskers sprouts. "Let's get in and get a window open. I'm sure it's stuffy in there."

"Thanks for doing this, Don."

"My pleasure. Does she have any idea?"

"I don't know how she would."

Halverson winks. "Go get her, kid."

The vaulted great room is very warm, having taken the sun through the high windows all day. Halverson hurries to open the terrace doors. Kenyon tries a switch and the old Tiffany fixture glitters overhead. There's a decorative oval molding of laurel leaves up there. The space feels even vaster than when he first saw it, but still not overly grand, and he's glad for that. The room's paneled woodwork all washed in pristine white, the mottled parquet that crackles with every step. It was the conceivable elegance of the place that pleased him from the start. It isn't a showpiece. It can be lived in. Before he'd even seen the bedrooms, what won him over were the hidden compartments in these walls. Halverson had run a hand down the seams of the paneling, opening each in turn along the entire length of the room. Each compartment was nearly as tall as Kenyon and lined with shelves. As if the house had been built expressly to enfold and protect a private library of the kind he's always wanted but never had the space for.

"Any minute now," says Halverson, eyebrows up. "Better make myself scarce. Good luck, my boy." He lumbers off down the hall, to wait in a back bedroom.

Kenyon breathes deep, checks his watch again, checks himself.

When Ernestine approaches along the sidewalk under the plane trees, she finds him standing in the open door.

"Come up," he says.

"Have you already started? You didn't say six, did you? I was sure it was six-fifteen."

"No, no, you're right on time."

He takes her hand and leads her through the entry into the pure white spaciousness of the great room.

"Kenyon, what on earth..." She's turning about, disoriented in the windowlight and the sparkling Tiffany glass. He'd told her dinner at the Fadimans, that was all. "What on earth?"

"The Fadimans aren't expecting us," he says. "I'm sorry to deceive you. But I wanted to bring you here. It's Kip who first told me about this, actually. His house is down the block. I came last week, and the minute I stepped through this door I felt certain. I could just picture... Anyway, I'm buying it, Ernestine."

"Oh! Are you?"

"Yes. As a home for us."

"Us?"

"I hope you'll live here with me. I hope you'll marry me and we'll make this our home. Will you?"

He watches as something inside her stops. She falls very still. She breathes out a small breath.

"I haven't bought a ring," he says, and turns up his hands. "I thought... this instead."

"This is yours?" she says, almost in disbelief.

"It will be," he says. "Ours."

They stand there a minute, looking at one another.

"Would you like to see the rooms?" says Kenyon.

She only nods, seeming to hold back her words, then sweeps forward and takes him by his sides, and he sees her eyes are glittering, wet.

"But first, yes," she says. "And not only because of this. Yes. Yes."

AND NOW A WORD FROM OUR SPONSORS

"Thank you very much. Thank you, thank you, you're supposed to clap right there, right there is where you clap! That's right. Jeez!"

"Boys and girls, whoever has the Magic Red Crayon, I want you to come on up to the Magic Window right now…"

"The line between performer and performance is long gone."

"This almost perfect man, this almost perfect gentleman, is in this play never the gentleman or the man that he is, paradoxically enough."

"You've gotta tell 'em to clap! Hey, watch the applause sign! Thank you."

"We understand that he *was* that man."

"And now, with a complete grasp of the English language, I explain to you the game."

"We all sense that somehow, without budging ourselves, we are living more life per second."

"This may be the most important answer you will ever have to give. You have twenty seconds, so think clearly and write fast."

"The goal is usually to make only enough sense to permit the senses to take over."

"If you were to meet a mesmerist, would he be a memory expert, a hypnotist, or a religious fanatic?"

"Now what I want you to do is take your Magic Red Crayon and put it right up against my finger. Would you do that? Right here. OK? You ready to follow me now?"

"Will you repeat the question, please?"

"Time's a little tired these days. Time needs a minute."

"A memory expert, a hypnotist, or a religious fanatic?"

"At critical junctures, ordinary people make choices, even if among a range of choices not of their own making."

"To the very end he never did perform the ethical free act of making up his mind."

"Who is prepared to take arms against a sea of amusements?"

"I'm gonna go slowly and draw a line across here, and you come right along with me. OK? That's fine. We're gonna have a swell trip."

"If we go on as we are, history will take its revenge."

"Gosh, that tub was so white it looked new!"

"In your Frigidaire Cold Pantry there's a place for all your foods: fresh and frozen, canned, bottled, and wrapped, new-bought and leftover. They're all right there, and they're all at your fingertips."

"…in a time that is no time and only time and all times, all the time."

"Consolation prizes on *Tic Tac Dough* are the wonderful Polaroid Lan cameras, which develop pictures in one minute."

"Ladies and gentlemen, I think it's very important to point out right now that all the problems on Juvenile Jury that we present to the children—they are presented for the first time, they are completely spontaneous."

"Television begins by being entertaining and ends by becoming authoritative."

"You following right along with me, boys and girls? All the way up to the top now. That's right. Gee, I think you're doing a fine job."

"This is an instance in which the asking of the questions is sufficient."

"Everything on this program is completely spontaneous and unrehearsed."

"To ask is to break the spell."

"What are you gonna do with the $700 after you've bought some tranquilizer pills?"

"Just follow my finger…"

SIDNEY

He's an honest guy, Sidney Winfeld. Nobody's ever gonna say different. He's upstanding, a husband and father to be, which never would he go ahead and become a father under deceptive conditions, not of any nature, so it's time to clear the air, time to tell Bernice their situation. Natural enough he hasn't done it already, what with May the 6th always on the horizon before now, which he hoped that meeting with Greenmarch might solve his worries and look how that panned out. Well, c'est la vie. He'll just hafta take a different tack from here forward—he's sure not gonna suggest to Bernice he's taking anything lying down. And the fact he *is* honest, whereas none of the other persons have any interest to be apparently—not the Greenmarch people, not the other contestants— won't that be what fixes it in the end? Honesty. Who else of any of them is ready to just be honest like Sidney?

Bernice is squinting into the menu, but Sidney comes right out with it— better not to leave it for later and suffer through dinner with his thoughts, the worries, knowing how she'll receive it. So he just says it, says how he's met with Greenmarch and that situation being what it is, now's the time she oughta know the extent of their financial circumstances, his winnings no longer available and etcetera, etcetera.

It's not desperate, sweetie, he's telling her. *We have my savings, it's not even close to any kind of desperate situation, OK, don't misunderstand me on that point.*

It's going on a few weeks now since she started to show. First it was a tightening look in her blouses, then the bulge you only saw in profile, then the riding up of the skirt fronts, and now Sidney and anyone can see the roundness even when she's facing you. She's got one hand on the roundness right now, the palm of her hand moving there in little circles while she hears him out.

But the disappointing nature of Ray's news, which there won't be the extra salary we were counting on—now I know it's a letdown, but in actual fact it has strengthened my resolve, Bernice, these TV people and their shenanigans, doctoring up these shows putting words in everybody's mouth, making Kenny Saint Claire into some kind of hero, some kind of godsend to America, reneging on their guarantees, it's time it comes into the open, time they get their comeuppance...

She's hearing him out, that hand on her belly, other hand still holding the edge of the menu which she's sort of let collapse in front of her, and now here comes the waiter with the wine, the white linen napkin, to do his little show of the bottle, the corkscrew, the one pour and then the other, which the wine all served he then sticks around to see if they're ready to order.

"Not just yet," Sidney tells him. "Could we have a few minutes, please."

Sidney chose a white napkin kind of place in case Bernice might wanna make a scene and she'd hafta think better of it. But he goes on talking and she doesn't even try to cut in, she's hearing him out still, patting her belly still and seems as calm as any business, and he wonders if he wouldn't rather have a scene—wonders, too, should he have spared this expense? But isn't that just the point, though? Why should they start tiptoeing around every nice thing? He's not gonna be that type. He's a husband and now a father to be and nobody's gonna push him around or tell him they don't owe him just basic decent *dignity*. He *made* that quiz show, Sidney Winfeld did. *Sidney's* the reason Greenmarch could sell—and sell for how many *millions?* Even Kenyon Saint Shithead, what would *he* be without Sidney? Sidney who honored his part of the bargain the whole way through, they can't tell him he didn't play it up and keep those TVs tuned in all those living rooms.

I won't stand for it, Bernice, is what I'm saying. I won't stand for it, you can be sure of that, honey. And I have recourse, honey. I have the recourse of the truth which I've already called up and spoke to a reporter at the Journal American...

He'd walked straight from Greenmarch's office into a phone booth right there on Madison Avenue, stood in the booth telling the whole story into the handset, the reporter going *really my goodness please tell again the name and title of this person or that person,* and Sidney staring all the time through the booth glass at the building at number 667 and thinking, *this time this time this time the story's gonna stick.*

Now as calm as any business Bernice comes out and says it, says, "Sidney, honey, as far as the money is concerned we both know as always that my mother is more than happy to help—" which she knows his feelings on that matter already, and why she'd tell him such a thing right now is more than he can figure, so he cuts her off, puts up a hand saying, "You know I won't have that, Bernice, and that damned well ain't necessary as I'm *trying* to explain right now, I have the answer to this situation already, honey, and it ain't about money anymore. This is about things of much greater significance, honey, much bigger than fiscal considerations and nor should you worry for that matter, I have the answer, and that's the only thing you need to remember."

And, yes, it would have been better, probably, if she'd gone and made a scene. Better a scene than this cool calm business of *the old lady'll bail us out, the old lady's got the dough you haven't,* which is she's saying in other words, *I never did expect I could rely on you, Sidney, I never did.*

But sure enough, the very next afternoon Sidney's at his desk in the transit office looking at the new issue of *Life* magazine with its so-called "personal account" by Kenyon Saint Claire, which the lies and mistruths of this account are just plainly outrageous—and here comes a phone call from the *Journal American.* It ain't the fellow Sidney spoke to prior but a different fellow called O'Brien who says he's on the paper's special services staff and just wants Sidney to know that there's a story in the works, a three-part serial in fact, and the paper very much wishes to continue its cooperation with Sidney on this story which they are confident is going to "blow the top off" the television game show industry.

Of course, Sidney tells him. *Of course, of course you can count on my full cooperation. I got nothing to hide I just wanna see these guys brought to light, I wanna see that the truth is known to the American public. And what I just said, any of it, you can put that on record if you want.*

Q:
Mr. Winfeld, did you ever
see me before today?

A:
Never in my life, sir.

Q:
In other words, the questions
and answers you are now giving
have not been rehearsed with me?

A:
That is correct, sir.

Q:

And they are truthful?

A:

Under oath, sir, I am telling
exactly what the story is.

Q:

If I understand this correctly,
you made ten or eleven different
appearances on the quiz program?

A:

Eight appearances.

Q:

So that the record will be clear,
for each and every one of those eight
appearances you were supplied with
the questions and the answers?

A:

Yes, sir, from the first to the last.

Q:

You were in school at that time?

A:

Yes, sir, I was a senior at the
City College of New York.

Q:

Were you using the program to
obtain financial resources
for your education?

A:

It's a municipal college, sir.
Mainly I wanted to obtain a sort of
financial independence from my in-laws.

Q:

For your in-laws?

A:

From my in-laws, sir.

Q:

A commendable trait, I should say.
One thing further, Mr. Winfeld. Have you
ever at any time had any psychiatric treatment?

A:

I have, sir. That was after I
left the program, sir.

Q:

You had none before that?

A:

I had never had any before in my life.
But I felt…I feel that we all can use some help.
I was very nervous during that time.

Q:

During the period following your interactions
with Mr. Greenmarch, is it true that Mr. Greenmarch
had control of the program for the other contestants
who subsequently appeared?

A:

That is correct, sir.

Q:

Including Mr. Saint Claire?

A:

That is correct.

Q:

Mr. Saint Claire has built himself up
as an intellectual giant in the eyes of the
American people and is making a lot of money today
thanks to his contract with NBC. Is it reasonable

to assume based upon your information, that Mr. Saint
Claire also got the Greenmarch preparation and treatment
throughout his time on the quiz program?

A:

May I say, sir—I believe you watched the kinescopes and
could see as well as anybody the identical actions
that I and Mr. Saint Claire were making all the time.
In other words, patting our brows and biting our lips,
etcetera. In other words, sir, I would usually
assume that two gentlemen under pressure do not have the
exact same patterns when they are nervous…

Q:

You would say, then, that Mr. Saint Claire was also given the
answers? That is, we may say that Mr. Saint Claire is also,
as you have referred to yourself previously in these
hearings, a "paid actor"?

A:

I must leave it for the committee to decide, sir.
I am just saying what I know to be factual.

Q:

Mr. Winfeld, as you will understand, the reason I point out
Mr. Saint Claire is because in the United States we are concerned
about education and salutary standards for our children. Here is a man
revered for his presumable knowledge and intellectual capacity. I want
to be sure that he is not perpetrating a fraud, you understand,
on the American people and the students who look to him
as a man with knowledge—

A:

I cannot make any accusations—

Q:

—when in fact he may have been fixed.

A:

I can only speak to the facts as I know them to be, sir. *

---

* Congressional Record, House Subcommittee on Legislative Oversight, October 6, 1959

KENYON

Now, now my life has really started, thinks Kenyon Saint Claire, as he stands in the half-dark at the back of the cameras, out of the brilliant beams of the canister lights that scour away every last shadow on the stage. His face is made up, he's miked and ready, watching the monitors with the crew, finishing a smoke back here on the stone studio floor crisscrossed with cables. The microphone, slung on its low wire loop around his neck, rests like an awkward phallus against his tie. His first few turns on the air, he kept knocking it when he gestured. The producer, Mr. Grant, chalked it up to nerves and gave him a little pep talk about deep breaths and taking his time—"But not too much time!" Mr. Grant was onto something there, for it was never Kenyon's nerves, really, so much as a wish to get it all out in the time—the very limited time—permitted him. He'd been talking about the stoics, Seneca and Aurelius mainly, and had been given exactly two three-minute segments (interrupted by an advertisement) to make his points, to win the viewer over to the idea of sitting down and reading the *Meditations* or *On the Shortness of Life*. Well, he managed it in the end, and he'll continue to tailor and refine his delivery, he's sure, till he can make the absolute most of this fairly rigid and demanding medium.

But these are the minor challenges of this lucky work, and what Kenyon is really thinking as he draws the last of the smoke and drops the butt to the studio floor and squashes it underfoot is that now, now his life is really starting. He'll get the hang of this business of boiling down ideas, gleaning the most intriguing parts, putting it all across in as concise and captivating way as possible—*selling it*, as Mr. Grant says—figuring out how to do so *visually*, for benefit of the *general viewer*, as Mr. Grant has encouraged. He'll get a handle on it all, and then he'll see what other opportunities may lay in store: perhaps some "special programming" as mentioned in his contract… He bends to retrieve the flattened cigarette, but before he can pluck it up the cumbersome microphone swings on its wire and jams him in the cheek.

His cue is coming up. He straightens himself, fixes the mike, and rubs his cheek (is it going to leave a mark?) as he watches Frank Blair on the monitor reading the news. Kenyon's segment follows.

And there's Garroway on the monitor now, on his feet and doing his easy walk across the studio floor with the camera following as he talks. So Kenyon steps into the light, finds his mark in front of the bank of technicians, and Garroway meets him there right in time, his dialogue with the camera just now melting into the proper segue.

LIVING ROOM

"And here's our good friend Kenyon Saint Claire, *TODAY Show* cultural correspondent, ready to share with us a little more about Herman Melville. Isn't that right, Kenyon?"

"Yes. Good morning, Dave."

"Good morning. So it was *Moby-Dick* on Friday and now to start off this week you'll be discussing—"

"'Bartleby, the Scrivener.'"

"Old Bartelby, yes. But before you start on Bartelby, I think our viewers should know, you have very recently had a major life change—and not of the television variety—isn't that right?"

"That's right, Dave. I've just been married."

"Just this weekend, wasn't it?"

"Yes. Only this weekend. My fiancée Ernestine and I were married in a very small ceremony with the justice of the peace, a few flowers, and, uh, our loved ones."

"Nothing too fancy then, huh, Kenyon? Just short and sweet."

"Yes, well, we wanted the wedding to be very private, just us and our closest loved ones."

"Isn't that nice. But now, there's the matter of the honeymoon. I hope we aren't keeping you from that."

"No, no. Since the wedding wasn't any too long in the planning stage, we're still deciding exactly where we'd care to go on honeymoon."

"You can't go wrong this time of year. I'm sure it will be a perfectly wonderful time, whenever you do get the chance to go, which I hope can be soon, and I'm sure our viewers join me and everyone here at NBC in congratulating you and wishing you and Ernestine every happiness."

"Thank you, Dave."

"Now, this Bartelby you'll be talking about today, we can't really call *him* the happiest fellow, now can we?"

"Well, no, I'm afraid Mister Melville's story isn't the happiest one ever told, but I do believe it's one of the most memorable and moving."

"Tell us why, tell us all about it."

KENYON

And here comes the camera, gliding in tight as Kenyon begins. And there he is, or someone like him, reflected in the cylindrical lens: a man, a teacher, speaking from the heart on national television, sharing literature— literature!—with the nation at 7:45 a.m. on a Monday. There he is, whoever he is, and he's just getting started.

Q:

Mr. Winfeld, do you have any
personal knowledge that
Mr. Saint Claire was fixed?

A:

Only by the other testimony, sir.

Q:

No, I am asking if you have
personal knowledge.

A:

No, sir. But look, in the seventy-two weeks
that the program was on the air, to the best of my
knowledge I don't believe it ever ran overtime one time.
I believe this can be pretty well verified.
Now isn't that a pretty astonishing thing to consider—
never once going overtime?

Q:

I don't follow.

A:

It's a kind of logical proof, sir.
You see, it proves that the whole thing
must have been pretty well planned ahead all along,
whoever the contestants may have been
at any particular time.

Q:

But you have no personal knowledge whatsoever
concerning Mr. Saint Claire and any
arrangements made between
him and the producers?

A:

That is correct.

Q:

He could very well have answered these
questions without coaching?

A:

Yes, sir.

Q:

He is widely acknowledged, is he not,
to be a man of intellectual ability?

A:

Yes, sir.

Q:

Mr. Winfeld, is any of your testimony in this
hearing motivated by an animosity?

A:

Toward whom, sir?

Q:

Toward Mr. Greenmarch or Mr. Mint or any
other person who failed to live up to what you
considered to be an agreement.

A:

I would say this, sir: I have no animosity toward Mr. Mint,
who has in no way hurt me. As for Mr. Greenmarch, I feel that here's
a man who has not lived up to his agreements. But you see, for me
it all extends even further. I have been bothered very deeply by my
conscience with regard to this business of the school vendetta
that was staged between me and Mr. Saint Claire.

Q:

School vendetta, you say?

A:

Yes, sir, in other words that I am City College and he is Columbia
University and for that reason he should be the winner, etcetera etcetera.

I was very hurt at being forced—I am sort of funny that way—to miss questions which to me were quite easy. This sort of hurt me, I don't know why.

Q:

Beyond that you have no feeling in this matter?

A:

I just want—this has become a hearing which I want to end and tell my story and finish.

Q:

I have no further questions.[*]

*Congressional Record, House Subcommittee on Legislative Oversight, October 6, 1959

SIDNEY

"Hello. Sidney here."

"Sid, it's Ray Greenmarch."

"Ray?"

"Yes, well, I'm sure you weren't expecting the call, Sid, but listen, do you have a minute?"

"Uh, I suppose a minute, OK, but I'm not so confident, Ray, that there's much to discuss between us."

"That's exactly why I called you up. You see, Sid, I've continued to have rather mixed feelings concerning our last meeting, May sixth, and, well, I've come to the conclusion that it oughtn't to have turned out the way it did. I still feel that there's some measure of unfinished business between us, and I regret that this was left where we left it on May sixth."

"Ray, look, if you're calling just to apologize—"

"No, no, this is more than an apology, Sidney, there's real substance to why I'm calling you tonight—and I hope it's not too late to be calling, by the way."

"I'm awake anyhow."

"Right. OK, well I don't want to keep you any longer than necessary, Sid, only I did want to…you'll recall that when that May sixth meeting of ours ended—well, it ended on a rather unfortunately blunt kind of note, but you will recall I hope that I did try to extend to you the assurance that I would still reach out on your behalf."

"Ray, to be honest with you, I don't have any further wish to entertain—"

"I can't say I blame you in the least. I really can't. But I did want to give you a call and make it known to you as plainly as I can, Sid, that I do think an appearance of some kind can be arranged."

"Excuse me?"

"A television appearance. For you. It's all pretty well arranged already, if you're still of a mind to take advantage of such an opportunity."

"You're offering me a TV spot?"

"Well, it would be an appearance anyhow. See, although NBC now owns the properties, our creative input does *occasionally* carry some weight. Anyhow, the upshot is that there's a vacancy on another quiz program, *High Low*, for next week. Are you familiar with *High Low*?"

"You're offering me a one-time appearance?"

"It would be an initial opportunity for you, Sid, and would entail a half-hour on the air for which we would pay you five hundred dollars—"

"You're fucking kidding me, Ray, right?"

"Pardon me?"

"You do know that as we speak the *Journal American* is writing a three-part story on the hanky panky—"

"I spoke with the reporter, yes."

"And now you call me up with the bright idea of a one-time appearance and five hundred dollars—"

"As I say, Sid, I've continued to feel badly about the way things were left between us. I did try to tell you on May sixth—"

"Isn't this a sorry situation."

"Sidney, listen, I don't see what possible good you think you'll be doing if you—"

"The story is being written, Ray. As I speak to you, they are writing the story in the paper."

"Don't you share my confidence that this is a matter we can work out between us, Sidney? Don't you see the damage you'll be doing to your own self with such a…cockamamie allegation in the papers?"

"Goodbye, Ray."

"I'm here to help you, Sid. I've always been here to help."

"I'm sorry, Ray."

"Remember that, won't you?"

"I do not wish to appear on your show, Ray."

"Just call me up—"

"Goodbye."

COMMENTATORS

"Please go look into a mirror. As you gaze at yourself, try to get a sense of what is lost between the mirror image of you and *you*.

"You might ask someone to join you facing the mirror. If so, you will surely feel that other person's presence as you stand there. But in the reflection, this feeling will be lost. You will be left with only the image, possibly an expressive one, but only an image. What is missing from the reflection is life, or essence."

LIVING ROOM

"Good evening. I'm Ed Murrow."

The picture is very close on Murrow's face, cigarette smoke coiling in his hair. Even through the screen you can smell the smoke coming off him.

"The name of the program is *Person to Person*. Tonight we'll be dropping in on Kenyon Saint Claire and his wife here in New York. We'll also be going to California for a visit with actress Ginger Rogers. We'll be ready to go in exactly thirty seconds."

KENYON

They've got two cameras running, one here in the study, one out in the great room where Ernestine waits on the sofa. The cables snake everywhere underfoot, the camera crew all chattering. "That's thirty seconds!" calls out the Assistant Director, in earphones, and the crew begins to quiet down. "Ready, Kenyon?"

"Ready as possible," says Kenyon. He's seated at his desk as rehearsed.

They did a run-through earlier this evening, before the cameras arrived. He and Ernestine know pretty well what to expect, how their fourteen minutes will likely transpire. "Ed sticks to the script usually," the A/D has assured him.

Still he's strangely nervous. The presence of those cameras, so bulky, so invasive-seeming now that they're in his home, and the popping and crackling of so many crew members' feet on the parquet, and the heat of the lights with which the crew is blasting all the upper shadows from the rooms—it sets his nerves aglow. And then there's Ernestine, poor thing, sitting out there on the sofa awaiting their "scene" together. Kenyon now feels beyond a doubt that he's coaxed her into this, pressured her even. She seemed so torn between supporting him and her natural wish to stay on the sidelines. He could have given her the space to step back like she wanted—instead he'd all but pleaded for her involvement. *My parents did the program just last year,* he'd told her, *my father and mother together, and it was fine. Ed Murrow makes it very easy. You'll see.* But what did his parents have to do with it, really? Why should he expect their participation to mean anything to Ernestine? She knew her own preferences and he'd compelled her to ignore them in the interest of making this spousal "appearance."

Now, from the small transistor just out of camera view, he hears the voice of Bob Dixon, the program announcer, talking Amoco: *All other gasolines contain lead. Yes, all other gasolines contain lead that really gets into your motor and causes it to become full of residue, of lead, that doesn't help your car one bit…*

What awkward phrasing. Did someone drop the cue cards? Are they having technical difficulties over there? Kenyon spots a few crew members exchanging looks that seem to ask the same questions.

But now the A/D, from just behind the camera, calls, "Ready! We're here in five!"

So Kenyon, straightening his tie yet again, takes one more deep breath…

LIVING ROOM

"And now," says Bob Dixon, "here's Ed Murrow."

And from the Amoco insignia there's a split second of darkness before Murrow's lit face materializes, the familiar hangdog brows arched above the trustworthy eyes. That face is here to tell you the truth. No matter what the subject, this man has never lied to you.

"Kenyon Saint Claire," says Murrow, "is a thirty-two-year-old instructor at Columbia. He teaches English and Comparative Literature. Very recently, he won a $129,000 in a television quiz contest, to become the newest of the Saint Claires in the public eye."

There's the hint of a smile, a wink-like glimmer in Murrow's delivery. He's saying, without exactly saying it, *Ain't it something, though, how fame works?*

"Kenyon's parents, Maynard and Emily, whom we visited on *Person to Person* some time ago, have long been known for their novels and poetry, and Kenyon's father has won the highest national literary prizes. Kenyon's late uncle, Curtis Saint Claire, was a top literary critic and biographer. Young Kenyon and his brother George grew up in Greenwich Village here in New York and on the family farm in Connecticut."

The picture switches to a view over Murrow's shoulder from where he sits in his armchair, elbow propped and debonair cigarette burning beside his ear. Between the curtains of the faux living room window before him is the image of Kenyon Saint Claire's house front.

"Mister and Missus Kenyon Saint Claire, who were married soon after the quiz game ended, now live in this handsome rowhouse not far from Washington Square."

Now the housefront dissolves to the live image of Kenyon Saint Claire himself, seated beside a desk piled with papers and books.

"Evening, Kenyon."

And the image of the man in the window replies: "Evening, Mister Murrow."

KENYON

And now they are live, and behind the invasive bulk of the camera, silent amid the sea of cables, the crew is huddled and stiff as Kenyon takes up the easy dialogue.

Just remember to look in the camera, the A/D told him and Ernestine. *Talk to the camera the whole time.* For there's no one to look at, no one to see, only the circular glass of the lens where his own reflection lurks, reduced and slightly distorted. That, and Murrow's fuzzy voice in the transistor.

Now the transistor says: "Tell us, Kenyon, what've you been up to since those eventful Mondays in the isolation booth?"

"Well, I've been busy," says Kenyon. "Lots of things. Let's see: I'm still teaching the classes I taught last year. I'm doing a good amount of television work and hope to do even more. I've still got a dissertation to write, as it happens."

The transistor replies: "Goodness, it sounds as if you're a little busier today, even if under a bit less pressure, than you were while on the quiz program."

"I am awfully busy, Ed, yes. I can tell you, by the way, that the pressure hasn't…gone down much either. There's still television and, uh, you know how exciting and, uh, tense those last few minutes and seconds before a television show are."

His own voice projects weirdly through the house. He can hear it resounding in the hallway. And he's aware, keenly aware of the many ears of the crew members, and of Ernestine, listening from the other room, aware of the flow of life in the house standing at a pause, suspended and waiting, all for the sake of broadcasting house and life over the network.

There is also, ever so audible, an echo of his own voice in the transistor, his words coming back in slight delay through Murrow's microphone.

Kenyon suddenly feels very dizzy.

But the transistor says: "From that current schedule of yours, Kenny, I gather you've had done with quiz shows now, except for some wonderful memories and a few dollars. Right?"

And that's his cue. "Wonderful memories, yes, and one other thing: a wonderful wife. I'd like you to meet her."

"Of course. Where is Ernestine?"

"She's in the great room."

He's getting up now, and the camera eases back to let him pass.

LIVING ROOM

The picture changes. And here in your living room is the living room of Kenyon and Ernestine Saint Claire, miles and miles—perhaps thousands of miles—away. A whole other sphere of existence.

Mrs. Saint Claire, in a smart collared blouse and skirt, is seated on the sofa in the expansive white-walled room, a cold fireplace behind her. And in comes Kenyon Saint Claire, fresh from the study where you saw him just a second ago.

"Mister Murrow, this is Ernestine." He takes a seat on the sofa cushion close beside her.

"Good evening, Ernestine."

"Good evening, Mister Murrow."

"Now I understand," says Murrow, whose charming face now fills the screen again, "that you two elected to have just a very small wedding, and that your honeymoon is yet to come, is that right?"

"Yes, that's true," says Ernestine. "We concluded together, Kenyon and I, that if we waited a little we'd be able to enjoy a much longer getaway than if we rushed into the honeymoon now, in the midst of Kenyon's several commitments."

She speaks quite softly, this Mrs. Saint Claire, in an even tone—almost as if speaking to herself, to remind herself of something. Though the picture has come very close to her face, she doesn't look out at you through the screen. Her eyes stay in the middle distance. Something very shy about her.

"I see," says Murrow. "That's very wise of you, I'm sure. Uh, Kenyon, if I remember the rumors, you married your secretary who was helping you handle, oh, some 20,000 fan letters, right?"

KENYON

Sitting beside Ernestine now, Kenyon finds it suddenly more difficult to look into the lens as advised. The second camera holds them, steady and predatorial in its stillness. He can feel Ernestine's tension beside him. But they've rehearsed this. It isn't this question alone, it's the many silent strangers watching from behind the camera, behind the lights, it's the falsity of this dialogue with a fuzzing voice in a box, it's the strange spell this whole broadcast is putting on the house.

Kenyon smiles a little, then tries his answer deadpan. "Well, what you've heard is only partly true, Ed. She wasn't my secretary, exactly, but worked at the production office. And in reality she'd only been handling my mail for a few months."

The transistor says: "Well, whatever the circumstances, we're all charmed, and you two are delightful. Now, Kenyon, when you walked into the living room there, I didn't notice any of the tools of the scholar—books. Do you have a special room for them?"

"No, no," says Kenyon, getting up. "They're actually just here."

The camera drifts along with him as he crosses to one of the panels in the wall behind the sofa.

"You see, this is a wonderful room, and all these walls are hollow—"

But now in the corner of his eye Kenyon catches a flurry of motion. The A/D is whirling a finger before him like a wheel, one hand on his earphones. And something has started the crew members whispering and shifting about.

"Look at this, Ed," says Kenyon. "Each section of the wall here is a hidden door, and when I open it you can see…that it's full of books. And that's the way with the wall all around."

The transistor says nothing.

The A/D keeps whirling his finger, eyes wide to urge Kenyon on. He's pointing to his earphones, shaking his head.

Kenyon stops. "Are we … are you still there, Ed?"

He turns full-front to the camera, watching the A/D's alarmed eyes, speaking *into* the A/D as if through a magical telephone. "Ed? Can you hear me? Can you hear me now?"

The transistor is silent. The A/D shakes his head. No signal.

Kenyon glances to Ernestine, rigid on the sofa. He freezes in place. They're only four minutes in, but something is wrong, and he mustn't walk back in Ernestine's direction. He must spare her that and hold the camera where it is. Only four minutes in.

"Can anybody hear me?… Anybody?… Are you there?"

The A/D is conferring with the crew. The camera doesn't move, but it seems they're still broadcasting live. They have ten minutes to go.

"I don't know what to say here, Ed. You're not coming through. I'm not hearing a thing, is anyone hearing me? Should we—is that it?—is our time up? I don't know what to… Should we cease transmission?… Should we turn the camera off? Ed? … Should we just turn it off now?"

Someone turn it off please …
      someone someone turn it off   the lights

            these cameras the cables the disembodied   voice

stiff silent crowd   crowded silence

and deafening   echo

                              turn it off now
now   turn it off

turn it   off   and   go!

7.

THE BLOW-UP

Summer/Fall 1958

"Our only error was that we were too successful."

—Albert Freedman, quiz show producer

KENYON

"Mister Saint Claire?"

"This is he."

"Kenyon Saint Claire?"

"Oh, I'm afraid you've reached his father. This is Maynard Saint Claire."

"I'm sorry, sir. I meant to dial Kenyon Saint Claire's office at Columbia College."

"Yes, and you have. We share the office, Kenny and I. But I'm afraid he isn't in just now."

"Well, Mister Saint Claire, my name is Colin O'Brien. I'm a reporter for the New York *Journal American*. Would you please tell Mister Saint Claire that I called?"

"Of course, just let me take down your number. Oh, wait a minute now. As it happens, you're in luck. Kenny just walked in." *[sound garbled]* "Kenny, it's a newspaper fellow…"

"…Hello. Kenyon Saint Claire here."

"Mister Saint Claire, this is Colin O'Brien from the New York *Journal American*."

"I'm sorry, Mister O'Brien, but this isn't the best time, and in any case I'm not giving interviews right now—"

"It's a little more serious than that, sir, if you have just a minute for me to explain."

"Oh? All right. A minute or two."

"I don't suppose you've heard of a fellow called Terrence Higgenfritz, Mister Saint Claire?"

"I have not."

"Didn't think so. You see, he was a standby contestant on a CBS quiz program called *Dotto*. On the other hand, though, Sidney Winfeld is a name you'll recognize immediately."

"Of course. But how can I help you, Mister O'Brien?"

"There's no way you could know this, Mister Saint Claire, but recently Mister Higgenfritz and Mister Winfeld have both brought to the New York County District Attorney's office separate allegations claiming that their TV quiz programs were fixed."

"Fixed?"

"Mm. And you see, since the testimony by both of these men has caused the D.A. to open investigations into the quiz shows, the *Journal American* will run a story on the subject in tomorrow's paper."

"Oh, I see. Well, in any event, I'm not sure where I come into any of this…"

"Well, Mister Saint Claire, we can be pretty certain that your name—as one of the biggest quiz show winners—your name is likely to come up."

"What is Winfeld saying exactly?"

"He claims that for every one of his appearances on the program the producers supplied him the answers and directed him in detail how to behave."

"Goodness. Why would he—"

"And he says—I was hoping to have a comment from you, Mister Saint Claire, for tomorrow's story—would you mind if we go on record here?"

"Hang on now. First finish what you were…"

"Sure, OK. Winfeld says that on the night he lost to you, he was ordered to 'take a dive' as he puts it, on an answer he knew perfectly well."

"Oh, does he? Well…I don't know what…and you would like a comment from me?"

"Yes, sir, seeing as the DA's probe is likely to widen in the coming days. And after tomorrow's story—I mean, your name as a winner is sure to—"

"And this Higginson character—"

"Higgenfritz."

"Yes, what is it that he's claiming?"

"He has a page from a notepad, a fellow *Dotto* contestant's notepad, where she'd written down all the answers ahead of time."

"And that and Winfeld—that's enough to start an investigation?"

"No, sir, there's more to the story. They've both testified at length to the DA It's a pretty deep story, frankly."

"But what does the DA hope to achieve with this…"

"With the probe?"

"Yes. I mean, for the D.A. to be involved, wouldn't there need to be criminal implications of some kind?"

"Sure, yes, and among other things there's the claim from Higgenfritz that he was paid fifteen hundred dollars by CBS producers in 'hush money,' as he calls it."

"My goodness. And Winfeld?"

"He claims to have his share of circumstantial evidence, including demonstrating that the producers coerced him in the rigging of the show and in keeping quiet afterward."

"Well…this is quite bizarre, I must say."

"Can I quote you on that, sir? Would you allow me to quote that as your comment on the matter?"

"I'm not sure I care to comment, really. This has nothing to do with me, after all."

"Mister Saint Claire, Winfeld has already referred to your win as a fix. And I'm sorry to tell you, but your name is going to be a big part of this story and these events. It's very likely you'll be asked to testify. We'd like to give you the chance to comment now, before it all starts."

"I don't know what to say, except—"

"Is this your on-record comment, sir? Can I quote this in the story?"

"All right, yes. What I'd like to say is…I am sad and shocked. And I don't know what to say except that I thought I won honestly. It's silly and distressing to think that people don't have more faith in quiz shows."

"Would you also comment, Mister Saint Claire, on the nature of your own experience on the quiz program?"

"There's nothing to remark, really—"

"In light of Sidney Winfeld's claims, after all, the question arises concerning what sorts of pressure other contestants may have experienced, what kinds of coaching, say. Were you ever pressured or directed in any manner?"

"Never."

Dad's at the desk an arm's-length away. The telephone sits atop Dad's file cabinet, and he's been at his desk all the while, a witness, while Kenyon stands with the receiver to his ear, listening, babbling, fiercely aware of everything Dad can hear.

Now Kenyon drops the handset back into its cradle, a muted chime as it falls. His scalp is tingling, his face feels somewhat stretched, as if someone's been pulling his hair. Otherwise he's fairly numb, not quite trembling, not quite alarmed.

He turns toward the window, digs out a cigarette.

Softly Dad says, "More than an interview, by the sounds of it."

Kenyon lights his smoke, draws deep, shakes his head. "Very strange. That Winfeld character, the fellow I first played against—he's made some…wild claims, apparently."

"The district attorney's involved, did you say?"

"Somehow, yes. And the *Journal American*, they're running a story on the whole thing tomorrow."

The calming column of smoke inside of him, Kenyon turns now, ready to find Dad's face looking back. And there he is, the old man in shirtsleeves at the desk, a white paper in his hand, his reading glasses lowered to the end of his nose. And the look in his face shows his wish to understand.

Dad says, "They wanted you to—"

"They wanted me to comment because Winfeld, he's told the D.A., apparently, that he lost to me on purpose. That the producers talked him into it."

Dad's hand sinks to the desk, the paper laid by. He straightens in his chair.

"It's a little confusing," says Kenyon. "I don't understand. Why would he lose if he knew the answer?"

"Very odd, yes."

"What was to keep him from just answering correctly? It makes no sense. And for that matter, why would he claim, for everyone to know, that he was given all the answers?"

"He says they gave him the answers?"

"Apparently, yes, that's his other claim. But why would he say that? Why would he want everyone to know? I mean if it were true…"

But presently, as he drops to his chair, as he sits and smokes with Dad mirroring his thoughtful silence, Kenyon senses a momentary weight easing off, the lifting of a small cloud, the arrival of a relieved and peaceable clarity of mind. He'll be OK. What did he ever do wrong? It's a story in the paper, that's all. And what harm is Sidney Winfeld? As for the DA's involvement, that's a matter of due diligence. Surely that's all it is.

"I just realized," says Dad. "I happen to know him."

"Winfeld? Who?"

"Frank Hogan. The DA He's a Columbia man."

Kenyon smiles, shrugs. He leans and stubs his cigarette into the glass ashtray on the windowsill. "Anyhow," he says. "It'll sort itself out."

It'll sort itself out. Of course it will. Hasn't he come through the worst of it already? Standing in that booth, piping out the answers, sweating and pretending. What could be worse than that?

SIDNEY

Didn't Sidney tell them? Didn't he say it? Hasn't he been saying it all along? For more than a year he's been saying it, but would they hear it from him? Oh no, he could tell them more than a year ago, but they weren't gonna have it, not from Sidney Winfeld, and then this Higgenfritz comes along, which *who the hell is Higgenfritz after all?*—the guy appears out of nowhere and who the hell is he supposed to be?—never even been on TV, wasn't even a *contestant*, was never more than a *standby*—and on a different show, different network—never had to answer a single question on the air, not one, but he's some kind of truth-teller, by some dumb luck he stumbles on somebody's notepad left lying backstage, by dumb luck looks at the little paper and finds all the answers written down before the show's even started and tells the same story Sidney's been telling all along, but whereas Sidney is just a bug in their ears, just a nuisance like, this Higgenfritz is some great truth-teller come down from on high to take the wool from everybody's eyes.

Sidney's at the newsstand now and here's the paper, my god, right here on the Front Fucking Page the words *BIG QUIZ SHOWS FIXED, CONTESTANTS CLAIM*, right there under the *Journal American* eagle, the bird with the banner flying out from its claws which the banner reads *An American Paper for the American People.* For years Sidney's been reading the *Journal*, years, and never until today has he noticed those words, which by god they're a good set of words for this particular story because after all this is Big-Time, this is bound to go very big since the American people, don't they deserve to know the true nature of their television programs, those smiling faces those audiences all that cheering and applause those studio orchestras and continuity cards and isolation booths? Well, here it is, Sidney Winfeld's own message finally brought to the American People courtesy of the New York Fucking District Attorney—and how's *that* for all you numb-fucks who wouldn't listen more than a year ago? OK, OK, so it took Higgenfritz to *corroborate*, so-called, OK, so what, anyhow the story is out now, *out out out* and those production studio twits those network ignoramuses they won't get this ugly genie back into their little lamp, not anytime soon, not until the American people get to have a look around at the real and actual nature of things in show business. *BIG QUIZ SHOWS FIXED*—there it is, says it right there in plain old big-letter English and Sidney can hardly believe it.

It's first thing in the morning and the paper's stacked nice and fat right there on the newsstand counter—even displayed on the stand-up rack.

Sidney picks one up, turns it to show Bert behind the counter in his smudged apron. "You seen this, Bert?"

"Sidney! I was gonna ask you the same thing!"

"*Seen* it? Me? I'm quoted! Right here. I'm the *reason* for it!"

"No kidding?"

"No joke, Bert. You're gonna hear more on this too, don't you doubt it."

"OK, Sidney, well, you'll want to be having a copy, I suppose. For posterity and all."

"I'll take five copies, Bert. Here's a dollar. No, no, keep it. You keep it now. It's a good day, Bert."

BIG QUIZ SHOWS FIXED, CONTESTANTS CLAIM

NEW YORK, Aug. 28, 1958—New York County District Attorney Frank S. Hogan said Wednesday that testimony by big-money quiz contestant Sidney Winfeld brings television's biggest quiz show into the DA's newly opened investigation of TV quiz programs. Mr. Hogan's quiz show probe was instigated last week, after former *Dotto* contestant Terrence Higgenfritz presented evidence of that program's rigging: a page from a fellow contestant's notepad on which she had written out the answers beforehand.

Mr. Winfeld, who won $50,000 on NBC's hottest property, alleges that producers gave him answers prior to each of his eight appearances on the air. He said he was then instructed to miss a question that "any schoolboy could answer" in order for Kenyon Saint Claire to defeat him.

Mr. Saint Claire, who proceeded to win $129,000, was reached at his Columbia University office for comment yesterday: "I'm sad and I'm shocked," he said. "I don't know what to say except that I thought I won honestly. It's silly and distressing to think that people don't have more faith in quiz shows." He added that during his nearly three-month winning streak on the program, he was never directed by the producers in how to answer or subjected to any pressure.

Meanwhile Mr. Hogan commented: "I'm convinced we have a lot more digging to do," suggesting that the probe was only beginning. "TV viewers," he said, "certainly have a right to be angry about the misrepresentations, if what is suggested is true."

CONT'D. ON PAGE 2

But back home in the narrow kitchen, slapping down the paper on the table for Bernice to see, well, it ain't exactly a hero's welcome, and seeing her pick the paper up and seeing the change in her face, which she looks to be almost sick, for all practical purposes almost ill so Sidney wonders if she isn't gonna lunge to the kitchen sink any second.

"Honey," he says. "What's the matter? What is it?"

"I didn't know," she says, but stops herself, stops herself and breathes like she needs to swallow something down. "I knew you'd gone to the district attorney, but I didn't know…" She pinches the paper's edge—never has liked the feeling of newsprint in her hands—and lifts it to one side of her to show him the headline as if he hadn't seen it already. "*This* I didn't know was coming."

"You didn't know? But how didn't you know? I went to the D.A., so what did you think?"

"It's a surprise, Sidney. I'm rather surprised is what I mean to tell you."

She's having her morning yogurt, the baby asleep in the other room, the bassinet at the foot of their bed, and they're talking in quiet tones, and the yogurt it's a pooled white spiral in her bowl, and now one corner of the newspaper is resting in the yogurt, soaking there, a tiny discoloration seeping into the whiteness around the paper's darkening corner. She doesn't notice.

"But this is good," he says. "Bernice, this is a good thing."

"How can you mean that, Sidney? You can't want this. This is public knowledge now. How is this good?"

"It's justice, honey. They can't just…they can't do whatever they want and nobody's the wiser, you see?"

"But it says about you right here, Sidney, it says 'producers gave him the answers prior.'"

She's all but gray now, her bottom lip is trembling, which he can't yet say for certain if she's angry or sad.

"Sure," he says. "That's true after all. That's the truth so that's what I told them. The show was fixed, that's the point, Bernice. Why the surprise? You knew it was fixed all the time, honey."

"*I* knew, Sidney. *Me. Me and you.* Here in the privacy of our home we both knew. But I didn't know it would come to this. I didn't expect that everybody, everybody else would know it too, any old stranger out there…"

"That's news, honey. That's how it works, it's public information. I'm not ashamed, why should I be, I'm the only person willing to tell the truth, why should we be ashamed of that?"

He moves close to her now, bends and embraces her as she sits, presses himself against her chair with arms stretched out around her and saying "Shhh, shhh," and kissing her hair which smells of the baby, "This is no cause to worry now, honey. This is good, we are good."

"Why?" she mutters, kind of crumbling in his arms, still confused, the paper still drooping from one hand. "Why good? Why do you say that, Sidney?"

"Because don't you see, Bernice, it's *my* story. It's *my* name there in the paper. This is Sidney Winfeld standing up to say the truth, it's *my* name they're speaking, not some other guy. Don't you see?"

"Sidney, these television men, they could really hurt you, honey, they could just snap their fingers and…and you a new father with our baby girl to care for."

"No, Bernice, because it is not their story anymore. This is *my* story now. They won't take it away. Not this time. Not from us, honey."

From the bedroom now the baby begins to cry.

COMMENTATORS

"Never before in history, one could argue, have individuals been so acutely conscious of the extent to which personhood is performed…. 'Our culture demands total transparency, at the same time that it demands near-constant performance,' the philosopher Michel de Certau writes… 'So, how can you know a person?'"

"You have to make allowances for the fact that everything we see tonight is real. There's a lot of polishing we still have to do. But that's what this exercise is all about."

LIVING ROOM

"I really like him. I can't stand the guy. I could eat her up. He's such a pain. I'd do anything he asked. She deserves a good slap around the face. Bighead. He's lying. She's just pretending to feel pity. He's going to find life really tough. What a wanker. She's an angel. He's so conceited, so proud. They're such phonies, those two. Poor thing, poor thing. I'd shoot him this minute, without batting an eyelid. I feel so sorry for her. He drives me bloody mad. She's pretending. How can he be so naïve. What a cheek. She's such an intelligent woman. He disgusts me. He really tickles me."

KENYON

In the earliest hour, Kenyon Saint Claire walks the length of Washington Square, heading back, the newspaper tucked under one arm. Daylight hasn't quite stretched above the buildings yet, all the streets a smoky purple, most everyone still indoors. At the corner of West Fourth and Broadway a crisp morning wind confronts him, the end of summer inside it. Somehow the sidewalk here is blanketed in small yellow leaves by the thousands. Honey locust, always the first trees to go. There's a pale swirl at his ankles with every step.

BIG QUIZ SHOWS FIXED, CONTESTANTS CLAIM

Stock-still at the newsstand on Washington Place, he'd read the whole thing through, turning the pages to the harsh light of the vendor's bulb.

... With the opening of the investigation by Mr. Hogan, C.B.S. was quick to scuttle *Dotto*, its most popular daytime show.

Meanwhile, in the face of Sidney Winfeld's claims of behind-the-scenes manipulation on NBC's own wildly successful quiz program, that network's executives and the show's production staff are flatly denying any foul play.

"It's a tired old story and it's already been laid to rest. We're disappointed to see such baseless accusations being made all over again," said Raymond Greenmarch, of Mint and Greenmarch Productions, Inc., the show's originating company.

When asked to comment on whether Terrence Higgenfritz's *Dotto* notebook corroborates Mr. Winfeld's claims, Mr. Greenmarch said, "I don't see how that has anything to do with our program. That is a different network, different show entirely. That is solely C.B.S.'s concern. Should it cast doubt upon the whole of television? I don't think it should." Would TV viewers agree with that perspective? Mr. Greenmarch: "I believe they would. Our viewership is very loyal and they have no reason whatsoever to doubt the genuineness of our programming."

To read these mistruths—to see Greenmarch's words in plain newsprint, all the while *hearing* Greenmarch's voice in your head—it's much like those glaring studio lights again, those Klieg lights—*Krieg* lights, war lights!—burning down on you through the isolation booth glass. That flayed-open nakedness under the brutally concentrated wattage: aimed, fixed, and focused. How that made you shrink. How it made you move and gesture, sweating all the while, how it made you search out the answer, the fake answer in the liquefying heat of pretend, how it made you say the words, the fake words, exactly as you'd practiced.

> …Mr. Greenmarch added that his
> company and NBC are working in full
> cooperation with the district attorney's
> office. …

Now Kenyon climbs the steps to his door. He'll show Ernestine the paper—he's already told her the story was coming—and they'll talk it over. He'll leave for the studio soon, his morning appearance on the *TODAY Show*, but they still have time. They'll talk it out.

In the kitchen the coffee is hot, but she's not there. He checks the terrace. No, she's gone back to the bedroom. Newspaper in hand, he steers himself down the hall, hears the hissing of the pipes before he gets there. Her bathrobe is thrown across the foot of their bed. The bathroom door stands ajar, steam escaping.

For a moment Kenyon stands just outside that door, still in his coat, newspaper in hand.

> *I don't know what to say except that I thought I won honestly.*

He doesn't want to bother her, but she knows he went to get the paper. He'd told her this was coming.

> *It's silly and distressing to think that people don't have more faith in quiz shows.*

And here he is, newspaper in hand.

He steps forward and taps at the door. "Knock knock."

From inside the spray she says, "Oh, you're back."

"I'm back."

"And? Is it out?"

He nudges the door, pokes his head around, and finds her shape blurred behind frosted glass, glaucoma of color and steam in a field of pink tile. Her voice, too, is muffled behind the opaque screen.

"Kenyon? Is it out?"

"It's out," he says. And he stands looking at her, or trying to, and already in the humidor of the bathroom the newspaper seems to be wilting in his hand.

"What does it say?" she says.

He can make out the shape of her arms. She's raising them to her head, running her hands through her hair. Then she seems to turn her head, to look at him through the distortion of glass, her own face a watery mask.

And him? What must he look like through the glass?

"Well," he says. "It's what we expected, pretty much."

"Is it big?"

"Yes," he says. "Pretty big. Front page. You can read it yourself. I'll leave it in the kitchen."

"Oh, are you going?"

"I'd better..." he says. "I'll see you this afternoon. Love you."

And before she can answer, he's moving through the bedroom toward the hall and then, remembering, turning just long enough to whip a tie from the rack on the back of the closet door.

Then he is going—he's out of the house and down the steps and heading up the street, knotting his tie as he walks. He'll have to shave at the studio. He'll be early enough. Hopefully not too early. Hopefully they'll let him in, somebody. He checks his watch. No, no, he's far too early. It's still barely daylight. Goodness, he's out of sorts. What was he thinking, charging from the house like that? He thought they'd talk it through. He'd fully intended... Now he's practically on the run, like a fugitive...

On the sidewalk at Broadway and Bleecker he stops, turns about. But no, no going home right now. Instead he checks himself, stooping a little to see his own clothing. Gray trousers, brown coat. Well, they'll have to do for today's appearance. At least they're clean. He hasn't eaten, but he hardly thinks of that, lets it flit like a little morning bird right through his head and out again. What he needs is to walk, to move, to charge on down the pavement, small—*so comforting, somehow, to be so small!*—at the foot of one massive building after another. They go on forever, the buildings, they pay you no thought, they hide you so nicely in their shadows. He's heading north, he could stay on Broadway all the way up. But no, the newsstands won't let him. They're far too numerous. That headline in stark black lettering, reproduced in impossible numbers, distributed everywhere. He's still below Washington Square, and he turns toward Mercer now. Can he get through NYU without being recognized? If only he'd brought a hat...

No, but what he needs is a phone. He needs, suddenly he realizes it, to call Lacky. Maybe they've tried him already, back at home. Oh, how many people are going to call after this? And how many will come to his door? And who?

There's Mom and Dad, of course. Of course, he'll need to speak to them...

He's not quite frantic, not quite panicked, but as quickly as possible he needs to find a telephone booth...

. . .

Greenmarch answers, though the secretary said she'd put Kenny through to Lacky.

"Kenny," says Greenmarch, "it's good of you to call. I just tried you at home."

"I left early today. I'm in a telephone booth."

"I spoke with your wife. She seemed a little concerned."

"Shouldn't she be? Wait, you mean you told her about fixing…"

"I mean she seemed confused…as to your whereabouts. What I told her was I'd try you at NBC."

"I'm on my way there now."

"Where are you exactly?"

"Uh, West Fifteenth, I think. A telephone booth."

"Now, Kenny, I understand you've seen the headlines."

"Yes. And everyone's going to—"

"Now, now, Kenny, let's hang on right there," Greenmarch's voice in a deliberately mellow register. "Let's make sure you take some deep breaths. Have you stopped a minute to breathe?"

Does Kenyon sound that frantic? He does, he realizes. He does. "Ray, don't patronize me, not today. I called to see what you're—"

"—how we're handling the situation, yes, of course. And we *are* handling it, Kenny. Don't you worry. We're convening a press conference, for one. And Fred will make a statement on the program very soon. But first, before all that, just look at the accusations, consider the source."

What can Kenyon say to this? The *accusations*, as it happens, are true.

"Now, Kenny, we've just heard, you should know, that it's going to be a grand jury. We just got the news over here. And listen, there's no reason for alarm. That part will hit the papers tomorrow and we didn't want it to alarm you. What you need to know at this point is that Mister Lacky and myself have been called to testify and you have nothing to fear from any of this. We'd *die* for you, Kenny. They could *break our legs*."

"I'll be called too."

"You're probably right. They'll be calling all the contestants, no doubt."

"I'll have to tell the truth."

"Yes, OK, but let's wait a minute here, Kenny. Let's think about what you mean by that. You mean, of course, the truth *as you understand it*. Let's be clear on this point, nobody's done any wrong here."

"I'll have to, Ray. I won't have a choice."

"Listen, Kenny, this may feel big to you, right at this moment, I can see that, but you need to bear in mind the reality of this situation. We've got all our public relations people on this, Kenny, and so does NBC, and the *reality* is that this isn't—this brouhaha—it is not going to go far."

Kenyon hangs up, his coin jangling down at the mechanical gulp of the phone box. He's enclosed in the musty booth, wind sweeping in through the three-inch gap below the folding door. He stares through scratched glass down the barren street toward Fifth. People are crossing there from corner to corner, their numbers increasing, the city waking up. But still, here on this little street a spirit of calm is hiding, stubborn, still gray, all gray here between the buildings. It will last a few minutes more at least.

For a few minutes more, if no one comes along, Kenyon is safe in this little cell.

Picking up the phone, he clinks another coin into the slot and dials and then Ernestine's voice is in his ear, bewilderingly rich and full. She's relieved he called, she says. She's read the paper and was starting to worry—the way he rushed out, she's never seen him like that.

"I'm sorry," he says.

"It's OK now. Now I know where you are."

"I mean for all of it, Ernestine. For all of it, I'm sorry."

"I'm not the only one concerned about you, Kenyon. Kip called this morning, your parents called, your brother, Mister Greenmarch…"

"I spoke with Greenmarch. Listen, Ernestine, I don't know what's going to happen now. This won't end any time soon."

"I know," she says. "Let's not get ahead of ourselves."

"People will see this story. You understand."

"They're seeing it now, yes."

"And not only see it, they'll believe it."

"Why shouldn't they?" she says. "It's the truth."

Shut away inside the telephone booth, Kenyon closes his eyes, willing the outside world to disappear. Something sinking inside of him.

"Isn't it, Kenyon? It's the truth."

"Yes."

"We can say that now. *You* can say it."

"But I haven't said it, Ernestine. I already lied. To the journalist."

"You're not lying to me, Kenyon. This minute, right now, you've told me the truth. That makes things better already. One thing at a time."

She's right, he thinks.

"Anyway, who do you mean, people will see it? What people?"

Kenyon breathes deep. He goes on staring through the gouged and blemished glass. All the morning people on the street. He's remembering now, remembering for no particular reason—and finds himself speaking the memory into the phone: how in the parlor of the farmhouse they would rig up a rope and bedsheet, he and George, and stage their little theatricals for Mom and Dad. Sometimes the sheet was a curtain to be drawn back. Kenny, costumed in one of Dad's old suits, stepping out on the braided parlor carpet to say his part. Dad's sleeves gathered in thick rolls at Kenny's wrists, Dad's collar swimming about his chest. Sometimes the bedsheet was a screen and he and George would hunker behind it with a lamp, making shadows. Mom and Dad indulged them, the most patient audience.

"They loved you," says Ernestine. "They still love you, Kenyon."

"You know," he says, "I'll be asked to testify. Sooner or later I'll be asked."

"One day at a time, darling. As for this morning, are you going to be all right?"

"I think I will be, yes. They'll have heard at the *TODAY Show*—Garroway and everyone."

"They respect you."

"Mm. I was going to talk about Renaissance Man. I can't do that now. How can I?"

"You should say what you want to say."

"Listen, Ernestine, I still want to take you on that honeymoon. Let's make it Paris. Will you come?" He's to join the cast of the *TODAY Show* in reporting from Paris next month. They hadn't planned on Ernestine accompanying, but why shouldn't she? Why shouldn't they finally take some time for themselves? "I won't be a liar," he says. "Not about that, Ernestine. Not to you."

"Kenyon," she says, "you're the most truthful person I know."

CONTROL

CAMERA ONE: close on Dave Garroway and pulling back as he rises from his desk. Follow as he moves slow across the studio floor, the wide-awake stage-lights glinting in his pomaded hair. He talks to the lens as he goes:

"As you may have seen already in today's newspapers, ladies and gentlemen, there have arisen some doubts about the management of a few television quiz programs. It happens that one such program was lucky enough to have the *TODAY Show*'s own Kenyon Saint Claire as its reigning champ for…well, it was for more than a few weeks, wasn't it, Kenyon?"

Pull in on two-shot of Garroway and Saint Claire. Saint Claire poised on a stool, the *TODAY Show* sign aglow in neon just over his shoulder.

"Good morning, Dave. Yes, I played for fifteen weeks."

"A terribly captivating fifteen weeks it was too. Quite literally so for you, isn't that right, having to stand in that isolation chamber?"

"Captivating is a good word for it, yes."

"Well, as you said yourself to the reporters, this hullabaloo about the quiz shows, it's all come as something of a surprise."

"That's right, Dave. It's caught me quite off guard, to be honest."

"I imagine so. Being a Columbia professor yourself, having shared so abundantly of your knowledge with our viewers this past year, I'm sure these accusations of cheating are—well, they must be dismaying."

"Yes, Dave, as our viewers may know by now, I have had my doubts about the educational value of quiz programs, but this sort of business—cheating and whatnot—that would be something else entirely."

"In any case, this morning you're going to tell us about the Renaissance."

"I am. In fact it relates to the subject of education. You see, it's during the Renaissance that the idea of liberal education first begins."

"Tell us, please."

CAMERA TWO: Pull in on Saint Claire as Garroway takes his next mark.

IN LIVING ROOMS ACROSS AMERICA

The television keeps talking as if it has the household's full attention. But in the house on Grove and McConnell Street in suburban New Jersey other business is afoot. Your daughter runs past the set where Kenyon Saint Claire, fixed in closeup, is saying, *A Renaissance man is neither an expert nor a specialist. He or she knows more than just a little about 'everything' instead of knowing 'everything' about a small part of the entire spectrum of modern knowledge.* Your son runs past. Young Genevieve, young Isaac, they're in their school clothes, they've just finished the cream of wheat and milk you set out.

It is universally believed that no one really can be a Renaissance man in the true meaning of the term, says the television.

Isaac is in a hurry to find his sweater. Genevieve has misplaced a shoe.

Was there ever a Renaissance man, even during the Renaissance, in that sense of the term? The answer is no. We shall even have to examine the question whether it is not possible for Renaissance men in the true sense to exist today....

And in apartment 26A in Queens, the dog is scratching at the door to be let out.

And in the Virginia rowhouse on Hillman Avenue, the milkman's crate clatters down on the stoop.

The teapot is shrieking. A black strand of smoke trails in from the kitchen—you've burnt the toast.

Originally, says the television, *the student would be taught seven arts or skills, consisting of the trivium—grammar, rhetoric, and logic...*

In the stucco duplex on San Francisco's Geary Street, you can't find your cigarettes. Damn it all, has the wife tossed them out again?

...and the quadrivium—arithmetic, geometry, astronomy, and music. The names are antique, but the seven 'subjects' were comparable to a modern liberal curriculum of languages, philosophy, mathematics, history, and science.

In Boston, on Garden Street, your husband paces the living room, brushing his teeth as he goes.

The television says, *The arts or skills were 'liberal' because they were liberating.*

Your husband calls out about his green tie. Did you iron it? It's not on its rack.

That is, they freed their possessor from the ignorance that bound the uneducated. The twentieth century has seen radical change in this traditional scheme of education.

The telephone rings. The ironing board skirls loud as it opens.

Someone's buzzing at the intercom.

The failure of the Renaissance, says the television, *to produce successful "Renaissance men" did not go unnoticed.*

The downstairs neighbor, apartment 26, comes knocking at your door, still in his bathrobe, still unshaven, to hand you the *Journal-American* and say how they keep mixing up the apartment numbers.

All that remained, in the popular consciousness, was the sometimes admiring, sometimes ironic, and sometimes contemptuous phrase "Renaissance man," says the television.

The pipes are rattling. A siren blares just below the window. The kids are shouting at each other. The cat is mewing at the door. Johnny keeps banging the kitchen cupboards. Carolyn is grinding coffee.

...which was applied to almost anyone who manifested an ability to do more than one thing well. Even then, the phrase was never used in its original, Aristotelian sense.

BIG QUIZ SHOWS FIXED, CONTESTANTS CLAIM

Kenyon Saint Claire, compact in the neat gray frame of the television screen, continues to look at the camera as if staring you straight in the eye.

Hey, wait a minute now. He's the front page news—*him*, Kenyon Saint Claire.

> Mr. Saint Claire, who proceeded to win $129,000, was reached at his Columbia University office for comment yesterday: "I'm sad and I'm shocked," he said.

They're saying somebody was giving him the answers all along.

In the television, he keeps talking. *That ideal and idea*, he says, *have been lost completely.*

AND NOW A WORD FROM OUR SPONSORS

"The charges made by Sidney Winfeld against our quiz program first came to the attention of our staff at NBC over a year ago. At that time our network made a thorough investigation and found them to be utterly baseless and untrue..."

"We go live now to the Biltmore Hotel for a press conference concerning the events and investigations surrounding the television quiz shows..."

> The whole gloss and excitement of the quiz shows has been badly tarnished this week by evidence of corner-carnival showmanship and petty scheming. The increasingly loud question among TV viewers is: Are the shows fixed?

"Good morning, I'm Raymond Greenmarch and this is my production partner Fred Mint. We've convened this morning's conference because it is our desire to refute and conclusively disprove the allegations made against our program by one disgruntled individual, an ex-contestant on the show. In fact, I may say—and I know Mister Mint feels very much as I do—that we have been pushed this week beyond all reasonableness of professional and human endurance by the malicious statements of Mister Winfeld."

> From unquestionably crooked *Dotto*, ruined by the revelations of standby contestant Terrence Higgenfritz, suspicion spread fast to NBC and the biggest program of all, the hallowed battleground defended for nearly three months last year by Kenyon Saint Claire.

"...All of us at NBC were completely convinced of the integrity of the program and of its producers, Mint and Greenmarch..."

> Sidney Winfeld, 31, one of the show's earliest big-money winners ($49,500), claims to be out to establish the facts. He is hardly a confidence-inspiring witness. He seems bent on destroying the reputations of everyone connected with the show.

"And now, presented by Geritol, America's Number One Tonic, your master of ceremonies, Fred Mint!"

"Thank you, ladies and gentlemen, thank you and good evening..."

> Mr. Winfeld admits to bitterly envying Kenyon Saint Claire, the man who defeated him, and appears to choke with bile at the very mention of producer Ray Greenmarch. But for all his vindictiveness, Mr. Winfeld's detail-packed story continues to command attention.

"Ladies and gentlemen, this is a bit unusual, but before we begin our show tonight there is something I must say to all of you. I am talking about the stories that you have read attacking my partner, Raymond Greenmarch, and me. All I want to say is this. The stories are wholly untrue. I repeat, they are wholly untrue..."

"...At the time these charges were first brought to our attention at NBC and shortly thereafter, two major New York newspapers made thorough investigations of them and apparently concluded, as did our executive staff, that they had no basis in fact. As a result they printed nothing."

"...There are two items this morning that Mister Mint and I would especially like to make known to the public, each relating to Mister Winfeld's wild claims..."

"...Now, ladies and gentlemen, every week for nearly two years we have presented for you the quiz program you are watching right now. You have come to know and depend on us for programming that is quite different from the standard fare, and I trust that we have been in every way reliable in showing you great contests of knowledge, one after another. You have every reason to believe me when I tell you that at no time, ladies and gentlemen, has any contestant ever been given advance information about any questions ever used on this program..."

"...In the first instance, we have in our records at Mint and Greenmarch Productions a signed statement from Mister Winfeld dated more than eighteen months ago. This is a statement which we have shared with the district attorney in the course of investigations into this matter, and I'd like to ask Mister Mint to read this statement now."

"I'd be happy to, Ray. Good morning, gentlemen. This statement from Mister Winfeld is dated February 11, 1957. It reads: 'I do hereby state and declare to whomever may be now or in the future concerned that Raymond Greenmarch, producer of Mint and Greenmarch Productions, has never in any way, shape, nor form, given imparted or suggested to me any questions or answers connected with the NBC television quiz program...'"

> "I was forced to say Gothic architecture
> originated in Germany, for instance, when I
> know damn well it was France."

"'...Any questions or answers I gave on the program were entirely my own and no aid or assistance was rendered to me by Mister Greenmarch nor any of his staff. ...'"

> "See, that's the trend now. You pretend
> to be a little bit dumb, which that makes
> the American public feel better about
> themselves."

"'…As a token of this statement and affirming it to be entirely true, I place my signature freely and without any mental or physical duress on the paper below. Signed, Sidney Winfeld.'"

> Why did he sign a retraction? Says Mr. Winfeld: "Simple. I did it in return for the promise of a job on another Mint and Greenmarch show. That's the part of the tape recording you never heard. And it was a job I never got."

"Thank you, Fred. Now, gentleman, if you'll hold your questions till the end, please, there is as I said a second item we'd very much like to share with you this morning. I am going to play for you now a tape recording made in my office on the very same day that Mister Winfeld signed the statement Mister Mint has just read out to you."

Click. Whir.

Tape plays:

Voice 1: I'll admit I flipped. And I'm saying to myself now, I'm saying, I'm perfectly willing to need help, that's why I'm here. I'm saying, ahhh, Ray gave me a damn good break.

Voice 2: You're welcome, Sid, of course.

Voice 1: But see, it all went back much further for me. I felt in the end that here was this guy Saint Claire with his fancy name, Ivy League education, parents of distinction all his life, and I had just the opposite, the hard way up. Here was my own sort of mental delusion that this should all be coming to me. …

Voice 2: You're owning up to it, then? That you've been acting badly. It's a good first step, Sid, to be able to say it. To just say, yes, there was a blackmail scheme afoot.

Voice 1: Uh *[pause]* yes.

> Yesterday Mr. Winfeld charged that "the tape recordings have been doctored." He admitted having a conversation with Mr. Greenmarch on the date specified, but added: "I insist that I did not say yes when Greenmarch asked me the question about blackmail."

> When asked what he had said, Mr. Winfeld
> declared: "I don't remember. I might have
> said no or emphatically not."
>
> Mr. Winfeld says that Mr. Greenmarch
> coached him in grimace and gesture, taught
> him how to "think" expressively in the TV
> isolation booth....
>
> This week New York District Attorney
> Frank Hogan announced that a grand jury
> will be convened to settle the many questions
> raised concerning TV's quiz programs. That
> jury will decide whether or not Mr. Winfeld,
> and other contestants like him, are telling
> the truth.

"...It has been a terrible experience, for everyone on this program, to have to combat the unfounded charges that have been flying at us, but, ladies and gentlemen, tonight we do consider ourselves lucky in one respect. So many of you have expressed your faith in us and in this program..."

> Is it true, as Mr. Greenmarch ominously
> suggests, that Mr. Winfeld has been under
> psychiatric care? Says Mr. Winfeld: "Sure
> I've been to a psychiatrist. I suffered from
> an acute anxiety neurosis after my time in
> that booth."

"...A wise man once said that the truth will win out. I know that it will, ladies and gentlemen, for we have not betrayed your trust in us. We never will."

> "You can't possibly be caught knowing where Gothic
> architecture began. God forbid."

"Now let's return to our contest of knowledge, shall we?"

Applause.

Q:

What'd he just say?

A:

Which part?
The contest of knowledge part?

Q:

No, right before that.

A:

Oh, about the truth?
He said the truth will win out.

Q:

The *truth* will win out?

A:

Yeah.

Q:

That's funny. For a minute I
thought he said the *booth* will win out.

A:

The booth?

Q:

Yeah, you know,
like the *isolation booth*.

A:

That's funny.

Q:

Yeah.

A:

The *isolation booth* will win out. Ha.
That is funny.

KENYON

"Everything all right, son?" Dad's face is pained, even a bit pale. "We tried to reach you this morning. Ernestine didn't know where you'd—but we saw you on television, of course. Do you need a cigarette?"

"I'd love one, thanks."

Kenyon doesn't even have his valise. Only upon leaving the NBC building did he realize he'd been without it all morning, left it behind when he hurried from the house at the crack of dawn. From West Fiftieth he continued on to the college, empty-handed.

"What about you, Dad? How are you and Mom taking all this?"

Kenyon's managed to shave, though—did so at the studio before going on the air. Can Dad see the wrinkles in his suit?

The first thing Kenny did in this house...

"Don't worry about us, son. Do you have a seminar? Are you sure you're up for it? I could fill in—"

"No, no. I mean, I'm a little out of sorts. But..." God, the smoke in his airway—what a blessing! He sucks it way down until it fizzes beautifully in his diaphragm. Breathes out. "Right now I need to be here, Dad. This is exactly where I need to be."

Dad's face clears somewhat, but he doesn't quite smile. "OK then. And there's no need to talk it all through, not right now."

No valise. And he'd taken pains to avoid colleagues on his way along College Walk. Even waited to climb the steps to Hamilton Hall when he saw Barzun come out through the main doors—made one more circuit of the paths just to delay his own entry. Then came into the building moving at top speed, eyes kept low.

"I'll have to borrow your Emerson. Can I?"

Dad gets up. "Let me just find it." Standing before the shelves, back turned in his trim blue suit jacket, he scans the many spines, innumerable books crammed in or stacked two-deep along the sagging planks of the bookcase.

...fall down the stairs...

"I'll testify," says Kenyon.

"Oh, they've called you?"

"Not yet. They will."

A slight man, thinks Kenyon as he looks at Dad standing there. So slim and unassuming a figure, especially before those high shelves. Modest in his simple suit.

What can I tell them, Dad? In the anxious confines of his mind Kenyon phrases the question. But when he speaks, the words are different. "I'm sure they'll have more questions than I can ever answer."

Dad's looking up at the highest shelf and in his gray neatly parted hair Kenyon can see the whorl. Something boyish and vulnerable about it. Innocent.

Dad reaches up. He grips a stack of four or five volumes, moves them aside, peers into the space they've cleared. "Ah, here. The *Portable*, Malcolm's edition."

He means Malcolm Cowley, a Saint Claire family friend. Malcolm's *Emerson* was a re-edited selection of the *Portable Emerson* that Dad himself was the first to edit some years before. In his introduction Malcolm openly criticized Dad's choice of selections, claiming that his own selections were more representative.

Dad brings the fat volume over, places it in Kenyon's hands.

"Malcolm's?" says Kenyon.

"Yes. He was right to include more of the essays, 'The Over-Soul' in particular."

And then, for a moment, Dad remains there before him. "No answer in words," he recites, "can reply to a question of things. That which we are, we shall teach, not voluntarily but involuntarily." He winks, says, "Listen, we can talk later. But, Kenyon, whatever it is that you must do, it'll be... for the best."

Kenyon nods, looking down at his own hands. He does not say: *Dad, my first instinct was to run.* He doesn't say, as he holds the Emerson: *Dad, we love words, you and I. It is words that we live by. But I've betrayed them, Dad, words, and now words will betray me—the words with which I answered all those questions on-air, words in the newspapers.*

BIG QUIZ SHOWS FIXED, CONTESTANTS CLAIM...

Kenyon does not say: *Dad, they've torn me away from words, just as everyone will be torn. They've made a picture out of me.* He doesn't say: *Dad, they make so many pictures now, day and night, so many pictures, just so they can cut them up, cut them up or smash them.* He doesn't say: *Dad, I can hardly picture* myself *anymore, except inside a frame. Except behind a screen. Except staring out through glass—unheard unless miked, unseen unless lit...*

Atop Dad's filing cabinet the telephone rings and Dad steps aside to take up the receiver. "Maynard Saint Claire here."

His eyes skate back to Kenyon as the voice in the phone makes its request. "Uh, no, no, I'm afraid Kenyon isn't here just now. No, I've no comment at this time, thank you."

The receiver clatters to its cradle. Before the phone can ring again, he stoops and pulls the plug from the wall.

"No comment," he mutters, and shows Kenyon a harried smile.

Kenyon doesn't say: *I still might run. That instinct hasn't gone.*

What he says is, "Thanks, Dad."

CONTROL

Cut to:

Kenyon Saint Claire walking, an autumn afternoon in Manhattan, 1958. Leaves swirling, the trees all turning. He's walking fast, full strides, a great distance before him...

Cut to:

Kenyon in a very long shot, small figure moving east along Cathedral Parkway. Turning south down Central Park West. We pull back even further, and all the steel and stone of the spire-like buildings rears up around him.

Cut to:

Kenyon accosted in the street. Men and women, men and women, they have something to say to him, they claim a right to approach. They seem to believe themselves shareholders of a kind—shareholders in something he represents or something he seems to threaten. They have cruel words, some of them, kind words, some. Again and again they address him, though he keeps on walking, shakes them off each time, saying, *I'm sorry* or *thank you* or *excuse me*, trots farther along, occasionally checking his shoulder.

Cut to:

Wide view of Kenyon Saint Claire in the dusky marble of the Forty-Second Street library, climbing the stairs. A small figure, a shadow, his feet clattering in vast quietude.

Cut to:

Kenyon standing in a wood-paneled room on the library's second floor, stationary before an illuminated glass case as tall as himself. Inside the case on a white satin pedestal, aglow in the soft display light, is a Gutenberg Bible. It lies open to a page in *Revelation*.

We see the gothic Latin typeface, the double columns, the dropped capitals hand-painted, shimmering gold.

Cut to:

Very close on the gothic print, words scrolling before the lens. In Maynard Saint Claire's voice, the voice of Kenyon's thoughts, we hear the words spoken in translation: *I know your works, your toil, and your patient endurance. But I have this against you, that you have abandoned the love you had at first. Remember then from what you have fallen; repent, and do the works you did at first.*

Cut to:

The book's perspective: a gaze pitched upward from the page itself. Kenyon Saint Claire looming above, staring down through the glass, his face half in shadow.

Cut to:

Evening at home. Kenyon in lamplight at the telephone table, receiver at his ear. The room behind him is dark.

Tom Grant's voice in the phone, the *TODAY Show* producer. *You deserve a chance to make a statement on the air. Garroway agrees. Will you prepare some words for tomorrow? Explain the outrageous nature of these Winfeld charges. Take a full two minutes if you need to. The viewers will appreciate it. NBC will appreciate it.*

Kenyon hangs up. From the darkness comes Ernestine, in nightgown.

"Coming to bed?"

"I can't just yet. Need to write something first."

She buries her hand in his hair, cradles his head at her breast. "You're going to be OK, aren't you?"

What can he promise her? He wishes so badly not to lie. "Well, I'm tired."

"Our longest day yet, hm? Did you talk to your father?"

"Mm-hm. We had a few minutes."

"He understands," she says. "He already understands."

"Mm."

Cut to:

Kenyon, alone again beside the lamp, pen in hand. He is writing.

Cut to:

Kenyon's hand moving across the page: *My colleagues here at the TODAY Show have generously offered me this chance to say a few words to you concerning the so-called quiz show investigations… I of course intend to cooperate with this investigation, and because I have nothing but the highest respect for all the good people with whom I've worked here at NBC since my first appearance on the quiz program, I fully expect that these charges will be found to be…*

The hand stops. The pen hovers above the paper.

For one minute…two…three…the hand remains very still.

Cut to:

Kenyon, still alone in the dark room, phone receiver in hand. Number by number he turns the rotary dial.

Sam Lacky's voice: *We won't betray you, Kenny, not a chance. They've got nothing, there's nothing illegal here, it's entertainment, for Christsake. Nobody here is ever gonna betray you, OK? We'd die for you, pal.*

Cut to:

Kenyon Saint Claire, in plaid pajama suit, settling into bed beside his sleeping wife…

Cut to:

Later. Kenyon in bed, on his back, eyes open and staring up through the darkness.

Cut to:

Still later. Kenyon throws back the blankets, gets up in the dark, creeps down the hall to his study, where he opens his desk drawer. In the drawer we see a modest stack of pages, rubber-banded. *Country of the Father* in typescript. His novel-in-progress.

Kenyon stands staring into the open drawer.

LIVING ROOM

In the neat black-rimmed box of the screen, Kenyon Saint Claire's face is moon-like, ghostly. He is perched on a stool in his customary suit and tie, the *TODAY Show* logo aglow in neon behind him. But now the camera moves in very close and his face fills the screen—bright gray, fuzzy at the edges.

"I believe in the honesty of the contestants on that program," he is saying. "I also believe in the honesty of the questions used on that program."

"I myself," he says, "was never given any answers or told any questions beforehand."

"And as far as I know," he says, "none of the contestants received any coaching of this sort."

MAILBAG

Dear Kenyon,
I still watch the quiz program every week. I can't seem to stop, even though it's never been the same since you left....

Kenyon Saint Claire,
If it's a fraud that you put over onto the American people all that time, I pray that you will receive the stiffest penalties of the law which hopefully means jailtime or worse....

Dear Mr. Saint Claire,
Is there any chance of you and the current champ Mrs. Von Nardroff staging a contest of knowledge on television? That would be something to see!

Kenny,
You will face the truth and the music soon enough.

ALL CHANNELS LIVE

I am frightened, says Edward R. Murrow's voice in the evening radio. He's delivering a speech in response to an industry honor just conferred upon him. *I am frightened by the imbalance, the constant striving to reach the largest possible audience for everything—by the absence of a sustained study of the state of the nation.*

In the grand jury room, as soon as Sam Lacky of Mint and Greenmarch Productions, Inc. takes the oath and settles into the witness chair, the assistant DA comes to the point:

Q:

Mr. Lacky, did you reveal to any contestant, prior to his or her appearance on any television quiz program, any questions that were later asked of him or her, for point value, on the same program?

A:

No, sir. Never.

Murrow says: *No body politic is healthy until it begins to itch. I would like television to produce some itching powder, rather than this endless outpouring of tranquilizers. It can be done. Maybe it won't be. But it could…*

Q:

Mr. Lacky, I must remind you that you are under oath.
I will repeat the question.

Murrow says: *Do not be deluded into believing that the titular heads of the networks control what appears on their network. They all have better taste.… But they must schedule what they can sell in the public market.…*

"Golden Fluffo, the first all-new shortening in forty years! Richer looking, better tasting, more appetizing!"

Murrow says: *The sponsor of an hour's television program is not merely buying the six minutes devoted to his commercial message. He is determining within broad limits the sum total of the impact of the entire hour.*

"Let's hear what Mrs. Thelma Styra, Indiana State Fair Baking Champion, had to say about Fluffo…"

Q:

And, Mr. Lacky, bearing in mind again that you are under oath,
a second question: did you reveal to any contestant, prior to his
or her appearance on any television quiz program,
any *answers* to any of the questions that later were
asked of him or her, for point value, on the same program?

A:

Never. Not once.

Murrow says: *If the sponsor always invariably reaches for the largest possible audience, then this process of insulation, of escape from reality, will continue to be massively financed...*

"I love Fluffo! It makes such a golden-brown pie!"

...and its apologists will continue to make winsome speeches about giving the public what it wants, or letting the public decide....

"Oh, man, that's some apple pie!"

Murrow says: *We are currently wealthy, fat, comfortable, and complacent. We have currently a built-in allergy to unpleasant or disturbing information, and our mass media reflect this.*

The day after Lacky's testimony, NBC issues a public statement:

"In light of the intense scrutiny brought upon the quiz programs produced by their firm, we have temporarily relieved the personnel of Mint and Greenmarch Productions, Inc. from the day-to-day administrative responsibilities relating to the quiz programs aired on our network. This decision has been made at the direct request of Fred Mint and Raymond Greenmarch, in order that they may devote more time to disproving the charges against the programs. NBC remains confident of the absolute integrity of Mint and Greenmarch Productions..."

"You'll wonder where the yellow went / when you brush your teeth with Pepsodent!"

Murrow says: *But unless we get up off our fat surpluses and recognize that television in the main is being used to distract, delude, amuse, and insulate us, then television and those who finance it, those who look at it, and those who work at it may see a totally different picture too late....*

"For our next problem," says *Play Your Hunch* host Merv Griffin, velvet-voiced, debonair in his dark gray suit, "we go into the art world. Observe three classic-looking busts here. Of course, they are labeled *X*, *Y*, and *Z*. Now two of these gentlemen were famous Roman emperors, the third is just nobody in particular. Look closely and tell me, which is the bust of Mister Nobody?"

From the district attorney's office, Kenyon Saint Claire receives by

mail—not a summons—but a request to be interviewed. A rush of relief
overcomes him.

"Maybe I won't have to testify after all," he tells Ernestine.

"Should you have a lawyer?"

"It says here it's just an interview."

One October morning, Kenyon finds himself in the D.A.'s office, seated
on one side of a gleaming maplewood table. Across the table, with stacks
of green legal files at hand, Assistant D.A. Joseph Stone undertakes the
questioning while a court reporter makes a record. Also on the other side
of the table, a Mr. Donnelly and a Mr. Barrett attend, though Kenyon is
unsure of either man's function.

Meanwhile, in the book-lined office of his home, Jacques Barzun,
Columbia colleague to Maynard Saint Claire, writes the first chapter of a
cultural study to be entitled *The House of Intellect:*

> *The truth is that Intellect can be diminished in its own eyes only with its own
> consent; its troubles become obsessions, its presence a canker, only from within…*

"Now, boys and girls, I need your help. We're gonna show Winky some
real magic…"

Murrow says: *I cannot believe that radio and television, or the corporations that
finance the programs, are serving well or truly their viewers, their listeners, or themselves.*

"Now this is gonna call for some really super magic. Got your Magic Red
Crayons?

I want you to put your Magic Red Crayon right where my finger is. You
ready?"

Q:

Mister Saint Claire, have you read the *Time* magazine cover story
about yourself, which was published on February 11th of last year?

A:

I have not. But I have spoken with several people who have read it—
my wife and family members and so on—and from what they've said
I've gathered that the story was substantially correct.

Q:

I am particularly interested in one short section of the *Time* story,
which I'm sure you'll allow me to read to you right now.

A:

Of course.

Q:

[reading]

"Saint Claire is the first to admit that he is no genius and
claims neither a photographic memory nor total recall. Indeed
most of his education was in schools that had little interest
in memory work or tests, regarded facts as mere accessories in the
handling of ideas and the development of taste and reasoning."
Now is this an accurate portrayal of your education, Mister Saint
Claire?

A:

All that is true. But I should add that, for whatever reason, I've
always had an excellent memory. I've always been fond of reference
books, for example, and a great many facts and figures from such books
have stuck in my memory over many years of reading.

Q:

Mister Saint Claire, our calculation is that in your fifteen appearances
on the quiz program you played twenty-nine games, and sixteen of these
were ties. Do you have any explanation for that extraordinary ratio?

A:

Well, the large number of ties is not all that extraordinary, really.
Not when you consider that most contestants are going to shoot for
twenty-one points within two rounds. If both players make it, there's a
tie.

Q:

Did you meet regularly with any of the program's producers
prior to your appearances on the show?

"That's the signal, folks," says Merv Griffin. "I need to ask you for your
answer now."

Murrow says: *If we go on as we are, then history will take its revenge, and retribution will not limp in catching up with us....*

"What's the question again?" asks the contestant.

"The question is: Which one is Mister Nobody?"

A:

No, sir.

Q:

No? You never met with any producers
or other personnel before your appearances?

A:

Sometimes before my appearances Mister Lacky met with me
in my dressing room. His advice was always the same: to relax,
to be natural, to take my time. He said to never
give an answer before I was sure of it.

Q:

Did Mister Lacky at that time or any other time
give you instructions about how to breathe or speak or
what facial expressions you should use?

A:

No, never.

"One of them is Nobody. Which one is Nobody?"

Murrow says: *If this instrument is good for nothing but to entertain, amuse, and insulate, then the tube is flickering now, and we will soon see that the whole struggle is lost.*

Q:

Did you receive assistance of any kind from any personnel of
Mint and Greenmarch Productions—questions, answers,
categories, or point values to request?

A:

No, never. Absolutely never.

"Which one is Mister Nobody? You'll win the game if you get it right."

Q:

Mister Saint Claire, do you have any explanation for the difference
between your answers today and the things that Sidney Winfeld and
some other former quiz contestants have said
in the newspapers about the quiz programs?

A:

I can't comment on Mister Winfeld's or
anybody else's motivations. All I can do is
speak for myself.

Jacques Barzun continues:

> *...the alienation, the disinheriting, the loss of authority have occurred, not
> between the intellectuals and the rest—the commercial rump—of society, but
> among the intellectuals themselves and as a result of their own acts.*

"Now here we go, boys and girls, follow me right around.... And this'll
be a very very big surprise at the end!"

Q:

I would point out one final time, Mister Saint Claire,
the large number of quite difficult questions you answered
correctly on the program, as well as the very broad range of subjects
covered in those questions. Now don't you see why we should think it
extraordinary that you were capable of answering every one of those
questions?

A:

I don't know what to say except to repeat that I have always
had an exceptional memory, and also that I have spent a
great part of my life reading.

Q:

Mister Saint Claire, thank you for agreeing to
this interview, but I must say to you frankly that I
cannot believe you've told us the truth today.
You will have need of a lawyer for your appearance
before the grand jury. You will hear from us again when
we've settled the date of that appearance.

Murrow says: *This instrument can teach, it can illuminate, yes, and even it can inspire. But it can do so only to the extent that humans are determined to use it to those ends.*

"You think it's Z. Let's turn over the card please...."

Otherwise, Murrow says, *it's nothing but wires and lights in a box.*

"...You're right, it's Nobody! You've won *Play Your Hunch!*"

Jacques Barzun concludes:
> *They have abdicated but live on, self-exiled.*

"We still lead the world in stimuli."

"In this new landscape, everyone gets a channel."

FORMERLY REIGNING
QUIZ PROGRAM
CANCELED

NEW YORK, Oct. 16, 1958—In the latest result of the continuing investigation into the quiz shows, it was confirmed today that NBC has canceled the program that once commanded the largest television audience of any. The cancellation, effective immediately, was decided after a study of Trendex ratings which show an irreversible downward trend. From its peak rating of 54.7 percent of "television homes" tuning in during contestant Kenyon Saint Claire's three-month winning streak last year, the show had fallen precipitously to 21 percent by the time of recent champ Mrs. Von Nardroff's defeat. Now, six weeks after former quiz show contestants began to report foul play behind the scenes, the program's ratings have bottomed out at a dismal 10.3 percent. According to many in the industry, this plummet can only be

interpreted as a consequence of the public's
loss of faith in quiz programs.

. . .

In early November, Sidney Winfeld testifies before the grand jury.

On November 5th, it is reported in all the papers that CBS has canceled
The $64,000 Question, effective immediately.

On November 8th, the *New York Times* prints a picture of Sam Lacky in
handcuffs.

KENYON

God help me, thinks Kenyon Saint Claire. He's seated on the morning train, headed uptown, holding the newspaper open before him.

TV QUIZ SHOW PRODUCER
CHARGED WITH PERJURY
NEW YORK, Nov. 8, 1958—The producer of television's most successful quiz show was indicted yesterday on charges that he had lied when he denied giving questions or answers to contestants in advance of their appearance on the program...

The train skirls along through darkness, the underground utility lights a sickening blur in the black windows, the bodies of all the passengers swaying, and the shrill screeching of the wheels is the noise of his own anxiety rising. He reads: *Detectives led him on foot to the Fifth Police Precinct on Elizabeth Street for booking.*

A criminal, thinks Kenyon. *Handcuffs and all!*

Lacky has a family, a wife and two kids. They'll see this.

Mr. Lacky appeared stricken with shock and embarrassment as detectives led him on foot to the Fifth Police Precinct on Elizabeth Street for booking, and was overheard to say of the handcuffs restraining him, "Can't somebody at least put a coat over those? I'm not an armed convict."

"Excuse me, aren't you Kenyon Saint Claire?"

It's a woman seated across the aisle, her hands gloved, her gray hair kerchiefed.

"You are, aren't you? You're *him.*"

Other faces are turning now.

"I'm sorry," says Kenyon. "I can't—"

"*Sorry.* Oh, sure, you're sorry. Well, there's more to life than apologies, young man. There's consequences. A person's actions have consequences."

Her voice is loud, even amid the train's noise.

"I saw you on television this morning. You may act as if there's no consequences. But most of us here know better. And you should be ashamed. *Ashamed.* Shame on you!"

The other faces, looking on, are grim now, stern, some smiling sardonically. A tattered sound of applause begins. Then a few roars of agreement arise, and the applause grows. And now they're all but jeering, jeering, as Kenyon folds the paper in his lap and waits for the slowing train to stop. They're chanting, "Shame! Shame!" as he stands and wedges his way forward between their crushing bodies. "Shame! Shame!" as he waits for the doors to open, though he's three stops short of his destination.

Then he's out onto the platform, pushing forward against the crowd pouring into the car. And now at his back they're cheering anew as the doors slide closed and the train pulls away.

He's breathing again. He's shaken but walking, heading for the light of the street above. And burned into his mind now is that photo of Lacky, handcuffed. Kenyon would never have thought, only two years ago while taking his first turn in the isolation booth, that a person could be arrested for…television. They can get Kenyon now too. They got Lacky for lying. And if Kenyon testifies—no matter what he says, lies or tells the truth— they'll get him too.

Up in daylight, on the street, he feels a new malevolence in every motion of the busy city around him, everything—the taxis and bustling bodies, the piles of trash along the curbs, the doors of buildings opening, shutting— all of it laced with an unforeseen brutality. He walks the remaining ten blocks to Columbia in a stupor, head down, his whole system aflood with confusion and fright.

Alone in Dad's office, he plugs in the telephone and calls Ernestine. He's on the verge of losing control. It's a kind of primal state. His tie is choking him, his shirt damp, his heart racing.

"They'll get me too," he says. "No matter what I tell the grand jury, that's it. I'm hung. What's to keep them from charging *me* with perjury for what I said before? Putting *me* in handcuffs? They *want* to get me, Ernestine, I see that now."

She tells him to slow down. He's scaring her, she says. He needs to get himself under control. Nobody is chasing him.

"We could lose everything, Ernestine."

"Let's think clearly," she says. "Take a minute now and think clearly, Kenyon."

Why did I lie? At the DA's office, during the interview. Why?

"Did they swear you in for your interview? Were you under oath?"

"I don't know. I can't remember. I must have been. There was a court reporter, I'm sure of that."

Why did he lie? He wanted to tell the truth from the beginning. Ernestine wanted that too, though she never said as much—never needed to say it—so why did he lie?

Because he'd already lied on television, the *TODAY Show*. Because telling the truth on television—was there anything more unnatural? With the network and the whole apparatus hanging over you. Because at the D.A.'s it was only an interview, or that's what he told himself. Because who was Kenyon to undermine the testimony he knew Lacky had given? Because why would Kenyon change the story and put Lacky at risk, along with the other contestants—they'd *all* lied, after all—*all of them* except that damned Winfeld.

It's entertainment, for Christsake. We'd die for you.

And now it spills out, the question itself: "Why did I lie, Ernestine?" From his mouth it spills into the telephone and travels unencumbered through the wires south along the length of Manhattan to arrive instantaneously at her ear.

He wants her to answer for him, on his behalf. To stand between him and his own actions.

She breathes.

"That I can't tell you, Kenyon. That only you know."

SIDNEY

Sonofabitch, thinks Sidney, the newspaper in his hands and the thought itself a smile in his brain—in actual fact it's like his whole body is smiling as he reads.

They got Lacky. Yes, they got Lacky, which this means they can get Greenmarch too. And as for Kenyon Saint Clueless, you can go right on lying, Professor, your own turn is coming.

But next morning Sidney wakes thinking, *Why wait? Why wait even longer now, haven't I waited long enough?* They'll catch Saint Claire lying, sure, maybe that's inevitable even, but knowing how these things go, that'll be later rather than sooner, but meanwhile, right now there's still the matter of impressions, the problem of public opinion, so-called, which for example Sidney goes to the grocery or the post office or the butcher's and everywhere it's "hey, Sidney, so it was one big sham all along, huh, like one big setup? Like fake from start to finish?" and what can he say—once, twice, ten times a day—what can he say but sure, sure, unfortunately it is true—and then, quick-like, "The funny thing though is that I coulda won it straight probably," or in other words: "I knew a lotta those answers already I am not after all an unlearned man"—or, speaking of public opinion and the matter of impressions, for another example: there every morning on the television is Kenyon Saint Claire—and sometimes nights too—Steve Allen, Jack Paar—Saint Claire in that suit and tie every time, the favorite champ and professor, the Daddy's Boy and winner in that Family of Winners, and even with the grand jury and with Lacky's arrest and with the quiz fix in the papers every day, still Kenny Boy wins and goes on winning, which isn't it time somebody asks him to try winning on his own merits for once and for once for a good cause? Surely the guy won't refuse—surely he'll want to show his so-called intellectual prowess. And as for Sidney, he knows he can beat him, he just knows it, and that'll be his chance to show himself capable, to show everybody that hey, he's more than just rigged, more than just some actor in this fix, and if he'd so chosen he could've gone right on winning.

Sidney picks up the phone and speaks with Marvin in the office at City College confirming, yes, sure—*certainly, if it can be arranged*, says Marvin, *we'd put it on the calendar right away*, and Sidney says, *That's great, thanks, Marvin. I'll see what I can do. I do believe this could be good for all those concerned: for the college first of all, but also as a message, you know, to young people, about learning and knowledge.*

A Visit

Sidney Winfeld knocks on the door of the house on Prince Street.
Ernestine Saint Claire: [opening the door] Can I help you?
Sidney: Missus Saint Claire, good evening. I believe you may know me from—

Ernestine: Oh, of course! My goodness, I didn't recognize you at first.

Sidney: Yes, that's on account of my hairstyle, probably. I've changed it since I was on TV. I realize this is unexpected. Me coming here, I mean.

Ernestine: Would you care to come in?

Sidney: Yes, thank you. It's sort of a funny thing, I never did wear my hair that other way, not in my whole life.

Ernestine: Have you come to see my husband?

Sidney: I had a question for him, yes. Only take a second. Is Mister Saint Claire at home?

Ernestine: I expect him back any minute.

Sidney: Oh, well, I wouldn't want to keep you…

Ernestine: It's no trouble, Mister Winfeld. Can I get you some coffee or tea?

They move together through the entry into the living room.

Sidney: What a beautiful old place this is. I'd have a cup of tea, sure, if it wouldn't be much trouble. You're very kind.

Ernestine: Not at all.

Sidney: They put me in an old suit too, you know. Used to be my father-in-law's, that suit. A full size too big at least. But, hey, when they're paying you…

Ernestine: I'm sure.

       [Awkward pause]

Ernestine: I'll just put the kettle on. Please have a seat. Make yourself comfortable.

Sidney, still wearing his coat, perches on the edge of the sofa cushion.

Sidney: It's funny, I know this sofa—this whole room actually—from *Person to Person.*

Ernestine: [from the kitchen] Oh goodness, wasn't that a disaster?

On the sofa Sidney waits, alone in the room, looking about. Ernestine reappears.

Ernestine: Do you live nearby, Mister Winfeld?

Sidney: Forest Hills. Not so close.

They hear the front door opening. Sidney stands. Ernestine steps away to greet Kenyon coming in. They murmur briefly in the entry. Then Kenyon steps into the living room.

Kenyon: Well, well. Here's a familiar face. [Extending a hand] What a surprise, Mister Winfeld.

Sidney: [Shaking Kenyon's hand] Pretty unexpected, I realize.

Kenyon: You're most welcome. It's been a rather strange couple of months, hasn't it?

Sidney: A strange couple of *years*, yes it has.

Kenyon: Have a seat, please.

Sidney perches again on the cushion edge. Kenyon sits in the reading chair opposite.

Kenyon: You've been well, I hope, since the show. It occurs to me now, actually, how little we ever saw of one another, shut up in those booths like we were.

Sidney: Well, it was part of the casting, wasn't it? Opponents and all that. … I've been well enough. My wife and I, we have a baby daughter now.

Kenyon: Isn't that nice. Congratulations.

Sidney: And you've been very well, I've noticed. I was telling your wife what a beautiful old home. It's like I knew the place already, I was telling her, from *Person to Person*.

Kenyon: How embarrassing. I'd rather forget that little mishap. What can we do for you, Mister Winfeld?

Sidney: Well, I come here with a kind of a proposal, which with the news about the quiz shows and all, I think this could be an opportunity you'd welcome. What I had in mind is a quiz match, a new one, like a rematch, between you and me.

Kenyon: Do you mean on television?

Sidney: TV or not, wouldn't matter. What I picture would be a public event for charitable purposes. We already have a kind of invitation, in fact, from CCNY. I don't know if you'd recall, but I was a City College student.

Kenyon: This would be a benefit, so to speak, for the college?

Sidney: Exactly, all the proceeds to CCNY. And we'd play it straight, just fair and square, as it goes without saying, I suppose.

Kenyon: Well, Mister Winfeld, it's an awfully nice idea.

Sidney: I wouldn't have any trouble, naturally, answering the questions. Which is to say, that's not why it was played fixed, you understand. The TV program.

Kenyon: Yes, I've heard, of course, about your charges.

Sidney: It was the producers' decision to play it fixed. From the start that's how they wanted it. I think I coulda won it on my own though. [smiles]

Kenyon: [Also smiling] I'm sure that's true. Well, this benefit match, it's a very nice idea—

Sidney: And I figured you'd welcome the chance to show your own true colors in a quiz situation—I mean a situation of a different nature than what they put us through on those Wednesday nights.

Kenyon: [demurring] I have to admit, Mister Winfeld, that with the news, as you say, being what it is right now...I'm afraid I'm not inclined to do so public an event.

Sidney: No? Well, you can think it over. How about you think it over? I mean, if it's the public nature of the event, I mean, you're on national television every day.

Kenyon: In a different capacity.

Sidney: Sure, in a different capacity. This quiz match, it's an opportunity, is all. Which, that's the reason I thought to extend to you the invitation...

Kenyon: I'm not sure the timing is right. I'm sorry.

Sidney: I see.

Pause. They sit, silent. After a moment, Ernestine enters.

Ernestine: The kettle's ready. Kenyon, Mister Winfeld is having a cup of tea. Will you have one?

Sidney: Thank you very much, Missus Saint Claire, but I'm afraid I won't have the time after all.

Sidney rises, and so does Kenyon.

Kenyon: [Walking Sidney to the door] I do appreciate the proposal, Mister Winfeld, and the idea, as I say, is a very nice one. I only wish the timing were better.

They arrive at the door. Kenyon lowers his voice.

Kenyon: Before you go, do you mind if I ask...why did you...I mean, what was it that made you go to the newspapers?

Sidney: [Pausing, taken aback] I'm an honest guy. What can I say? All that money, and putting one over on the public every week. It all just didn't sit right.

Kenyon: What I mean to ask is... I'm trying to understand...why would you admit to being fixed, for everyone to know? There must have been something...

Sidney: I'm an honest guy, like I said. Unlike Ray Greenmarch, I'm an honest person who keeps his promises. (*Pause*) What I am not is a loser.

Kenyon: I see.

Sidney: They said to me, *We don't want you, we want the TV you.* Well, I am not the person the TV represented me as.

Kenyon: Sure. I see.

Sidney: What about you, Mister Saint Claire, since we're discussing this.

Kenyon: Pardon me?

Sidney: Myself, this TV business, at various times and occasions I've been angry about this and I've been jealous and I've been vengeful—across the board, you name it. But now? Now I just want to be *me* again. How about you?

Kenyon: Well, Mister Winfeld, there you have me. That's something worth thinking about.

Sidney is out the door and gone.

8.
GLASS
1959

KENYON

They didn't call. They didn't summon. No telegram, no letter by registered mail. Months went by, and he'd begun to think that, just perhaps, it might all slide away into the past: the DA's interview, the suggestion that he'd be called to testify—an episode of uncouth intimidation, of legalistic power-mongering, a momentary scare. Maybe they wouldn't come after Kenyon after all. What anyway would they gain from doing so? Maybe they'd taken a clear look at last, seen the honorableness of his aims in being on television: education, always education. Since the beginning he'd had good intentions. Since the beginning all he'd wanted to do was make a difference for the better. Surely anybody reasonable could see that—and maybe they had.

He'd gone to Paris with the *TODAY Show*, bringing Ernestine along. It was a promise kept, if not exactly a honeymoon. He joined the cast and crew broadcasting from the very boulevards—*un homme de la rue*, a televised *flâneur*, although harnessed as he was to his microphone cable and the bulky camera he couldn't wander more than a few feet in any one direction. He and Ernestine had the afternoons and walked the city together. Now and then he spoke to her of his time in Paris years ago, leaving out certain parts. Somehow the place seemed not nearly as real to him now as it did back then—all its visions more remote, the sensations dulled. He could hardly believe in that time of his life anymore. That raw hopefulness. Himself as a writer: a novelist! Had that dream faded completely? What did he have to show for it? Ernestine seemed happy to be there, in Paris, even if forced to share him with the TV people.

When they got back home the grand jury was still underway, as far as he knew. But it seemed bogged down in the drudgery of legal process. The longer it plodded on, the less furor it aroused. Sam Lacky, he'd heard, had spent no more than a few hours in jail, released on bail almost immediately. He'd relocated with his family to Mexico. The quiz program itself was off the air, a thing of the past—and now Kenyon hoped it could be forgotten altogether.

Kenyon's mail continued to bring a mix of affection and damnation, but with Ernestine's help he could screen the worst of it. And by avoiding the newspapers, too, he found he could almost put the whole two-year episode out of mind. Almost.

He began to relax again into his pleasant reality: *TODAY Show* in the morning, then Columbia, and here and there a special appearance on nighttime TV: Jack Paar, Jack Benny, Steve Allen. Mostly he wasn't asked about the Winfield charges anymore, but he got to speak about the things he loved, the things that mattered: literature, history, philosophy—even on "primetime," as they called it. Hadn't that been his accomplishment: to elevate the medium? The rest of the time was his and Ernestine's to share, at home together in their beautiful old house, or with his family at the farm.

And then, in January, the summons did arrive.

Strangely, its appearance did not revive the crushing dread right away. Instead, with surprising equanimity and clarity, he showed the summons to Ernestine and said, "I want to protect us here. That's what matters most. I need to do what will best protect us."

Did that mean he should tell the truth? Kenyon himself didn't yet know, and Ernestine didn't ask—not out loud, at any rate (but she kept looking at him in a way only she could do). Somehow even not knowing what he would do did not unsteady Kenyon—he felt sure he *would* know soon enough. For now, he could put it all out of his mind. When the day of his testimony arrived, he would know.

One evening, a week or so after the summons came, Kenyon found himself alone in the house, Ernestine away at her monthly book club meeting. This month's book was Fitzgerald's *Gatsby*—a novel Kenyon had always found troubling, both in its substance and because of its exaltation in the literary world. He took out the summons and looked at it, then folded it away in the inside pocket of his jacket and went out for a brisk walk around the neighborhood, bundled in scarf and overcoat and woolen hat.

It was January's early twilight, the trees mostly skeletal and the sky leaden and lamps beginning to come on in the windows of shops and residences. He moved in widening circles, rounding his own block before branching off deeper into the Village. He'd grown up on these blocks, and yet on this night the city felt alien, inhospitable. The bodies swarming along the sidewalks, the roar of accelerating cars, the unrestrained after-hours laughter, the slammed doors, the shouts and odors—it was a pandemonium of clashing motives, of desperate private destinies all striving to outpace each other—dreams and fears entangled at an urban crossroads.

How does one city bear so much stranger-to-stranger proximity? How does any person ever cross the gulf to knowing and caring for any other? In the dioramas of the windows Kenyon could see faces—faces in profile, faces in passing, faces staring into twilight. Across the darkening streets these windows, and the faces in the windows, faced each other—without greeting, without so much as acknowledgment.

You learned to look *through* your fellow citizen, your neighbor. Life in the city demanded this. And meanwhile, more and more, you fixed your attention—fixed your attention with ardent, blinding hopefulness—on the *inside* window, the small glinting box abuzz in your living room.

In the many windows now as Kenyon walked, there were flickering projections: the restless broadcast. *That* window, because its knobs and buttons promised empowerment, was more and more a source of light and warmth and affirmation and reassurance. A new technological community: illimitable, immediately accessible.

In fact, it was no window at all, but a mirror—no community, but a congregation of mirrors—and like some mythological tool, the mirror held every fantasy, every nightmare, every secret aspiration.

Once inside that mirror, once reflected there, how did one get out again? *I want to protect us...*

Later that evening Kenyon called Dad, asked to be put in touch with Ruben Carlino, his lawyer.

I need to do what will best protect us.

At their first meeting, before even opening his briefcase, Ruben calmly folded his hands on the tabletop, leaned forward, and said, "I can best advise you only by knowing exactly what happened. So tell me, Kenyon, did they give you the answers?"

Kenyon paused. How could he compound his lie yet again? On the other hand, how could he not? Ruben had known his father for decades, another Columbia man.

"No," he said.

But even as he spoke the lie, Kenyon preserved in his own mind and imagination the awareness that he could just as well, when the day of his grand jury testimony arrived next week, speak the truth.

He wanted to keep in reserve every possibility—orchestrate and command every possible outcome. He wanted to hold onto the freedom to choose.

...

Now it's the night before his testimony, and as he lies in bed beside Ernestine, Kenyon's mind begins to clear. He feels himself visited—in his very limbs there's some powerful surge of confidence.

He says: "It's a performance. Just like the quiz program was. And I survived that. I survived the isolation booth. I'll survive this."

Ernestine, silent, moves closer, embracing him more tightly. But hers is a plangent, reproving silence, and as quick as it came Kenyon's confidence ebbs. Then he lies stranded in their bed, in her arms, alone and adrift though she embraces him.

In his mind Kenyon Saint Claire is saying to himself: *I survived, I survived— but did I win?*

Did I ever truly win?

And can I win this now?

Truth or lie, can this be won at all?

"Part of you," says Ernestine, after several minutes.

"Mm?"

"Some part of you will survive, yes." She's talking into his neck, quietly, her head nestled into his shoulder. Slow, slow words. "Go before that jury and give one more little performance. Say the lines the producers expect. Protect these people who make a game of everything. Some part of you will survive that, sure. But I want more, Kenyon. I want more than *part* of you."

"Darling, there's not much choice here. What can I do? It isn't even about principles. *They're* all lying: Greenmarch, Lacky, all the other contestants."

"Not Winfeld—not *all* the others."

"No, but the rest. Is it my place to put them at risk? Or *this*—am I to put *all this* at risk? We could lose it all, you know, if I misstep now. Everything. It could be…just stripped away. This house, everything."

"It's what you *do* that matters, Kenyon. Not whatever happens to you."

The first thing Kenny did was fall down the stairs.

"Whatever happens," he says, "happens to *us*."

"Yes," she says. "To us."

"Ernestine, this is a grand jury."

"That's right. Not television. You say Mint and Greenmarch want you to go on performing, to just go on speaking their lines. I say you are realer than every one of them. Than all of them put together."

We help you be you. Even on television.

"You always have been realer, Kenyon."

And what if the impression one made is not one's own?

"Being real," he says, "to be real…" but his words drift off into silence, his brooding thought.

The person we're creating here, that'll be you.

"Go on," says Ernestine. She's reading his mind. All along, always, she's had this way of reading his mind. "Say it, Kenyon."

You know what you know, and we know what you know. It's simple, see?

He says: "How…how is a person ever real again? After all the faking."

"You break the pattern," she says. "You tell them."

"Tell them?"

"Yes. Then they'll see you. Let them see you, Kenyon. Show them."

Let them see you.

In the morning Kenyon is ready. He passes through the doors of the wood-paneled grand jury room—he's dry-cleaned and freshly shaven, collar starched and woolen tie carefully knotted—and takes his seat in the burnished witness chair. He feels rejuvenated, refreshed, lucid-of-mind. His purpose here is crisp and certain. He can hold his head high.

Show them.

They swear him in—his hand on the book—and then Assistant D.A. Joseph Stone stands before him.

"Mister Saint Claire, we'll move directly to the most pertinent questions. You appeared on the quiz program fifteen times between the dates of November twenty-eighth, nineteen fifty-six and March eleventh, nineteen fifty-seven. Is that correct?"

"Yes, sir."

"Over the course of those fifteen appearances, your cash winnings amounted to what total exactly?"

"$129,000."

"Of the twenty-nine games you played to win this money, sixteen of the games ended in ties. Sixteen in twenty-nine. Is that correct?"

"That sounds correct to me. I don't remember the precise number."

"Mister Saint Claire, in all your appearances on the program, did you ever receive assistance…"

While phrasing the question, Mr. Stone turns his back, stepping across the room to his table, his files lying open there—transcripts of prior testimonies, no doubt, sworn affidavits, evidence various and thorough.

"…did you ever receive assistance of *any* kind from *any* personnel of Mint and Greenmarch Productions…"

Kenyon's eyes drift across the cleared space before him. The men of the grand jury are seated along the risers to his right—and among them, immediately, he recognizes a face.

"…assistance such as questions, answers, categories, or point values to request?"

Kenyon has seen that face before. He doesn't know the man's name, they've never spoken, but yes, he's seen that broad face, no question—it's the face of a retired Columbia man, Kenyon's sure—he's a man Dad must know…

You break the pattern. You tell them.

"I can repeat the question, Mister Saint Claire, if you wish. Shall I repeat the question?"

Again Mr. Stone is before him, holding a piece of paper.

"No, sir," blurts Kenyon.

Who is that broad-faced man? Dad knows him.

"No?" says Mr. Stone. "Do you mean to say—"

"No, I did not receive assistance. Never, sir."

Mr. Stone's face darkens—whether in dismay or gratification, Kenyon's unsure. Mr. Stone turns his back again. "The witness states that he never received any questions or answers. Would you assert, then, Mister Saint Claire, that all the money you won was won fair and square?"

"Of course."

"The witness states that he won the prize money fairly. Now, Mister Saint Claire, I have here a number of questions—all trivia questions, and I would like for you, as a demonstration of kinds, to answer these questions."

"Now?"

"Yes, sir. The first is this: Pizarro was an early Spanish explorer who discovered and conquered an advanced civilization. Tell us the civilization he discovered, the country this civilization was in, and the leader of the civilization at the time of the conquest."

"May I ask for how many points?"

The room erupts in laughter.

Kenyon says, "I don't mean to be facetious, sir. The point values indicate the difficulty. Helps me tackle the question."

"I believe," says Mr. Stone, "this is an eleven-point question."

"Let me see," says Kenyon. "Pizarro, Pizarro..."

Is he truly being asked to do this, to perform like the man in the glass booth?—even here in this hall of justice? He feels the sweat accumulating under his arms.

"They were the Incan dynasties he discovered," says Kenyon. "Weren't they? And that of course was in Peru."

"And the question's third part, Mister Saint Claire?"

"Will you repeat that part please?"

"The leader of the civilization at the time of the conquest."

Kenyon shifts in his seat, boxed in, and he can all but feel the booth's encasement again—that isolation behind the hot glass.

Will you ever come out from behind the glass?

"I'm afraid I don't know the answer to that."

"I beg your pardon? You don't know the answer, you say?"

Will you be forever mediated *now?*

"I do not."

The glass between you and the world? Between you and yourself...

"But surely you recall answering this correctly, this very question, on the quiz program."

"Perhaps. It's possible I did. I don't know. There were so many questions."

Glass between you and those you love...

"Here's another for you, Mister Saint Claire: Name each of the six Balearic Islands."

Under oath and confined to his seat, Kenyon fumbles about for the answers. Three of the islands he gets. Three he can't even guess.

"Name five members of George Washington's cabinet."

He's perspiring very badly now—under his coat, along his brow, in the cavities of his cheekbones. He's trembling too. He says, "Sir, must I really? Is it necessary?"

Mr. Stone simply nods, impassive. "Please."

"Well, there was Jefferson."

"Yes."

"And Hamilton."

"Correct."

Mr. Stone is eyeing the paper in his hand, waiting, waiting as Kenyon strives to dredge up another name.

"I knew them all at one point. I studied so much at that time, you see. Let me think a minute.... Oh, McHenry!"

"Yes."

"And Knox, of course."

"Yes."

But there are more, and still Mr. Stone stands waiting.

"How many more are there, sir?"

"You've named four of the five we need. There are seven more names to choose from."

"Seven, goodness…. Well, I'm afraid I don't have one more."

"Mister Saint Claire, you gave five names on the quiz program. Do you recall that?"

"Certainly. It's been more than a year since then, as you know."

Mr. Stone's eyes remain on the paper. He half-turns to the jury. "The witness, we may note, is having great difficulty answering fully any of the questions that he answered with remarkable success during his winning streak on television. But I have a few more for you, Mister Saint Claire…"

Mister Saint Claire…

Mister Saint Claire…

Who are you here? Are you this face? This name?

Isolated in the witness box, Kenyon cannot articulate these thoughts—no, but the ambient anxiety of the thoughts besieges him.

Are you merely who they take you to be, and in this moment only?

Do you answer to the name as they speak it?

Or in their mouths does the name become another word altogether?

Meanwhile, relentlessly, the transmissions of the culture swirl on. Even confined in the witness box, Kenyon stands amid the swirl, like anyone.

The culture never rests, the sponsors never quit reaping.

Who are the sponsors?

And is he someone wholly isolated—in body, in time? A face?—still only a face from the screen? A name broadcast into the dark room of a mass mind, a mass memory.

The scores are very close now. His own face in closeup—but the frame is split: it's Kenyon Saint Claire against *himself.*

A face against a name.

Look, you're a teacher, we understand that—we're not looking for actors here if that's your concern, you go on the show as yourself, you're the educator, the man of good family that's you. We help you be you even on television—'cause television it's a different dimension—what we do for the program, Kenny, is create people.

Who are the sponsors?

The frame is split—his face in two places …
and the scores so very close now…

Still the assistant DA stands before him. "Might it be, Mister Saint Claire, that you don't know everything you have claimed to know?"
What did you ever know?
And still the quiz questions keep coming.
This show isn't over.
Who are the sponsors?

. . .

Rain pours down, the sidewalks awash, all the gutters running high. Pedestrians keep close to the sides of the buildings. From the Criminal Courts building Kenyon heads up Centre Street toward Canal.

He's one person amid this city's millions, only one, and he's feeling that personhood now—the vulnerability—while the rain seeps through the shoulders of his overcoat. He's now as exposed as anybody in this city, except more so. He's alive to the dread truth that anything can happen: a cab can run you down, you can slip and break your neck on the subway stairs, these buildings, any of these buildings, can topple and crush you, the rivers can rise—the East River, the Hudson—and sweep you right off this frantic island. You can become famous.

Kenyon is trapped inside the possibilities, alone. He's lied again—what choice did he have, with that broad-faced man looking on from the jury?
What choice did you ever have?
He's locked in the glass isolation booth. Kenyon is in the booth and they've shut off the lights. It won't be much longer now until…

He keeps walking. This is his city, but he is far—very far—from home. From the city in which he was born, the city of his father and mother. From Ernestine.

He keeps walking, wetter by the minute, no stopping.

Somewhere on the air, in the atmosphere, in the whisking of taxi tires, amid the drenched steel and concrete, from the bridges, the basements, the alleys, the towers, the open windows, the subways, the limousines— there's a voice.

The voice is electronic: *Stay with us.*

The voice is in the ears of every hunched and hustling citizen: *We'll be right back.*

In Kenyon's ears, in everyone's, the voice is saying:

DON'T

GO

AWAY.

TV NOW

On a stadium floor beside a wrestling ring, the favorite blond billionaire—stocky in suit and tie, his hair a wavy golden pelt—bodyslams a second billionaire in suit and tie.

From the tiered seats, tens of thousands roar as the camera zooms and retracts.

Zooms and retracts.

Sprawled over him on the floor, the favorite blond billionaire repeatedly slams his fist into the second billionaire's head.

Minutes later, spot-lit at the center of the wrestling ring, the defeated billionaire is strapped into a barber's chair. The favorite blond billionaire stands over him, thrusting high in one hand a pair of electric barber clippers.

The camera zooms and retracts.

Wrestler henchmen hold the man's head still. The favorite blond billionaire bears down with the clippers.

The defeated billionaire's hair comes away in clumps, which the favorite blond billionaire flings to the floor of the ring.

The defeated billionaire is wailing, crying, his face histrionically wracked.

Zoom and retract.

From the tiered seats, tens of thousands roar.

TIME MAGAZINE
MARCH 23, 1959
Show Biz:
No Longer Embarrassing

Until very recently, you would have been hard-pressed to find a self-respecting intellectual who might admit to owning a television. The cathode-ray set was faux-pas, or was at least a cause for mild embarrassment, something like professing an admiration for Norman Vincent Peale or California burgundy. These days the TV is all but taken for granted as a household fixture even in the homes of high-brows, and even a literary and academic intellectual can admit, without too much irony, to TV addiction. A surprising case in point: ever since his son Kenyon triumphed on a TV quiz show, Columbia University's Maynard Saint Claire has become an avid TV consumer.

In her new book, *Marriage of Minds* (Appleton-Century-Crofts; $3.95), wife Emily Saint Claire reveals that her husband is an addict "not of informative or egghead programs…but of pulpy and high-pulse offerings like noir mysteries, shoot-out westerns, crime stories, and quizzes. He is done for. I settle in by the hearth with my book, and soon the idiot commercials are blaring and I know he's up to it again. Occasionally I join him, it's true; often I remain with my book. But the professor is more and more faithful to 'prime-time.' There was, one particular evening, a great deal of shouting and carrying on. I waited for it to pass, and when I asked, 'Whatever was that ruckus?' the professor was red-cheeked, like a boy caught in some no-no. 'Wrestling,' he admitted. 'I just wanted to see what it was like.'"

9.
ENTR'ACTE:
The News, 1959

"The historical situation is not a background,
a stage set before which human situations unfold;
it is itself a human situation, a growing
existential situation."
—Milan Kundera

TV QUIZ INQUIRY
SEALED BY JUDGE

Jury Foreman Angered—
Insists Findings Be
Made Public

Quiz Show Legal Teams
Oppose Report

June 11, 1959—The New York grand jury which for the last nine months has investigated television quiz shows was officially discharged yesterday by General Sessions Judge Mitchell D. Schweitzer.

During its long investigation, the panel sat for more than 150 hours and heard more than 200 witnesses. The grand jury's findings on rigging of the shows were handed up in a 12,000 word presentment to Judge Schweitzer, but the judge said today that he felt the report was "expungable prima facie," which means he thought it should be stricken from the record on its face value.

A presentment is a grand jury finding that calls attention to illegal activity but does not include an indictment. After lawyers for several quiz shows filed objections, Judge Schweitzer has ordered the presentment sealed and kept secret on the ground that such a report makes accusations without offering a forum for denials.

"An indictment may be challenged by the accused," he said, "but a presentment is immune. It is like a hit-and-run motorist. The damage is done. The injury it may unjustly inflict may never be healed."

Yesterday, Louis M. Hacker, foreman of

the grand jury, expressed anger over Judge Schweitzer's decision. "I disagree in a most serious way with the court," Mr. Hacker said. "Our presentment does not contain the names of any individual contestants, quiz shows, producers, or television networks." He added that the grand jury, hearing its testimony in secret, was able to protect the contestants who testified. He said that if the presentment were impounded, "society would not be satisfied" and open hearings by the Federal Communications Commission or Federal or state investigating bodies would result. "Testimony would then be taken in public and many people would be hurt."

The Grand Jury Association, in a brief filed today, also took issue with Judge Schweitzer's decision. Grand jury reports are subject to judicial scrutiny, the association said, but once a grand jury has reported, "the suppression of its report fosters a dangerous policy of depriving the public of any knowledge of its investigations."

Of the 497 grand jury presentments returned in New York since 1869, every one has been made public.

IN LIVING ROOMS ACROSS AMERICA

American Vice President Richard Nixon jabs a finger into the vest of the man before him: "*You* don't know *everything!*"

Soviet Premiere Nikita Khruschev and the vice president are inside the geodesic dome of the American National Exhibition in Moscow—or so the anchor person has said. The picture on your screen limits itself to the two men standing before a single microphone, members of the press crowding in around them. Khruschev is a short, fat man with a warty nose. Beside him Nixon is lean and swarthy.

The picture wavers in black and white, but the men have been looking together at the RCA Company's exhibit: a new color television camera, accompanied by a color monitor. Any who pass before the RCA camera, said the anchor, can see themselves transmitted in full color on the monitor. You have to take their word for it. The picture on your screen limits itself to black and white.

"How long has America existed?" Khruschev says. "Three hundred years?"

During the awkward delay in which Khruschev's translator relays the question, the noise of many camera shutters is heard.

"One hundred and fifty years," says Nixon.

But is that correct? Isn't it in fact one hundred and eighty-odd years?

"Well then, we will say that America has been in existence for one hundred and fifty years and this is the level she has reached." Khruschev gestures off-screen, presumably to the color monitor. "*We* have existed for not quite forty-two years and in another seven years we will be on the same level as America. When we catch up to you, in passing by we will wave to you." Grinning, the gap-toothed Khruschev wiggles a hand in the air and swivels his head as if watching America recede into the past.

"I can only say," says Nixon, "that if this competition in which you plan to outstrip us is to do the best for both our peoples and for peoples everywhere, there must be a free exchange of ideas."

The two men, each eager to make best use of the microphone, are standing very close together, and now, without even needing to extend his arm, Nixon jabs a stark finger directly at Khruschev's vest.

"After all, *you don't know everything!*"

Q:

What is meant by the American dream?

A:

That all men shall be free to seek
a better life, with free worship, thought,
assembly, expression of belief, and
universal suffrage and education.

Q:

What is the wardrobe of an
average American woman in the
middle-income group?

A:

Winter coat, spring coat, raincoat,
five house dresses, four afternoon "dressy"
dresses, three suits, three skirts, six blouses,
three sweaters, six slips, two petticoats, five nightgowns,
eight panties, five brassieres, two corsets,
two robes, six pairs of nylon stockings,
two pairs of sports socks, three
pairs of dress gloves, one bathing suit,
three pairs of play shorts, one
pair of slacks, one play suit,
and accessories *

---

* IBM RAMAC 305 computer, Moscow Exhibition, July 1959

CONGRESSIONAL SUBCOMMITTEE SEEKS TV QUIZ DATA

Chairman Moves
For Release of Sealed
Jury Presentment

July 31, 1959—The chairman of the Congressional House Legislative Oversight subcommittee, Representative Owen Marcus, Democrat of Arkansas, said yesterday that members of his group would seek copies of the recently impounded grand jury presentment on television quiz shows. Mr. Marcus announced that his subcommittee plans to investigate charges that shows were rigged on a large scale. He said he already has information "leading us to suspect" that certain quiz show contestants were primed "to enhance their audience appeal."

"If this is true, then the American people have been defrauded on a large scale," Mr. Marcus said. "It is a matter of intense and paramount Federal interest" that a nation-wide mass communications media not be used to perpetrate "fraudulent advertising schemes on the public," he said.

The presentment handed up this June 10 by the grand jury had been ordered sealed by Judge Mitchell Schweitzer.

NEWSREEL, AUGUST 1959

[Fanfare of trumpets]

UNIVERSAL-INTERNATIONAL NEWS:

NEW DIPLOMACY

Khrushchev to Visit U.S.A.

VOICE: **Ed Herlihy**

In a special White House conference, President Eisenhower makes official the hints and rumors of a dramatic visit by Soviet Premier Nikita Khrushchev this fall, to further the cause of peace. Ike reads the text of a joint announcement released simultaneously in Moscow.

Eisenhower:

The President of the United States has invited Mister Nikita Khrushchev, Chairman of the Council of Ministers of the USSR, to pay an official visit to the United States in September. Mister Khrushchev has accepted with pleasure. Mister Krushchev will visit Washington for two or three days, and will also spend ten days or so traveling in the United States. He will be able at first hand to see the country, its people, and to acquaint himself with their life....

HOUSE TV INQUIRY
WILL GET GRAND JURY'S DATA

Aug. 5, 1959—Judge Mitchell Schweitzer directed yesterday that the minutes of a grand jury investigation into the alleged rigging of television quiz shows be turned over to a House subcommittee.

The group that asked to inspect the minutes is the Legislative Oversight subcommittee headed by Representative Owen Marcus, Democrat of Arkansas. Last week the subcommittee announced that it planned to look into charges that shows had been rigged on a large scale.

"The committee seeks the minutes to facilitate the holding of its own hearings and the making of its own findings," said Judge Schweitzer, in a press conference in his chambers. He added that in reviewing the committee's supporting affidavit requesting the minutes he felt there was a "note of urgency. And there was a clear showing that the release of this data is in the public interest."

OPEN HEARING SET
ON TV QUIZ SHOWS

Aug. 6, 1959—The subcommittee of the House of Representatives that will investigate television quiz shows made it clear yesterday that it would bring into the open the complete story of any "scandals" it uncovered.

Robert Lishman, special counsel to the subcommittee, said in Washington that the "entire story of these scandals" must be brought out "if Congress is to ascertain what corrective measures may be needed to prevent a future hoax on the public."

He also explained that while it would be impossible now to say who would be called to testify, if a hoax had been perpetrated on the public, "a whole cast" of witnesses would be needed to get all the facts on the record.

NEWSREEL, SEPTEMBER 1959

UNITED STATES INFORMATION SERVICE

presents

KHRUSHCHEV'S AMERICAN JOURNEY

VOICE:

Soviet Premier Nikita Khrushchev, on his grand tour of the United States, arrives in Hollywood for a star-studded luncheon at the studios of Twentieth Century Fox. Bob Hope, Elizabeth Taylor, Charlton Heston, Shirley MacLaine, Gary Cooper, Ginger Rogers, Kirk Douglas, and more of the industry's brightest join the Premier for a lavish meal. In remarks for the crowd, Khrushchev expresses disappointment that his time in California will not include a visit to Disneyland. The Premier's disappointment turns to confusion, and then to anger.

Khrushchev:

Just now I was told I couldn't go to Disneyland. I asked, why not? What is it, do you have rocket launching pads there? I don't know! And just listen—just listen to what I was told. *We*—which means the American authorities—*cannot guarantee your security if you go there.* What is it, is there an epidemic of cholera there or something? Or have gangsters taken hold of the place? *[Shouting now]* I say, I would very much like to go and see Disneyland! That's the situation I'm in, your guest. For me, such a situation is inconceivable. *[Appearing outraged]* I cannot find words to explain this to my people.

VOICE:

Afterward it is off to the sound stage, where Khrushchev
and his party are treated to the filming of a song-and-dance scene
from a new production, *Can-Can*, introduced by Frank Sinatra. Next
on Khrushchev's itinerary, a short jaunt north to San Francisco,
where the Premier makes an unexpected stop in one of the country's
newest supermarkets, Quality Foods of Daly City. The Soviet
leader inspects capitalism's potatoes and grapefruit on his tour of
the supermarket, while the commotion of his arrival causes one
surprised lady shopper to faint. Meanwhile, eager photographers
create havoc climbing instant coffee displays, freezer cases, and
checkout counters trying to get the perfect photo...

COMMENTATORS

"Khrushchev, a natural ham, instinctively understood this new reality.
He recognized that his trip was not just a diplomatic journey; it was an
opportunity to put on a TV show starring himself."

10.

THE CAMERA EYE, THE CAMERA I:

Fall 1959

"A television-radio system is like a nervous system.
It sorts and distributes information, igniting memories.
It can speed or slow the pulse of society. The impulses it
transmits can stir the juices of emotion, and can
trigger action. As in the case of a central nervous system,
aberrations can deeply disturb the body politic."

—Erik Barnouw, *The Image Empire*

LIVING ROOM

Here on the screen is matronly Nina Krushchev in dowdy floral dress and coat, hair barretted, all smiles, as she tours Maryland's National Institute of Dry Cleaning with her small entourage of Soviet security and a larger entourage of reporters and cameramen.

"She was shown a large room full of moths, where the institute can test out its newest mothballs," explains the *TODAY Show*'s Dave Garroway as the footage plays. "She was given a first-hand demonstration of a stain removal technique by this gentlemen here, hard at work on what looks to be a wedding gown. Is that a wedding gown?"

The picture shifts to Garroway, seated at his *TODAY Show* desk in his trademark tortoise-shell glasses and bow tie and beige jacket, the *TODAY Show*'s multiple clocks ticking away on the wall behind him. He continues in his easy, friendly, inviting way (he's just the kind of fellow you wouldn't mind having to dinner).

"Well, it proved to be an interesting outing for the First Lady of the USSR. Meanwhile, of course, her husband was engaged in informal talks with the President back at Camp David..."

CONTROL

Cut to full shot of the *TODAY Show* commentators seated side by side along the wide anchor's desk, adjacent to Garroway. He turns to the group. "The Khrushchev tour has made for quite a packed and interesting week, hasn't it?"

Pamela Harrison, in the middle seat between Frank Blair and Kenyon Saint Claire, pipes up: "Indeed it has, Dave. I think all the way back to Mister Khrushchev's arrival at Andrews Air Base on the 15th—it seems like forever ago—and the way he embraced that little girl who brought the flowers out to him, the way he patted her head. Theatrical from the start!"

"He's quite the performer," says Garroway. "We've learned that much about him this week."

"He's the biggest television star there ever was," says Frank Blair. "I mean, have we ever seen anything like him?"

"He understands the cameras," says Kenyon Saint Claire. "He knows how to use the medium—how to use television, doesn't he? I mean, putting his arm around the president in the car from the airport. Upstaging whoever it is that's making a speech of welcome—"

"Shouting about Disneyland," says Garroway.

"Exactly."

"Yes, well, our coverage of the Khrushchev visit, here on *TODAY*, will continue right to the end…"

KENYON

In a dim rear corner of the *TODAY Show* studio, Kenyon sits before the mirror at his small dressing table scrubbing off this morning's makeup. From the mirror's depths two figures approach.

"Kenny, you should meet Mister Godfrey."

Kenyon swivels in his seat and there stands Tom Grant, *TODAY Show* producer, with a short black-haired man at his side. The man extends his hand.

"Daniel Godfrey," says the man, with a large smile. "Nice to meet you, Mister Saint Claire."

"Mister Godfrey is here from Washington. From Congress."

"Not a Congressman," says Godfrey. "Just working for one. I'm with the House Subcommittee on Legislative Oversight. Representative Owen Marcus, the committee chair, is my employer."

"I see," says Kenyon. "I'm afraid I was just getting ready to leave. I have a class. I teach at Columbia."

"Yes, I'm aware of that. I won't keep you. But I thought I'd stop and say hello. Since I was in the neighborhood."

"I apologize," says Kenyon. "You've caught me in an unusually busy week, what with the Khrushchev visit and all. Isn't that right, Tom? Tom asked me to do some extra appearances this week, in the nature of a commentator."

"Madness," says Tom. "A week like we haven't seen since…"

"Since the birth of television," says Kenyon.

"It's been a circus to watch," says Godfrey. "That's for sure."

"What brings you to New York, Mister Godfrey?"

"Oh, a little research. I guess you may have heard about the Congressional investigation—"

"Of the quiz programs. Of course."

"Listen, do you mind if I—?" Godfrey pulls a stool from the neighboring dressing table. "Since I was in the neighborhood, I thought I'd—the committee's getting ready for the public hearings, you see."

"Yes, I've heard."

"And your name is sure to come up. You know, Kenyon Saint Claire's situation with regard to the quiz program, Kenyon Saint Claire's consequent notoriety—you understand it's inevitable."

"Do you mean I'll have to testify?"

"Well, no, there's no hard plan to ask you to do so. Not yet."

"I do appreciate that. I already went before the grand jury—"

"Yes—"

"—so my testimony is on record."

"Sure. And you see, Mister Marcus feels strongly—if at all possible, he wants to avoid laying any undue hardships on those contestants who have already testified, or appearing to single out any one person. He's a little…deferential that way. He even said to me, *We're not going after Saint Claire*. Now, what happens when the hearings start and more information is brought to light and your name inevitably comes up, well, that's another matter, that could change matters considerably."

"I see. So you're here to—"

"To give you a bit of a heads-up, yes. But also, besides to meet you like I said, I thought I could offer you the courtesy of a little information."

"Oh?"

"Mister Saint Claire, I'm not sure you'd know this, but some time ago there was a development involving Mister Lacky, the producer I think you're acquainted with—"

"Sure. Sam Lacky."

"Yes, Samuel Lacky, the quiz program producer. Well, I thought it would interest you to know, Mister Saint Claire, that Mister Lacky went back some time ago—this past spring, I believe it was—he went back to the D.A. and changed his testimony."

Reflexively Kenyon glances up at Tom Grant, still standing there listening.

"Changed his testimony?" says Kenyon, confused.

"Yep. His earlier testimony had gotten him arrested, you'll remember."

"Of course. But how do you mean, changed?"

"Unfortunately, I can't say much here—no more than what I've just told you. It's the role of the subcommittee to bring these things to light during the hearings. But I thought that fact might interest you. Thought I could offer it, you know, as a courtesy to you."

Godfrey's meaning is clear. Kenyon is dumbstruck.

Changed his testimony, he thinks, *from perjury to...*

The opposite of perjury is the truth, he thinks.

A person can change his testimony?

Suddenly in his gut there's a cold cube of dread—hard-edged, invasive, sharp corners jabbing his lungs. He doesn't look up again but he knows: above him, looming there, Tom Grant watches his every move.

At a loss, Kenyon turns back to the mirror. "Well. That's very interesting. When did you say this was?"

"Oh, in the spring. And Lacky, being a producer, being so involved in the course of these television programs, he *will* testify before the committee."

"I see."

So Kenyon's grand jury testimony is, by implication, void—and will continue to be. And yet the D.A.'s office hasn't come after him.

There in the mirror is Tom Grant, watching.

Why haven't they come after Kenyon?

Godfrey rises, slides his stool back to where he found it. "Well, it's nice to meet you, Mister Saint Claire," he says.

They haven't come after him because Congress will.

Blindly, numbly, Kenyon says, "Nice to meet you."

For a moment Godfrey doesn't move. Instead, with hands in his pockets, he stands watching as Kenyon swabs the last of the makeup from his forehead. Then he says: "That stuff come off as easy as it goes on?" But he doesn't wait for an answer. His flicks out his card, clicks it down on the dressing table. "Well, maybe I'll see you in Washington some time."

Godfrey turns and heads back across the studio, Tom Grant following.

Kenyon watches them disappear in the mirror's shadows.

SIDNEY

They took forever, these guys and their legal beagle ways with their politics and processes and questions and answers and affidavits and depositions and due diligence and you name it on and on, which what is all that but splitting hairs really, and which even when you know how long it takes doesn't make waiting it out any easier.

October the sixth of fifty-nine today. That makes it three years ago Sidney first went public—*three years!*—but now finally it's come to this, to Washington and to Sidney appearing in this hot hearing room overpacked with spectators—Sidney sitting at this witness table under all these lights— the photographer's bulbs flashing and the lights glaring for the TV cameras just like the ones on the quiz show, and sitting here right now Sidney can't help but think how he's come full circle. He's back on television. One more time he's being broadcast, one more time he's prompted to answer the questions, only this time the questions come from the long wall of Congressmen seated before him, and there's no glass to separate him and this time he's not here to *perform*, so to speak, but to perform a public service.

Bernice couldn't come; they couldn't bring the baby along and best for her and the baby both to stay home in Forest Hills—but she'll see him on TV. Sure, he got back on TV after all—and this time he's *himself*, Sidney Winfeld, the real one, not some poor schmuck in a bad haircut and oversized jacket—and won't he make her proud?

They've got a screen and projector set up right there, just off to one side, and it's loaded up and ready to show the kinescopes of his own appearances, his performances in the isolation booth, which Sidney expects he'll get his chance in the course of testifying to lay out all the ways he's nothing like that guy they asked him to play for TV.

But this ain't about him at all. This ain't about Sidney Winfeld. And he knows this. And it ain't about what happens on TV even. What it's about is TV, *period*. It's about being on it, being on it by any means possible and playing a part, which that's exactly what these Congressmen are doing, let's not kid ourselves, and anyway what was Sidney himself doing all that time except playing the part they asked of him? What was he on the quiz show but a paid stooge in a sense?—a sop to the public at large. Sure, there's no shame admitting it, but, hey, if you're the very first stooge then are you really a stooge? Which, speaking of first and second stooges, what would that make Saint Claire?

The goddamn ulcer or whatever it is hasn't gotten any better either. Sidney this morning in the lavatory at the back of the lobby choking down antacids hoping he wouldn't wince through all the proceedings, and sure enough there's a twinge in his gut every minute or two but he sits it out, pays attention, does his best to get at the answers they're looking for.

He's here, isn't he? He's here and he's himself, the real Sidney Winfeld. And what about Saint Claire? Where the hell is *he*?

No, Sidney's right here in front of them—why not, what's he gotta hide?—and didn't this all begin with *him*?—the public enlightenment of these proceedings, isn't *Sidney* responsible? And has anybody said as much? Has anybody in all these proceedings said so much as a *thank you*?

And what do they all wanna talk about but Kenyon Saint Claire?

Saint Claire this Saint Claire that. Saint Claire who when he comes out in public to stand there in suit and tie and say nothing except that he's got nothing to say—and he's positively mobbed with reporters and camera guys every time, but meanwhile Sidney can't help but notice that there's comparatively few journalists crowding around whenever *he* stands—Sidney Winfeld stands—at a mike.

Which, isn't it clear that Sidney's part here even now is to play the loser after all? That even though Saint Claire was the bigger stooge, it's Saint Claire that comes away with more so-called *points* in the public mind.

Sidney continues his testimony, answering their questions and illuminating for them the situation and nature of this whole charade as if he didn't first do this very thing an entire three years ago, but what he's thinking all the time—he can't help but think it—is how maybe someday there'll be a point system for everything, for *all of us*. Someday we'll all have numbers attached to us and no one'll have much choice. Everybody will know, by the numbers, who are the winners and who are the losers.

Can't you just see that happening?

KENYON

It's after hours, the NBC building mostly dark, but Kenyon rides the elevator to the thirtieth floor, alone in the musty cube of paneled plywood and metal, cables hissing in the quiet shaft whose blackness deepens and deepens beneath his feet, the car rocking on its tether as it rises, shuddering, its walls brushing the walls of the shaft, the dial above the doors creeping upward through the numerals. In the sheeted bronze before him stands Kenyon's double: a squeezed and elongated figure, the lines of the arms and legs a little wavy and the grim face weirdly skeletal.

Hello, Winky Dink.

They called him at home. Never before have they asked him to come in on the same day, let alone within the hour.

Higher and higher he goes and more and more he feels the slimming and narrowing of the brick tower surrounding him—its stacked windows, its sheer height, and the numb removal of the twentieth, the twenty-fifth, thirtieth floor from the noise and bustle of the street.

This afternoon in Dad's office, on a small TV set borrowed from the student lounge, Kenyon and Dad watched Sidney Winfeld testifying in Washington. In that distant field of black and white, among the shrunken but somehow still authoritative men of Congress, their suited figures seated in one long row behind placards (each placard sternly engraved with the man's name), Kenyon's own name kept coming up.

Watching beside him, Dad was very quiet and still, even as the words *Kenyon Saint Claire* recurred and recurred, echoing first in the contained space of the televised hall, and again from the television itself into the room where father and son sat side by side. But even while his name was spoken, what most amazed and transfixed Kenyon as he watched were the form and features of the man at the witness table. Trim, well-groomed, thoughtful, articulate, even urbane at times, Sidney Winfeld was a figure entirely new—nothing, nothing like the man from the televised isolation booth.

The sheeted bronze slides away before him and the distortion is gone. Mr. Bigler is there in the reception area, awaiting him. All Kenyon's perceptions are painfully lucid now. He and Mr. Bigler are walking, walking the length of the vacant offices, their steps soundless in the carpet, the only noise a soft chuttering of the ventilation system up here—those long sheet-metal tubes hidden in wall and ceiling and coiling floor-to-floor up and down the fretted framework lobby to roof.

In the conference room they find Mr. Denning, Tom Grant, Mr. Einsler, and Miss Gray.

Q:
Kenny, come sit down here.
I imagine you know why we called you tonight.

A:
I imagine I do.

Q:

We need you to tell us, Kenny—because,
you understand, Mint and Greenmarch Productions
operated with a great deal of autonomy and there
was much that this network knew nothing about—
we need you to tell us, did *you* know about the fix?

A:

(*after a long pause*)
Not really, no. There was some talk
about "controls," that sort of thing.
But that just seemed to be
the way TV worked.

Q:

Were you given the answers?

A:

(*pause*)
No.

Q:

And that is the truth?

A:

Of course.

Q:

Did you—did you receive
assistance of any kind?

A:

No. I mean…

Q:

Kenny, this is now a Congressional matter.
The network, as you can appreciate, I'm
sure, is very eager to protect and maintain
its positive image in the public mind,
the mind of our tens of millions of viewers—

A:

I *was* offered assistance, it's true. But I refused it.

Q:

Who offered you assistance?

A:

Sam Lacky. The program producers.

Q:

It's important that the truth come out.
It's important, Kenny, that this network
demonstrate to the committee its
full cooperation.

A:

Yes. I see.

Q:

And especially the full cooperation—
the *forthcomingness*—of any person
strongly associated with this
network in the public mind.

A:

Yes, of course.

Q:

You are one such person, Kenny.

A:

I see.

Q:

Kenny, we need you to contact that committee.

A:

Sir, I haven't been asked to testify. The Chairman
wants to avoid any unnecessary hardships
for former contestants—

Q:

You need to send them a wire.
You need to tell them what you've
told us tonight. You need to make yourself
available. You need to do this within
twenty-four hours. Those hearings
have started already.

A:

What should the telegram say?

Q:

Talk to your lawyer, but it should
say what you've told us tonight, since
that, as you've said, is the truth.

A:

This has been a very strange year.

Q:

Kenny, you understand what you are, yes?
You understand what your face is, yes?
You are strongly associated in the public
mind with the integrity of television
programming—and more importantly, the
integrity of this great and fine network.

TELEGRAM

To: House Subcommittee on Legislative Oversight

Respectfully request you read following statement into the record of the proceedings before your committee. "Mr. Saint Claire was at no time supplied any questions or answers with respect to his appearances on the quiz program. He was never assisted in any form and he has no knowledge of any assistance having been given to any other contestant. Mr. Saint Claire voluntarily appeared before the New York County grand jury and told that body under oath that he never received any assistance in any form from any person at any time. Mr. Saint Claire is available to the committee to reiterate what he has told the New York County grand jury under oath."

(Signed) Kenyon Saint Claire

SUBCOMMITTEE

CHAIRMAN MARCUS: Yesterday morning, Wednesday, October 7, the Chair received a wire signed by one Kenyon Saint Claire. Among other things it advised that he is available to this committee. This committee wired Mister Saint Claire yesterday—last night—acknowledging his wire, advised that this committee would be glad to comply with his request to appear and testify, and respectfully invited him to come before this committee either Thursday afternoon, October 8, which is *this* afternoon, or Friday morning, October 9. It requested him to advise the time that we may expect him.

It is now late in the afternoon and we have been expecting some reply, in view of the fact that he initiated the matter himself. We have not received any reply and consequently we are not at this time advised whether Mister Saint Claire will, as he suggested, make himself available.

KENYON

He asks for leave and gets it. Discreetly, while Dad is out of his office, Kenyon goes to the English Department Chair. In light of the unusual public pressures, he says, he needs time to think. He pleads for a week—a full week is what he needs—and he gets it.

A few hours later he and Ernestine are in a taxi en route to New Jersey to collect the 190 in its garage. And soon enough they're alone together in the car, tires humming on the highway beneath them as they bear north, their bags in the trunk and the city at their backs and far ahead out of sight, at the end of the black road ribboning before them, are the barns and pastures, stone walls and falling colors of New England.

In Kenyon's pocket, wadded up into a small tight square, is the telegram from Washington. He hasn't shown it to Ernestine.

They never did take their honeymoon—their real honeymoon, the one Kenyon had promised her. Their last time away was Paris—with the cameras, the crew, the *TODAY Show* team. The story of the riggings was in the papers by then, the news intensifying every day, but in Paris they could at least pretend—the *TODAY* folks weren't going to harp on the subject, god knows, their own network.

There's no pretending now, with the stir in Washington and every day's headlines and the public sentiment turning sour, as Kenyon's mail demonstrates—still that heap of letters arrives daily (delivered now to a post office box) but the tone of those letters, how it's changed.

So much has changed. And now he's fleeing not only that subcommittee but the network—television itself. But no, they'll find some peace. For a week at least.

If they drive fast enough, and far enough north...

Wind roars along the sides of the car. They are fleeing television itself—and his *television self*. Kenyon's foot pushes hard at the accelerator.

A week of peace, the telegram out of mind...

They stop at a filling station about an hour north of New Haven. Thankfully, blessedly, Kenyon is not recognized. At least he gets no indication from the man who handles the pump: steadily moving old fellow, stocky arms unhurried in flannel sleeves, stocky legs in their stained overalls anchoring him firmly to graveled ground. Salt of the earth.

Kenyon wonders: Do they watch as much TV, folks up here?

While Ernestine is in the ladies' room Kenyon takes out the telegram, unfolding it as if to read it again, but he can't bear to read it, doesn't intend to—instead he rips the telegram clean across, shuffles the ripped pieces together in his hand and rips again, sprinkles the pieces into a trashcan.

"Bad news?" says the attendant, hanging up the pump handle, and winks a wrinkled eye.

SUBCOMMITTEE

CHAIRMAN MARCUS: Now permit me to state that it was not this committee's intention at the outset to require the attendance of *all* contestants. We have had many contestants—a good number of contestants—here, most of them in public session. But *this* contestant, as it was with others who were reluctant to appear, seems to have *challenged* this committee and the facts which have been developed....

KENYON

"Why New England?" Ernestine had asked while they were hurriedly packing the suitcases.

"The time of year," Kenyon said. "The changing. I want to catch those glorious colors. The whole countryside changes so fast, have you ever seen it? Two weeks from now, it'll be like a different countryside altogether."

Ernestine didn't approve—still doesn't, though they're nearly three hours along on I-91.

She kept looking at him—while they were still at home, throwing their clothing into suitcases, like fugitives already—and clearly she saw something worrisome. So she's come along, disapproving but concerned for his well-being.

He doesn't mean to scare her. Was it desperation she saw in his face? That's exactly what he's escaping, as the car hurls them north, north, north. Desperation, entrapment in the city with his whereabouts always known, his fame and his face betraying him on every sidewalk.

His only want, for the week ahead, is to be unwanted. His only want is…peace.

They've crossed the Massachusetts line and the country is opening up, white-barked groves and plush greens and autumnal golds racing past their windows.

We could live here someday, Kenyon thinks as they rush ahead.

Someday. A little farm plot. No bigger than Mom and Dad's…

How the fan letters changed—and how quick and stark the difference. Even the salutations turned icy: no more "Dear Kenyon." Most of them merely said "To Kenyon Saint Claire" now. The most hateful bore no salutation at all, nothing to delay the excoriation:

I knew you were a goddam fake

they ought to take away those college degrees of yours

all you ever did was show how cheap and easy they can buy a man's soul

what kind of teacher does these horrid things

do you have any idea the corrupting influence

what have you ever done with your life but sponge off the honest hardworking people?

what do I say to my 15-year-old daughter (she adored you)

to my 17-year-old son (he emulated you, Professor)

SUBCOMMITTEE

CHAIRMAN MARCUS: This committee has received no reply and has no further word from Mister Saint Claire. In view of the facts established in these hearings, this committee feels that the testimony of Mister Saint

Claire is most important. He has failed to make himself available as he said he would. Efforts have been made to locate Mister Saint Claire without success.

KENYON

Yesterday on their arrival at this little motel outside Montpelier, he signed the registration book "Mr. and Mrs. Westhouse"—and felt himself blush when he turned to find Ernestine looking on: a strange cold ferocity in her eyes. For a moment he could imagine her slapping him. But surely she knows the consequences of using their real names.

She went straight to sleep without so much as a *goodnight*, turned on her side facing away.

No *good morning* today either, and without a comment she hands him the day's paper, then goes alone to the breakfast room.

SAINT CLAIRE TAKEN
OFF AIR BY NBC IN
TV QUIZ INQUIRY

*Winner of $129,000 Relieved of Jobs
Pending 'Final Determination'*

HIS TESTIMONY SOUGHT

*House Group Hears of Fix on Other
Big Quiz Programs*

WASHINGTON, Oct. 9—Kenyon Saint Claire was relieved of all his work assignments by the National Broadcasting Company today.

The NBC announcement, in which the network stated its judgement that retaining Mr. Saint Claire would be "improper in light of the Congressional inquiry," came almost simultaneously with an announcement by the House Special Subcommittee

on Legislative Oversight that Mr. Saint
Claire had not replied to a request that he
appear today or tomorrow.

The action was taken as House investigators heard more testimony of the fixing of television quiz shows. Mr. Saint
Claire, who until his suspension was a
$50,000-a-year consultant and televi-
sion commentator for NBC, and teaches literature at Columbia University, won
$129,000 in 1956-57 on TV's highest-rated
quiz program. House witnesses have said
this program was fixed, but they have so
far made no accusations against Mr. Saint
Claire.

After their few nights in Vermont Kenyon drove them east into Maine.
Ernestine had stopped asking where they were going. She could see he
had no idea.

He turns the car down winding forest roads, down tiny highways
blanketed in reds and golds, through farmland, through villages comprising
no more than a general store, a cluster of barns, and a cattle crossing. They
push farther into thicker woods. They don't bother with the map.

There's that mountain up here, Mount Ktaadn, thinks Kenyon.
Somewhere deep in the trees there are moose-haunted lakes. The seashore,
too, isn't far. Maybe they'll end up there. Is it mostly beach or cliff in
Maine?

Ernestine, still disapproving, softens a little. She seems to pity him,
mostly. She can't find it in herself, he knows, to be fully present and awake
to their surroundings—not under these conditions. She doesn't lecture
him, doesn't insist. She is giving him this time. But he knows what she's
expecting him to do. Even with every turn taking them farther down every
little road, he knows.

As if to avoid abetting him in his shameful flight, she does not offer to
drive. She tucks up her knees, nestling into the passenger seat, staring out
at the blurred foliage. A second conscience—softer, more generous than
his own—riding always at his side.

He's mostly silent, and she leaves him to it. When they speak, it's discontinuous—spurts of observation, half-disembodied. Or their words concern the strict necessities of travel: stopping at the next nearest restroom, filling station, restaurant, finding a motel or inn for the night.

He's asked her not to look at the newspapers anymore. Not for the next few days. He doesn't want to see them.

She simply nods.

Inquiry Says Saint Claire Eludes TV-Quiz Subpoena

Hearings Are Recessed Until Nov. 2

WASHINGTON, Oct. 12, 1959—Congressional investigators charged today that Kenyon Saint Claire had dodged a subpoena for his appearance in the investigation of rigged television quiz shows.

Representative Owen Marcus, chairman of the House Special Subcommittee on Legislative Oversight, said that subcommittee investigators had been unable to find the Columbia University English Literature instructor. Mr. Marcus described the search for Mr. Saint Claire as "diligent" and said that the subcommittee had been aided by "others also interested." Asked if the "others" included a United States Marshall, Mr. Marcus replied, "That's another question." He noted that the subcommittee would reconvene on November 2, the date on which Mr. Saint Claire must appear or face the full consequences of the law.

Columbia University announced in New York that it had given Mr. Saint Claire a week's leave. He did not appear for sched-

uled classes either Friday or yesterday.
Inquiries then disclosed that he had been
given the leave at his own request.

Reporters have been unable to find him
in New York, and there has been no answer at his home telephone number.

They've meandered through Maine for two days, going as far north as
Augusta, then turning south again, coming down through Portland and
crossing into northern New Hampshire. They've been sleeping in quaint
little roadhouses along the way, the autumn colors seeming to blaze more
brilliantly each afternoon, and now, six days since they set off in search of
peace, they are on a country road somewhere near the Connecticut state
line when Kenyon slows and pulls the car to the shoulder. He turns off
the motor and gets out, steps around the car and stands at the edge of a
grassy clearing, arms spread wide.

High deciduous trees line the clearing. Their canopies, waving in the
wind, are stupendously yellow and orange in the October sunlight, as if
recently set afire.

Ernestine gets out and stands beside him.

"Do you see?" he says. "Total contrast!"

Contrast, he means, to the city they left nearly a week ago. To everything
preying on their thoughts during these days.

He walks ahead into the field, the blowing grass pale green and rustling
up to his knees, dampening his pant legs.

"Someday I want to buy some land, Ernestine," he says, not turning, still
moving forward. "A place in the trees, just like this."

He keeps walking, wading toward the far center of the field, nothing
but the great whooshing in his ears, and the call of birds. He continues
past the center toward the line of trees. And maybe he'll walk right into
the forest.

He feels, right now, like a man intending never to go back.

"Kenyon!"

He turns and there is Ernestine, far away now on the shoulder of the
road, her hands cupped to her mouth.

Between them the pale green expanse of the field is waving, waving.

Again he hears his name, and then she's saying something more, but her
voice is half-lost amid the rushing leaves and grass. He hears *father*. She is

saying something about his father. He lifts his knees again, moving back across the field toward her, returning.

"Couldn't hear!" he calls, from the center of the field.

Again she cups her hands and cries out. And this time her voice arrives with perfect clarity: "You're going to be a father!"

Kenyon stands motionless in the field. Her words in his ears. He feels the wind very keenly, and remnants of mild warmth in the slant sunlight.

Ernestine is watching him across the grass. They are entirely alone together in a world of color. And through a kind of ultimate transparency Kenyon can see, in the shape of her shoulders as she stands there awaiting him, the profound *fact* of her. How firm and patient and loyal a person can be. It overwhelms him now to think of the innumerable contingencies, synchronicities, and alignments that have by mysterious accumulation delivered them to this moment in time and in themselves. He cannot understand how they have come to arrive here, facing each other in this privacy so immaculate, so consequential—but he understands the moment. That he understands. It's time to live this life, no more pretending.

He walks toward her. She waits, unmoving as he comes, and he feels himself a man stepping out of a picture or through a window into the elucidation of time and the trees and his body and hers.

He embraces her. For a long time they stand there in the noisy silence of the field, amid the fiery leaves.

"A father," he says.

The word repeats and repeats in his mind.

"Yes," says Ernestine. "Here's where it stops. No running anymore."

And he knows she's right.

"It's your turn now, Kenyon. You're ready for this."

Here's where he stops. No more dragging Ernestine highway to highway, inn to inn. She always knew there could be no hiding, but she suffered him, trusting. And now he's ready. They'll turn around, he'll go back and testify, that's the first thing. Then he and Ernestine will raise their child in truth, just as Mom and Dad raised him.

"Let's go back now," she says.

He nods and then she squeezes his hand and kisses him hard.

At the farmhouse door, Mom and Dad smile large and take them in, arms wide, hugely relieved but with never so much as a word about their worries these last seven days. Still, Mom insists they spend the night, and Dad concurs. Protective, parental, they've perceived the situation in its entirety and by instinct they act quickly to offer harbor. Their immediacy, their discernment amazes Kenyon anew. To have come from people like this.

Before long it's very late and the women have gone to bed. Kenyon is exhausted but he'd rather sit up with Dad than sleep. In the den they smoke together, and though Dad has said nothing on the subject, Kenyon begins: "I'll be going down to Washington. To testify."

Silent, Dad just draws on his cigarette, listening with lifted brows.

"First, though, I'll need to go to the D.A. Fix the answers I gave him."

"I see."

"Set that record straight."

"Yes."

"Sometimes, Dad, I have no idea—how it all happened. I just don't know."

"You made a mistake, Kenny. A mistake only."

"Yes. I thought I could deceive you, everyone, so many people."

"You thought you could deceive yourself, son."

In the lamplight Dad's eyes are glimmering—a deep, steady look—and Kenyon sees now, reflected in that focused glimmer, the liquid image of a man—himself—very small.

He says, "Dad, tell me, did I really fall down the stairs?"

"Hm?"

"In the Bleecker house, when I was five or six. Did I really fall down the stairs, or is that just...just a story?"

Dad's eyes narrow now. He's puzzled. "I don't recall that. What do you mean, son?"

"You know, there was that story in the family..."

"I don't remember you falling, Kenny. And I don't remember a story."

"No?"

"No. What makes you ask?"

"Oh, a little memory I've had. Just a memory, I guess."

Only in the morning does Kenyon learn of the subpoena.

"We thought it could wait," says Dad. "Last night wasn't the time to tell you."

But this news is almost irrelevant now. Kenyon's resolve to go to Washington is his own. He asks Dad to come with him. From his rocker by the fire, Maynard Saint Claire rises. He crosses the parlor carpet to the sofa where Kenyon sits. Pinching up the thighs of his pant legs, he sits down, wraps one arm around Kenyon's shoulder, and pulls him close. With a single word he answers: "Proudly."

Saint Claire Alters Replies Given New York D.A.

NEW YORK, Oct. 24, 1959—Kenyon St. Claire, big money television quiz show winner, made "substantial changes" yesterday in earlier statements he had given to the office of District Attorney Frank S. Hogan.

Mr. Hogan declined to say whether the contestant admitted to receiving questions or answers prior to appearing on the program.

Mr. St. Claire appeared voluntarily at Mr. Hogan's office at 11 a.m. with his lawyer, Ruben Carlino. He spoke with Assistant District Attorney Joseph Stone for about an hour and with Mr. Hogan for several minutes.

Shortly after Mr. St. Claire left Mr. Hogan's office, the prosecutor met with reporters. The following points were brought out at this meeting:

Mr. St. Claire made a complete statement in which he admitted that he had not told the complete truth in assertions he had made previously. It was indicated that Mr. St. Claire's earlier statements were the same ones he had also made before the grand jury that investigated the quiz shows.

A number of other quiz winners have called Mr. Hogan's office and indicated a desire to change previous statements.

The question of action by Mr. Hogan on the possibility of perjury is being considered.

When Mr. St. Claire emerged from the District Attorney's office, he appeared distressed. Observers speculated that he was about to cry or that he had already been crying.

"I'm in a hurry," he said. "I have classes. I can't say anything at this time."

He hurried into a taxicab with Mr. Carlino.

Mr. Hogan spoke of Mr. St. Claire sympathetically.

"He's been through a harrowing ordeal," he said. "In my judgement he will give completely truthful answers to the Congressional committee."

Asked what he meant by "harrowing," Mr. Hogan said he meant a "mental struggle." But he would go no further on that subject.

Mr. St. Claire will appear before the Congressional committee at Washington Nov. 2.

KENYON

Washington, D.C., November 2, '59

"Into the fishbowl," said Ernestine.

They were standing in the lobby just outside the crowded hearing room, just minutes ago—reporters, photographers, and cameramen swarming on all sides calling *Kenny! Kenny!*—but Ernestine leaned very close, her eyes held firmly on his, and looping her purse to her arm, she reached up with both hands to fix his tie.

"You're ready," she told him. "We're all ready. So into the fishbowl."

And here is Kenyon Saint Claire seated in the great stuffy room overpacked with spectators, and here are hundreds of cameras surrounding him, and they will televise the whole proceeding. And at one side of the room stand the big screen and projector, and so it is happening, even here in the capitol of this republic—his own life, his own self, his own work are transmuted into the moving image, luminous spectacle in the dark democratic hall—and this, all along, this transmutation is what he's been a part of. All along. Even him!

The public eye, he's thinking, as he stands before the men of Congress, one hand raised and one hand on the book while they swear him in.

"Do you swear to tell the truth?" etc.

"I do."

The public *I....*

Let them see you.

And then it's begun. And in time the projector will play and the images recapitulate the whole thing, and Kenyon will turn his head and watch Dad, in his seat up front, as Dad watches with all the rest, the bright moving images—shadows and light shifting on the old man's face...

The camera eye...the camera I. ...

Tell them. Show them.

Sworn and ready, Kenyon asks if he may read the statement he's prepared. Chairman Marcus permits this. So Kenyon reads aloud, before the five hundred in this hall, before the many millions more in living rooms across the country, before Dad and Ernestine sitting just there. He reads out the story of how he came to appear on the quiz program, how he agreed to Lacky's arrangement of supplying him the answers in advance, how quickly the success of the show, his own success, grew past all reckoning, how the money got bigger and bigger and the letters poured in, the offers and solicitations. How he could almost tell himself then that it was all good and well, for he was setting a positive example—wasn't he?—reflecting to the whole country the value of learning and education.

But no, now he couldn't help seeing how he'd created a *false* impression. How he'd represented knowledge as one's ability to get the answers right always, always the answers, and always for more and more money. How he'd further solidified that false impression every time he appeared on the air—what an *insincere* and *inauthentic* performance he'd given. How he'd acted as somebody other than himself, and in his worst moments had believed it was all for the good. How the mass entertainment and technological spectacle cajoled him more and more toward self-deception.

But then, at last, the quiz program was behind him and he'd moved on to his work with the *TODAY Show*, where finally, he'd thought, finally he could believe entirely in his role. But soon came the first exposure of

Sidney Winfeld's story in the papers—and all Kenyon could think about were the many thousands of letters people had sent him, good everyday Americans who believed in him and valued his television performances. How he couldn't endure the thought of failing these people. How he couldn't, in the end, ever seem to find an answer to his dilemma—though of course the answer was always simple.

And so he had run away. He'd run from everything: from his work at the university, from television, from the newsmen that mobbed his door, even from his own family. Everywhere he turned he was wanted for a comment, an interview, a photograph, a few candid minutes on television. But he kept running. With his wife he drove up into New England. He was in a state of desperate confusion, and he was running from himself most of all. He'd been doing it for longer than he knew.

And all this time, all along, the truth was the only answer. The only way. His own father had said as much to him. Very early on his father had said it, even though Dad couldn't have known the nature of Kenyon's deceptions. But finally now, finally, Kenyon has come, ashamedly and in humility and much too late, to see that his father was right. The answer, at last, was for Kenyon to admit to everything, to admit to his own self-deception, his own fear, his own wish to run away—to come home to himself and his family and to face these truths, and then to appeal to the people of America, to all those viewers who had trusted, praised, and encouraged him. And that's what he hopes to do now with this statement: to promise them he's learned his lesson well, and to appeal for their forgiveness.

Finished, he breathes. His hands are trembling very badly—he had to lay the paper before him on the table as he read, so disruptive was this trembling.

He feels his lawyer's hand heavy on his arm, squeezing.

He reaches for his water glass.

Q:

Mr. Saint Claire, I want to compliment you for
the statement that you have just made.
Those of us who have known a great deal about this
problem over this period of time can, I think, appreciate
more than the average person your remarks today.

I do have a couple of questions I'd like to ask.
Was there anything, in the lead up to your first appearance
on the quiz program, that caused you any concern?

A:

Concern about my own performance, you mean?

Q:

No. I mean concern about the way the program
was run or the conduct of the producers.

A:

Well, beyond the answers being given to me, my one concern,
as I recall, was about the nature of some of the questions.

Q:

The questions themselves concerned you?

A:

Yes. I'll tell you what I mean. In one of my first meetings
with a staff member—I forget who it was exactly—the man read a
number of questions to me from cards, just as Fred Mint
reads them on the show. These were examples of the types of things
that might be asked on the show. I remember feeling some worry later
on, going into my first broadcast, that some of the hardest of those
questions could not be answered so readily. For example, I remember
one question: "What was Shakespeare's first play?" Well, there is
scholarly disagreement about this. So there is no real answer.

Q:

Your participation in this program, Mr. Saint Claire, has vaulted
you into the entertainment field. It is of concern
to many of us on this committee, concerning entertainment
generally—many of us wonder at times if it is necessary
to have a phony or deceptive arrangement
in order for one to gain this national popularity,
particularly on television?

A:

I don't know much about show business, about the entertainment
business. As far as this program is concerned, sir, I wish it had been
done honestly.

Q:

Do you mean to say, you wish you had performed it honestly?

A:

I wish it had been possible to do so, yes.

Q:

If it is our nature, as a society, as human beings, men and women, your
nature and mine, to lie, to love to lie, to lie to others,
to lie to ourselves, and to lie about whether we lie—if
this is our nature, where does the truth emerge?

A:

Do you mean, where in terms of television, sir?

Q:

I mean, I was wondering, since the television stations
operate theoretically as a public service and in the public interest,
if you feel there is any obligation for them to more or less clear
themselves with all of the people that have been deceived on
these quiz programs—if they should not offer some public
service time for the purpose of clarifying.

A:

I believe very strongly in public service programming.
But it would probably be presumptuous of me
to say what the networks should do in this case.

Q:

Who did you talk to at NBC about your $50,000 contract?

A:

Mr. Bigler and Mr. Denning, I believe.

Q:

What were the nature of these discussions?

A:

There wasn't much discussion, really. I was to be what is
called a public programming consultant, but nobody had
any ideas, and I hadn't any either.

Q:

But they signed the contract?

A:

Yes.

Q:

And agreed to pay you $50,000 for what they
did not know—not knowing what you would do?

A:

They knew—we knew—I would
appear on the *TODAY Show.*

Q:

Did you conclude, Mr. Saint Claire, that actually what
they were buying was your popularity that had been
created on the quiz show?

A:

That occurred to me, sir.
I was inclined to believe that.

Q:

I'm sorry, Mr. Saint Claire, but
we must pause for a moment here.

A:

Pause, sir?

Q:

Yes, we need to pause here for
a word from our sponsors.

[*advertisement:* dog food]

Q:

We are back. Now, a point of order. I had thought
that everyone who would consider himself or herself
a photographer was familiar with the rules. While I am
speaking, you are to keep me firmly in frame. Gather
around now. There. That's more like it. Now,
Mr. Saint Claire, I suppose it would not be any excuse or
consolation or justification for your part in this, but certainly
it seems to me that the people most responsible for this

kind of deception are those who produced the program and
who apparently were much more experienced in the art of
deception than you were.

A:

Well sir, I did my share of deceiving.
I even believed I could deceive *myself*.

Q:

You imagined so, yes. And what will be the future of the individual
imagination, Mr. Saint Claire, in what is usually called
the 'civilization of the image'?

A:

The montage is the message, and the message
is that the torrent *feels good*.

Q:

Isn't TV a kind of trickster?
Aren't screens of all kinds?

A:

A trickster, sir?

Q:

Yes, insofar as the trickster is always
between his victim and reality.

A:

Well, yes, sir, what we have is culture recast as data.

Q:

I'm sorry, we must pause here for another
word from our sponsors.

[advertisement: household cleaning agent*]*

Q:

We are back. And you were saying, Mr. Saint Claire,
something about culture…

A:

Well, at present, sir, America is a nation where
at the same time cultural freedom is promised and
mass culture is produced.

Q:

Mass culture?

A:

Popular culture, if you will.

Q:

That's a very benign-seeming moniker.

A:

In the first place, not everyone believes a cure is needed,
and in the second, there probably isn't any.

Q:

If I'm following you, Mr. Saint Claire, you mean to say that
entertainment has shed its pejorative stench. In other words,
for example: a movie based on a comic book that was invented for the
sole purpose of spawning a movie that could then make the
illustrious claim of having been based on a comic book.

A:

Most of all, sir, I was running from myself. I realized
that I had been doing it for a long time.

Q:

Or, say, movie adaptations that end with
the main character, who is a writer, writing
the book that the movie will be based upon.

A:

Yes, sir.

Q:

Do you recall, Mr. Saint Claire, the origins
of the word "broadcast"?

A:

It was first an agricultural term, wasn't it?

Q:

You are correct. It referred to a method of
distributing seed. Of planting.

A:

Yes, I do remember that.

Q:

Mr. Saint Claire, I do not need to state that you
come from a long line of outstanding citizens and
family in this nation of ours, great literary and
educational geniuses. And your father is with us
today, I believe…

A:

My father is a teacher and writer, yes. His students
will tell you how he spoke without notes, pausing at times
to ask opinions or to listen to questions. When asked
a question he would listen carefully, then think a moment,
often with his thumbs hooked into his lapels, before answering.

Q:

And you, you've captured the imagination of the public by
exhibiting the mastery of information, earning money, and
redefining culture as performance.

A:

Well, sir, they have not seen my heart, they've seen only
my demeanor. For three years of this unreal and imaginary life
shall I lose my true and essential life?

Q:

The audience gets to know you inside and outside.
The television camera, they say, is like a magnifying glass
and you can't enjoy looking at anything blown up for too long.

A:

And at home, in the living room, the TV screen—you
can only look into it, sir. You can't see *through* it.

Q:

What does it show?

A:

It's a mirror, sir. Not a window. It reflects.
Or it lets us retreat or turn away.

Q:

And if it were a window rather?

A:

Well, a window—a real window—can be opened. You
can reach *through* a window, can't you?
You can extend yourself.

Q:

Open your consciousness, in other words?

A:

That's correct.

Q:

Mr. Saint Claire, there have been some witnesses that have
testified who have taken the position that this was entertainment,
that no one was hurt and that everybody was entertained and
everybody was making money and it was all right. That is what
Mr. Lacky tried to sell you, was it not?

A:

Yes.

Q:

At the time when you were considering going on
the quiz show in order to "do a great service to the
intellectual life, to teachers and to education" in general,
were you thinking at all about the effect of your appearance
on the children of this country?

A:

Yes, sir, I was.

Q:

Do you mean you thought that your *performances*, as they have
come out now, would be a good thing for the children
and their respect for education?

A:

I'm sorry, I misunderstood your question.

Q:

We're taking another break here. Don't go away.

[advertisement: life insurance*]*

Q:

Welcome back to the proceeding. Are we on? OK, proceeding.
Mr. Saint Claire, did you not realize at that time the bad
effect this television hoax would have on the
children of the country?

A:

Unfortunately, I did not. Not everyone grows up. Many, perhaps
most people, refuse to face the darkness in them and remain in
a disguise of perpetual childishness. That's a perilous condition.
You don't know how such people will react in a crisis....
We all require a medium through which we can see
our own heart of darkness.

Q:

Boiled down, Mr. Saint Claire, to the essentials,
your statement indicates to me that what you did,
you did for money. Do you agree?

A:

I'm sorry, sir, that was not the only reason. Of course, that *was* a
reason, but there was also the promise of winning.
The temptation to win.

Q:

And all throughout your testimony you indicate
that you did not want to lose your $50,000 contract.
On page five of your statement you stated that Mr. Lacky
guaranteed that you would end up winning no less
than a certain amount. Are you in a position to
state what that amount was?

A:

This amount changed from week to week. It was,
before my first appearance, $1,000, before my second $8,000,
and, if I remember correctly, it then went to twelve, fifteen,
twenty-five. I think it was never again discussed after I had been
on the program six or eight times. I assumed thereafter that
I would receive what I had won on the program.

Q:

You assumed you would win both in appearance and in fact—

that whatever amount you had won in appearance
would also be yours in fact?

A:

That's correct, sir.

Q:

Mr. Saint Claire, do you feel now
that you *have* won, or do you feel you have lost?

A:

I've learned that these things—winning,
losing—they're not what we think them to be.

Q:

Are you still on the payroll of NBC?

A:

I believe that I was as of the time that I walked
in here today. I don't know if I am now.

Q:

Are you in fact still employed
by Columbia University?

A:

I believe so, sir, yes.

Q:

Have you any information that they are
in fact intending to relieve you permanently
of your duties at Columbia? Answer in ten seconds,
please—we have another commercial break coming.

A:

I have heard that they probably will relieve me, sir,
although the decision, I understand, has not yet been made.

Q:

Back in a minute, folks.

[advertisement: women's cosmetics*]*

Q:

We are back and live in Washington. Kenyon Saint

Claire is our guest. Did you, Mr. Saint Claire, at
any time have any conversation with any sponsor
of any quiz program on which you appeared?

A:

While I was on the program?

Q:

Yes.

A:

No, sir.

Q:

You had no conversation
with Pharmaceuticals, Inc.?

A:

No, sir.

Q:

Or any representative of that company?

A:

No, sir.

Q:

Do you currently take pharmaceuticals yourself?

A:

No, sir. Although many, many people do so, I understand.
More people every day.

Q:

A nation breathed each breath with you,
and went out and bought another vial of Geritol.

A:

It's my understanding that many people did so, sir.
That many people still do so.

Q:

Buy Geritol, you mean?

A:

Geritol, Zarumin, Sominex. Wouldn't you agree,
sir, that we're a very tired, very nervous people?

Q & A   327

We want safe sleep, wouldn't you agree?

Q:

Mr. Saint Claire, would *you* agree that the quest
for self-realization through consumption has hardened
into a virtual science of impression management?

A:

Presto change-o, sir, that's a thing of the past.

Q:

Wink-o, wink-o, you mean to say, works twice as fast?

A:

Yes, sir.

Q:

The raw meat of actuality, shall we say...

A:

The raw meat of actuality finally has succumbed, sir,
to tidy and manageable packaging.

Q:

What is a screen, Mr. Saint Claire?

A:

A thing that divides. A thing people undress behind. A thing
every computer has, in fact a thing computing has distilled itself
increasingly into. Shall I go on, sir?

Q:

Yes please.

A:

A thing we'll all carry around with us in our pockets one day,
a thing fundamental to western-world human information gathering.
A thing that has an appearance of transparency and that divides us from
bankers, ticket sellers, post office workers, people with money. A thing
people project onto.... Now, may I ask you a question, sir?

Q:

It's rather irregular.

A:

Allow me to ask, sir. What good

is knowledge if it just…floats in the air?

Q:
It goes from computer to computer.
It changes and grows every second of every day.

A:
But nobody actually knows anything.

Q:
I have no further questions.

A:
Sir, before we finish here, can I thank this committee?
I didn't think anyone would ever want to thank this
committee, but I owe this committee
a great deal in my own heart.

Q:
Mr. Saint Claire, you certainly have
helped clarify the record for the committee's
benefit and consideration. Maybe this unfortunate
experience will reveal a great deal out of which we
all may get a lot of benefit.

A:
I hope so, sir.

Q:
God bless you, young man.
We are adjourned.
And that's a wrap.

[advertisement: indigestion powder*]*

NOVEMBER 3, 1959

The Herald Tribune—The argument in favor of television's operations as presently constituted is that they give the people what they want. And there is truth in this contention, as can be demonstrated by ratings and sales charts. But the truth is only partial. For television doesn't give all the people what they want. In its race for ratings it deliberately ignores the needs of the intelligent adult, the inquiring child, the nation which requires intellectual nourishment as well as empty diversion. Who can say how large or how small this audience is—or whether its importance is measured by its size? Who can say what price may eventually have to be paid for the current debasement of taste and deterioration of all standards except the fast sell? The quiz shows may well represent only the first installment of the bill, and not the largest one.

The Post and Times-Herald—At this point in his shattered young life, nothing said about Kenyon Saint Claire can scar him more than he has scarred himself and the good name of his family. For the moment, our question is this: how many men identified with the big and little fixes of life, with the spurious commercial, the fake promotion and all the other artifices of financial salesmanship, are resuming business as usual this morning now that Kenyon Saint Claire has walked into his lonely exile?

The Baltimore Sun—What matters is the set of circumstances that made this particular temptation possible: the time-salesman state of mind that allowed television networks to turn a blind eye to the use of their time on the air so long as they got a good price for it; the scramble for sales which drives advertisers to seek the lowest common denominator of public appeal; the attitude of television producers who, with their eyes fixed on viewer ratings, do not scruple to slaughter truth on the altar of spectacle.

The Pittsburgh Post-Gazette—One must conclude sorrowfully that the financial temptations put before a poorly paid teacher were more than he could resist. He fell victim to the always tempting notion that one could get something for nothing, and that one could be whatever one needed for a price or a prize to be. There but for the grace of not having been asked to appear on television may go altogether too many of us.

The New York Times—It remains to be seen whether the aftermath of the quiz scandal is not going to prove just as distasteful as the actual rigging of the contest.

As of the present, the record still shows that a duly constituted grand jury, one of the basic foundations of a democratic society, was treated almost with contempt. To judge by the available evidence, apparently many witnesses felt that going before a grand jury was just another little quiz game to which the answers could be rigged in advance.

Much more than the TV industry has been tarnished. The seriousness of the grand jury's investigative role has been beclouded.

For many youngsters addicted to television, the Saint Claire case may be their first exposure to a genuine moral issue.

But the problem of television entertainment remains precisely what it was before the contestants showed up: how to make a practical case for higher standards in programming when the public will look at whatever it receives free of charge rather than turn a set off.

The Saint Claire episode, bad as it is, is but symptomatic of a disease in the radio and television world, a disease that seems sure to touch not only the whole gamut of programs from public speeches to private advertising, but to spread outward to all the innocent souls of our new videoland. It is a disease which permits things to be presented not quite as they are.

To the solution of that dilemma of the video age the quiz scandal and its aftermath may very well contribute nothing.

The Portland Oregonian—Had Kenyon Saint Claire not perpetrated his treason against the intellectual life, his family name might never have been discolored. On the other hand, had he never treasoned, could we be certain that Americans decades from now will remember the Saint Claire name at all?

By standing in that isolation booth, by err-

ing so publicly, by being the kind of prodigal son that he is in this brave new world
in which he lives, Kenyon Saint Claire has
unwittingly made of himself and his family
name a lasting symbol—a symbol of what
we were, and what we became. We can be
certain that decades hence, for those Americans looking back through the latter half of
this century, the Saint Claire family will stand
like a landmark, a collective lesser Rushmore
perhaps, at a clear turning in our road as a
nation and a people.

CONSEQUENCES FOR
SAINT CLAIRE

Text of NBC Statement,
Swift Response by Columbia

Perjury Charges Likely
for Saint Claire and Others

Nov. 4, 1959—*Following is the text of the statement issued yesterday by the National Broadcasting Company in announcing its dismissal of Kenyon Saint Claire:*

In light of the facts that have now emerged, it is clear that Mr. Saint Claire abused the confidence of the viewing public as a performer as well as a quiz show contestant. As an example, more than a year ago, after the start of the New York District Attorney's investigation, Mr. Saint Claire prepared a statement and requested permission to read it on the *TODAY Show....* This statement is typical of the repeated assurances through which Mr. Saint Claire masked his participation in the rigging. On this record, we feel we cannot continue to present him over our facilities as a representative of NBC....

Ousted by Columbia

Monday evening, the same day of Mr. Saint Claire's Congressional testimony, the Columbia University Board of Trustees announced that they had accepted his resignation....

New York D.A. Reviewing Situation

District Attorney Frank S. Hogan said yesterday that he would consult with a grand jury on the question of untruthful testimony given under oath in the grand jury investigations into the quiz shows.

"It would seem from the conflicting statements in Washington," the prosecutor said, "that there was grand jury testimony given under oath which wasn't true."

Questioned about the possibility of a perjury indictment being returned against Kenyon Saint Claire, Mr. Hogan said:

"I can't think of this in terms of one contestant. Many people appear to have lied." He added, "We will use the full recourse of the law. Perjury is a serious crime and we so regard it."

LIVING ROOM

The *TODAY Show* Dave Garroway's face full upon the screen in closeup. He speaks with strong emotion, even shedding tears: "I am still a friend of Kenyon Saint Claire....I can only say I'm heartbroken. He was one of our family. We are a little family on this show, strange as it may seem....Whatever Kenyon did was wrong, of course. I cannot condone or defend it. But we will never forget the Leonardo DaVinci notebooks or the poetry of William Blake which Kenyon left us with."

COMMENTATORS

"Later it was learned that Garroway's outburst, though genuine, was taped several hours before its broadcast."

"As a special bonus to the viewing public in a gesture to wipe the slate clean, NBC offered to donate time for a series of debates between the major presidential candidates of 1960, which eventually resulted in the televised confrontations between Kennedy and Nixon.... Two adversaries faced each other and tried to give point-scoring answers to questions fired at them under the glare of Klieg lights."

---

* Afterward, it was widely understood that the telegenic Kennedy was the winner of this debate.

EPILOGUE

LONGSHOT MAGAZINE, 1994

Jared Florence is a familiar face in front of the camera. One of our finest American actors of the last half-century, Florence has enjoyed his share of top-drawer roles in some of Hollywood's most notable movies, a few of which are now regarded as modern classics. Over the last twenty years, however, with a string of infrequent but memorable films, Florence has distinguished himself as a fine American producer and director.

His newest directorial opus is *Contestant,* a morality tale about TV corruption at the top, set during a game show scandal of the 1950s. Opening this month in wide release, *Contestant* has already generated its fair share of Oscar buzz. Florence sat down with *Longshot Magazine* after the movie's Washington, D.C., premiere.

Q:

Mr. Florence, thanks so much for taking the time to talk with *Longshot.*

A:

Happy to do it.

Q:

Your new film *Contestant* attacks corrupt TV by looking at game show hoaxes in the 1950s. Did you grow up watching game shows yourself?

A:

Some, sure.

Q:

Did you watch Kenyon Saint Claire? *

A:

Well, who didn't? I mean TV sucked you in.

Q:

It seems incredible that the real
Kenyon Saint Claire became a major celebrity.

A:

Worse. He became a role model.

Q:

I understand you did not have Saint Claire's—
the *real* Saint Claire's—cooperation on this project.

A:

We did not. You know, he's never spoken
publicly about those events. Not in
the 35 years since they happened.

Q:

He'd lied under oath.

A:

He lied to TV audiences every night he
was on that game show. He lied to a grand
jury. He lied to Congress. And in real life—the
movie doesn't show this part—but in real life
he was charged with perjury.

Q:

Did he go to jail?

A:

No, they suspended his sentence.
Same for the producers who'd lied.
They were symbolic charges, if anything.
And Saint Claire became a recluse. He moved to

---

* Saint Claire is played brilliantly in *Contestant* by screen newcomer Ralph Tuttle,
for whom an Oscar nomination looks likely.

Minneapolis for many years. Worked as
an encyclopedia editor out there. He's
spent his life hiding and ashamed,
as far as anyone can tell.

Q:

Now, there's been some early controversy in
reaction to *Contestant*, and the way you've chosen
to dramatize certain events.

A:

Well, it's not a documentary. We've taken some creative
license, for dramatic effect. The idea is to make the story into
something that people will want to see. And maybe they'll
learn something from it too, who knows? But the movie, any
movie, needs to be enjoyable to watch. I'm proud of the film,
but in the end, it's entertainment—and any movie,
you know, needs to earn back its investment.

KENYON, 1992 (AGE 66)

The phone call comes on a Sunday.

"Is this Kenyon Saint Claire?"

"Who's calling?"

"Mister Saint Claire, my name is Alex Parksdale. I'm a film producer—"

"I'll have to stop you right there, Mister Parksdale—"

"Wait now, if you'll wait just a minute, Mister Saint Claire, please, and let me just explain."

Silence, while Kenyon holds the receiver to his ear.

"Mister Saint Claire? Are you still there?"

"I'm here," says Kenyon. "I'm sure you've heard that I don't grant interviews or—"

"I have heard that. At the very least, I want to let you know that we're making a film—it's in pre-production now—a film about the quiz show events."

Another silence, then:

"I see."

"It's a drama, and I think you'd find that the story is very well handled, sir. It's a Jared Florence production and Jared's directing, so you can be sure that the story is in very good hands."

"Well, thank you for calling."

"Now, Mister Saint Claire, I understand your reticence all these years— myself and my team, we all do, and we respect that, and we respect your privacy, sir. However, if you were to give it some thought—"

"I can't participate, I'm sorry."

"If you were to just give it some thought, just consider being involved in the capacity of a consultant, well, we'd welcome your input."

"I appreciate your calling, but I'm afraid I—"

"And, Mister Saint Claire, the film is very well financed, I can assure you. We'd be prepared to offer you $200,000."

They have Sidney Winfeld's cooperation, Parksdale told him.

"And we'd come to you, sir—the whole production team—no need for your contribution to be of a public nature, and no need for you to travel.

We're talking behind-the-scenes involvement only. Of course we would credit you…"

On an index card from her recipe box Kenyon writes the figure down for Ernestine, brings it to her.

$200,000

With the figure jointly in mind they walk together out across the field that Dad used to mow so proudly, then out along the property line and into the neighboring stand of trees where Kenyon, on their first summer in residence here, passed the months cutting a path through the beechwoods—first with axe and saw, then with scythe, then with mower. His shirts pleasantly sweat-soaked, his arms and hands rewardingly sore, Ernestine's iced tea awaiting him back on the sun porch. The following summer he'd gathered and stacked the stones that make the rough-hewn wall which follows the path on one side. For a week or so their son Maynard had helped him, here on a visit from college: Mayney was just growing into his own strong limbs then, and he astonished his father and mother both, with his ease and assurance in work, conversation, and simple companionship. Somehow he'd become, in the three or four months since they'd seen him last, a man. He was studying mathematics. He hoped to teach.

These days, the stone wall is thick with moss, the many small crannies festooned with ferns, and in some places it needs repair. As they stroll alongside it, Kenyon steps away to inspect a spot where the rocks have tumbled. He stoops to fit a few back in place. Why so satisfying, the grit and clack of stones nestled one atop the other? Something about the vibration through the hands, and the sound in the ears. *Stonechat.* He's heard of a bird with that name, they say it makes a call like stones knocked together.…

They amble along, he and Ernestine, hand in hand, their familiar woods enclosing them.

They don't even discuss the figure, the money.

Parksdale said he would send a contract by overnight courier.

Somehow this man, whom Kenyon had never met—this quick, clipped voice in the phone—had brought the conversation to that. "Just for your consideration," he'd told Kenyon. "What do you say? You can look it over and think about it, OK?"

The document arrives before lunch the next day. From the kitchen window they watch the brightly lettered van swooping in along the drive, the delivery man scurrying from van to doorstep, rapping the old iron knocker hard on its iron plate—and gone by the time Kenyon opens the door.

But there at Kenyon's feet, in its slim cardboard mailer, is the contract.

Kenyon carries the contract through the parlor, stops in the kitchen to give Ernestine a kiss—she only glances at the mailer under his arm—and heads to the den. From the top drawer of Dad's old desk he withdraws the letter opener. He pierces the cardboard corner, pries the blade upward along the mailer's seam. The creamy contract paper is heavy in his hand. And in one smooth motion he tears the paper top to bottom and drops it in the waste can beside the desk.

SIDNEY, 2019 (AGE 90)

But anyway, when the movie people called him up—what, twenty-five years ago—Sidney concluded he'd cooperate. They *asked* him, after all. He'd be a "Consultant" in the credits, they said, which OK, why wouldn't he cooperate? Wasn't it a chance, one more time, one more chance to make sure the record got straight? $30,000 they paid him too, which considering it wasn't even like a part-time job, not nearly a commitment of that nature, well, who'd complain?

The movie wasn't so bad either as far as Sidney thought. And because it was very well received Sidney found himself in some respects back in the limelight—kind of funny after thirty-odd years, but so it was.

There was something about the whole business, however—something strange in the way his life just went right on but also in some respects never quite felt the same after that—after the movie and all.

For instance, every so often, even now, somebody or other'll ask Sidney for his two cents on the whole brouhaha, the scandal and Congress and all that. It happens again today—a regular Wednesday and he's at the coffee shop and somebody—an older fella of course, not too many younger folks even know the story anymore—this older fella, he recognizes Sidney, says he's heard something about a book, like a fiction book, coming out, which this is the first Sidney's heard of it, and so this fella asks in so many words, "What's your two cents on *that*?" and Sidney, well, what can he do but shrug a little and tell the fella: "My two cents? My two cents is, first it was my life and then it was a movie and now it's gonna be a book—like a novel? Is that what you're telling me?—and all I can say is, Why would you do that? It was already a movie, or didn't you know? All anyone's gonna say is, *Oh, that? Well, hell, there was already a movie about that.* Believe me. This happened to me. This was my *life*, but now people say, *Hey!*—they say, *Hey, that's like the movie!*—they look at me and go, *Wait, that was you?* It's like … it's like once that picture's on the screen all the rest is not so real anymore, you know?"

KENYON, 2019 (AGE 92)

Nights now, Kenyon sleeps soundly in the back bedroom of the old family home, Ernestine by his side. They've grown old, and their Maynard has raised a family all his own. Twice a year Mayney and his wife Alberta come to visit. And sometimes their two daughters and son will come, if they can get away from their busy jobs in the city. They've always been thoughtful kids, those grandchildren, and their parents too. And even now they breathe such life into the place.

Kenyon's own folks are long gone. Dad died in 1972, Mom several years after, 1980. And that's when he and Ernestine left Minneapolis, moved back here to the old family farm. As for George, he moved into the old house on Bleecker Street, where he raised his own family. He still lives there, a widower now. Life in the city, he's been saying for years, is not what it used to be.

Often now, on very still and cloudless nights like this one, for a long time before falling asleep Kenyon will lie with his head pitched back on the pillow, staring up past the curtain valance through the window glass at the moon as thoughts swim in and out of his mind. These nights the moon's hard silver glints down on the farms and cities of Connecticut, on New York and Minneapolis and many places besides, places large and small with names Kenyon's never heard—glints down, amidst everything else, on Kenyon's own life, his loved ones, and all the anonymous people everywhere.

This moonlight, it's almost too real to bear. It's the clearest broadcast imaginable.

NOTES & ACKNOWLEDGEMENTS

Attribution for Quotations in Q&A:

page

12 *Some people have said our contestants*: Steve Carlin, TV quiz show producer, 1958

13 *After I did the pilot*: Sonny Fox, host of *The $64,000 Challenge*

13 *The individual*: Ihab Hassan, "The Way We Have Become," *Georgia Review*, summer 2009

13 *It was the most impactful show*: Daniel Enright, TV producer

13 *The sponsors probably quadrupled*: Joseph Cates, TV producer

13 *It was a con game*: Reverend Stoney Jackson, contestant, *The $64,000 Question*

13 *I'm telling you*: Jack Narz, quiz show host

13 *As a matter of fact…millions of living rooms*: Clifton Fadiman, "The Decline of Attention"

13 *The deception we best understand*: Lionel Trilling, *Sincerity & Authenticity*

13 *I remember one night*: Sonny Fox, host of *The $64,000 Challenge*

14 *Every two minutes*: Steven Shaviro, *Stranded in the Jungle*

14 *We're all secretly practicing*: David Shields, *Reality Hunger*

14 *The camera begins to attract…people it records*: Stanley Milgram, played by Peter Sarsgaard in *Experimenter*

14 *Tell me the large technologies*: David Thomson, *Television: A Biography*

14 *I've often been tormented…and they're all tuned in…Well, I'm all for the multiplication*: Clifton Fadiman, *Conversation*, NBC Radio, 1954

14 *She laughed in a sweet*: David Thomson, *Television: A Biography*

14 *Reality, to be profitable*: Mark Slouka, *War of the Worlds*

15 *The world was becoming a television studio*: Peter Carlson, *K Blows Top*

15 *The age of humanism*: David Thomson, *Television: A Biography*

20 *Good art weighs nothing*: The *Autobiography of Mark Van Doren*

28 *We call it trivia*: Jeopardy! champ Ken Jennings

31 *The rewards, I don't need to tell you*: The *Selected Letters of Mark Van Doren*

40 *Everyone knows who the sponsor is*: Clifton Fadiman, "Ladies & Gentlemen, Your Host"

40 *We'd sit in the sponsor's meetings*: Merton Koplin, TV producer

40 *You cannot ask random questions*: Edward Jurist, TV producer

40 *Sponsor, agency, network*: Clifton Fadiman, "Ladies & Gentlemen, Your Host"

45 *You want the viewer to react*: Dan Enright, TV producer

50 *The living rooms were hushed*: Patricia Hampl, *A Romantic Education*

82 *The emcee is not precisely dishonest*: Clifton Fadiman, "Ladies & Gentlemen, Your Host"

87 *Praise little boys*: Mark Van Doren, "Psalm 3," *That Shining Place*

98 *In frenetic quest*: Daniel Boorstin, *The Image*

99 *It was the picture that mattered*: Don DeLillo, *White Noise*

99 *Everything on TV*: straw poll comment, *Miami Herald*, circa 1959

134 *The great networks are sharpening their weapons*: *Chicago Sun Times*, March 12, 1961

146 *He is an engaging*: *Time Magazine*, February 1957

147 *The St. Claires represent a tradition of people*: ibid, quoting family friend Clifton Fadiman

147 *In our senior year*: *Time Magazine*, February 1957

155 *The controversy about the effect of TV*: *The Victoria Advocate*, 1957

155 *Well of course we want problems*: Mark Van Doren, *Book of Praise*

155 *Like a good American*: Erik Goldman

163 *Remember, we're not selling the program*: *New York Times*, October 5, 2015

164 *We're here to deliver the audience*: ibid

173 *A degree of deception*: Dan Enright, TV producer, in *Time Magazine*, 1959

173 *Those concerned with this matter*: *The Victoria Advocate*, 1957

185 *Kenny is almost a Greek tragic hero*: *Time Magazine*, February 11, 1957

195 *Thank you very much, thank you, thank you*: Jack Bailey, as host of *Queen for a Day*

195 *The line between performer and performance*: Michelle Orange, *This Is Running for Your Life*

195 *This almost perfect man*: Mark Van Doren, *The New Invitation to Learning*

195 *And now, with a complete grasp of the English language*: Ernie Kovacs, as host of *Take a Good Look*

195 *We all sense that somehow*: Todd Gitlin, *Media Unlimited*

195 *This may be the most important*: Edgar Bergen, as host of *Do You Trust Your Wife?*

195 *The goal is usually*: Todd Gitlin, *Media Unlimited*

196 *Who is prepared to take arms*: Neil Postman, *Amusing Ourselves to Death*

196 *If we go on as we are*: Edward R. Murrow

196 *In a time that is no time:* Michelle Orange, *This Is Running for Your Life*

196 *Ladies and gentlemen:* Jack Barry, as host of *Juvenile Jury*

196 *Television begins by being entertaining:* Clifton Fadiman, *Any Number Can Play*

196 *This is an instance:* Neil Postman, *Amusing Ourselves to Death*

196 *To ask is to break the spell:* ibid

196 *What are you gonna do:* Jack Barry, as host of *Tic Tac Dough*

210 *Please go look into a mirror:* Jerry Mander, *Four Arguments for the Elimination of Television*

227 *Never before in history:* Barrett Swanson, *Los Angeles Review of Books*, August 15, 2016

227 *You have to make allowances:* Don DeLillo, *White Noise*

227 *I really like him:* Javier Marias, *Your Face Tomorrow*, Vol. 1 (translator Margaret Jull Costa)

236 *The whole gloss and excitement:* Time Magazine, September 8, 1958

237 *Ladies and gentlemen, this is a bit unusual:* NBC television, September 8, 1958

247 *I am frightened:* Edward R. Murrow's "Wires in a box" speech to the Radio & Television News Directors Association, October 15, 1958

254 *We still lead the world in stimuli:* Don DeLillo, *White Noise*

254 *In this new landscape:* David Shields, *Reality Hunger*

289 *Khruschev, a natural ham:* Peter Carlson, *K Blows Top*

318 *If it is our nature:* David Mamet, *Three Uses of the Knife*

320 *And what will be the future of the individual imagination:* Italo Calvino, *Six Memos for the Next Millennium*

320 *The montage is the message:* Todd Gitlin, *Media Unlimited*

320 *The trickster is always between:* John Berger, *A Seventh Man*

320 *Culture recast as data:* Joan Shelley Rubin, *The Making of Middlebrow Culture*

320 *America is a nation where:* Partisan Review, May-June 1952

321 *In the first place:* Neil Postman, *Amusing Ourselves to Death*

321 *A movie based on a comic book:* Michelle Orange, *This Is Running for Your Life*

322 *He spoke without notes:* Donald Keene, Columbia class of 1942, quoted in David Lehman's introduction to Mark Van Doren's *Shakespeare*, New York Review Books

322 *Captured the imagination of the public:* Joan Shelley Rubin, *The Making of Middlebrow Culture*

322 *The audience gets to know you.* Jack Benny, quoted in David Halberstam's *The Fifties*

324 *Not everyone grows up...heart of darkness.* Charles Van Doren, Encyclopedia Britannica film "The Secret Sharer" (1973)

326 *A nation breathed each breath.* Jack Gould, *New York Times*, September 28, 1958

327 *The quest for self-realization.* Joan Shelley Rubin, *The Making of Middlebrow Culture*

327 *The raw meat of actuality has finally succumbed.* Jack Gould, *New York Times*, Sept 28, 1958

327 *A thing that divides...people project onto.* Ali Smith, *Artful*

328 *What good is knowledge...knows anything.* Don DeLillo, *White Noise*

334 *Later it was learned.* Joseph Stone, *Prime Time & Misdemeanors*

334 *As a special bonus.* Richard S. Tedlow, *American Quarterly*, autumn 1976

340 *It seems incredible...role model.* "New Again: Robert Redford," *Interview Magazine*, September 1994

Additional Sources:

-Kip Fadiman's comments during dinner at the Saint Claire house are based on, and sometimes quotations from, Fadiman's delightful and prophetic essay "The Decline of Attention," found in his book *Party of One* (1955).

-Kenyon and Maynard's talk during their night-walk on the farm draws upon, and includes quotations from, Charles Van Doren's article "All the Answers" in the July 28, 2008 issue of *The New Yorker*.

-Maynard Saint Claire's Don Quixote speech consists of verbatim extracts from Mark Van Doren's remarks on WNYC Radio's Books & Authors Luncheon, March 10, 1957 http://www.wnyc.org/story/mark-van-doren-clifton-fadiman-and-sir-charles-snow

-Kenyon's remarks at the Boston conference, as well as some of the details in the section entitled "LIFE (Attempt)," are based on, or quotations from, Charles Van Doren's article, "Junk Wins TV Quiz Shows," *Life Magazine*, Sept. 23, 1957

-Kenyon's remarks on the *Today Show* about Renaissance Man consist of quotations from Charles Van Doren, *A History of Knowledge*.

-Kenyon's statement before Congress is based on the statement made by Charles Van Doren before Congress on November 2, 1959.

-Many of the newspaper extracts throughout *Q&A* are written in close emulation of—and some contain verbatim text from—actual newspaper articles of the day.

-The following publications were extremely useful to me while writing *Q&A: Television Fraud* by Kent Anderson; *The Image Empire* by Erik Barnouw; *K Blows Top* by Peter Carlson; *The Fifties* by David Halberstam; *Prime Time & Misdemeanors* by Joseph Stone; and "Investigation of Television Quiz Shows: Hearings before a Subcommittee of the Committee on Interstate and Foreign Commerce, House of Representatives, Eighty-sixth Congress, First Session," National Archives.

Special thanks to Jane Klain at the Paley Center for Media in New York, for pointing me to additional resources and allowing me the use of a copy machine. Thank you to Robert Antoni, Dave Roth, Keija Parssinen, Jaynie Royal, and Pam Van Dyk. And thank you to The Corporation of Yaddo, which provided me shelter, nourishment, and quietude during the writing of this book.

Made in the USA
Las Vegas, NV
22 January 2021